It began with
LABYRINTH
in which Jon Land drew a terrifyingly real picture of a nuclear age gone mad.

It continued with
THE OMEGA COMMAND
in which this enormously talented young writer shattered the nerves of readers everywhere with a vision of technological disaster.

It sizzled with
THE COUNCIL OF TEN
in which all the enemies of freedom united to destroy the world forever.

Now it explodes with
THE ALPHA DECEPTION
in which a powerful, invisible enemy threatens America with a simple choice: surrender or total annihilation. . . .

Also by Jon Land:

THE DOOMSDAY SPIRAL
THE LUCIFER DIRECTIVE
VORTEX
LABYRINTH*
THE OMEGA COMMAND*
THE COUNCIL OF TEN*

*Published by Fawcett Books

THE ALPHA DECEPTION

Jon Land

FAWCETT GOLD MEDAL • NEW YORK

A Fawcett Gold Medal Book
Published by Ballantine Books

Library of Congress Catalog Card Number: 87-91013

ISBN 0-449-13118-1

Manufactured in the United States of America

First Edition: February 1988

For Mort Korn and Emery Pineo
and so many others who have given so much

ACKNOWLEDGMENTS

With all my books, the list of those deserving mention and thanks would make up a book of its own, so just a small sampling will have to suffice.

First and foremost, I am blessed with a truly supportive team at Fawcett headed by Leona Nevler.

Daniel Zitin is an editor in every sense of the word, bringing a compassion and objectivity that has often been thought missing from the contemporary publishing industry.

The wondrous Toni Mendez and Ann Maurer complete a team which sweats over every page and detail and forces me to reach higher with each effort.

My deepest appreciation to the McGreeveys for help with the Colorado landscape and to Shihan John Saviano, as always, for aiding in the choreography of the many fight scenes.

Finally, my thanks to Paul Hargraves for unlocking the mysteries of the deep, and to Gene Carpenter for the seed from which this book was born.

PROLOGUE

THE town of Hope Valley died without protest.

Sunday morning dawned lazily, with the sun sneaking over the mountains of Oregon unseen by the one thousand residents who had gone to bed expecting rain. The first rays fell upon the black roads and neatly manicured lawns set between driveways complete with basketball hoops and two-car garages. A layer of dew coated those vehicles left out to bear the elements and, after negotiating a dozen lawns with papers tucked under his arm, a lone newsboy found his high-tops soaked through to the cuffs of his jeans.

The Sunday edition was by far the most cumbersome of the week, its bulk bending his bike's twin steel cages outward, with the overflow jammed in a sack over his shoulder. The boy kick-stood his bike and padded toward the next door on his route, sneakers sloshing through the grass and then squeaking on pavement as he climbed the front steps. The paper landed with a thud that sent color ad-inserts flying into the air.

The end came before they had a chance to drift to earth.

In his last instant of life, the boy had time to register an explosion of light like that of a flashbulb that didn't vanish with a click. A bluish-white beam poured from the sky in a moving arc across Hope Valley. It had impacted first at the town's western perimeter. By the time the boy's mind recorded it, a cloud of charcoal-black dust had already formed, following the beam as if attached by a leash and swallowing everything in its path.

The wind picked up fiercely, whipped up like a whirlpool tossing about the remnants of ruptured buildings with ease. At the last, the boy's ears caught the sounds of crumbling and crackling. He was about to scream when all the breath in him was sucked out. His blood, flesh, bones, even his clothes turned to dark dust and joined the spreading black cloud as the town of Hope Valley vanished into oblivion.

PART ONE

OBLIVION

Nicaragua: Sunday, nine A.M.

CHAPTER 1

"LIEUTENANT Ortiz is here, Major Paz," shouted the young soldier as he ran down the runway. "He's just been checked through the gate."

"Hurry him up, then," ordered Guillermo Paz. "And be quick about it."

The young Nicaraguan stopped long enough to make a semblance of a salute and ran back in the other direction.

Major Guillermo Paz too was a native Nicaraguan but no longer felt it. He had spent his late teens in the hell of the Samoza dictatorship and had seen his father tortured and killed. He had become one of many Sandinista rebel leaders, and when the revolution was over, Soviet advisers picked him out to go to Moscow to master the rudiments of true soldiering, killing, and leading. He became, in effect, a troubleshooter for them, a spy in his own country—though that was not how he saw it. Three years in the Soviet Union with some of the best military minds in the world had spoiled him. Sent back here to command a crucial air base on the Lago de Nicaragua just south of Acoyapa, Paz realized all at once how backward and infantile his country was. The soldiers were inept and unreliable. If not for the even greater ineptitude on the part of the Contras, the present government would have gone the way of the last.

Major Paz stood rigidly as the jeep carrying the latest Soviet-trained pilot approached. Although Paz was of average height, he was of anything-but-average build. A near-lifetime of weightlifting, which started with his hoisting feed onto trucks as a boy, had given him a midsection that was essentially a single solid block. He had no neck to speak of, and a tremendous chest made him an impossible fit for standard-issue uniforms. He wore his black hair never more than a quarter-inch long, in a stubble cut that showed off the thick scar which ran across the right side of his scalp. The only luxury Paz allowed himself was the thick mustache he groomed twice daily and stroked constantly. He was stroking it now as the jeep's brakes squealed before him.

The Acoyapa base was important for its new supply of fifteen Soviet-made Hind-D helicopters, the most awesome warships in the world of guerrilla fighting. The general consensus in Moscow was that twenty Hinds could do more damage to the Contras' jungle strongholds than twenty thousand Soviet troops. Each ship was fitted for 128 27-millimeter unguided rockets and six laser-guided antitank missiles. Add to this the six machine-gun cannons perched beneath both of the strangely curved wings, aimed by sights located in the pilot's helmet, and the result was a truly incredible fighting machine.

Paz could never help but gawk when his eyes fell upon one of his Hinds. Its ponderous-looking, squat frame gave the ship a slow, lumbering appearance—a hulking, overloaded menace which in reality was a quick and agile flying tank. Armor plating rendered it safe from anything but a perfectly placed missile. Its handling was so precise that any decent pilot could slide it between a pair of trees with only inches to spare. Its navigational system was laser-based and its turbo boosters could achieve speeds exceeding 250 knots. All this considered, Paz supposed the best thing about the Hind-D was that the Americans had nothing like it and desperately sought a prototype to copy. There were even rumors afloat that a million-dollar bounty had been offered to any man who could bring one back to the United States intact. But outside of Russia the only fifteen in existence were right here on this base, and the security employed by Paz day and night made theft or even approach impossible. Even Cuba was without the warships. Paz was not about to disappoint the Soviet "advisers" who had arranged this command for him.

The latest pilot climbed down from the back of the jeep dressed in full flying gear and approached Paz directly.

"Manuel Ortiz reporting for duty, sir."

Paz returned his salute. "You're late."

"Rebels blew up another bridge. Traffic had to be rerouted."

Paz grunted his displeasure.

Ortiz looked at him dutifully. "I could take her out over their camps if you wish," he offered, gazing over the major's shoulder at the Hind.

"Not authorized."

"Who's to know?" Ortiz returned with enough seriousness to make Paz smile with pride. There was something about this man he liked. Dedication. Professionalism. Qualities the major had seen all too infrequently since his return to Nicaragua. And this pilot was a cut above the regular troops in appearance as well. Older to start with, easily over six feet and well muscled. His beard was neatly trimmed and speckled with gray. His worn features were framed by rather long brown hair. His face was ruddy, creased, and punctuated with scars, the most prominent of which ran through his left eyebrow. Ortiz was obviously a veteran of several wars previous; maybe he was even a native Soviet. He certainly had the eyes for it: black, piercing, and empty like those of a shark. Paz looked into them and saw enough of himself to be content.

"Stick to the flight plan," Paz instructed.

"It would be an honor to have you join me, Major."

"Regulations insist I remain on the base for the duration of your test flight."

Ortiz smiled warmly, standing at ease. "There was a time, sir, when we fought without regulations. Survival was all that mattered, rules no more than what our hearts told us were right for the time."

"You're a poet as well as a pilot, Lieutenant."

"Late nights in the jungles, Major, make our thoughts turn inward."

"Yes," Paz agreed easily. Give him another hundred men like Ortiz and he'd have the rebel bastards whipped in no time.

"I'd better get moving," said Ortiz, starting for the Hind's cockpit ladder after another salute.

"You know the reporting procedure," Paz advised. "Take good care of her."

Ortiz saluted yet again. "Like a virgin on her wedding night, Major."

Paz watched Ortiz climb into the cockpit and fire up the jet-powered engines. Seconds later, the Hind lifted gracefully, straight up with a slight list to the right. Paz held the green cap over his stubble-covered head as the ship's huge propellers sliced through the wind, driving it straight forward. Ortiz steadied her fifty feet up and headed out over the airfield as he climbed gracefully on his planned northeasterly course.

Paz was still watching the Hind's shrinking shape vanish in the distance when a jeep pulled up alongside him. Its single passenger, garbed in flight gear, emerged from the backseat.

"Lieutenant Manuel Ortiz, sir, reporting for flight duty," the man announced, saluting.

The major's mouth dropped as he looked back once more at the horizon where the Hind had already disappeared.

Blaine McCracken cut in the turbo boosters and watched the Hind-D's airspeed indicator climb toward 250 knots. The cockpit was still strange to him. He had spent several weeks drilling on the basics of the mission, from perfecting his Spanish to mastering the Hind's elaborate control panel from reconstructed pictures.

Damn Russians, though, didn't know when to leave well enough alone. The control panel he was facing now was altogether different from the one he had drilled on, which wouldn't have been so bad if not for the fact that all labels and instructions were in Russian. He had already lost critical time trying to pick up airspeed while keeping his altitude low to avoid being tracked on radar. The plan was intricate, the timing much too fine to lose even a second.

"Move it, girl," he said under his breath, "or I'll have to pinch your behind."

Blaine checked his coordinates: an hour of flying time to the landing site where he would be meeting his partner on the mission, Johnny Wareagle. Blaine was heading fast for the Tuma Grande River when a warning panel he recognized as the intruder alert screen flashed with three green blips.

"Well, girl," he said softly, "looks like we got company."

"Red leader to base. Red leader to base."

"This is base," returned Guillermo Paz.

"We have the enemy in our sights. Repeat, the enemy is in our sights. Should we engage?"

"Negative, Red leader. I will have Green, Blue, and Yellow units rendezvous in your sector immediately. Stay on his tail. Repeat, stay on his tail."

Paz gave the appropriate instructions to the rest of his units and breathed easier. Imagine losing a Hind. . . . His career would be ruined. He had resisted the initial temptation to stalk the stolen Hind with more of her sisters, opting instead for four units of three standard helicopter gunships each. Certainly they would be sufficient to get the job done in this case. After all, where did the thief plan to fly the stolen Hind? There was no possible way he could get out of the country, none at all. Paz reminded himself that he must remain calm. If need be, he could still order his gunships to destroy the Hind and then fabricate a story to cover the truth. Accidents did happen.

Paz stroked his mustache and dialed up a fresh frequency. "Acoyapa base to Falcon One," he said to the man piloting the Hind. "Surrender or die."

McCracken did not acknowledge the warning. The three choppers were holding their positions behind him as he expected they would, waiting for others to mass from different directions to box him into a forced landing. He had no chance of reaching his destination. Unless. . . .

Blaine turned his eyes to the targeting controls, range finders, and dual joystick handles. Thankfully, the weapons systems' positioning remained just as he had studied it. He switched on the AUTO switch and practiced rotating his head. Beneath the wings the air cannons turned with him. His 128 unguided missiles were laser-aimed and made for air-to-air combat. Comfortable with the control panel, Blaine took a deep breath and brought the big agile bird around.

"Red leader to base! Falcon One has turned and is coming at us in an attack run. Repeat, attack run!"

Paz slammed his callused hand down on the desktop. This thief was surely insane. What could he possibly hope to gain from such a display? Reenforcements would be closing by now. The thief would know that. An act of desperation obviously. Well, Paz would just have to stop him here.

"Destroy him, Red Unit," Paz ordered. "Repeat, destroy Falcon One."

"Roger, base."

The three choppers had moved into an attack spread when Blaine locked the middle one into the firing grid sketched over his face mask. Blaine fired a burst from his wing-mounted air cannons; the chopper exploded into a jet of orange flames as the remaining two converged on him from opposing angles, guns clacking. It would take a perfect shot, however, to disable the heavily armored Hind. Blaine could feel the bullets banging off the ship's steel hull, but he knew they were merely distractions to allow the smaller ships to draw close enough to achieve sure hits with their missiles.

The strategy was wise. Each carried two missiles and only one of the four would have to impact to force the Hind-D into an unscheduled landing or worse.

The choppers whirled closer.

Blaine could take one out easily, but in the impossibly short period of time for a man unfamiliar with the controls, two seemed a long shot. But there was a chance.

McCracken dipped evasively to buy the time he needed, swinging round to the north once more. The choppers corrected their attack angle and started in again.

Blaine went into his swing. It was not something an intelligent pilot would have done, but then Blaine was hardly a pilot at all. Gnashing his teeth from the G-forces, he somehow kept both thumbs poised on the firing buttons of his twin cannons, sending a non-stop barrage that scarred the sky as Blaine circled around behind his targets.

Blaine could only hope he had figured the remaining choppers' positions properly. An explosion pounded his eardrums and shook him forward against the safety straps. He felt the Hind whirling out of control, and when the second explosion came it was all he could do to keep his hands on the navigational stick. His trembling hands held on to it desperately as the Hind swooned lower, treetops directly beneath him now, a vast green blanket into which he seemed sure to be wrapped.

Guillermo Paz sat anxiously by the radio. Over one minute had passed since Red Unit's last report, an eternity in battle. Already he was dreading the call he would have to make to Managua if the impossible happened and the bastard somehow got away. More than his career was at stake.

Crackle, crackle, crackle. . . .

"Base, do you read?" came a garbled voice through the static.

"This is Base," Paz returned, squeezing the microphone's base.

"He's down, Base. We got him. Down ourselves but. . . ."

Crackle. . . .

"Where? Request coordinates."

Crackle. . .

"North of . . . north . . ." *crackle* . . . "of Santo Domingo. . . ."

It was enough to go on, plenty. Somewhere north of the town of Santo Domingo. The rest of Paz's fleet was already in the area. He might be able to salvage this mess after all.

The Green Unit leader saw the white wing protruding from the ground brush and radioed in.

"We've got him, sir. Down in the brush, two miles north of Santo Domingo."

"Land and report."

Six of the nine choppers landed in an open field eighty yards from the brush that concealed the stolen Hind's carcass. The soldiers grouped together and approached, warily, with leveled guns.

The Hind's wing sharpened as they drew closer, poking up from the thick brush where the rest of its corpse must have been scattered in the crash. Strange there was no smoke, the leader reckoned, nor any evidence of explosion or smell of fuel. It was not until he came upon the wing that he realized why.

"Por Dios," he muttered, touching it. "It's made of wood!"

It had been nearly an hour since Blaine had passed over the Ditch Point after issuing the report of his own demise. The static had been the touch that clinched the authenticity of his words, he figured, managed through a means no more elaborate than crumpling sections of navigational maps one after the other. Johnny Wareagle had planted the fake wing at the Ditch Point, the idea being that in case of an emergency, the wing would distract pursuers long enough to allow Blaine to reach the border. Things hadn't gone exactly as planned, but they had gone well enough.

McCracken didn't need any of his crumpled maps to tell him he was coming up on Honduras and the landing site just west of Bocay where the rest of his team had established a small camp and had a Hercules transport waiting. He landed the Hind next to the Hercules without further incident and waited for Johnny, who would be making his way here by jeep from the Ditch Point.

Two hours later, a huge figure appeared in the opening of the small tent where Blaine was resting. He gazed up into the eyes of the giant Indian.

"Musta drove pretty damn fast, Indian."

"Speed is relative, Blainey. For some a mile is the same as a step. For others . . ."

Blaine nodded his understanding, still gazing up. Wareagle admitted to seven feet and might have easily exceeded that by an inch or two. His hair was tied in a ponytail, and his flesh was baked bronze by years of living in the outdoors following four tours of duty in Nam in Captain Blaine McCracken's commando unit. For the first time since those years, Wareagle was garbed in a set of camouflage fatigues.

"The uniform suits you, Johnny."

"A reminder of the hellfire. In the jungle today it tried to come back to me until the spirits chased it away."

"I figure those same spirits moved the Honduras border a bit to make life easy for me in the end."

"It would not be beyond them."

McCracken nodded at that. He had seen Johnny's mystical powers at work too often to challenge them, first in Nam and then much later on a snow-swept night in Maine when the fate of the country had hung in the balance.

"What next, Blainey?" the big Indian wondered.

"First off, I'm going to make sure that Hind-D gets delivered safely to Ben Metcalf in Colorado Springs. I didn't spend two months of my life preparing for this to see it get fucked up somehow. I like seeing things through to the end."

Wareagle nodded knowingly. "Sometimes the ends are not ours to control, Blainey. Man is a creature of constant beginnings. Your constant obsession with finishing leads you on an empty journey that can never end. We are nothing more than creatures of our destinies unless the spirits guide us."

"You sound like a travel agent for the soul."

"The spirits are the agents. I am just the interpreter."

"They furnish your words concerning me this time?"

"They furnish all." Wareagle hesitated. "I worry for you still, Blainey. So restless is your manitou. So driven are you to pursue that which you cannot identify."

"But we *have* identified it, Indian; it's what lured you out of your retirement villa up in Maine and got me away from sorting paper clips in France: the world's gone nuts. Innocent people are dropping dead all the time. The madmen are taking over and there are only a few of us left to keep the balance straight."

"You did not throw it off by yourself, Blainey," Wareagle told him. "And yet that is how you seek to restore it. Ever since the hellfire . . ."

"The real hellfire was the five years I was out, Indian. Now I'm back but I'm doing things my way, on my terms. Ben wanted a Hind. I owed him. Straight and simple." He paused. "Hope I didn't forget to tell you how great it is working with you again. No one else could have pulled off that trick with the fake wing."

"Men see what they expect to. The trick is to give it to them."

"The trick is to stay alive, Indian. Where you off to from here, back to the wilds of Maine?"

"A national convention of Sioux in Oklahoma, Blainey.

The time has come to accept my heritage once more, to accept myself as *Wanblee-Isnala*."

"Wan *what*?"

"My Sioux name as christened by Chief Silver Cloud."

"And what's *his* Sioux name?"

"Unah Tah Seh Deh Koni-Sehgehwagin."

"Give him my best."

CHAPTER 2

PRESIDENT Lyman Scott didn't stop to remove his overcoat upon reaching the White House. Instead he made straight for the elevator, located ten yards from his private entrance, that would whisk him down to the secret conference room, deep underground. Scott was a big, raw-boned, athletic man, and even his exceptionally fit Secret Service guards had to struggle to keep up with him.

Especially today.

A man with thick glasses and thinning hair was waiting for him at the elevator.

"Are they all here, Ben?" the President asked.

"Yes, Mr. President."

The aide waited until the three Secret Service men had entered the compartment after the President before pressing the down arrow. The elevator had only two stops, one underground and another at ground level where they had just entered.

Lyman Scott stripped off his overcoat and scarf. He had been president for just over two years and for a portion of that period seemed well in control of his duties. He had run on a platform of sanity and sense, especially when dealing with the Soviets. Upon taking office he initiated a series of summits with a progressive Soviet leader who felt, as he did, that a constant dialogue was the most efficient way of ensuring future peace. The country rallied behind him, a long-sought-after goal at last to be achieved. But there were costs. As a show of good faith, Scott kept his campaign pledge to drastically cut back on defense spending and reorganize the military community. There was grumbling and resistance, but the process nonetheless was underway.

Then came firm evidence of an active Soviet presence in Central America, Syria, and Iran. While claiming to bargain in good faith, the Soviets had been building up foreign divisions throughout the entire duration of the peace talks. Russian leaders insisted they were even then pulling back, but the damage had already been done. When Scott refused to respond strongly, even militarily, the polls came up squarely against him. The country believed its President had been played for a fool, and men Scott should have been able to trust failed him at every turn, feeling betrayed themselves by his earlier policies. He was labeled weak. A cartoon picturing a chicken cowering from a bullying bear made the op-ed pages of several major newspapers. For the past two months, Scott had weathered a storm which showed no signs of letting up.

The elevator doors slid open. The President left his aide and guards out in the corridor and passed through a high-security door into the Tomb.

The four men already present immediately stood.

"Forget the formality, gentlemen," Scott said by way of greeting. He tossed his overcoat and scarf onto a couch and moved to his customary seat at the head of the conference table. It was built to accommodate up to twenty, but today only five chairs were taken, the occupants of the other ones having disappeared one at a time over the past few weeks with the evaporation of the President's trust in his own advisers. It had been paranoia, in fact, that had led him to convene this meeting here in the Tomb instead of in the usual briefing room. The isolation was devastatingly apparent; each word spoken seemed to echo through the narrow emptiness of the chamber. The Tomb was barren but for the maps that hung on the walls and for the single red phone perched on the conference table within the President's reach. The light came harsh and bright from the recessed ceiling; for some unknown reason there was no dimmer switch.

Scott sighed deeply and met, in turn, the gazes of each of the four men before him. To his left was William Wyler Stamp, a career intelligence officer who had revitalized a CIA that had come under fire during the last administration. Stamp was urbane and dapper, with a quiet demeanor more befitting a professor than a spymaster.

Sitting opposite each other, and just as ideologically divergent, were Secretary of Defense George Kappel and Secretary of State Edmund Mercheson. Kappel was a lifelong friend of the President, which kept him in the administration despite his perpetual hawkishness and seemingly congenital distrust of the Soviets. On the other hand, Lyman Scott had known Mercheson for only one year longer than he'd been president. A former senator from Michigan, Mercheson's pointed nose and slight German accent doomed him to be forever likened to the legendary Henry Kissinger. The press often labeled him "Merchinger" or "Kisseson." He was Scott's chief supporter when it came to Soviet relations and the architect of a controversial disarmament treaty the President had been on the verge of signing before the rug had been pulled out from under his administration. Past sixty now and generally thought to be past his prime, Mercheson nonetheless enjoyed a comfortable grasp of the issues and the unusual ability to pass on his opinions in clear, concise terms.

The last occupant of the Tomb was Ryan Sundowner, director of the Bureau of Scientific Intelligence; BSI for short, but better known as the Toy Factory. By far the youngest of the group, Sundowner wore his brown wavy hair long and opted for a tattered tweed sports jacket rather than the traditional Washington suit. He looked as uncomfortable in the jacket as he did in the Tomb itself. This was his first visit ever.

"Mr. Sundowner," the President said, "tell us about Hope Valley."

Sundowner cleared his throat. He rose from his chair, holding tight to a black remote control device in his hand.

"I believe, sir," he started, "that the pictures we're about to see speak for themselves. If they don't, there's an accompanying narration that says it better than I can."

Sundowner pressed one button on the remote and the Tomb's recessed lights darkened. He pressed another one and the map in the center of the side wall parted to reveal a forty-five-inch video monitor. The device was familiar to him but had been custom-altered for the Tomb, and Sundowner had a vision of pushing the wrong button and sending missiles hurtling from their silos. He pushed a third button and the screen filled with a videotaped flyover shot of what had been Hope Valley.

Nothing but a black cloud. Everywhere, everything, from one side of the screen to the other.

"My God," the President muttered, rising as if to gain a better view in the darkness of the Tomb, a dimness diffused only by the glow of the video screen and the light over the door.

Sundowner froze the frame. "The military alerted the BSI after being alerted themselves by a highway patrolman who saw the cloud. Thought it was smoke at first."

"You mean he *entered* the town?" raised Secretary of Defense Kappel, aware of the possible implications.

"He came close enough. We've got him in seclusion now, more to keep him quiet than as an anticontamination precaution. There's no danger of infection here," Sundowner explained, pointing at the screen. "I only wish it were that simple."

The scientist started the tape again. Different angles and views of the cloud were displayed, showing no trace of the town.

"What about the perimeter?" CIA chief Stamp wanted to know.

"Hope Valley's as isolated as they come," Sundowner told him. "Just a single main access road which we cordoned off and set the appropriate buffer in place. The military and BSI personnel are working together under Firewatch conditions. That much has been contained."

"That much," echoed Mercheson, mimicking the obvious understatement.

There was a brief glitch in the tape after which the screen filled with a moving shot down the road approaching Hope Valley.

"The thickness of the cloud made it impossible for any of our flyovers to tell us anything. Our next phase called for an observer to be sent in. The picture you're seeing now comes courtesy of a camera built into his helmet. He had to look through the windshield of the van he was driving, so excuse the graininess."

"Who made the decision to enter?" the President demanded as the murky mass loomed larger on the screen.

"I did, sir," admitted Sundowner without hesitation.

"Rather large responsibility to take on yourself, considering the potential risks."

"There was more risk involved, sir, by *not* investigating the scene itself. We had no idea what evidence might be lost on the wind and I was satisfied by on-scene reports that the biological reactions were of negligible consequence."

"Meaning?"

"No dizziness, nausea, or wooziness from the soldiers enforcing the five-mile sealing and buffer zone. No symptoms of anything at all. Except fear."

On the screen, the van had reached the outer borders of the cloud, headlights barely making a dent in the blackness as it crawled on.

"Nevertheless, the driver is wearing a POTMC suit," Sundowner elaborated. "Stands for Protective Outfit, Toxicological and Microclimate Controlled."

Sundowner paused long enough to touch a button that brought up the volume on the screen's hidden speakers. "The driver's narration begins here, so I'll let him take over."

The softly whirling sounds of an engine came on before the voice, words slightly garbled by the Tomb's echo, forcing the occupants to strain their ears.

"Base, this is Watch One. I'm almost to the edge of town. Whatever's in this cloud, it's playing hell with the windshield. As you can see I've got the wipers on steady now but they're not doing much good. A gritty residue full of flakes and dust is building up in layers, so whatever this cloud is it's got plenty of solid makeup to it. It's still hard to tell if—wait a minute. Jesus Christ . . ."

The picture on the screen buckled as the driver jammed on the brakes, seeing something his helmet-contained camera could not yet pick up. Remembering this, he accelerated the vehicle again.

"I'm going to try to rotate my head regularly to make sure everything I'm looking at comes through. I'm entering the town now . . . or what used to be the town."

Narration continued and the men in the Tomb sat listening, looking, mesmerized. The tape was shot in color but it might as well not have been; black powder dominated what had been the center of Hope Valley. It lay in piles everywhere, all different sizes, no pattern whatsoever, and it seemed to shift in the wind even as they watched. It was so powdery that the van rolled easily over it. The narrator drew his vehicle to a halt to allow for the clearest possible picture.

"Checking instruments now," he said and for a time only engine sounds filled the speakers with the camera's view of the town lost as the driver lowered his helmet. *"Instruments show only a slight flux in heat levels. I read no evidence of explosion. Repeat, no evidence of explosion. Whatever caused this wasn't nuclear or even remotely fulminatory."* Another pause. *"Instruments indicate the area of direct effect is cylindrical and, my God, symmetrical."*

"Symmetrical," broke in Secretary of State Mercheson, "what exactly does that mean?"

Sundowner hit the PAUSE key and the screen froze again. "Any kind of ground-level explosion would spread outward like water spilled on a table. Ragged edges and a generally irregular pattern. Symmetrical means we're facing an impetus from above ground level."

"Push the PLAY button, Mr. Sundowner," Lyman Scott ordered.

The scientist obliged and the narrator's voice returned, the screen blurring as he lowered his head closer to the instruments.

"I'm checking the range finders now. I read no evidence whatsoever of any remains. Nothing's even standing. It doesn't make sense. Whatever happened here should have left residue I could fix on, yet there's nothing except for that black dust. Sensors show no signs of movement indicative of life. I'm checking oxygen levels now. . . . Machines say the air's breathable. They don't say it's sooty but I can assure you of that much. I'm going to start driving again." The screen grew dark once again, and the Tomb's occupants squinted their eyes trying to see through the sooty cloud. "*It's my estima—*"

There was a thud and the picture rocked.

"What the hell . . ."

"You're not going to believe this," the narrator's voice said as if in reply, "*but I just hit another car. I'm getting out to inspect the damage. Better take my lantern. . . .*"

The screen blurred again, then filled briefly with a shot of the driver's door opening out into the blackness. The narrator's breathing quickened as his boots met the pavement and he started around to the front of the van with the lantern's beam focused directly before him.

"What the hell?"

The car he had struck was missing all four of its tires.

"I hope it's thieves because—wait a minute . . . I don't know if you can make this out but I'm looking inside the car

and the interior's just a shell. No trace of cloth or plastic. Long as I'm out, I might as well take a little walk. . . ."

Sundowner pressed the MUTE key and picked up the narration himself as the helmet-mounted camera looked into the dent carved in the sooty blackness by the powerful lantern.

"Two more cars here," he started when the screen displayed them, "also missing their tires."

"Busy thieves," observed Stamp.

Sundowner's words rolled over him. "Here we have a pile of bricks where a building once was."

"Looks like it just crumbled in on itself," said Kappel. "No semblance of structure, just like the instruments recorded."

"There's no trace of most other buildings at all," continued Sundowner when the camera locked on what had been one. "Just holes in the ground filled with that black dust."

"What about people?" the President wanted to know.

"None."

"I was talking about traces, remains."

"None," Sundowner said without elaborating further. He hit the MUTE key and the narrator's voice picked up again as he headed back for the van.

". . . now. I've got the layout of Hope Valley memorized and I want to check out the residential neighborhoods. . . ."

Sundowner fastforwarded, watching the counter for the proper cue when to stop.

"I'm in what used to be a neighborhood. It's the same as the commercial district—nothing left. But hold on. In the detailed maps I studied before entering there were plenty of trees and grass." He cocked his head to the left and held it. *"There was a park over there, I'm sure of it. But now, as you can see, there's nothing but black dust. Looks like the stuff just swooped in and swallowed everything. . . ."*

The foundations of several houses were still visible, but nothing rested on top of them. There was just the black dust, rising up from the excavations and whipping about in the stiff wind. The scene looked to be that of a distant planet with a violent, unsettled landscape unfit for habitation. No plants, buildings, or life. Not even any death.

"What about the people, goddamnit!" the President blared suddenly. "What happened to the people?"

Sundowner pressed STOP. "They were attacked, sir."

The President leaned over the table, the fear in his face caught by the glow coming off the screen. "You had better be prepared to explain yourself, Mr. Sundowner."

"I'm not, Mr. President, and I'm not sure I ever will be able to do so satisfactorily, because what happened to Hope Valley *can't be* explained."

Lyman Scott moved back into the darkness, safe from the screen's light. "Your report indicates otherwise. You said *symmetrical*. You said *attacked*. But there's no weapon on this planet that could bring about what we just witnessed."

"You mean, sir, there didn't used to be."

CHAPTER 3

BLAINE McCracken watched the Hind-D being wheeled down the ramp from the cargo bay of the C-130 transport plane that had flown it to the Air Force test lab in Colorado Springs.

"You're late," Lieutenant Colonel Ben Metcalf barked cheerfully, striding across the airfield toward him.

"Next time call Federal Express. They're the only ones who'll absolutely, positively do business with bastards like you."

The two men met at the foot of the ramp and shook hands firmly. Metcalf's eyes fell fondly on the Hind.

"I can't tell you what it means to us to finally get our hands on one of these."

"Forget the plural," Blaine scolded. "I did this for *you*, Ben, you and you only. For services rendered, remember?" Fifteen years ago, Metcalf had run interference for Blaine with the brass back in Vietnam so that Blaine's unit could cut through enemy lines instead of red tape.

"But in this case there's the matter of the million-dollar bounty on this bird. That money now officially belongs to you."

"Except I don't plan on claiming it, not when it'll probably mean having my picture plastered across the cover of some half-assed war-lover's magazine.''

''Would probably boost circulation a bundle to showcase that beautiful mug of yours.''

''Yeah. People'd have to buy a copy to find out if I was human or not. If anyone asks, just tell them you inherited the Hind after it was left in a tow zone.''

They started walking down the tarmac.

''You still think about the war, Blaine?''

''Never stopped. Johnny says I'm obsessed with bringing things to a finish. Maybe in this case it's because over there we never finished anything; we never really knew we started.'' Blaine gazed at the Hind as it was towed toward a hangar. ''You gonna keep her here awhile?''

''Couple months at least. I'm going to take care of the flight testing myself, just as soon as I patch up the holes you put in her.''

''Wouldn't mind sticking around for that myself.''

''You're more than welcome to but there's a message waiting for you in my office. From a woman.''

''And I told her never to call me at the office. . . .''

Metcalf laughed briefly. ''Figured you'd be a harder man to track down.''

''Somebody needs me, it's not that hard. That's the way I want it.''

''Message said it was important. No name, just a number. Massachusetts exchange, I think.''

''Terry Catherine Hayes,'' Blaine said, mostly to himself.

''Know her?''

''I used to.''

Ben Metcalf insisted on flying Blaine across the country in an Air Force jet. McCracken sat in the cockpit and tried to remember what piloting a jet was like.

And what Terry Catherine might be like now. They hadn't seen each other in over eight years, almost nine, after a brief and intense romantic interlude that had been Blaine's last. It had been quite an item for a month at least. The daughter of a rich Bostonian banker taking up with a mysterious government agent no queries could find any record of. They had met at a cocktail party when Blaine deliberately mistook her for the woman he was there to protect.

T.C. . . . He was the only one who called her that, and she pretended to hate it for those weeks McCracken had shared with her, shared more than he had with most women. Sustained attachments were impossible in Blaine's chosen profession. Too easy for the woman to be hurt or used as leverage by an opponent seeking any possible advantage. And just as dangerous, attachments could provide too seductive a picture of what the other side of life was like. Normalcy, settling down, living under your real name and without the fear that anyone's eyes you met might belong to a person about to kill you.

In this case, though, it hadn't been McCracken who had broken things off, it had been Terry Catherine. He hadn't told her much about himself but it was enough to let her know the commitment might last only until the next phone call. T.C. chose to accept the pain on her own terms. She was just twenty-two then, a kid fresh out of Brown University with the whole world before her. McCracken, three months past thirty, knew what the world was really like. Vietnam had interrupted college for him after just one year and he had never gone back. His life was made for him in what Johnny Wareagle called the hellfire, such events as the Phoenix project and the Tet Offensive.

The emotional hellfire came when T.C. broke things off. He probably would have done so himself before too much longer but understanding the strength it had required for her to do it made him love her more. It was impossible for him to forget her. He wanted her so much more once it was certain that he couldn't have her.

They hadn't as much as spoken in the eight-and-a-half years since parting, which was all the more reason to believe that something in T.C.'s life must be desperately wrong for her to seek him out. He tried to tell himself the fire of her youth's beauty would be long gone, but he was destined to be surprised by her yet again.

Their meeting that night was set for the Plaza Bar in Boston's Copley Plaza Hotel, not far from Terry Catherine's Back Bay townhouse. The Plaza Bar was located off the hotel's lobby, on the right of the main entrance. On most nights it featured the nimble piano work of the famed Dave McKenna, his fingers sliding across ivory in the bar's back right corner. Blaine entered through the handcarved archway just as the last chords of a McKenna favorite were greeted by applause. The ceilings were high, and the fresh smell of leather couches and low armchairs mingled with cigarette smoke and perfume. He scanned the room for T.C., but she wasn't at any of the nearby tables. He headed for the far wall, where more tables were secluded behind a Japanese screen. As he approached, she stepped out to meet him.

She was undoubtedly the most beautiful woman in the bar. Her figure had remained tall and lean. She wore only traces of makeup and a dress that highlighted her model's body. There was nothing pretentious about her appearance. Blaine immediately felt all the old attraction he had tried to forget. She stood there uneasily, her smile slight and nervous, and Blaine knew more was behind the tension than simply their reunion.

He kissed her lightly on the lips, let his squeeze of her hand linger.

"You promised me you'd stay beautiful," he said through the lump in his throat. "And you have."

"Still working the old charm, eh McCracken?"

"Some things don't change, T.C."

"Been a long time since anyone called me that. I still hate it."

"Well, Terry Catherine, that's why I say it."

"I see time hasn't mellowed you in the least. As I always used to tell you, if God had meant us to use initials, he wouldn't have bothered with names in the first place."

Blaine let go of her hand and together they walked to her table, set back against the wall where there was nothing to disturb their privacy. Through a nearby window they could see people passing on the sidewalk outside.

"I do plenty of things God probably never meant," he told her when they were seated.

"And I understand one of those colorful escapades," she followed without missing a beat, "earned you the title of McCrackenballs. I was offended when I heard about it. They could have come to me for a reference."

"Your memory that good?"

"Some things you don't forget."

"That ring I felt on your finger means you forgot one promise you made to yourself."

She nodded emotionlessly. "An unfortunate misstep. Lasted three years. The divorce was a much happier day than the wedding. I keep the ring as a reminder to avoid similar missteps in the future."

"Why bother making one?"

She didn't answer him right away, and that gave Blaine a chance to gaze into her eyes. She really was beautiful, even more so now than eight years ago. The little her face had aged made it seem fuller, less dominated by the high cheekbones she had always been sensitive about. She wore her hair shorter now, shaggy, neither in fashion nor out—just her.

"Because I was scared," she said finally. "Twenty-seven years old, all dressed up, and nowhere to go. I panicked. Promised myself I'd say yes to the next man who popped the question. Could've been worse. It could have been you, McCracken."

Blaine winked. "Anything but that."

"Anyway, I'm now determined to die single."

"But not a virgin."

"Thanks to you."

"If I was the first, I'll eat your mattress cover."

"You were the first that mattered, the first who wasn't a juvenile, or who didn't come ready packaged from my family, or who wasn't a horny Brown undergrad. It's the same thing."

A waitress came and T.C. ordered a glass of wine by name and vintage. McCracken said he'd take the same.

"Red and white," he noted with a shrug. "All just colors to me."

"A man in your position really should pay more attention to such things, McCracken."

"A man in my position shouldn't be drinking at all. You should see me. I'm really good at swirling the contents of a glass around so no one can tell I'm not drinking it."

"The wine you just ordered is twenty dollars a glass."

"I'll swirl slower."

She laughed and looked at ease for the first time. "You're a hard man to keep track of."

"You found me."

"I never stopped keeping tabs, you know. I know all about your trouble in England and your subsequent banishment to the office pool in France. Learning of your resurrection was second only to my divorce as the best day ever."

"But you didn't call until now."

The waitress came with their drinks, saving T.C. the trouble of responding right away. She sipped. McCracken swirled.

"I thought it would be much harder to reach you."

"I make sure it isn't for people who know me. It's what I'm doing these days—paying back old debts, settling scores. Makes me feel I'm worth something."

"Doing favors for friends . . ."

"Something like that. The freedom's priceless. I've sworn off Washington. But, of course, you'd know that."

"I heard."

"How's Back Bay?"

"Crumbling. Water table rose and the townhouse is sinking. Literally. It's cost me more in repairs than what my parents paid for it." She paused. "I found a phone number for you, but no address."

"Got six of them—apartments. Two don't even have any furniture, but they're scattered conveniently all over the country. What I really want is to own a car. You know I've never really had my own. Pretty incredible for a man of my advanced years."

T.C. sipped some of the wine, and the goblet trembled in her hand. Blaine grasped her other one in his.

"What's wrong, T.C.?"

"I hate asking you for something, after so long I mean."

"Favors for friends, remember?"

She placed the wine goblet on the table. "It's my grandfather. He's . . . in danger."

"Cotter Hayes? You're kidding."

"Not Cotter Hayes. My grandfather on my mother's side." She paused. "Erich Earnst."

"Hmmmmmm, not your average Boston yankee name."

"Anything but. German Jewish. World War II specifically. An escapee from Sobibor."

"If the gossip columnists could hear you now. . . ."

"It's one of Boston's best-kept secrets, I assure you." Another piano rendition by Dave McKenna ended, and T.C. waited for the applause to die down before continuing. "That Rawley Hayes would consent to marry a woman of Jewish persuasion . . . well, fortunately the truth never came out. Might have ruined him if it had." A sad smile crossed her lips. "Truth was, though, that Grandpa Erich was always infinitely more fun and interesting than Grandpa Cotter, especially when I grew old enough to appreciate him and all he'd been through."

"But now you're saying he's in danger."

"Because *he* says so. And I believe him. It's all very recent. The police don't buy it—nothing to go on. I . . . didn't know where else to turn."

McCracken swirled his wine some more. "I need to hear the specifics."

"There aren't many, Blaine; that's the problem. He's certain he's being followed. He should know, after all he's been through." Her mind strayed. "My mother's not really Jewish. Grandpa Erich found her wandering the streets of Poland and brought her to America with him and his wife. Never forced their religion on her because they didn't want her subjected to the persecution they had undergone. But, in addition to bringing my mother over, he also brought along a sack of diamonds the size of a tote bag. His gem parlor is still one of the best in Manhattan. The money made his daughter enough of a somebody for my father to take notice of her."

"You sound bitter."

"I hate pretenses; you know that."

"All too well. And that's why if you believe your grandfather, I believe you." The relief on her face was obvious. Her need for the wine seemed to evaporate, and she too, began swirling her glass.

"Trouble is I'm not exactly sure what I can do about it, T.C. This isn't exactly the kind of work I specialize in."

"You could talk to him."

"Which I'm sure you've done already. You're a sensible person. Is there anything he says I can make use of?"

"You'll ask the right questions. You always do."

"Except once. Might have saved you the bother of that divorce otherwise."

She shook her head sadly. "It would have happened anyway, Blaine, probably well before the three years were out, and that day would have been a bad one instead of a good one."

"In a twisted sense, I suppose that's a compliment."

"Not so twisted."

Blaine put his hand over hers. "Call your grandfather. Tell him I'm coming to talk to him."

She smiled. "I already did. He's expecting you tomorrow morning at his gem parlor in the diamond district."

"You know me too well, T.C."

"Some things don't change."

"Did you also mean to leave us the night?"

She hedged. "The morning was his idea, not mine."

"Then I suppose—"

"Dinner, Blaine. Some more of this wine probably; I'll drink while you swirl. That'll be as far as it goes, but it'll be plenty far for me because just having you here means enough. I don't want to spoil it. I want to hold it just the way it is."

"I love it when you talk dirty."

CHAPTER 4

"Is your report ready, Mr. Sundowner?"

When the scientist answered, his voice was hoarse with fatigue. In the past eighteen hours there had been time only for a quick change of clothes. Once again, the Tomb felt large and devastatingly empty to him. As he spoke, he was distracted by the echo of his own words.

"I'm not sure it will ever be totally complete, sir," he told the President, "at least not in the foreseeable future. To be honest, I know no more than I did yesterday; I've just confirmed my original feelings."

The other men in the room—Kappel, Stamp, Mercheson, and Lyman Scott himself—stared at him with laymen's confusion and disdain.

"Then get on with it," urged the President.

Sundowner didn't know where to start. Or rather, he did—and that was the problem.

"It all comes down to the symmetry of the destroyed radius. I'll spare you the explanatory details. Suffice it to say that the town of Hope Valley was destroyed by a hostile action in the form of a particle-beam weapon fired from between ten to twenty thousand feet above the Earth's surface."

"*Beam* weapon?" raised Secretary of Defense George Kappel. "You mean like a laser?"

"Not at all. Lasers fire focused beams of *energy*. A particle beam fires *matter*, subatomic particles accelerated to the speed of light. The mass of these particles increases with speed, and the energy produced goes up by the square."

"In English please, Ryan," requested the President.

Sundowner sighed. "An ordinary television set is actually a particle-beam generator which utilizes a gun to shoot particles in the form of electrons through two magnets. Presto! You've got a picture, the density of which is directly related to the concentration of particles fired from the set's gun. If it was too dense, the beam would obliterate the screen and everything in front of it. Now picture that on a much larger scale with a gun firing particles other than electrons. On the subatomic level almost anything is possible."

"As yesterday would seem to attest to," advanced Secretary of State Edmund Mercheson. "But how could this beam we're facing leave no trace whatsoever of people's remains, wood, plants, trees, grass, even rubber and cloth?"

"Organic matter," Sundowner stated flatly, rotating his stare from one to the other. "The subatomic particles break up organic matter."

"Speak plainly," ordered Lyman Scott.

Sundowner swallowed some air hoping the dull fear rising in him would slide down with it. "All life on Earth is based on the carbon atom. The subatomic particles composing the Hope Valley beam have the capacity to destroy the glue which holds that atom together. It breaks down the carbon chains into their basic elements. Separates the oxygen from the hydrogen on a molecular level which reduces organic matter to black carbon dust."

"The cloud," realized the President.

Sundowner nodded. "I had my suspicions after viewing the tape the very first time. But I wanted to put off my report until I had time to examine the evidence further—what did survive, as well as what didn't. Steel, brick, and all other forms of *in*organic matter in the town were themselves unaffected by the beam. Buildings composed of these materials collapsed, but only because the bonds holding the inorganic materials in place were carbon-based."

Lyman Scott felt his lips trembling and fought to still them. "What exactly would be needed to generate such a beam?"

"Two things, essentially. One, the discovery of a subatomic particle that disrupts the carbon chain. Two, a power source capable of focusing those particles into a beam on the level that wiped out Hope Valley. Without the second discovery, the first is useless in terms of a large-scale weapon."

"The *ultimate* weapon," Lyman Scott muttered. "Quick and absolute destruction."

"Not as absolute as it might have been," continued Sundowner. "The death ray traveled across Hope Valley from west to east in a beam three miles across, starting roughly at one border of the town and finishing at the other."

"Are you saying, Mr. Sundowner," raised Secretary of State Mercheson, "that the beam could just as easily have drawn a line of destruction straight across the entire country?"

"Theoretically, yes."

"Satellite delivery, then," from Kappel.

"*Whose* satellite?" the President demanded. "*Whose* weapon? Somebody has it, and for some reason they wanted to demonstrate its potency to us without letting us know who they are."

CIA chief Stamp leaned forward, almost reluctantly. "I may have a lead, sir. Just past midnight Saturday, six hours before the destruction of Hope Valley, our Turkish station received a message on a closed channel warning that an American town was going to be . . . destroyed."

"Why didn't you tell us this yesterday?"

"The message was only just relayed to me. Our Turkish station delayed transmission because, as I said, the channel was closed. Should have been inactive and had been for months. Our security had been penetrated, forcing us to re-route."

"Get to the point."

"It was a Soviet penetration."

A few long moments of silence passed before Secretary of Defense Kappel's voice sliced through the Tomb's heavy air. "Wait a minute," he shot out, "are you telling me that the *Russians* have a weapon that can melt people where they stand?"

"Not at all," said the man from the CIA. "But the fact remains they were the only ones who knew about the Turkish channel."

"Mr. President," began Edmund Mercheson in a typically droll, Kissinger-like tone, "a single instance of penetration of a single channel is hardly sufficient basis to adopt an accusatory posture. My feeling is we are more likely facing an enemy seeking to utilize this penetration to make us *think* the Soviets are behind everything, so as to severely limit our field of responses."

"We're severely limited in any case," noted the President grimly.

"But we have one option clearly open to us," Kappel followed almost before Lyman Scott had finished speaking. "I'd advise bumping DEF-CON status up to two, three at the very least. We've been *attacked*."

"But," argued Mercheson, "DEF-CON functions as a signal to no one else *but* the Soviets. It insinuates escalation, a tough atmosphere in which to initiate dialogue."

"I'd submit we're already past that."

"Which may well be exactly what the true wielder of this particle beam wants," said the man from State.

"I'm inclined to see Ed's side of things," broke in Lyman Scott. "No offense, George," he added, as if afraid of offending one of the last men whose trust he enjoyed. "But I can't see the point of the Soviets advertising the existence of such a superweapon *and* warning us in advance through such roundabout means. Even stranger, utilizing a weapon in this manner would seem to me to negate its ultimate purpose. If they've got and plan to use it, why not just draw the line all the way across the country? Why stop at Hope Valley?"

"Your point's well taken, sir," agreed Sundowner. "And the answer may lie in the reasons why we abandoned research aimed at developing this sort of weapon. The scientific limitations presented us were insurmountable. . . ."

"But apparently overcome by *somebody*," shot out Kappel.

"Maybe not," Sundowner continued. "There might be a very good reason why their deployment didn't extend beyond Hope Valley and why they bothered to warn us in the first place. The power source required to generate a beam of this nature is immense. Maybe they're only capable of effecting it on a small scale, so they risked a contained open demonstration complete with warning to make us think otherwise."

"Yes," echoed Mercheson. "We've heard from them once. Under that scenario they've set us up to hear from them again, fully convinced of the efficacy of their threat."

"Blackmail," realized Lyman Scott. "Hope Valley employed to hold us hostage to some sort of demands."

"And, Soviet or not," began Stamp, "they would certainly be well aware of the problems facing Washington at present. We're vulnerable, and our response is limited by that vulnerability."

"Words well chosen," said the President, "but too minced. A nice gesture, Willie, but we're all friends here. This administration isn't just vulnerable, it's under siege from all sides. We're not just lame ducks, we're sitting ducks for our enemies at home as well as abroad. Might be some, a few who once occupied these empty chairs, who'd welcome the whole business to finish the job of bringing us down."

"The Soviets would like nothing better," reminded George Kappel. "It's possible they've used this means to manufacture a crisis, destroy us from the inside without ever having to use their weapon again. Screens and inconsistencies thrown up in our path to force us to go in circles. They know our grip is tenuous. If we handle this situation poorly, we could face collapse."

"Gentlemen," said the President strongly, "if this government is out of control, I'll accept responsibility. But I won't, can't, sit here and admit we've lost."

"That's not what I was saying, sir," insisted Kappel.

"But it comes down to that, doesn't it?"

"Maybe we should hope it does," put forth Sundowner suddenly, "because under that scenario we would at least be granted time to formulate a response. If we could negate the weapon, we can negate the threat."

"Ever so simple, assuming we had such a response."

"I believe we do, potentially anyway: Bugzapper."

"I thought we had determined its activation to be technologically infeasible," said Kappel after a brief pause.

"Not anymore," the scientist told him.

Upon taking over as head of the Toy Factory four years before, Sundowner had inherited the remains of the Strategic Defense Initiative, better known as the Star Wars system. Problems both financial and technological had already stripped the program bare. What had originally been envisioned as a seven-layer defensive shield against all incoming missile attacks had been peeled away one layer at a time until all that remained was a ground-based laser system which utilized mirrors in space and had tested out as being woefully inadequate against anything but a small-scale strike—hardly a layer at all.

For years Sundowner had maintained his own theories and finally had the chance to set them to work. He called his program "Bugzapper" after those deadly bright lights that fry any insect that wanders too close. His system functioned on the same general basis. Sundowner envisioned a fleet of three or four dozen satellites poised in geosynchronistic orbits over the United States, attached to each other by invisible energy fields. Any object that attempted to penetrate such a field would suffer the same fate that awaited the nagging mosquito on a summer evening. In effect, an impenetrable shield would be erected over the nation, rendering it invincible to any major attack—a shield without the complexities of Star Wars.

"The major problem with Bugzapper from the beginning," Sundowner was saying, "was that for the shield to be effective, the energy fields erected between the various satellites had to be constantly active. The power drain would thus be enormous. And since the satellites would have to possess the capacity to recharge themselves in outer space, solar energy was the only possibility. But it was impossible until recently to find a sufficient power storage capability."

"Don't tell me," quipped George Kappel. "You've discovered a way to lay cable connecting your satellites with the sun itself."

"Not exactly," said Sundowner, "but close enough."

The red phone buzzed twice and the President leaned forward over the table and lifted the receiver.

"Yes?" he said, holding it to his ear. His lower lip dropped as he listened attentively, his face seeming to grow progressively paler. "And that's it?" he asked at the end. "I see. . . . No, we'll handle it from here. . . . Yes, tell them to keep monitoring." Lyman Scott turned to the men before him, still clutching the receiver to his ear. "We've been contacted in Turkey again; same channel, same code."

"Sir?" one of them raised, speaking for all, hoping to learn the contents of the communiqué just received.

But the President simply looked toward Sundowner. "Lay your cable, Ryan. And lay it fast."

The two figures sat alone in the rearmost row of the Bangkok movie house, the light cast by the celluloid images barely reaching them.

"I am instructed to require your name and status before any further discussion can take place," said the smaller of the two.

"My name is Katlov and my status is renegade," said the other softly, turning enough so a patch over his left eye was visible in the darkness. The rest of his features were indistinguishable.

"Strange for a renegade to seek out a KGB station chief."

On the screen an American western, dubbed in Thai, was nearing its climax.

"To me you are simply a messenger, Station Chief."

The KGB man grunted. "I am a busy man."

"And a small one."

"Get to the point."

"You will deliver a message for me to Moscow."

"Really?"

"You will tell them that I can give them Raskowski."

The KGB man's mouth dropped.

"You will tell them I have no time for games or delays. The *world* has no time. I will meet their emissary here."

"This is my station," the KGB man said defensively.

"There are terms you will not be able to meet."

"But—"

"I won't have this!" Katlov snapped. "I will give you the key we used for the Turkish channel. That will be all the proof they require. It will show I am what I claim to be."

"I know nothing of such a channel's significance."

"*They* will know, you fool! You will relay to them my instructions. You will stress the importance of immediate action and that I alone hold the means to end this madness."

"What madness?" the station chief asked, pensive now.

Katlov made a motion to rise. The KGB man restrained him gently.

"Please. I'll . . . do as you say."

Katlov settled back in his chair.

CHAPTER 5

NEW York's famed diamond district occupies only one block, West 47th Street between Fifth and Sixth Avenues. From across the street, at first glance, Earnst's Gem Parlor looked small and unassuming, its narrow shape squeezed between a pair of larger and more openly aggressive merchants. But at second glance, McCracken reckoned from his position fronting the jar-filled window of Kaplan's Delicatessen, it stood a cut above the others in class as well as clientele. The fact that it need not stack its front windows with rows of diamonds revealed this, as did a front entrance cubicle complete with armed guard.

McCracken and T.C. had taken Eastern's nine A.M. shuttle from Boston. She had insisted on accompanying him and he had reluctantly agreed only after she promised to do nothing but remain in her room at the Waldorf and wait for his call. The cab dropped them both off at the hotel, and Blaine walked the short distance to Earnst's.

He should have used the opportunity to check for tails but he was distracted by thoughts still lingering from the night before. T.C. had left him at the Copley Plaza just past one A.M. but called as soon as she got back to her crumbling townhouse, and they talked for another hour. Blaine didn't know which he regretted more: the fact that she wasn't lying beside him then or that she had broken off their relationship all those years before. He slept fitfully, dreaming of her, and hating it once he awoke because only in dreams could he bring her as near to him as he wished.

With those thoughts chasing him again, Blaine dashed across the street through westbound traffic. Seventy West 47th was embroidered in plated gold over the entrance. McCracken stepped through the first door and faced the uniformed security officer squeezed behind a counter.

"Good morning, sir," the guard said cheerfully. "I'll need an I.D. card to hold while you're inside."

Blaine produced one of his many driver's licenses and handed it over. The guard fumbled beneath his counter, finally locating the entry button. There was an ear-scratching buzz, and Blaine watched the inner glass door snap electronically open. He passed inside and found himself within the long, narrow, and elegantly appointed confines of Earnst's. A crystal chandelier cast shimmering light over the whole quiet scene, reflecting off the many glass counters and display cases. Instead of standard stools behind the various counters, Earnst's were covered in rich velour that matched the color of the carpeting.

McCracken ambled past a series of display cases and was surprised not to see any hidden wires strung through the glass. Then he realized that it was not here but on the upper levels of the store that gems of greater value were kept and traded. Access to these was limited, and strictly by appointment.

"Can I help you?" a clerk asked him as he stood before a case layered with diamond sapphire necklaces.

"I'm here to see Mr. Earnst. He's expecting me. Tell him it's Blaine McCracken."

"One moment."

The clerk turned and disappeared up a set of stairs situated behind one of the counters. A minute later he returned with an older man by his side.

Erich Earnst must have been closer to eighty than seventy.

His thinning white hair was wild, and his flesh was grayish. He walked with a slight limp. Blaine moved forward to greet him.

"Mr. McCracken," the old man said gratefully, extending his hand. "I'm so glad you've come. Please, let's go upstairs."

Blaine freed himself from the old man's surprisingly strong handshake, aware that the rapid shifting of Earnst's eyes was due more to fear than age. T.C. had said her grandfather was in danger and that was good enough for him. Given the vast sums Earnst dealt with every day, anything was possible. Blaine owed it to T.C. to follow every lead.

"We'll talk in my office," Erich Earnst said as they moved behind the counter to the staircase he had just descended.

Blaine followed the older man up the stairs. At the top they had to turn right and directly before them rose a high security steel-and-glass door. Earnst slid an electronic entry card into a slot and the door snapped open.

Obviously in a hurry now, Earnst stepped through and made sure the door caught behind them.

"This way," he beckoned, and Blaine moved with him down the hall into a beautiful office, furnished in the same colors as the display area downstairs. The old man closed the door and limped to his desk.

"My granddaughter has told me quite a lot about you, Mr. McCracken," he said. "Please sit down. Excuse me for being so nervous, but I haven't slept well in a month now."

Blaine sat down opposite Earnst in one of a pair of red velvet chairs facing the neat desk.

"A month ago," McCracken noted. "Was that when it started?"

"Yes. The feeling of being watched is well known to me. You develop a sense for such things when you spend years running for your life."

"I can understand that. It's why I'm here."

"The others didn't believe. The police . . . *ach*. I tell them and they listen, but they think I'm crazy."

McCracken leaned forward. "Mr. Earnst, you said you were being watched. Does that mean followed as well?"

"No. I don't go anywhere, so there would be no reason to follow me. I come here and I go home. Nothing else. I'm watched all day long. Nights sometimes, too."

"And it started one month ago."

"Yes."

"Does anything else about that time stand out in your mind?"

Earnst didn't have to think. "No. The robbery had happened two weeks earlier."

"T.C. didn't mention anything about a robbery."

"I'm not sure I mentioned it to her. There was nothing worth worrying her about. Only a few items were taken."

"Specifically?"

"Ruby-red crystals sent to me by a supplier in Greece."

"Rubies?"

"Only in color. I'd never seen anything like them. I thought they might be quite valuable and agreed to take them on consignment." The old man's stare turned distant. "Strange crystals they were, jagged and irregular. Unfinished. There was only one customer who showed any interest in them at all. Why is this important?"

"I'm not sure yet. Tell me about this customer."

Earnst pushed himself up from the chair and limped behind his desk where he extracted an appointment book from the top drawer. Flipping through it, he quickly came upon the day in question.

"Lydia Brandywine made me show her all five of the crystals. Said she was searching for something exotic and totally different. I showed her plenty of gems that afternoon, I remember now, but the crystals were the only items that interested her. She made an appointment to choose a setting but the crystals were stolen a few days later."

"*Just* the crystals?"

"Because of their potential as one-of-a-kinds, I kept them in a separate place." The old man shook his head. "My security was antiquated. The door we passed through was added after the robbery. My first, you know, in all these years."

"And ten days or so after that you started feeling you were being watched."

"Yes."

"I'll need Lydia Brandywine's address."

Earnst jotted it down in a large scrawl and handed it over. "Why bother?" he wanted to know.

"Because I don't believe in coincidence. I want to follow these crystals and see where they lead, so I'll speak with Mrs. Brandywine. If I get nowhere, I'll start over somewhere else."

That set Earnst thinking as he sat back down. "It's strange."

"What is?"

"The man who supplied me with the crystals requested their return shortly after the robbery. He sounded quite agitated, even frightened, when I told him they had been stolen."

"Tell me about him."

"He's a Greek named Kapo Stadipopolis. He's a prime dealer in artifacts and gems sometimes obtained through shady means. All merchants depend on the black market from time to time, including me."

"That's not the issue here, Mr. Earnst. Your safety is."

"Stadipopolis has a shop in Athens, on Monastiraki Square. He's good at what he does, seldom makes a mistake. But he claimed he shipped me the crystals by accident. Said he needed them back desperately."

"In your mind, what were they worth?"

"Whatever the market would bear for one-of-a-kind items. Believe me when I tell you, Mr. McCracken, that I had never seen anything quite like them before. A woman like Lydia Brandywine, well, there's no telling how high she might have gone for something no one else had."

"She was no stranger to you then."

"Hardly. All the merchants know her. She is always in search of the unusual."

"So the crystals were worth stealing."

"Even more so because they were untraceable. Once remade and refined into stones for setting, they wouldn't even resemble what I obtained from Greece." Earnst looked impatient. "I still don't see what this has to do with my being watched."

"T.C. also said you felt your life was in danger."

"An old man's exaggeration."

"Really?"

"I'm . . . not sure." He hesitated, groping for the words to express what he felt. "I can feel them out there waiting; for what, I don't know. A few times I walk to work, and I see faces I shouldn't recognize but do. My apartment building has a new doorman—all of a sudden. The guard service sends a new man to watch the—"

The intercom on Earnst's desk buzzed. "Yes?" the old man said into it.

"Mr. Obermeyer's man is here with the delivery, sir," a clerk's voice came back.

"Hmmmmm, early. Send him up." Then, to McCracken as he started for the door, "Forgive the interruption."

But Blaine reached out and restrained him by the arm, his mind working in another direction. "The fact that he was early bothered you. . . ."

"Yes, but—"

"It's not the routine. How early, damnit, how early?"

"An hour, perhaps two."

"And who would check his papers?"

"The guard at the main entrance, of course."

"The one your security service replaced," McCracken said softly, recalling the man's difficulty in finding the button beneath his desk.

Earnst nodded slowly, fear filling his eyes as he realized the same thing McCracken already had.

"What do we do? What do we do? They've come! Oh God, they've finally come!"

"They've done us a favor, Mr. Earnst, because they don't know I'm here, and even if they did they couldn't know who I am. What's the procedure?"

"A clerk will escort the delivery man to the security door."

"And then?"

"I open it and let them in."

"Follow the procedure."

"But—"

"Trust me, Mr. Earnst. I'll be right behind you all the way. But we've got to move now. Quickly!"

McCracken crouched low as soon as he was back in the corridor, and moved quickly to the security door so he couldn't be seen through the window two-thirds of the way up. When the old man was five yards away from the door, a face appeared against the glass.

"My clerk," Earnst said to McCracken who was now poised low against the wall adjacent to the door, so that when it opened it would obscure him.

Blaine motioned him to open the door, whispering, "Move toward me quick as you can when it gives."

Earnst punched a coded sequence into a keypad. The door snapped open and began to move inward.

The rest unfolded too fast for the old man's eyes to follow, but McCracken grasped it all. The clerk's frame shoved against the door and through it into the hallway with a large man behind him. There was a *fsssssst* and the clerk went down. Blaine noted the strange-looking pistol in the man's hand and sprang into action.

The man was going for Earnst, bringing the pistol up again, never seeing McCracken until he was upon him. Blaine used the man's weapon against him, turned it back into his gut and jammed the trigger. A second *fsssssssst* split the air and the man stiffened immediately.

"My God," muttered a trembling Earnst.

"Just tranquilizers," McCracken explained, jamming the

strange pistol into his pocket and sealing the door again. "Whoever it is must have wanted you alive." He grabbed the old man and led him back down the corridor. "But now we've changed the rules on them, which might change their plans. They still want you and there'll be more of them, the guard downstairs for instance. Is there another way out of the building from this level?"

Earnst nodded fearfully. "My private elevator connects with a common exit for mine and four other stores."

"Fine. Your office first and then we'll make use of it."

They reached Earnst's office. Blaine eased the old man inside and steered him toward a display case set against the wall. It was filled with small, unfinished diamonds.

"Grab as many of those as you can."

"What?"

"T.C. sent me here to keep you safe and alive and that's what I plan on doing."

The old man moved to the case and drained a measure of its contents into a small black jewelry box. "But the diamonds, why?"

"Insurance," Blaine replied and led the way back into the corridor, eyes peeled toward the security door. "They want you alive. We can make that work for us."

The elevator was located at the opposite end of the hallway from the door. Earnst could barely fit his security key in the special slot to activate it. McCracken helped him and eased the old man in first.

Blaine drew his gun and had moved ahead to shield Earnst by the time the doors slid open again. The lobby before them was empty. McCracken wasted no time, grasping the old man gently once more.

"Let's go."

Blaine led him forward toward a set of glass doors which opened out onto 47th. He held the gun low by his hip, partially hidden by his sports jacket. Earnst gripped the jewelry box with both hands to his chest as he moved behind Blaine out the door and into the street.

"Stay by my side," McCracken whispered and swung right, walking east.

West 47th was a snarl of pedestrians and vehicles. With the city clogged by the lunchtime rush, packs of humanity squeezed past each other, spilling into the street to merge with the gridlocked traffic. Horns blared. Tires went through a series of crazed stops and starts.

Blaine led Earnst on, moving with the flow of the crowd. A chill crept up his spine, warning him to beware of adversaries closing in even now, searching them out—but from where?

Up ahead the reason for the traffic tie-up became clear. A moving truck had wedged itself into an impossible position across the street. The slightest acceleration would crumple a car on one side of it or the other. Several individuals were helping the driver with his delicate maneuvers. Blaine slowed.

"What's wrong?" Earnst wondered.

"That truck up there, I don't like it."

"How can you tell? How can you *know*?"

Blaine's response was to grasp the old man's arm at the elbow to urge him to go faster. The gnawing feeling of an attack soon to come was tight in his stomach. Yet from where would it come? Who might the assailants be, if there were any here at all? Everywhere he turned another shoulder brushed his own. Too many to be sure of anything. But as long as they wanted Earnst alive, he—

Through the cool spring air, Blaine caught a sound. It was faint but terrifyingly distinct: the clang of a machine pistol bolt being yanked back followed by a sudden *click*.

Alive, damnit, you're supposed to want him alive!

From tranquilizers to real bullets. Something had changed. The drawing-back of the bolts meant the gunmen had spotted them and were closing even now.

Wait! The crowd! There was a way he could make use of it!

They were halfway to Fifth Avenue now. Just ahead a

temporary scaffolding was in place for construction on the upper floors of a building.

"Open your box of diamonds," McCracken whispered to Earnst.

"What?"

"Just do as I say. And when I tell you, fling the contents up in the air."

The old man gawked in disbelief. "Are you crazy? Millions of dollars, you're talking about. Millions!"

"Still not worth your life. There's no time. They've got us. This is our only chance. When the excitement starts, mix with the crowd and disappear. You've done it before. You can do it again."

"The killers will still chase *you*."

"That's the idea."

Somewhere behind him, Blaine felt footsteps pushing forward. Their pursuers were about to strike.

"Now!" McCracken ordered.

The old man lowered his eyes and hesitated. McCracken was about to knock the diamonds upward himself when Earnst flung the contents of the jewelry box back over his shoulder.

The diamonds flew into the air, shimmering in the noon sun. The entire street seemed to come to a halt; the gems cascaded down, as if from heaven. Then the chaos set in.

Men and women clawed past each other. Some lunged into the street or toward the sidewalk in pursuit of the slightest glimmer. Others dove around or through bodies for stones far smaller than a pinky fingernail. All was bedlam, screams, shouts of anger, threats. Bodies piled atop each other. Stronger men peeled them aside to clear a path for their arms.

Blaine helped Earnst move to the edge of the chaos and then took off against the flow, smacking into people rushing back toward the frenzy. He gazed to his rear and the sight stunned him.

Four men in the black garments, beards, wavy side curls, and homburgs of Hasidim had yanked machine pistols from beneath their overcoats. The Hasidim were fixtures on this street, but not normally with guns in their hands. Their first bursts split the air in Blaine's direction. Bodies collapsed with bloody punctures dotting their flesh. The screams intensified.

Blaine gnashed his teeth at the carnage. His strategy had exposed the gunmen all right, but now several people were dead as a result of it. He continued to run, blending with the crowd rushing from the gunfire and colliding with pedestrians who had stopped to gaze back toward the excitement. He sped under the scaffolding and past another delicatessen, heading for the street corner.

At least the killers were known to him now. Once through the scaffolding, he would draw them into the open. Any fire then would be clear of innocent bystanders, and Blaine would be able to take on his assailants commando-style. It wouldn't be easy; their silenced machine pistols attested to their professionalism, but—

A woman smacked into him from behind. The impact knocked his arm against a street lamp, and the gun went flying under a sea of rushing feet.

Behind him the four black coats loomed closer. Blaine had no choice but to run; escape was his only option.

But not at the expense of more innocent people. With that in mind, he darted straight into 47th Street, zigzagging through traffic in a diagonal toward Fifth Avenue; the subway perhaps, a cab or bus. Bullets chewed the air. Screams tore at his ears, joined now by the shrieks of brakes and the crash of steel on steel as cars swerved sharply to avoid him. He sped onto Fifth Avenue with the awareness that the gunmen were very close and a continued flight by him would almost surely claim more innocent lives. He had to narrow the battlefield in order to gain the advantage.

The service entrance to a spanking-new building at 590 Fifth Avenue had been propped open by deliverymen, and Blaine sped through it up a wide set of stairs. He heard what must have been singing and had climbed three flights before a collection of crates deposited on the landing blocked his way further up. He had no choice but to go through a door that brought him to the origin of the singing.

He was on the dais of a synagogue that occupied the second and third floors of the building. A robed man, apparently a rabbi, was standing next to a young boy, while a man in different robes, apparently a cantor, chanted from a scroll. Few others were present. It must have been a rehearsal, a rehearsal for the boy's upcoming Bar Mitzvah.

"Get out!" Blaine shouted, as he rushed forward, but his warning was barely complete when two of the Hasidim charged onto the dais after him. One stumbled and slipped but the other came straight for McCracken. The man aimed his machine gun.

Blaine grasped the heavy wooden ends of the Torah scrolls and swung the heavy object like a bat as he lunged toward the gun-wielding "Hasid." The sacred symbol cracked into his face and tore his feet out from under him as the second "Hasid" regained his balance and a third came through a door at the front of the synagogue.

McCracken dove to the floor of the dais and rolled. He grasped the machine pistol of the downed "Hasid" and fired a burst at the second man now charging toward him across the dais. The bullets caught the man in the gut and sent him careening into the Torah stand. The stand toppled to reveal the terrified boy who had sought cover behind it.

The third assassin's bullets flew wildly across the dais. A man screamed, then a woman. The boy crouched in fear.

Blaine leaped to cover the boy as the third "Hasid" fired a fire spray over the area where the boy had just been. The leap had separated Blaine from his gun and he swept the floor for it frantically. He found it just as the costumed killer, snapping a new clip into place, was charging up the synagogue's center aisle. Blaine fired at motion more than shape as the front door crashed open and the fourth "Hasid" burst through.

The third had stopped and crumbled in his tracks. Blaine

twisted to train his machine pistol on number four. He fired a split second before the last gunman and sent the man over two sets of seats. He was dead when he landed.

McCracken kept the boy tight beneath him as he checked the dais. A young woman was holding her arm. The rabbi was bleeding rather badly from a leg wound. Blaine eased the terrified boy gently up at the shoulders.

"Now," he told him, "you can live to become a man."

CHAPTER 6

"BLAINE, where have you been? What happened? I've been calling the parlor and—"

"Never mind, T.C. Your grandfather's safe, but it was close. I don't know what he's gotten involved in but it must be big. And unless I miss my guess, it's got something to do with some twice-stolen crystals."

"Crystals? You mean gems? *Stolen?* Blaine—"

"Listen to me. I'm not sure what these crystals are but they're part of the mystery and they're the only trail I can follow. But somebody might not want me to get very far, and it might not take them very long to put the pieces together. Just stay put at the Waldorf until you hear from me."

"No, I want to—"

"You'll do as I say," he insisted firmly, then lowered his voice. "I'm going to tell you how to reach an Indian friend of mine in case something happens to me. You'll be safe. He'll make sure of it."

"Blaine, you're scaring me. . . ."

"I just want you to appreciate me more when I come to pick you up."

* * *

McCracken rented a car at Hertz's midtown depot and headed out toward the home of Lydia Brandywine, which was in Woodmere. He wasn't sure how she connected with all this but a connection was plain; the robbery had occurred days after she had examined the crystals. So she had alerted someone, the force behind the "Hasidim" perhaps, to their existence. Whether she had done so on purpose or not Blaine didn't know. He intended to find out.

Lydia Brandywine lived in a large house, not quite large enough to be a mansion, off Chester Road. It was painted white, and its facade was dominated by a trio of pillars. The grounds were spacious, and a circular drive fronted the entrance. McCracken parked directly before it and climbed the steps. He rang the bell, waited a few seconds, and then rang it again. He heard locks being turned and then the door swung open.

"Have you seen my cat?" an old voice asked him through the crack left by the chain. "Have you seen Kitty?"

"No," McCracken said, flashing his best smile. "Erich Earnst sent me. He's recovered those crystals you were interested in, and he sent me out to inquire about possible settings for them."

She gazed beyond him. "Has he recovered my cat? She's disappeared before, though. Always comes back. Wants to eat."

"May I come in, Mrs. Brandywine?"

"Why?"

"To discuss possible settings for the crystals."

"Oh, yes." She started the door inward to unfasten the chain. "Certainly."

The door open, she bid Blaine to enter. He saw she was frail and wrinkled, her body hunched over. She was hardly the type he'd expect to be a second-floor customer of Erich Earnst and well known in the diamond district to boot. She wore a long dark dress with a shawl covering her shoulders.

"It's so nice to have company. If only I could find Kitty. Here, Kitty," she called. "Here, Kitty. . . ."

Blaine followed her through the huge marble foyer to a set of double doors. She thrust them open to reveal a grand wood-paneled library dominated by shelves of leatherbound books.

"I feed her in here. Sometimes she hides." She walked in, eyes peering about, voice higher. "Here, Kitty. I'm getting your dinner ready. It's your favorite. Here, Kitty. Oh, where *is* that damn cat!"

"Mrs. Brandywine," McCracken started, "if you could spare a few minutes. . . ."

"What'd you say your name was?"

"McCracken."

"First or last?"

"Last."

"You have cats, McCracken?"

"No."

"Don't. More bother than they're worth." She moved to an elegant brass-legged glass table with an antique bowl atop it and a can of cat food resting alongside. Leaning over, she began to spoon its contents into the bowl. "She'll smell the food and come running. That's my best hope. Here, Kitty."

"Mrs. Brandywine, about the setting . . ."

She swung toward him. "Yes. Wanted to make a collar for Kitty. Something different. Fell in love with the crystals at first glance. Just the kind of thing I had in mind."

"The expense didn't bother you?"

"Why should it?" She was spooning again now, tapping the last of the can's contents out onto the side of the antique bowl. "Here, Kitty!"

Blaine kept himself patient. "The crystals, Mrs. Brandywine, did you tell anyone else about them?"

"Just Kitty. She was very happy. Didn't run away for a week afterwards. Damn cat. Why do I bother?"

"Was there anyone else?"

She eyed him sharply. "Anyone else what?"

"That you discussed the crystals with."

"Who else would be interested? Don't get out much anymore you know." She was mixing the cat food up now. "Here, Kitty!"

"How did you get into the city the day you visited our shop?"

Lydia Brandywine had to stop and think. "My driver. Victor."

"Where is he?"

"With the car. I call him when I need him."

Blaine felt he might be on to something. "Do you have his number?"

"Somewhere."

"Did he ask you about the crystals when he drove you home from the parlor?"

"Kitty doesn't talk much," said Lydia Brandywine. "Sometimes, but not much. Ah, here she comes now. . . ."

McCracken had time only to register the fact that the padding of approaching paws was too loud and out of place. He swung, too late his eyes told him, and he froze in his tracks.

Kitty was a black panther.

The big cat opened its mouth and snarled from deep in its throat.

"You're carrying a gun," said Lydia Brandywine, no longer interested in the cat food and suddenly quite in command of her faculties. "I saw the bulge. Reach into your belt and pull it out slowly. Move too fast and she'll lunge. Don't challenge her."

As if to reinforce the old woman's words, the big cat snarled again and whipped its paw through the air, claws bared. A single lunge away, a lunge that could be covered in the shadow of an instant. Blaine slid the pistol he'd lifted from one of the 47th Street assassins out of his holster and let it drop to the floor.

"Very good, Mr. McCracken," Lydia Brandywine said. "Now slide it over here." When he had, she stooped to retrieve it, all the while keeping her eyes on him. "Now move backward very slowly and settle yourself in that chair Remember, slowly, and keep your hands by your sides."

Again Blaine did as he was told. He found the chair with the back of his legs and slowly settled into it. The big cat advanced a bit, staying a lunge away.

"I'm going to leave you briefly. Rise from that chair and she'll tear you apart. Move your hands from the arms and she'll tear you apart. She won't move so long as you don't."

Lydia Brandywine kept her eyes on him as she glided past, the gun clutched in her hand, no longer seeming as old. She petted the panther's head on the way out. There was no phone in this room and Blaine figured she was moving to another to summon reinforcements. More of the men behind the attack on 47th Street, no doubt, and they'd be on their way here in minutes.

The cat snarled again, stretching its lips wide to show its teeth and whipping its long tail from side to side. Blaine knew he could not possibly move before it was upon him. Panthers were in many respects the most dangerous jungle cats, the best fighters, and the most precise killers. He was certainly no match for Kitty, even though he might have been able to disarm the woman. Once she returned, though, there'd be two forces to contend with. So if he was going to move it had to be fast. But how?

He remembered he still had the tranquilizer pistol loaded with one more dart in his right pocket. If he could extract it and fire before the big cat was upon him. . . . No, even if he scored a perfect hit, the panther would have the second it needed to find his throat. Blaine had to buy himself that second, as well as shoot.

He knew Kitty would lunge at the first sign of motion. But if the motion was deceptive it might be fooled long enough for the tranquilizer to work. Blaine heard Lydia Brandywine's voice speaking to someone over a phone. He knew the conversation wouldn't last much longer.

Blaine braced his legs. He was depending on the big cat to be just as quick and deadly as legend had it, so when it attacked he could make the lunge work in his favor. He pushed his legs hard on the floor and tossed his body backward, giving the chair all his weight. As expected, it toppled over. The cat lunged but failed to adjust to his tumble backward. Its leap carried it short, buying him the second he needed.

The tranquilizer gun was in his hand, and he fired as the cat regained its footing and came for him. The slightest fumble would have meant death, but the dart shot out with a *fsssssst* and thudded into the animal's extended shoulders. The cat didn't falter and kept coming. The huge jaws opened wide and lowered over him, teeth bared and breath hot and dripping, and he closed his eyes in terror, latching on to the beast's throat instinctively.

But the panther was already limp with the weight of unconsciousness. Blaine heard Lydia Brandywine's heels clicking fast for the library and lurched back to his feet. She had his gun and he was out of darts. He had another weapon, though.

As she crossed through the double doors, McCracken hoisted the sleeping panther up by its neck and let its feet dangle above the floor. It took all his strength and he felt his shoulders popping from the strain. Lydia Brandywine lurched into the room and steadied the gun with both hands a dozen feet before him.

"The gun's a Brin-10, Mrs. Brandywine," Blaine said ever so calmly. "Packs quite a wallop. Difficult to keep steady. You might get lucky but then again you might not. Kitty's only stunned now but miss your first shot and I'll break her neck. Miss your second and I'll break yours."

"No!" the old woman screamed, more out of concern for the cat than herself.

"I'm an animal lover myself, Mrs. Brandywine. Never think of harming one unless I have to. She's just sleeping now. Still breathing," he said, making sure to display the contracting chest. "See? But that will change if you don't drop the gun and slide it over here."

Lydia Brandywine's old hands shook uncontrollably for a few seconds before she let the gun drop.

McCracken held fast to the cat. "You called someone. Who?"

"The party that hires me from time to time."

"To do what?"

"Search out rare, precious gems and then furnish detailed descriptions. The cat, you're hurting her!"

"No I'm not. You did that with the crystals you saw at Earnst's?"

"Yes."

"And then they were stolen."

"I had nothing to do with it. Please let the cat go!"

McCracken wasn't ready to do that yet. "Who are these men?"

"I don't know. I swear it! They sought me out, paid me enough money so I wouldn't have to move from my house. I never meant any harm!"

"These men did plenty today. They're coming, aren't they?"

"Yes."

"How long?"

"Let the cat down."

"How long?"

"A half hour. Twenty-five minutes maybe."

"I'll be going, then. I'll have to tie you up but I won't make the bonds too tight. I promise."

He let the panther down easy and tied Lydia Brandywine into a chair with drapery cords stripped from the wall. He checked to make sure they weren't too constricting and was halfway to the double doors when he headed back for the glass table.

"She'll probably be in a bad mood when she wakes up," he said, lifting the cat food dish up and placing it next to the snoring panther. "I hate to see a good meal go to waste."

* * *

The car screeched onto Lydia Brandywine's property exactly twenty-seven minutes later. McCracken watched it from a concealed position behind a tree with his Hertz rental stowed safely out of sight. After fifteen minutes the three men returned to their car, and Blaine climbed back into his and followed them all the way back into Manhattan. It was rush hour and he fought with his nerves as the car he was shadowing maneuvered ahead of him, out of sight on occasion. He couldn't risk being spotted by the men. If they were pros, it wouldn't take much. He had given Lydia Brandywine his real name and she would have passed it on to them. A check would be made, and the men would know they had problems.

He managed to keep their car in sight right until it swung off Park Avenue onto East 48th Street. They continued on past Lexington and slowed as they crossed over Third Avenue into the Turtle Bay neighborhood, parallel parking into a spot before the low 200s. Blaine pulled past them and double-parked. In his rearview mirror he watched the three men climb out of their car and ascend the steps to the right half of a slate-brown townhouse duplex squeezed between a pair of larger brick buildings. One of the men pulled the steel security grating open and another unlocked the townhouse's door. Seconds later all three men had disappeared inside.

McCracken saw a space open up almost directly across from the townhouse and reversed diagonally across the street to take it. Tires squeezed against the curb, he settled back against the seat. At this point his plan was to wait until the three men, or at least two of them, departed again before making his way inside the townhouse. Until then, he was alone with his thoughts.

The choice of Turtle Bay for a headquarters or meeting place struck him as strange. After all, this neighborhood was one of Manhattan's most fashionable, home to numerous celebrities and wealthy businessmen. The townhouses on the north side of the street enjoyed a common garden, Amster Yard, which was not visible from the front; just one of the many features which placed Turtle Bay among the city's most prestigious residential areas.

Two hours passed. Blaine watched the night fall soundly and the lights come on in the street, those inside the rows of townhouses slowly joining them. Cars continued to line both curbs but traffic had thinned markedly. Across the street, an entry light flashed on over the townhouse he was watching.

McCracken felt something was out of place and gazed up at the windows. None showed any light. Odd. If the men inside were still there, at least some of the lights should have been turned on. Their car was in place and Blaine was certain none of the men had left.

A familiar chill gripped him, a slow shudder following in its wake. He lunged from the car and hurried up the steps to the townhouse's entrance. The steel grating had not been locked, leaving him only the door to negotiate past. Just a single lock which Blaine had out of the way in under thirty seconds. The door opened into darkness. McCracken stepped inside and waited for his eyes to adjust before pressing on. His vision sharpened and he saw a front hall with narrow rooms on either side of it, one of them a kitchen, and none furnished. The stairs leading upward curved a few yards before him. Leaving the lights off, he started to ascend, silently in case someone might still be upstairs.

The steps broke to the right as they neared the second floor and Blaine froze. Before him a pair of shoes protruded from a door. At the top of the landing he saw the blood, a pool of it in the center of the room's hardwood floor. The room smelled of must, mold, emptiness.

And death.

The other two bodies had been propped up together along the wall in a neat posture, as if they had been searched after death. Each displayed a single bullet hole, like a ruby in the middle of the forehead. All three had been gut shot as well, which accounted for the blood on the floor. The bullets in their heads had been merely to finish them.

Whoever had done the shooting liked to inflict pain. Or had been ordered to.

McCracken stepped further inside. This room had a huge draped window overlooking the lush garden. The killer could have gained entry to the garden from another of the townhouses and once there could have made a straight route here, entering through the back. His task completed, he would have left the same way. That was why Blaine never saw him.

But had that task been completed satisfactorily? The killer had left the men alive long enough for questions, but they must not have pleased him; signs of a search were evident among the room's meager furnishings. The stuffing of the furniture had been sliced up and scattered. The drawers from the room's single desk had been pulled out and their contents tossed around.

McCracken had seen all this before. The apartment must have been a temporary headquarters for a team of agents. Right down to the black rotary telephone; standard issue in mobile operations.

These men had worked for the government!

And now they were dead. Killed by whom, though? McCracken felt the anxiety of confusion tearing through him. He had assumed all along the three men were part of the force behind the 47th Street assassins and the man with the tranquilizer pistol. Now, he wasn't sure. A second party had made itself known—a brutal and efficient killer.

His heart thudding now, Blaine noticed a yellow legal pad sticking out from under the desk. He moved over to inspect and found the remnants of tape just where he expected them. Yes, standard procedure would dictate that the assigned team make notes at all stages of the operation to ensure accurate reporting. These notes would be kept hidden, usually taped to the underside of a drawer where a casual search would leave them unnoticed. This too was procedure.

Unfortunately the killer must have also been aware of this; the ragged fringe at the pad's top indicated a number of pages had been torn free. All the pages that remained were blank.

But not totally. McCracken placed the pad atop the desk and grabbed for a pencil. Using the side of the point, he skimmed lightly over the top remaining blank page to trace out whatever had been written on the preceding sheet. The notes contained on it would have been the most recent. It took several minutes of very subtle work with the pencil before the outlines of words and phrases became visible. He found mention of the crystals, of Lydia Brandywine, and Earnst's gem parlor.

And at the bottom, by itself, a four-digit number. The very last entry the dead agents had made.

McCracken went ice cold.

The number was T.C.'s room at the Waldorf.

CHAPTER 7

BLAINE raced breathlessly the two blocks toward the Waldorf. His thoughts had shut off by the time he reached the hotel's majestic entrance. They brought only pain, the realization of a hurt too horrible to accept.

He sped through the Waldorf's doors and took the marble steps leading up two at a time. He rushed to the elevator bank and pressed the up arrow. A compartment slid open and he was inside it immediately, pounding the CLOSE DOOR button as if it would make the machine get started faster. Twelve floors later he stepped out and dashed to T.C.'s room. The door was locked, but the security bolts and chain were not in place. He had it swinging open over the carpet less than thirty seconds later.

T.C. sat in a chair by the window, propped up facing the television. Blaine held his breath as he approached and let it out only when he saw the small red hole in the center of her forehead.

Blaine came closer, chewing his lips, fighting back tears. He wanted her to be alive, to be playing possum to confuse the man who had come to kill her.

He had spoken to her five hours before, six maybe. Told

her to stay put. Maybe if he had sent her home they wouldn't have found her. Maybe she'd still be alive. Maybe . . .

He could see her rushing to the door not long before to respond to a knock, thinking it was him probably. The end would have happened very fast. No struggle. Little pain.

McCracken sank down on the bed, too shocked to cry. He fought to still his shaking.

"Damn," he moaned. "Damn. . . ."

T.C. was dead, and he had helped kill her. He accepted the responsibility because he needed the rage that went with it, needed the guilt to push the grief back. The pain in him was sharp and lingering, worse than any bullet or knife. He wanted her back. He wanted it to be eight years ago all over again so he could have another chance.

Why? She hadn't known anything, damnit!

Whoever was behind the killings in the townhouse was undoubtedly behind hers—the same killer, even, judging by the bullet wound. That there were two forces operating here was obvious. But which was responsible for what? Who was behind the "Hasidim," the man with the dart gun? What had happened to require such a killing spree? The wild bullets in the street, three dead government agents, T.C., and possibly more.

McCracken buried his rising grief and guilt and forced himself to think. The dead agents were his only lead. They would lead him to someone in the government who knew more of what was going on and how the crystals were connected.

Which would lead him to those behind T.C.'s killing. Making them pay was the only thing he could still do for T.C.

Revenge was no consolation but it would have to be consolation enough.

Blaine covered T.C.'s body with a bedspread. He knew now what wheels he had to set in motion. For situations like the townhouse, various government agencies jointly operated a cleanup service. The contact number was changed often but was readily available. Always an 800 number. He dialed it.

"Sanitation department," said a voice.

"There's dirt on 222 East 48th Street in New York City. Operation's probably on record."

"That's improper coding," the voice came back.

"Send a crew."

"State your designation please."

"Tell them it's going to be a long night."

"*What?* Who *is* this?"

McCracken hung up. He had said enough. He knew they would respond because only someone cleared would have the number. They would check the on-call operations roster and find that the townhouse was active. A crew would be dispatched.

He returned to East 48th Street, walking slowly to catch his breath and settle his nerves, knowing it would be awhile before the cleanup crew arrived. In fact it was ninety minutes after his return that a nondescript white van double-parked in front of the townhouse. Two men climbed out and moved up to the entrance. Blaine saw one of them pull the steel grating back while the other worked the door with a skeleton key. Took thirty seconds. Too long. They were dressed in dark blue overalls which looked innocuously like uniforms from the gas or electric company. No one would question them.

At last they had the door open and were moving inside. McCracken waited until the two men were out of sight before drawing close enough to the van to assure himself only the driver remained inside. His elbow was propped into the night air on the open window sill. Blaine came up along the side stealthily, grabbed the exposed arm and yanked it brutally toward him and down.

The driver's head struck the door frame hard. By the time he registered the pain, Blaine had him by the throat, squeezing just hard enough.

"One chance," he told the man. "Who do you report to?"

"Don't know," the man rasped, struggling to force the syllables out. "Upstairs, they're in charge."

McCracken squeezed harder on the driver's carotid artery until the man was unconscious. Then he made his way to the front door and pressed his shoulders to the left of the frame. Any second now one of the sanitation crew would return to the van for body bags or, more likely, a crate to remove the corpses. He saw a shadow sliding down the stairs inside and shrank further against the building, not even a flicker of his outline visible.

The sanitation man barely had time to open the door before Blaine was on him, hand ramming his face and forcing it backward as he hurled himself inside. He slammed the man hard against the wall, making sure he was out before letting him slump. The final team member was upstairs. The answers would come from him.

After closing the front door, he climbed the stairs and entered the room in silence. The third team member, his back to Blaine, was working on the bodies. Blaine grasped him from behind in a hold that shut off his wind.

He dragged the man to the nearest upright chair and plopped him down in it, easing up on the pressure enough for the man to breathe. He switched his position to the side so he could meet the man's eyes and let him see the determination in his own.

"I'm going to give you a chance not to die," Blaine said, maintaining a tight grip. "But only one chance."

The man regarded him with eyes bulging in terror, proclaiming innocence as well as fear.

"Which branch were they working for?" Blaine demanded.

The man caught his breath and seemed surprised by it. "I've got a phone number, just a phone number."

"I'm listening."

"585-6740."

"Area code?"

"Local exchange. New York City."

"Very convenient."

He tied the men up and left them in the van. He was functioning on automatic now, trying not to think about T.C.

From the townhouse, Blaine's next stop was a phone box three blocks down. He needed to learn the address attached to 585-6740 and required only a touchtone phone to obtain it. He still had friends in the CIA who owed him favors, and they repaid their debt partially by keeping him constantly updated on changes in coding and procedures concerning the acquisition of information over lines. He dialed a number in Langley, Virginia, which linked him with the Company data base. Next he pressed out his request code, waited for a beep, and then punched in the number in question as if he were dialing it normally.

"Hotel National," a mechanical, synthesized voice told him after twenty seconds. "42nd Street and Seventh Avenue, New York City."

Blaine replaced the receiver.

At midnight Times Square was alive with people, though not nearly as many as the old mythology would have it. Most were simply strolling through the night, looking for nothing more than a bright light to walk toward and then by. The Square offered this, plenty of food stops, and twenty-four-hour movie houses. In addition to pornography and prostitution, it now possessed such developments as the Newsday Building and the Marriott Hotel that aimed at washing the area clean of its traditional reputation. But a number of buildings clung stubbornly to the old ways or at least images of them.

The Hotel National was among these. Its signs advertised "Newly Renovated" and while this may have been the case, another sign advertising rooms-by-the-hour seemed more prominent. The hotel's front was well lit, except for a vertical lighted marquee with all its bulbs burned out. As Mc-

Cracken passed under it he could hear a fizzling electrical current refusing to give up.

He headed through the glass entrance doors and moved straight toward a glassed-in cubicle directly before him, behind which stood a black man in a white shirt only half-buttoned. The lobby did look good, he had to admit, and he wondered if the renovations stopped there.

The clerk didn't acknowledge his approach, and Blaine had to tap on the glass to get his attention. The man slid a section of the partition away.

"You wanna room?" he asked between puffs on a rank cigar.

Blaine had his pistol out, chambered, then through the opening and under the man's chin before he could finish his next puff.

"Not exactly," Blaine told him, pushing the gun up enough to force the clerk to his toes. "Don't fancy this gun myself," he said. "Not enough control. Need two hands to steady it, but I'm going to spare only one on you. You're going to cooperate, aren't you?"

The clerk struggled to nod.

"You rented a room tonight to some people who didn't look like they belonged here, right?"

Another semblance of a nod.

"How many?"

"Four. Only one up there now. Room twenty-four. Second floor."

"You sure?"

"Saw the others go out and they ain't come back. That over there's the only door."

Three, Blaine reflected, the same number that had perished in the townhouse. . . .

He freed a twenty-dollar bill from his pocket and placed it on the counter. "Thanks."

He sprinted for the staircase, gun still out. One man remained in the room upstairs, a man the cleanup crew would have reported to, a man who would have some answers. For him. For T.C.

He reached the room in question, the bottom half of the "2" and top half of the "4" missing. He could see the frame's wood was rotted too much to resist even a slight kick, never mind a full one.

He threw a full one into it. The door shattered at latch level and flew inward.

Blaine was through it while it was still in motion, gun raised before the crash against the wall sounded. In the back of his mind he had already recorded that the room was all wrong: too big, spacious, well furnished, even smelled decent. He had recorded all this even before the voice of the lone occupant reached him in the half light.

"Good evening, Mr. McCracken," said Ryan Sundowner. "I've been expecting you."

CHAPTER 8

McCRACKEN looked at the youngish man in the tattered sports jacket and then at himself holding the gun.

"I'm Ryan Sundowner," the man continued. "Head of the Bureau of Scientific Intelligence."

"The Toy Factory," McCracken followed. "I've heard of you. The fact that you knew I was coming doesn't bode well for our friendship."

Sundowner gazed at the pistol which Blaine had lowered only slightly. "If that statement was due to the fact that I'm a part of what you've become involved in, I accept the responsibility. Trouble is, I'm as confused and scared as you are."

"Not quite. You were expecting me, I wasn't expecting you. What the hell has the Toy Factory got to do with all this?"

"Long story." Sundowner stopped. "The gun, Mr. McCracken, you really don't need it."

"I'll be the judge of that."

"I dismissed my men to avoid any unpleasant incidents."

"Lucky for them."

"I know what you've been through. If it's any consolation, the three bodies you discovered in the brownstone belonged to my men."

"*Your* men? Then who—"

"Killed them and killed that woman? I don't know. But between the two of us, I'm hoping we can find out. I've got a car waiting downstairs. I'm heading back to Washington. I'd like you to come with me."

"I'll go with you as far as LaGuardia. The rest depends on how much I learn to love your company. How'd you know about the woman?"

"Your call into the Sanitation Department was traced to her room."

"Next question: why did she have to die?"

Sundowner didn't respond until they were in the backseat of the car and the driver had pulled out into traffic. "It starts with those crystals."

"Lydia Brandywine works for you," McCracken realized.

"Worked. Past tense. They got her, too."

"Efficient lot, aren't they?"

"This is all new to me, Mr. McCracken. If I sound calm, it's because I, you, all of us are facing something far more terrifying than a few deaths."

Blaine's eyes flared. "Not 'just' a few. You'd best remember that."

"I understand how you felt about the woman. I spent much of the night going over your complete file. She was included in it."

"That file was sealed after Omega. It was one of my conditions."

"I unsealed it. For reasons of national security, a person with authority can do just about anything."

"I don't have a thing to do with national security anymore. Or was that left out of the file?"

"No, it was quite clear on that point."

"Guess I made a mistake giving Lydia my real name. She passed it on to your goons and they passed it on to you before they died. Don't know enough to keep my big mouth shut." Blaine looked angry again. "Right now I'd like to shove those crystals down yours."

"I'd let you if you had enough of them. That's how important those crystals are to us. We've been looking for something like them for months, years really." He started to reach into his pocket. "Here. You of all people deserve to see what they look like."

Sundowner's hand emerged with a jagged piece of ruby-red crystal, perhaps six inches in length at its longest point. It was filled with grooves and ridges, seemed shiny even in the dull light of the backseat. McCracken took it in his hand. It felt cold, though it wasn't. He supposed the coldness was in his mind, emanating from the fact that he was now clutching what had led to T.C.'s death. He wanted to fling it out the window but squeezed it tight instead.

"We call it Atragon," Sundowner explained. "You are now holding in your hand the greatest natural power source ever known to man. We hope it will be the batteries to run Bugzapper."

"Bugzapper?"

"I'll give you a complete demonstration once we reach Washington."

"I don't remember agreeing to go. See, I've got my own trail to follow."

"It's the same one as mine, unless I miss my guess. Terry Catherine Hayes was killed by men who don't want us to find further stores of the Atragon crystals. Find the crystals, and you find the men."

"Is it really that simple?"

"In a sense, yes. But in another sense we're facing the most complicated threat to our very existence we have ever faced."

"You have a knack for being melodramatic."

"In this case, I'm understating, believe me. Three days ago a small town was obliterated by a particle beam with some rather unique properties. There wasn't a single carbon atom left. That includes the inhabitants."

McCracken looked at him closely.

"Mr. McCracken, your file emphasizes the fact that you are obsessed with saving the world one piece at a time, that you can't stand to see innocent people die. Well, over a thousand died in the town of Hope Valley, and that could be just the beginning. The wielder of the beam weapon is blackmailing us. Simply stated, we have three weeks to unilaterally begin the process of dismantling our nuclear arsenal or we will face annihilation."

"The Soviets?"

"The indications are there, too many of them probably. The point is somebody's got this death beam, and there's nothing we can do at present to stop it."

"I love phrases like 'at present'."

"It's accurate here, I assure you. In effect, Bugzapper is a shield of energy effectively enclosing the entire country and rendering it invulnerable to enemy attack."

"Missiles as well as death rays?"

"Under the right conditions, absolutely. But the right conditions include Atragon to power the shield. The crystal you're holding acts as a solar receptor with tremendous storage capacities. A virtual twin of it powered three floors of the Toy Factory last week for over an hour."

"Without burning up?"

"More than that, we had to shut the system down because our circuits were starting to overload."

"So it was *you* who had the crystals stolen from Earnst in the first place."

Sundowner nodded. "Yes. Standard procedure, I'm afraid, to avoid drawing attention to our experiments. There didn't seem to be any rush for completing them at the time."

"Until Hope Valley."

Another nod. "With the realization that the crystals might be our only shield against annihilation, Atragon became a very precious commodity indeed. I ordered our men to move on Earnst to learn his source for it."

"Only they failed, thanks to me. And then they got whacked by a first-class hitter a few hours after these four guys with beards and black coats traded in their prayer shawls for machine guns."

"Dispatched, no doubt, by whoever is so determined to stop our search for the Atragon reserves before it gets underway."

"And probably this same force is controlling the death ray that Atragon may be able to neutralize."

"Exactly."

"Fine. But you're asking the wrong questions. How did this mysterious force learn about your sudden pursuit of Atragon? No, let me rephrase that. Who did you tell about the crystals and when?"

"The crisis committee. Yesterday."

"Crisis committee, huh?"

Sundowner listed the occupants of the Tomb.

"One of them blew the whistle on you, Sundance. Fucked your plan up big-time and killed a girl I could have loved if she had let me."

"That can't be!"

"Wanna bet? Believe me, I've been there. The only one I'm ruling out is you because if you were the leak, I'd be dead already."

Sundowner's lips quivered. "But what you're saying, it's . . ."

"Welcome to life in the big city."

The first signs for LaGuardia appeared.

"Then if you agree to cooperate, I should keep it between just the two of us."

"Don't bother because too many people already know I'm involved. The mole, whoever he is, will learn soon enough anyway." Blaine changed his train of thinking. "I gather your operation at that fleabag hotel wasn't a last-minute setup."

"It's our New York field base."

"The clerk was yours then."

"Yes."

"Another mouth that could talk. Don't hold anything back about me, because as far as you're concerned I'm not helping. That's the way it's gotta be no matter what. See, Sundance, I took this sacred vow. Sort of like celibacy. The government fucked me too much, and I decided never to let them fuck me again. Somebody killed Terry Catherine Hayes, and if that person happens to know where the crystals for your Atragon shield are, that's fine. But right now the only use for your crystals I can see is ramming them up the ass of whoever ordered her death."

Another sign passed for LaGuardia Airport.

"Washington, Mr. McCracken?"

"Call me Blaine. Why not? I've got nothing better to do this morning."

> Hope Valley was just a sample of the awesome weapon we now possess. The United States of America has until midnight of April 21, three weeks from now, to unilaterally disarm and dismantle all nuclear devices or face annihilation from our death ray.

McCracken read the second communiqué that had come over the Turkish channel after they were en route to Washington by private jet.

"Mean business, don't they?" was his initial response.

"They seem to."

"We got any plans to actually capitulate and follow through with the disarming?"

"No."

"Could it be accomplished in three weeks even if we did?"

"Of course not."

"Don't you think the framer of the threat knows that? Don't you think he'd never actually believe we'd disarm unilaterally under any conditions?"

"Not unless he was very naive. What are you getting at?"

"Something smells here, Sundance. It's smelled right from the time Hope Valley got zapped and it stunk worst of all when an innocent woman bought it a few hours ago. Why would someone demonstrate a weapon to make us do something we never would anyway?"

"We've discussed that."

"Reach any brilliant conclusions?"

"We're hoping it means the weapon isn't deployed yet or perhaps isn't effective on a wide scale."

"Hoping isn't concluding. We've got to face the fact that whoever wrote that communiqué blackmailed us without ever believing we'd succumb to his demands. Which means his demonstration in Hope Valley had a different purpose altogether." Blaine paused. "Who possesses the kind of technology required to build such a beam?"

"Considering the research expense, the list stops at us . . . and the Soviets."

"What does the General Secretary say? I assume the President has talked to him."

"He denied all culpability and even knowledge of such a weapon. Offered to help in any way he could."

"Mindless rhetoric. Could just as easily be playing it cool to keep us off guard. But at least they're talking. That ought to delay World War III for a while."

"We're at DEF-CON 3 now. Might not delay it for long."

McCracken stroked his beard. "Assuming my route takes me to your crystals, how much time would I have to deliver them?"

"For reasons I'll explain in Washington, you'll have one week."

"Real generous with time, aren't you?"

"My estimates indicate that Hope Valley was obliterated in three seconds at most. The precedent's been set."

Dawn had come by the time they landed in Washington and proceeded straight to the Bethesda headquarters of the

Toy Factory. The Bureau of Scientific Intelligence blended with the countryside of which it was a part. The multiplex of buildings was unfenced, looking as much residential as commercial. McCracken and Sundowner drove through the well-sculptured grounds en route to the entrance.

A pair of marine guards held the door open for Sundowner, with McCracken right behind. Once in the lobby they made for an elevator that descended to the underground floors where the most sensitive experiments were carried out. They exited the elevator four floors later at a stop labeled D and moved straight for a door with yet another guard before it. This time, although the guard recognized Sundowner, the scientist was forced to key in the proper sequence on a pad to gain entry. Blaine entered in Sundowner's wake and found the two of them to be alone in the lab.

"Welcome to the home of Bugzapper," said Sundowner.

The lab was dominated by a scale model of the Earth nearly ten feet in diameter with the United States perpetually occupying the very center. Suspended over the stationary U.S., held in the air by wires running from a platform attached to the ceiling, were sixteen miniature satellites which looked to Blaine like fancy fluorescent light bulbs.

"A scale model," explained Sundowner. "Since the life-size Bugzapper satellites will achieve geosynchronistic orbit, there's no reason to add rotation."

He moved to a computer terminal near the globe and, still standing, pressed a few keys. Immediately the miniature fluorescents caught, casting a bright haze over the whole of the scale version of the United States. Blaine noted that the light emanated from all sides of the miniature satellites at once, seeming to link each up with others.

"The light is just for effect," Sundowner explained. "The real Bugzapper's energy shield will be invisible." He moved back alongside Blaine and led him up a set of stairs to a raised platform which looked down over and into the model. "What you're seeing is being powered by an Atragon crystal the size of a fly's wing."

McCracken could hear a faint humming.

Sundowner reached down to a dish placed next to another computer terminal on a table beneath them and grabbed a marble. Handing it to McCracken, he said, "A miniature Atragon shield is thus in place. Toss the marble down into the light and watch what happens."

Blaine dropped the marble down. There was a brief *pffffft* and it was gone.

"By scale," explained the scientist, "that marble was the size of a huge asteroid. You can see the potency involved here."

"Except your shield is going to be facing a death ray, not marbles or even asteroids."

Sundowner nodded as if expecting the comment. "Not really a ray, Mr. McCracken—a beam, specifically a particle beam composed of *matter*—subatomic in scope, to be sure, but focused into tremendous mass energy by the time it reaches the shield. Easily dense enough to activate the sensing mechanism."

"What do you mean activate? You mean it's not always on?"

"*Active* but not on. Otherwise the power drain would be immeasurable. Solving that problem, in fact, was the first major breakthrough we made." He stopped and looked at Blaine more intensely. "Think of the way Bugzapper's more mundane namesake functions. You've got a negative force confronting a positive force with the difference of potential not quite great enough to jump the gap—that is until a bug flies in and serves as a conductor between them. Energy passes through the bug and the fields are at last connected, with the bug paying the price for it, of course."

"Not as simple in your system, though, is it?"

"Hardly. Four dozen satellites will compose Bugzapper at completion. And by the rules of astrophysics, they can't possibly maintain a constant distance from each other. So we have to let them stray in their orbits. The distances will vary and it will be up to a super-computer to regulate the flow of energy emanating from each satellite to its neighbors to ensure the difference of potential is great enough so the gap can't be jumped until something, a missile or a particle beam, forms a conductor. The computer's judgments and instructions will be determined and made in microseconds."

Sundowner hesitated and started back down to floor level, with McCracken right behind. "Of course, it was the discovery of Atragon that turned all this theory into potential reality. Without those crystals to serve as a power source, the shield won't work."

"And," McCracken picked up, "you'll need a hell of a lot more of them to fit forty-eight satellites, never mind getting them launched in time for it to matter."

"Installation is no problem, since the satellites have already been fitted for some sort of solar storing receptacles. Adapting the Atragon once we've got it to the proper specifications won't take long at all, so my feeling is the satellites can be ready for launch within ten days of delivery, the shield fully operational forty-eight hours after that."

"Given the three-week time frame in the extortion note, that's cutting things close."

"At least, though, it gives us a chance." Sundowner stopped. "I've explained what we're up against. You can see how important this Atragon is to us."

"Hold on, Sundance, I already laid things out for you. I'd like nothing better than to bring back your Atragon so long as its trail leads me to the men who killed T.C. But if the trails break off somewhere, you know which one I'll follow."

"I'm willing to accept that."

"You don't have much of a choice. Don't try to follow me; your men won't stand a chance, and the attempt will aggravate me to no end. I'm difficult when I'm mad, Sundance."

"Can't you give me some idea where you're going?"

"Across the Atlantic."

"Narrows it down some. . . . I could still hold back word

of your involvement from the crisis committee, give you some room to move."

"We've discussed *that* already, too. No, I'm more worried about a certain fat man named Vasquez. He happens to be a major narcotics distributor I KO'd just before I got shoved into the secretarial pool in France. He's sworn to kill me if I ever set foot on his turf again."

"And just what is his turf?"

"Most of Europe."

"Terrific," Sundowner moaned. "You realize, of course, that if you're right about a leak in the Tomb, whoever killed my men and that woman might find you before you find them."

"That, Sundance, is precisely the idea."

Sundowner explained it all to the other men gathered in the Tomb, leaving out nothing but McCracken's assertion about the presence of a mole. He had to doctor the story a bit to make up for it.

"So is he working for us or not?" the President wondered at the end.

"I'd have to say not. But he's agreed to communicate with me regularly, and it's my guess he won't be able to resist finding the Atragon for us."

"Why?"

"The stakes, sir. If this death ray is unleashed, millions of innocent people will die, and that's the one thing McCracken can't tolerate."

"Don't turn him into a hero," cautioned CIA chief Stamp. Then, to the President, "Truth is, we're talking about a rogue here, a renegade, a killer."

"Killer's a bit strong," broke in Sundowner.

"Okay, I'll grant you that much. But the others fit him well. What has become known as the Omega Command business proved that much. He forced the ruin or resignation of many of our predecessors."

"That wasn't McCracken's doing, by my recollection,"

interjected Secretary of Defense Kappel. "It was the doing of those individuals who brought it on themselves by the way they handled the situation."

"Tried and sentenced by McCracken in Omega's aftermath," elaborated Mercheson. "Yes, it's starting to come back to me now. This McCracken is a menace beyond compare."

"Gentlemen," said the President, "I'm a bit confused here. You mean this McCracken doesn't work for us in some capacity?"

"McCracken doesn't work for anyone, *especially* not us," said Stamp.

"Why not?"

It was Sundowner who answered. "Long story. It starts back in Vietnam where McCracken was the best we had; an expert at infiltration, sabotage, all forms of counterespionage activities. He was a loner, yes, a rogue, by all respects couldn't handle the 'age of accountability' at all. We kept trying to farm him out, and while he was working with the British a hostage situation came to an unpleasant end. To show his displeasure with the way things had been handled, McCracken pulled an Uzi on Churchill's statue in Parliament Square and shot off certain sections of his marble anatomy. That's where he got his nickname."

"What nickname?"

"McCrackenballs."

"As in—"

"Yes."

"The point, sir," broke in Stamp, "is that the balls McCracken has broken over the years haven't all been ceramic. Plenty have been the flesh-and-blood privates of his superiors."

"And usually with good reason," argued Sundowner. "Omega was a case in point. The government called him out of exile to work for them and their subsequent treatment of him was inexcusable. Consequently, he's sworn never to work for us again. He went free-lance, started taking on assignments and missions that no one else wanted any part of, almost always to pay off old debts and favors."

"And now he's after the killer of this woman," the President reminded them, "not the reserves of the Atragon."

"His only route to the former is to follow the trail of the latter, and he can accomplish it infinitely better than any team we could dispatch in his place." Sundowner hesitated long enough for his words to sink in. "Either he'll find the crystals or he'll follow a path straight to the force that doesn't want us to get them—the force controlling the ray. We win either way."

"Nobody wins with McCracken," said Mercheson. "Except McCracken."

"I don't see what we have to lose by the attempt in this case," concluded the President, "or that we have much choice. McCracken is going out there anyway, and he's the only one Earnst pointed in the right direction. He's not working for us, so there's no culpability on our part for his actions. He was straight with us, and Ryan was straight with him. So as far as we know, Blaine McCracken doesn't exist anymore."

"For now," said Stamp.

Sergei Chernopolov, General Secretary of the Soviet Union, held the receiver tighter against his ear.

"There has been a change in plans, Tomachenko," he informed the person on the other end. "An American agent has entered the picture. Bangkok must be put on hold until he can be dealt with properly."

"Who is this agent?"

"Blaine—"

"McCracken," completed Tomachenko.

"You know of him then."

"I've heard of him."

"Is he as good as they say, good enough to make inroads and gains?"

"It is possible."

"Likely?"

"Hard to say under the circumstances."

Chernopolov nodded to himself. "Then you know what you must do. McCracken is priority one. Take any steps you feel are necessary. Forget accountability. You report only to me." He paused. "If you are successful, the slate will be wiped clean. You know what that means."

"Yes," was all Tomachenko replied.

Another assignment, another mission, and another success because it had to be. So much was riding on it. More than ever.

Strange how being a woman helped her so. Men underestimated her skills, perhaps hesitated in response to something as infantile as chivalry, or allowed a pleasing body or teasing smile to distract them. A nearly exposed set of breasts could make a finer weapon than any when wielded properly. And the woman used hers as she used whatever else was called for in the completion of her missions.

Her name was Natalya Illyevich Tomachenko. And she was the number one assassin for the KGB.

CHAPTER 9

THE town of Pamosa Springs lies at the foot of the San Juan Mountains as they wind their way through southwestern Colorado. The town's population, barely 700, is tucked into one of the gulleys between foothills that are dwarfed by the San Juans themselves. It's pretty easy to feel small with mountains stretching nearly three miles high on either side of you, but the people of Pamosa Springs don't look at it that way. Nor do they concern themselves with the fact that beyond a third side of town lies nothing but dry lands and open country all the way to Silverton. The only access road juts off Route 149; its only destination is Pamosa Springs. Being cut off from civilization on three sides makes for a solitude the residents call security.

The commercial center of Pamosa Springs, meanwhile, is barely a center at all. Just one main road with several buildings on each side, built for a time when the town was growing, and struggling for survival now that it wasn't. A restaurant and a bar owned by Hal Taggart sat on either side of a seventy-seat movie house. There was a general store which took care of most essentials, and a mini-mart attached to the two-pump gas station that took care of the rest. The bank doubled as a post office, and the municipal building included the jail, mayor's office, and no more. A small K Mart that had been in town for twenty years pulled out seven springs back, its space taken by a discount drugstore that stayed only long enough to learn it couldn't break even.

Back then, and before, Pamosa Springs wasn't exactly a boom town, but it certainly showed some of the signs. The natural hot springs running out of the Lake San Cristóbal area hadn't yet dried up, and a fair number of visitors passed through after sampling a bath with purported rejuvenating qualities. Silver veins in the San Juans kept miners busy enough to need a place to sleep, eat, and buy equipment, and the railroad built a freight yard in the town with plans to lay track to connect up with the Durango and Silverton narrow gauge. But then the silver veins went dry, and the railroad went bankrupt even before reaching the nearest reservoir. The population of Pamosa Springs shrank from just over 2,000, and there were soon almost as many vacant houses as occupied ones.

The town's present residents had stuck things out figuring there was still more good in Pamosa Springs than bad. Many had seasonal jobs at the neighboring ski resorts that kept them away for good parts of the season, which often stretched up to eight months. Others ran mail-order businesses or claimed to be artists. Still more commuted to work in cities up to 150 miles away. You could live like a king for practically nothing in Pamosa Springs as long as you didn't expect too much. Nobody ever died poor in the town, but nobody ever got rich, either.

Until now maybe, some of the residents might say guardedly.

It had been an especially harsh winter in this part of Colorado, and the runoff that accompanied the spring thaw caused massive erosion and several minor landslides through the San Juans and the accompanying hillsides. A few hills bled their bellies open.

With silver running high in the town's past, the first thought of the residents was that the shiny stones pulled from the dirt and rocks were more of the blessed mineral. Fact was, there were at least six different kinds of stones pulled from the mountainside and none of them was silver, which was not to say none of them was valuable. On the contrary, several held great promise, including some that looked like pink diamonds, and samples were sent off to the National Assayer's Office in Washington for identification. The residents of Pamosa Springs sat back patiently to wait for the results.

Nothing had been heard in three weeks now, and life in Pamosa Springs mostly held to its menial normalcy. The local movie house held over a double feature of *Rambo* and *Red Dawn* for the ninth consecutive week. The town's women composed their twentieth letter to Jerry Falwell, pleading with him to appear at their annual luncheon. Gearing up for the coming elections, a newsletter reminded residents that last time out, the Republican presidential candidate had carried Pamosa Springs with ninety-two percent of the vote.

And Hal Taggart continued losing customers. Since he operated the only sit-down restaurant in the Springs, this should have been impossible. But Taggart had detoured into misery and isolation since his son's death in Beirut four years back, and some would say he'd gone clear around the bend. He'd been gone for three weeks after getting the news and disappeared for another two a few months later. Since then his bar and grill had become strictly a grill, open at sporadic, unreliable hours. And now when it was open, no one showed up. But Taggart washed the dishes regardless and talked up a storm to himself. Some said there were nights when he served up platefuls of the daily special to customers who weren't there. And lately he had taken to shooting the rats in his storage room with an old .22 hunting rifle that hadn't fired straight in a decade. The rats survived, and the town grew used to the quick blasts coming from inside the grill.

It was a lazy Tuesday afternoon when Hal Taggart caught

a whole squadron of rats munching away at his cereal supplies. He was searching desperately for his rifle when the first of the army trucks pulled off the access road into the outskirts of town. The sight of what might have been an entire company rolling in with full battle dress and gear—jeeps, a dozen trucks, and squat-looking armored things with slats for machine gun barrels—grabbed the eyes and ears of just about everyone. Many ventured tentatively into the streets to watch the soldiers climb from the trucks and begin deployment, obeying the orders of a man dressed in fatigues but wearing a beret instead of a helmet.

Hal Taggart had located his rifle just as the company had pulled into town, but the damn rats had scurried before he could sight down on them. The smelly things were rushing out through a hole in the wall between the grain sacks. Taggart had just had enough. Gun ready, he rushed out the grill's back door and gave chase down Main Street in the rats' trail.

"You fucking bastards!"

Taggart's cry carried down Main Street, followed rapidly by his charging frame with gun cradled in his arms.

The rest happened so fast that it seemed not to be happening at all.

A pair of soldiers saw Taggart coming and leveled their guns at him. He slowed but didn't stop; his sad eyes were on the rats, and he was aware of nothing else. He was still giving chase when both soldiers fired. A pair of staccato bursts, and Hal Taggart was tossed backward, midsection and apron drenched in blood, arms and legs twitching when he landed.

The rest of the soldiers turned their weapons on the townspeople who were standing in the street in shock. Fingers grasped for triggers, uncertain of what to do next as people began rushing about with no clear sense of purpose.

"Cease fire!" screamed the bereted leader. "Cease fire!"

The echoes of a few random shots sifted down Main Street. Somewhere glass shattered. Then came stunned silence as the people of Pamosa Springs became prisoners in their own town.

PART TWO

INTO THE LABYRINTH

Athens: Wednesday, noon

CHAPTER 10

It was mid-afternoon Wednesday before McCracken was settled in Athens. The journey had taken twenty taxing hours, thanks to a trio of plane changes deemed necessary in case Sundowner tried to have him followed.

He checked into a small hotel located in the center of the city's modern section. The clerk spoke good enough English to help him ascertain that Kapo Stadipopolis, the antique dealer from whom Earnst had received the Atragon crystals, maintained his shop in the heart of the famed Monastiraki Square.

Blaine would head there as soon as he managed to get washed and changed.

Spring in the Mediterranean was traditionally warm, and once back in the streets he wore only a light jacket over his shirt to keep his shoulder holster concealed. He found the city of Athens to be a paradox, but a pleasant one. It blended the modern flavor, luxury, and sense of a national and commercial capital with the ancient traditions that provided the city its fame. From his hotel in Omonia Square, Blaine had intended to walk to Stadipopolis's shop, but he had underestimated the distance and hailed a cab instead. The driver proceeded due south down Athena Street and deposited him in the heart of the Athens shopping district.

In effect, Monastiraki Square marked the beginning of Old Athens or the *Plaka*. The Square itself was formed by three intersecting streets lined with shops and open-air markets of every kind. As usual, it was bustling with activity. The hot sun beat down, but the shoppers seemed not to mind, some simply strolling, others negotiating with shopkeepers in search of the best possible bargain. Waiters in long white aprons struggled to keep up with the flow of the many patrons in and out of the various outdoor cafes. Merchants selling their wares out of boxes or platforms in the street called eagerly to tourists as they passed, changing languages as frequently as smiles.

According to the hotel clerk, Kapo Stadipopolis' antique shop was located in the center of Pandrosos Street, and Blaine made his way toward it. He was feeling quite secure. No one could possibly know that he had gone to Greece, and he took considerable comfort in that.

Stadipopolis's shop, called "Kapo's," was as simple as Earnst's parlor had been lavish. It was wedged between two other buildings, one a fruit market and the other a bakery specializing in uniquely Greek creations. Blaine passed the shop twice from the outside and saw it was packed from floor to ceiling with artifacts at various prices, all labeled in both drachmas and dollars. There were voices coming from inside, a seller—Stadipopolis probably—arguing with a prospective buyer. Blaine entered and heard the slight tinkling of windchimes. There was little room to maneuver amid the clutter near the entrance, and he moved forward.

"Not a penny less, I tell you," a curly-haired Greek with a thick mustache was insisting. "One hundred American dollars."

"Fifty," replied a well-dressed man with a woman tight by his side. McCracken felt he was trying to impress her with his negotiating ability.

The Greek held up a vase. "Mister, this is hundreds of

years old. You want to go home and show off something authentic or go home and brag about how you talked a poor merchant into a bargain for something less? It's a crime what you do to us. You think I won't be able to sell this to the next person who walks through that door? You think I won't?"

"All right," the man relented, "seventy-five."

"Hah! Seventy-five, he says. I pay eighty for this and he offers seventy-five like he's doing me a favor. How are my children supposed to eat if I lose money on all my transactions? You have children perhaps?" he asked the woman.

"No," she replied, slightly embarrassed.

"Well, I do. Seven of them. Each looks like their mother, thank God. I tell you this, I been married to her twenty wonderful years, since I was seventeen. You married that long?"

The couple said nothing.

"We start young here. In Greece, you start young with everything. Even business. I can sell this to you for less than what I paid under no circumstances. Nothing personal. The next man through the door will jump at it for one hundred, even one-twenty-five." He noticed McCracken. "Hey you, come over here. What you think of this? Come, be honest. . . ."

Blaine walked over to the counter and squinted his eyes as he ran his fingers lightly over the vase. "Most impressive," he noted professionally. "I'd say from the Hadrian period. Yes, the Ionic propylon markings definitely date it back to the second century A.D., give or take a hundred years. I'll offer you five thousand American for it."

The young couple were already moving for the door, shaking their heads and not offering good-byes. The door opened and closed. The windchimes tolled softly again.

The curly-haired Greek was shaking Blaine's hand enthusiastically, eyes wide. "I tell you this, my friend. They say I know more history than anyone on the Square, but you know more even than me. I respect you, so I let you have this piece for only, well, I'm in a good mood, say two thousand American."

"I made it up," Blaine told him.

"Huh?"

"I doubt anything from the Hadrian period of Greece has 'Made in Japan' stamped on its bottom."

Stadipopolis found himself foolishly turning the vase upside down as McCracken ambled toward an open case of "authentic" Greek artifacts demanding incredible prices.

"I tell you this, my friend," the Greek said, following him out from behind the counter. "You cost me money a few minutes ago. You owe me for that. There is maybe something—"

"I'm not buying," Blaine said as he rotated a small green dish in his hand. Then he turned to the Greek. "I'm selling."

"As you can maybe see, my inventory is a bit overstocked."

"What I have to sell won't take up much room, Mr. Stadipopolis."

The Greek's expression turned apprehensive. McCracken moved back toward the counter, Kapo Stadipopolis right behind him.

"How you know me, American?"

"Only by reputation."

"How come I don't know you?"

"Because we haven't been introduced, nor are we about to be."

"I don't buy from strangers, I tell you this."

"Really?" said Blaine, placing the small piece of Atragon Sundowner had let him take on the counter top. "What a pity . . ."

Stadipopolis' eyes bulged. His lips trembled, and his olive skin paled.

"Wh-wh-where? H-h-how?"

"America. Erich Earnst. That's all you need to know. The rest of the questions are mine."

The Greek didn't seem to hear him. "Who you work for?" he demanded fearfully. "Who send you?"

"I told you no more questions. Tell me about the crystals."

"Nothing to tell."

"Earnst said you shipped them to him by accident, then requested their return after they had been stolen."

"Earnst is still *alive*?"

"He wouldn't have been, if not for me."

Another couple, this one older than the last, came through the door. The sound of windchimes followed them.

"Go away!" Stadipopolis roared. "Closed!"

The couple exited as quickly as they had entered.

"I kept Earnst alive," McCracken said, "and I'll keep you alive too—if you cooperate."

"What makes you think I am in danger?"

"Mostly that if you don't cooperate, I'll make it known on the streets that you sold these crystals to me this day. It's not hard to figure that you're scared of somebody. How long do you think it'll be before word filters from Monastiraki Square to them about what you sold me?"

"No!" Stadipopolis pleaded, hands clutching for his face. "You can't!"

"For reasons you can't begin to understand, I can. And I will unless we talk."

"Not here," the Greek said, eyes darting. "I might be watched. Is possible."

"Where? When?"

"Tonight. Ten o'clock at Kerameikos Cemetery. You know it?"

"I'll find it."

The Greek started to move away. Blaine grasped his arm in an iron grip. "Set me up, Kapo, and I'll know it. The man you're frightened of might be a match for me but then again he might not. I'm betting not. I'd hate to have to make Monastiraki Square poorer by losing you. Place just wouldn't be the same again.'' Then, in words spoken like ice, ''Don't call him, Kapo.''

''I wouldn't! I *couldn't*!''

Blaine nodded at him, satisfied, and started to turn for the door, pocketing his crystal again.

''No,'' Stadipopolis said. ''You must leave with something. Money must change hands. If I'm being watched, it would look strange if it didn't.''

''Might look stranger if it did.''

''Please! Just to be safe.''

McCracken handed over a twenty-dollar bill and grabbed the much-disputed vase. ''Got just the place for this. . . .''

''But—''

Blaine was on his way for the door. ''Ten o'clock tonight, Kapo, in that cemetery. You set the rules. Just don't break them.''

And the windchimes tumbled against each other once more.

Outside, across the street from Kapo's, a legless beggar who had been pushing himself along on a skate-wheel platform stopped suddenly. His eyes had to be deceiving him. He had to get a closer look. He tried to better his view of the man who had just stepped out of the antique store, but the flow of pedestrian traffic was too thick, forcing the beggar to risk a quick slide through moving traffic in the street.

Pedestrians lurched aside and cars were brought to grinding halts. He reached the other side of the street and caught one glimpse of the shrinking figure, then pushed himself through the door of a fruit market. A customer and his bag went reeling. A basket of oranges toppled to the floor.

The beggar didn't stop.

''Your phone, Andros!'' he screamed when he was halfway across the floor. ''Hand it to me quick!''

The befuddled proprietor pried the receiver from its hook and lowered it to the beggar.

''Now, dial this number! Come on, get ready!''

Andros dialed the number the beggar recited. The ringing started, stopped.

"I must speak with Vasquez," the beggar told the man who answered.

CHAPTER 11

KAPO Stadipopolis hummed to himself for distraction as a second minute ticked past ten o'clock. He'd been waiting as planned by the Tomb of Dionysios of Kollytos since five minutes of, and there was no sign of the American. Good. Maybe he wouldn't show up. Stadipopolis wouldn't be surprised if he was dead.

The Greek tried to light a cigarette but the stiff night breeze thwarted him. After a half dozen tries he gave up, returned to his humming, and wrapped his jacketed arms about himself to ward off the chill. Behind him the white stone bull, symbol of Dionysios, perched atop twin pillars. It seemed ready to pounce.

Stadipopolis kept humming, the only sound in the Kerameikos Cemetery.

"Boo," whispered a voice in his ear as an iron finger poked him like a gun in the back.

Stadipopolis swung around in utter surprise. "You want to give me heart attack, American?"

"You were making enough noise to wake the dead." Blaine glanced around him. "Literally."

"You're late," the Greek managed, steadying himself.

"Hardly. Been here since just after eight. Had to make sure you weren't planning anything."

"You don't trust me?" Stadipopolis seemed offended.

"I don't trust anyone until they give me a reason to."

"We must be quick."

"I couldn't agree more."

Blaine thought Kerameikos Cemetery a good choice for the meeting. It was more a testament to the past than the dead and was popular among tourists for good reason. The cemetery contained the excavated remains of the old Kerameikos quarter of Athens, along with monuments to great figures dating from the sub-Mycenean period to late antiquity. Within the excavated portions no two tombs were alike.

The cemetery was cut into sections by serpentine walkways which made it seem larger than it was. Just enough excavation had been performed to avoid clutter and promote atmosphere among the testaments to Greek history. The tomb of Dionysios was located due north from the Kerameikos Museum on the Pireos Street side. Just south of the gate through which McCracken had entered lay the Agora, the old market at the foot of the steep grassy hillside which led up to the famed Acropolis.

"You understand my meeting you might mean my death," Stadipopolis said fearfully.

"And not meeting me would have assured it."

The night was lit by a half moon, and the Greek moved back into the shadow cast by the ceramic bull atop the tomb.

"I want to know everything you do about the crystals," Blaine told him. "And I want it from the beginning."

"The beginning in this case is difficult to pin down. Before the dawn of civilization as we know it."

"Spare me the history lesson, and let's start with how you came to be in possession of the crystals."

"They were stolen from a man of great power. He is called the Lion of Crete. He is mad, but nobody dares cross him."

"What's his name?"

"He goes by many. The closest to the truth is Megilido Fass."

"So you stole the crystals from him and then shipped them to Earnst. . . ."

"No!" Stadipopolis insisted, drawing back against a pillar. "This I tell you, American, for the sake of my children, I would never dare cross a man like Megilido Fass. He has his own villa in the southwest of Crete, big as a town they say. People have been known to go there and never return. Boys mostly."

"Boys?"

The Greek nodded reluctantly. "Wealth has its luxuries, among them being the ability to indulge in whatever . . . pleasure suits you at the time. Fass is free to do as he wishes. As I said, no one ever crosses him, and that includes the authorities." He made a spitting motion. "Worthless pigs that they are. Corruption is their middle name in these parts."

"Not just in these parts, Greek. All right, so it was Fass who was originally in possession of these crystals. Then he was robbed."

Stadipopolis nodded. "On a dare, a foolish one. A young man whose family had been wronged by the heathen vowed revenge and was coaxed on by his friends. He intercepted a shipment from Fass bound for Morocco. The crystals were among it."

"And where do you come in?"

"How do you say, American—that in this city I am known as a man who can move merchandise that might burn one's hand. The foolish young man brought the stolen goods to me. I purchased them for a reasonable price, of course not knowing their source."

"Of course."

"Had I . . . well, no call for such speculating. To turn a profit and avoid entanglements, I wished to move the gems quickly. Through America, as always."

"And Erich Earnst."

''Exactly. The crystals were of special interest to me because I had never seen anything like them before. . . .''

''Just what Earnst said.''

''They were . . . mesmerizing.''

''Something obviously made you request that Earnst return them to you after you sent them along.''

''I tell you this, American. My dealings with Earnst over the years were never anything but profitable. He was a man of honor and integrity.''

''But that didn't stop you from asking for the crystals back.''

''I had no choice. A few weeks after I mailed the shipment, men came to my shop. They were well known in the Square as hired hands of Fass. They were very polite, sickeningly polite. They even purchased several items. Then they asked about the crystals. Since I knew there was no way they could know for sure that I had brokered them, of course I denied ever having seen them. They smiled and left peacefully, asking me to please contact them if I heard any talk.''

''But they still spooked you.''

Stadipopolis swallowed hard. ''Not then. It was a week later. The men returned to my shop just as polite as the first time. One was holding a box in his hand and I thought they had come just to return the merchandise they had purchased, perhaps even realize a small profit on the deal I would have been all too happy to grant. They told me to open the box.'' The Greek stopped, as if he had to force himself to go on. ''There was a head in the box, a head belonging to the boy who had robbed Megilido Fass and then sold his booty to me.''

''So you told them about Earnst.''

''No, American, I didn't. I would have, had they left the box containing the boy's head with me.''

''What's the difference?''

''The fact that they took it with them showed me they weren't sure I was the one who had brokered the crystals.

They were showing it all around the city to men like myself, waiting for one of us to break. Fass is an awful man but not prone to making unnecessary enemies in Athens. It would not suit his needs."

"Then Fass knew nothing about Earnst."

"He couldn't have. If he had, Earnst would have been dead months ago and the crystals stolen back."

"Except they were stolen . . . by someone else."

"Yes," said Stadipopolis knowingly, "and the fact that one of them is in your possession indicates you are working for that party."

"Working with, not for."

"It doesn't matter."

"It does to me."

"Then let me tell you what matters to me, American. You are here searching for more of these crystals because this party has discovered their potential as a power source."

Stadipopolis' statement took Blaine totally by surprise. He fought not to show it. How could this man have known?

"Might be a handsome profit involved for the man who helps us locate the reserves."

"The reserves should be buried forever, along with the rest of the crystals you possess." The Greek's voice was strained.

"No more riddles. I'm sick of them. What are these crystals?"

"Death has followed them everywhere, always. I didn't know. If I had—"

McCracken reached out and grabbed a fistful of Stadipopolis' shirt. "*What* are they?"

The Greek's lips quivered. "Their origins I learned later, too late. They are the product of myth."

"People don't get killed for myths."

"This myth may well turn out to be real." And he swallowed as much air as McCracken's squeeze allowed him. "Atlantis," he said.

It took a few seconds for Stadipopolis' words to sink in.

"Wait a minute," Blaine responded, releasing his hold. "Atlantis, as in the island that sank into the sea?"

"The very same."

"I came here for truth," McCracken snapped. "Not phony mythology."

"Truth, American, is a matter of perspective. Mine changed when I found a link I could not dismiss. Many believe that the people of Atlantis harnessed the sun to create a power stronger than atomic energy. They accomplished this by using a ruby-red crystal to store vast amounts of the sun's energy for later use. *Ruby red!* You've seen it. You possess it!"

"And you're going to help me find more."

"No! Atlantis destroyed itself by abusing the power of its crystals. They tried to use them as *weapons*. I have read about this. And now I hear you tell me in so many words, American, that someone you represent is doing it again. Trying to harness the power of something man was never meant to uncover, never meant to—"

"Wait! Quiet!"

"Why do—"

"I said quiet!" Blaine rasped.

He had heard something, a boot kicking pebbles. Then more sounds, soft thuds of car doors closing gently.

Blaine's eyes swung about him. The various tombs and monuments blocked his view of the nearby roads.

Where were they, damnit? Where?

The sounds stopped, which wasn't a good sign, for it meant whoever it was had drawn close enough to be satisfied. Blaine thought of New York. Perhaps the same party was behind the men on 47th Street. Or perhaps they'd been sent by Fass.

Stadipopolis came a little forward. "American, what is it? What's wrong?"

McCracken yanked his gun free of its holster. "Stay out of the light!"

"I'm not about to—"

"I said *stay out*—"

It was too late. The gunshots had begun.

CHAPTER 12

McCRACKEN had already hit the ground when Kapo Stadipopolis's face vanished. Blood and bone splattered everywhere, splashing up against a white stone pillar. The Greek's corpse struck dirt an instant after Blaine plunged to the ground.

More shots echoed through the cemetery air. Footsteps pounded earth, coming closer. McCracken thought fast. The darkness was his ally. All the killers would have seen after firing their burst was two bodies going down; it would have been impossible to tell if they had been hit or not. Blaine hugged the ground and began to crawl away, pushing with his elbows, around the back of Dionysios's tomb.

Two men in black rushed out of the darkness into the circle of light cast by one of the floodlights. McCracken fired and one gasped and crumbled. The other dove behind the cover of a monument. He called out for help, and Blaine recognized the language.

It was Russian!

Cars screeched forward on the nearby street. More doors pounded solidly. Footsteps smacked cement and then hard ground. If McCracken was going to move, it had to be now.

In the next instant, he was on his feet. The gunman behind

the monument fired his automatic rifle at Blaine as he ran, and Blaine returned the fire with random shots to keep the man at bay. Blaine passed behind another tomb, a larger one with DEXILEOS chiseled in huge letters. He emerged on the other side to a new volley of staccato bursts and chips of ancient marble flying into his face. Again Blaine dove, firing at shadows in the darkness. His pistol clicked on an empty chamber and he rolled aside to snap a fresh clip home.

He was under cover now, but the sound of the nearby traffic confused him and made it hard to judge the number and proximity of the whispering voices.

Russians, goddamnit, Russians!

But sent by whom?

Blaine pulled himself through the slick grass, using the floodlit Acropolis above as a landmark to guide him. His problem was not to defend himself but to escape. He could kill plenty of the enemy, but each bullet used would attract more live ones. Eventually they'd have him. It was inevitable. He kept crawling.

The voices around him grew louder as his pursuers grew more impatient. Each second he evaded them would work in his favor. With the increased possibility that their quarry might escape, desperation, and with it carelessness, would set in.

Blaine stopped behind a smaller row of tombs just before Sacred Way, which divides Kerameikos Cemetery in two. Looking up, he saw they housed among others, Pythagoras. Strange, he mused, that the slightest error on his part now and he would die atop the Greek father of precise mathematics. His plan was not yet formed. The point was now to just keep moving.

A little more than a hundred yards ahead lay the remains of the wall erected by Themistokles around Athens following the Persian invasion. If he could scale it, he might get away before the Russians had a chance to react.

Quiet, he urged himself, as footsteps stopped not more than a half-dozen feet away from the tombs that shielded him. Blaine readied his pistol, determined to avoid using it at all costs because of the attention it would draw.

Fortunately, the gunmen swung across Sacred Way toward the other side of the cemetery. McCracken crawled ten more yards and then slid beneath the raised platform of another monument and rested. It was sixty yards to the walls, and he could never hope to cover the distance on his belly. He had to create a distraction, something that would draw the gunmen away from the direction in which he planned to flee.

Blaine twisted in his confined space, fighting his cramped muscles, and considered his options. First he thought of using the fresh clip in his Heckler and Koch to chip a significant piece of a monument away. He could assume the opposition would converge on it, and then he could escape. But the marble might not splinter sufficiently, and he would have accomplished nothing but to alert the killers to his actual position. No, he had to do something else.

McCracken smiled when his eyes fell upon the Kerameikos Museum, the one modern building within the cemetery. He knew it was packed with the kind of artifacts that would make an advanced alarm system a necessity. A bullet or two through the windows should create the distraction he needed. Blaine aimed toward the largest window he could find. He fired only once.

The shrieking alarm started the instant the glass shattered. Huge floodlights atop the museum blazed suddenly, illuminating irregular patches of the cemetery with an eerie glow. Blaine watched the Russians shy away from the light, dodging and darting, yelling to each other in total confusion.

McCracken pushed himself from beneath the monument and was on his feet instantly. He sprang onto the Sacred Way toward the inner wall that would lead him to the gate and freedom.

The alarm continued to wail, and approaching sirens added to the chaos.

A pair of breathless Russians swung onto the road right

before him. He saw them long enough before they saw him to crack one solidly in the throat and launch a kick to the other's groin. Two blows later, both were unconscious.

"There! There!"

McCracken heard the calls in his wake as he reached the inner wall that stood between him and the Sacred Gate.

He had just reached the top when bullets chewed at the stone near his hands. Dust and chips coughed into the air. Blaine hurdled over and took the impact on both legs equally to save himself from spraining an ankle.

He dashed fifteen yards and reached the Sacred Gate. It was part of a wall at least ten feet high, and because the gate was locked Blaine knew he had no choice but to scale the wall. The gate itself had the most footholds, so he leaped upon it, aiming his hands for a slight ridge just two feet from the top. His legs churned and kicked to keep him from slipping. With the Russians as close as they were, he would get only one chance.

McCracken hoisted himself upward, one hand over the other in a rhythm his feet also fell into. His right hand had just reached over the top when riflemen reached the inner wall behind him and began firing. The Athens police were arriving too and seemed at the outset to be most concerned with taking cover. Blaine's vulnerability terrified him. A ricocheting bullet grazed his shoulder and the searing pain provided the last burst of adrenalin he needed to throw himself over the wall.

This time his fall was not nearly as graceful. He landed on the ground with a thud and lost his breath on impact. He tried to regain his feet and almost made it, but he fell again onto the knoll that bordered the eastern edge of the cemetery.

A pair of dark Mercedes sedans tore around a corner and headed toward him. With no other choice, Blaine forced himself to his feet and ran along the grass in a daze.

McCracken felt beaten. The cars hadn't spotted him yet but they would, and there were the many troops left in the cemetery to consider, too. The presence of the Athens police might deter some—but not all. It would only take a few to best him in this condition.

He stumbled on with his head down, but when he looked up he saw an amazing sight. Brilliantly lit by modern floodlights, the Parthenon stood majestically atop the Acropolis, Athens's ancient hill of state and commerce. The complex, open regularly for tours right up to midnight this time of year, might offer him a means of escape.

The rocky hill contained a set of ancient chiseled steps which provided access to the Acropolis. The majesty of the bright sight, its promise of hope, gave Blaine the energy he needed to run across the street and start up the ancient steps. The going was steep and many of the steps were chipped or rotted away. Blaine slipped regularly but never let himself lose his balance. If he could reach the Acropolis and mingle with the tourists. . . .

Bullets splintered the silence of the night, echoing against the hill. His thoughts were interrupted. Once again only the next second lay before him.

Now three-quarters of the way up the hill, he moved off the steps onto the grassy slope of the Acropolis. The darkness hid him. He struggled on upward, climbing diagonally toward the Propylaea, which formed the original five-gated entrance to the Acropolis. Tourists normally entered by way of Beule Gate, but that was far too bright a section for McCracken to risk.

His hands scraped against jagged rock as he climbed through a restricted area. Once on level ground, he made for the Temple of Athena. Further on he could see that the bulk of the tour group was now concentrated near the majestic Parthenon itself.

"Recent measures enacted by the Greek government have drastically reduced the damage to these artifacts caused by pollution," the tour guide, an olive-skinned woman, was explaining in English. "But still the rock surface and marble facing have been damaged beyond repair. Surviving through thousands of years of history only to be . . ."

Blaine found himself standing next to a mustachioed man with a camera dangling around his neck. The man turned suddenly, surprised by his sudden appearance.

"Hell taking a piss around here, isn't it?" Blaine quipped. "Nearly killed myself. Ancient Greece wasn't much when it came to plumbing, I guess."

The man smiled and returned his attention to the tour guide.

"The Parthenon was built as a temple to Athena and a statue of her stood in the east end until . . ."

McCracken heard the footsteps coming and didn't have to turn to know the Russians were approaching. He had to act fast. But what to do?

When in doubt do nothing, went the humorous teaching, but tonight Blaine found more than humor in it. The killers had never gotten a good look at him in the Kerameikos Cemetery, and he doubted they had been furnished with anything but vague descriptions. Their target was not supposed to be a figure in a crowd.

Blaine's escape had changed all that. His dusty clothes might have given him away but the night breeze had dusted other men as well. The only feature that could identify him was his wounded shoulder. The flow of blood had stopped, and the patch was drying. A skilled eye, though, might notice something out of the ordinary.

Blaine backed up so he was flanked by two women.

"That concludes our tour, ladies and gentlemen," the tour guide said, and the group applauded politely. "Now," she continued, starting to move through them, "if you'll follow me, we'll make our way down the east path back to the bus."

McCracken let himself be absorbed into the crowd. Turning, he saw the Russians for the first time in the light, suits looking out of place and soiled by their climb up the hill. Their eyes swept the tour members anxiously, holding briefly on each of the men as they too struggled to mix with the crowd. They gave Blaine the same visual inspections the others received and then conferred with each other, shrugging. Some of their fellows had drifted back among the relics, perhaps believing their quarry to be lurking somewhere in that area.

Blaine blessed his luck. If they thought he was still hiding, he might be able to slip by them by simply sticking with the tour group. He descended with the group down the well-lit east path of the hill. He did not look ahead to his next move; there was no reason to until he found what awaited the group at the end of his descent. He was aware of a pair of Russians lagging back a bit at the rear of the group. A third walked near the head of the procession. From his position in the center Blaine could easily neutralize all three with bullets if it came down to that.

With forty more yards to go until ground level, McCracken saw the tour bus for the first time. Along with something else.

A pair of black Mercedes sedans, windows lowering as the tour group came into view. The cars were ancient, as much relics of their kind as the structures he had just left at the Acropolis. Oversized monsters from a different age, they sat by the curb, one behind the other, waiting.

Blaine also noticed a number of well-dressed men on the sidewalk near the bus across the street. All wore overcoats on the warm spring night. The enemy's strategy was obvious: wait until the group reached the bottom of the hill and kill all the tour group patrons if their quarry had not showed himself. The media would call it a terrorist attack, and a half-dozen leftist groups would claim responsibility.

Blaine felt the cold sweat dripping down his face and soaking the skin beneath his shirt. His heart thudded against his rib cage, and his breathing suddenly felt labored. Clearly he had to act. He couldn't allow the slaughter of innocent people. He drew his right hand slowly inside his belt to feel for his Heckler and Koch P-7, which still had seven shots left. The key questions were when to move and where to move first. The street was coming up fast. Russians lay on all sides of him. He had to act before they did but not in a manner that drew their fire randomly into the crowd.

Think, damnit, think!

The bus was right in front of him now. The shape huddled behind the wheel was obviously the driver. The large vehicle could provide cover for him. It would certainly— No, not cover. . . . Blaine saw what he had to do, but there was still the crowd to consider.

Ten yards from the bus now. . . .

He had to make sure the tour patrons were safe before he acted. It was the only alternative.

Near the bus and across the street, the Russians were pulling out their automatic weapons. The windows in the black cars were all the way down. The signal to fire would come from them.

Blaine knew his next step had to come now and threw himself forward without further thought.

"AHHHHHHHHHHHHHHHHH!"

His scream pierced the night and froze the tour group in its tracks just as it was supposed to. In that same instant, he had his pistol out and was firing in the direction of the black cars, for distraction as much as anything. He had done the last thing the Russians would have expected, and the action allowed him to take control of the crowd's movement. As his gunshots resounded, the tour patrons hit the ground screaming, taking them out of the line of fire from the street.

The suddenness of McCracken's motion had stopped the men in the Mercedes from signalling and had forced the overcoated men to take cover. By the time the enemy had recovered their senses, Blaine had reached the side of the bus and fired four bullets up the hill at the charging figures who had stayed near the rear of the pack. Two of the men went down quickly, and then a third.

Just one bullet left, and no time to snap his last clip home. . . .

Automatic fire sliced into the side of the bus. Two overcoated men rushed across the street trying to better their angles as Blaine moved to the open door of the bus. McCracken climbed the steps with his frame low. He saw that the driver, slumped over the wheel, must have been hit by a stray bullet. Blaine pulled the man's head back, and saw the protruding tongue and purplish features in time to realize he had been strangled. Suddenly a figure rose out of the darkness in the back of the bus.

Blaine fired his last bullet, but he was still in motion himself, and the shot went off target. It hit the bolt of the Russian's machine gun and jammed it. More machine gun fire pounded the bus as McCracken yanked the dead driver away from the wheel and crouched low in his place. The keys were still in the ignition and he turned them. The bus engine coughed, then caught.

McCracken saw the Russian charging him from the rear, knife in hand now, and floored the accelerator pedal as he shifted into gear. The bus lurched forward suddenly and the attacking Russian toppled over backwards.

Enough bullets had found the tires to make for a bouncy, grinding ride. Blaine kept his head just above the dashboard as more automatic fire sliced through the few remaining windows. He concentrated on keeping the bus straight against its determined efforts to waver out of control. The big vehicle weaved one way and then the other, Blaine's frantic spins of the wheel inevitably an instant late. What remained of his side mirror showed the Mercedes sedans in hot pursuit with gun-wielding men hanging out windows in both. Blaine raced the bus past the Roman Market and the Library of Hadrian, then screeched into a left toward the familiar surroundings of Monastiraki Square. He had a fleeting sad thought of shopowner Stadipopolis's children, who would now grow up orphans after all.

It was the sound of a boot grinding against the steel floor behind him that made Blaine swing around, and the motion saved his life. The Russian's knife missed him and tore into the fabric of the seat back. The bus careened wildly out of control through Monastiraki Square, smashing through the outdoor tables and sheds. McCracken struggled to control the wheel with one hand while the other reached back for the Russian.

Behind him the two sedans weaved an ever-changing course to avoid the wreckage in the bus's wake. McCracken heard more than saw them as he fought the Russian behind him. The man was raising his knife once more and Blaine knew in that instant there was no way he could possibly deflect the blow. There was only one thing he could do.

He jammed on the brakes.

The Russian went flying toward the windshield, separated from the knife. Stomping on the accelerator again, Blaine grasped the man's hair with his free hand while his other hand worked the wheel frantically one way and then the other, tearing the front of a shop out on one side of the street and then weaving into a second across the way.

The two Mercedes sedans spun into each other, looking like bumper cars at an amusement park as they spun out of control. The skilled drivers managed to right the ruined vehicles and get them back on the bus's tail, but McCracken had widened the gap.

Blaine slammed the Russian's face into the bus's dashboard again and again until the man had gone limp. He watched the man slump to the floor, then turned his attention back to the road. He spun the wheel hard to the left onto one of many smaller side streets which cut through the Kerameikos district, looking for a place to dump the wounded Russian. He had lost sight of the Mercedes sedans and clung to the hope that they had given up the chase. Blaine turned the wheel just as hard to the right down yet another side street.

He saw the horse-drawn carriage much too late to do anything but slam on the brakes and work the wheel madly. But riding on two rims and two bad tires, the bus could do nothing but lock up and roll over onto its side, missing the carriage as it slid down the street into a row of parked cars and then a building. McCracken felt his consciousness wavering and realized the initial roll had slammed him against the door. The bus had come to a halt with the door on the bottom, so he pushed his aching body upward. Blood poured down his face from a nasty gash on his forehead. He used the steel first-aid kit to knock out the remnants of a window so he could pull himself out. He smelled gasoline and heard a hissing from the engine.

Blaine managed to get his torso through the shattered window and, with considerably more effort, his legs as well. But his balance was gone and he tumbled hard to the sidewalk with the world blurring in and out of blackness.

The sound of screeching tires had him moving again and the sight of the two approaching sedans had him trying for yet another escape. He stumbled and staggered, his body a mass of pain. His gun was gone, and it was empty in any case. Blaine limped toward a shop with its light still on.

Bullets hit the ground near his feet. Car doors opened and men poured out to give chase.

Damn! He shouldn't have tried running. He should have known they would spot him instantly.

Still staggering, he reached a sidewalk and nearly tripped on the curb. He pulled himself along the buildings now, refusing to give up. There had to be a way to survive. A weapon he could make use of, something . . .

A flood of automatic fire sent him diving to the sidewalk and crawling desperately for cover that didn't exist. It seemed over. By all rights it should have been.

The small car coming toward him with high beams blazing surprised him as much as it did the Russians. They swung suddenly, awash in the light, and darted aside when it seemed certain the small car was intent on running them over. At the last instant the car, a Volkswagen Beetle, swung away from them for the curb, and slowed down between the downed McCracken and his pursuers. In the next second, an Ingram machine gun poked out the driver's window and commenced firing at the shocked Russians. They returned the fire.

McCracken watched in a daze. If he was being rescued, this had to be a dream and soon he would wake up dead. But then the passenger door was thrown open and through the darkness he made out the coldest pair of eyes he had ever seen in a woman's face.

"Get in!" the woman shouted. She never stopped firing.

CHAPTER 13

THE car bucked as the woman jammed down on the accelerator. McCracken managed to get the door closed as the Beetle lurched toward the gun-wielding Russians.

"Who the he—"

The rest of Blaine's words were lost in a hail of gunfire and glass as the windshield shattered. He ducked low, head near the gearshift, and felt the shards spray him. The woman swung the wheel hard, still firing out the driver's side window with her Ingram.

"Shift into second!" she ordered Blaine.

He did as he was told, frozen by the fiercely resolved glare on the woman's face. He had seen enough professionals before to know he was looking at one now.

More gunshots sounded behind them, one shattering the rear window. The Volkswagen stayed straight, the Russians thus forced to rush back for their heavily damaged Mercedes sedans.

"Third," the woman started, hesitating as a corner came up. "Now!"

Again Blaine obliged and sat up in his seat. The woman pulled the Ingram back inside and handed it over to him, eyes alternating between the side and rearview mirrors.

"I want you to know I don't kiss on the first date," Blaine told her.

The woman seemed not to hear him. Her eyes maintained their intensity, narrowing suddenly.

"Damn," she uttered, "they're on us."

And the Beetle picked up speed. The woman swung right off Sari Street onto a narrow side road lacking a sign. The glare of headlights shimmered off the rearview mirror as the sedans screeched round in pursuit. The woman took another right and headed straight toward an alleyway connecting this street with another. When they were almost upon it, Blaine realized its narrowness, realized even the small Volkswagen would have no chance of negotiating through it.

"Hey," he started. "Hey!"

Again the woman ignored him, gritting her teeth and downshifting to lower the Beetle's speed as it sped into the alley with barely four inches to spare on either side. Sparks flew as the driver's door grazed the cement building on its side. The woman overcompensated a bit too much and Blaine's door smashed inward.

The woman remained expressionless. The end of the alley was just thirty yards ahead. Again headlights flashed in the rearview mirror, this time dimly. Blaine turned behind him, smiling.

"Come on, you fuckers," he urged the oncoming Russians. "Try it."

They did, but the driver of the lead Mercedes realized the narrow width of the alley too late to pull back. He managed to brake just before the Mercedes crashed into a pair of buildings. The second sedan smacked into it solidly from behind, compressing the back end to match the crushed front, so that the lead Mercedes resembled an accordion.

The woman swung right onto Evripidou Street and eased the Beetle's speed back with the appearance of more traffic.

"Next time I think I'll leave the driving to Greyhound," Blaine told her, wiping the blood and sweat from his eyes with a swipe of his sleeve.

"We have little time," she told him flatly and Blaine noticed her accent was foreign. He felt a chill.

"You're Russian, aren't you?" he managed.

"Since birth," the woman replied without looking at him.

"We have much to discuss," the woman said as she locked the door of the hotel room behind them.

"Like to know your name," Blaine said. "Might help avoid confusion during the course of our conversation."

The hotel was located three blocks from his but was not listed in any brochure or travel guide. It catered mostly to patrons who booked by the hour, perhaps night, and never in advance. There were no sheets on the bed, and there was barely any furniture besides a single chair and small dresser. The window was dirt-stained, with parts of its lower rim painted over.

"Natalya Illyevich Tomachenko," the woman said by way of belated introduction.

Blaine's eyes wandered. "KGB. I've heard of you."

"And I have heard of you, Mr. McCracken."

"My friends call me Blaine."

"We are not friends, just allies thrust together out of necessity."

"I've slept with women out of far less." McCracken winked.

"Your sense of humor is well known to us and not appropriate at this time."

" 'Us'?" Blaine raised. "I thought you were speaking for yourself."

"In the Soviet Union, the singular does not exist," she said, without bothering to hide a note of bitterness.

"An uncharacteristic tone for a top KGB agent. Yup, it's all coming back to me now. You retired. Then came out again."

"I had my reasons."

Blaine looked at her. "What have they got on you, Natalya?"

The remark stung her. She seemed about to speak, but then changed her mind.

"Relax," McCracken told her. "My government isn't exactly my biggest fan either."

"You would perhaps choose to blame them for your own foolish mistakes?" she shot back.

"Such as?"

"A hotel clerk with a big mouth and an empty wallet. My Russian friends bought your room number from him for twenty American dollars."

"Damn, I thought I was worth more than that. . . ."

"I paid forty for a key to your room two hours earlier," Natalya Tomachenko said, opening the single closet door to reveal Blaine's suitcases. "I knew you would be in no position to return to your room after tonight, so I took the liberty of removing your possessions."

"How considerate." Blaine found Natalya more than a little attractive. There was no denying her beauty. The dark Slavic features and wide, deep brown eyes made that impossible well before the shoulder-length black hair was even taken into consideration. Still, the implacable set of her jaw and her ice-cold stare kept her from being as ravishing as she might have been. Blaine wanted to call this nameless feature something almost masculine, but even that didn't suffice. Her coldness, an almost mechanical resolve, transcended gender. She was like a machine awaiting orders. But this machine was hiding something as well. Blaine was as certain of that as he was of her beauty.

"Your head and shoulder are still bleeding," she said in her most tender voice yet, as if reading his mind. "I have bandages and antiseptic."

"Did you anticipate my wounds as well?"

"Obtaining a few seemed unavoidable. You were vastly outnumbered."

"Only until you came along. You timed your entrance to perfection."

"That too was necessary. I couldn't enter the cemetery or

follow you up to the Acropolis. My face was too well known to your would-be killers."

"Then you were following me."

"No. Them. I knew you were in Athens, yes, but not where exactly, and your security precautions worked for a while."

"Okay, how did you know that much?"

Natalya started toward the doorless bathroom which consisted of a single sink and toilet. "First your wounds must be taken care of. Detail them for me."

"It would take all night."

"Just the worst ones."

"My shoulder's felt better," he said, grimacing as he pulled off his jacket to reveal the bloody tear caused by the bullet that grazed him. "And my head, of course."

"Anything else?"

"Give me a few hours and I'm sure a few other spots will turn up."

Ten minutes later, Blaine's shoulder was swabbed and wrapped tightly with gauze stripping. The head wound, more bloody than serious, was handled with a simple strip bandage. It was already starting to clot. He sat down uneasily on the bed, with Natalya Tomachenko seated stiffly across from him on a wooden chair.

"When we left off," Blaine started, "you were about to explain how you knew I was in Athens."

"When word reached us—"

"Who's us?"

"One question at a time. When we learned you had been retained by—"

"Not retained by anyone. I'm operating on my own here."

"A poor choice of words. I'm sorry. When we learned of your involvement, agents were dispatched to various airports."

"Plural?"

"Your sense of security is well known to us. The one stationed at Kennedy learned you were flying to Paris."

"But the ticket I bought was for London."

"He, too, was made aware of your methods. We had agents stationed all over Europe; virtually every major international terminal was covered."

"Quite an operation. I dîdn't realize I was being tailed because technically I wasn't. I must be very important to you."

"More than you realize," Natalya told him. "Your importance to us began in New York. The men in the diamond district were Soviets."

"Yours?" Blaine was confused.

"Not at all. The force controlling them was behind the attack tonight as well, along with the murders of those government men in New York. And the woman."

Blaine fought to control his feelings. "A *Soviet* force?"

Natalya nodded reluctantly. "The force knew where Earnst had obtained the crystals and thus where you would be going next. Stadipopolis was allowed to live this long only to trap you."

"I sense a polarity here. . . ."

"I'm coming to the explanation now." She rose and moved to the dirt-encased window, gazing half out it and half at McCracken as she spoke. "Five days ago, a town in your state of Oregon was obliterated by what your scientists have accurately termed a carbon-decimating death ray. It was developed in the Soviet Union several years ago but abandoned when General Secretary Chernopolov realized the mad track it would place us on. The operation was known as the Alpha project."

"Alpha as in the Greek letter?"

Natalya nodded. "Because the research was to mark the beginning of a new kind of weapon."

"Well, I guess the world won't be safe until the Greek alphabet's been expended. . . ."

"Even as the project neared its successful completion, General Secretary Chernopolov determined the only conceivable upshot of such a weapon would be war. He knew there was a strong faction in Moscow that would have insisted on the weapon's utilization had it been allowed to become operational. His only way of averting war, then, was to cancel the Alpha project before its completion. The decision was tremendously unpopular, causing a rift through the Kremlin."

"And thanks to this rift the Alpha project managed to continue."

"Through General Secretary Chernopolov's greatest rival and the man who headed up Alpha: General Vladimir Raskowski."

"I've heard of him," McCracken said. "Sees himself as the second coming of Alexander the Great."

"Worse now that he is in possession of the means to fulfil that destiny. Raskowski was—*is*—an outcast, a madman. He pushed forth the ethic that it was Soviet destiny to overrun Europe and crush whatever meager resistance NATO forces could muster. There was a time when his ideas had considerable support in the Kremlin. But the new leadership under Chernopolov shunned Raskowski and his insane schemes that would have certainly landed us in the midst of global nuclear war. The Alpha project was canceled. Raskowski's career was ended. He was exiled, all his KGB titles and military rank officially stripped."

"Rather extreme for you people."

"Not extreme enough. A little more than a year ago, Raskowski vanished."

"Along with all the records of the Alpha project, I assume."

"Of course. The general had never gotten over the fact that when we were able to destroy America we chose not to do it. There were some in Moscow who supported his views. Several of them disappeared at the same time as the general. Others continued to work, gathering intelligence for Raskowski's plans before they, too, vanished."

"Traitors in the Kremlin? Pinch me, I must be dreaming."

"Moscow is not immune and neither, as I mentioned before, is Washington. Raskowski controls the highest-placed mole in intelligence history, a man with the confidence of the President himself."

"That would explain a lot," Blaine nodded, recalling his own certainty that a leak had sprung within the crisis committee. "I don't suppose you could tell me who this mole is."

"Only by the code name Raskowski has used for him in the past: the Farmer Boy. Supposedly he was born on a Soviet farm to an American mother and Russian father. The Farmer Boy was handpicked along with dozens of other young Soviets to be groomed as spies *within* America. They were sent there as children. Raskowski has buried all the agents he controls so deeply that their identities, the Farmer Boy's included, remain a mystery even to us."

McCracken thought briefly. "Okay, so after learning through the Farmer Boy that certain crystals had been discovered which could power an energy field that could stop his death ray, Raskowski ordered Earnst's death to destroy the trail."

She nodded. "Because he couldn't let his plan be stopped. There is a progression, you see, and either the destruction or disgrace of your country is a vital part of it."

"Do us in one way or another and they'll roll a red carpet out to him from Moscow leading straight to Chernopolov's chair."

"Unfortunately, yes. The destruction of the United States would propel him into power, just as your unilateral disarmament would if you accede to his demands. And if you decide to fight, the Kremlin might have no choice but to turn to him for the certain victory his death ray would guarantee."

"In every scenario he wins and we lose," noted Blaine somberly. "And your government can't admit any of this because to do so would be to admit they've lost control. Unthinkable in the Soviet Union."

"Because it would force the government to topple, thus accomplishing Raskowski's goal for him. Unthinkable *any-*

where. I was dispatched by General Secretary Chernopolov personally to ensure that none of these scenarios comes to pass. He cannot afford to mobilize traditional forces, just as your government cannot."

"And where exactly do I come into your scenario?"

"Two days ago we obtained a lead as to Raskowski's whereabouts, at least the means by which his death beam has been deployed. If I . . . fail, our only hope will be that your search for the Atragon crystals either succeeds or flushes him out."

"Long shots at best."

"But you'll take the chance, just as I will, because more is at stake here for both of us."

Blaine let the statement pass and scratched at the bandage on his forehead. "I met with a Greek antique dealer tonight who pointed me in the direction of a man named Megilido Fass. He seems to possess some unusual sexual leanings which may provide my in to him. Think you might be able to dig up some more details for me?"

"I'll make the necessary calls."

Blaine shook his head. "Ironic, isn't it? Two superpowers compromised by their own inadequacies. What's left? Us . . . two outcasts charged with returning sanity to an insane world."

"Let it stay insane. So long as it survives."

CHAPTER 14

NIGHT came early in Pamosa Springs on the second day of the occupation. Jeep and foot patrols swept through the streets to enforce curfew and by eight P.M. not a soul out of uniform could be seen anywhere. The drapes and curtains in every house were drawn, as if whatever was happening to the town could be simply blocked out.

Those residents peeking between the cracks saw a huge break in the darkness, thanks to a host of floodlights on the hillside that three weeks before had yielded up its minerals. What they couldn't see from this distance was the large complement of men at work with hydraulic drills and manual tools, lifting and rummaging through huge slabs of the hillside. Nor could they see five truckloads of machinery and equipment still being unloaded and set up in the gulley beyond the floodlit hill.

The four members of the Pamosa Springs town council were gathered by candlelight in the attic of the oldest member's house just after one A.M. No one took the meeting's minutes and everyone whispered, the only sound other than their voices being the jackhammer pounding coming from the hillside.

"Well," said Mayor Jake "Dog-ear" McCluskey, "anyone want to get this meeting started?"

"As I see it," responded Clara Buhl, trying to shift her bulky legs in the cramped confines of the attic, "we were supposed to figure they were the real army, Corps of Engineers probably. They musta had a cover story all set that woulda made plenty of sense to us . . . till Hal Taggart appeared on the scene."

"And their story got shot to hell," from McCluskey.

"Along with Taggart," added Sheriff Pete Heep.

"So all hell breaks loose," picked up Clara, "and it's pretty obvious to us that they're not the real army. They forget all about the niceties and take us all prisoner."

"Which still don't tell us what they're here for," the mayor raised. McCluskey was a beefy man with a belly that had long since fallen over his waist. He had once been a football star and pictures of him in various poses plastered his office walls. They made quite a collection, and most of Pamosa Springs had been given the tour often enough to be able to recite the year and day each shot had been snapped. McCluskey had a square face and straight jaw, both of which seemed even more rectangular thanks to his crew-cut. The nickname Dog-ear was due to the fact that he was missing a hefty chunk of his left lobe courtesy of a murderous beagle that had gone crazy on him as a child.

Sheriff Pete Heep, on the other hand, was rail thin, all knees and elbows, which cracked and squeaked with almost every move. A tour in Korea had sent him home with shrapnel in three of his four limbs. Heep kept his sense of humor about the squeaking—and the pain—giving himself the nickname of "Junk" Heep to describe his battered body, which took twenty minutes to stir out of bed every morning.

"Did it real organized like, too," added Sheriff Junk. "They're experienced, whoever they are, and damn well armed." He moved his elbow with a resounding *pop*. "Can't expect to keep us prisoners forever, though. I mean this is a town."

"Maybe not forever," chipped in Clara Buhl, "but long enough. Judgin' by the pace they been working at, I'd say they don't want to stay here any longer than they have to. They got a roadblock set up on the only road leading into the Springs and who would question the army? All they have to say is something about hazardous waste or some nuclear test gone wrong and people'll steer clear for miles."

Clara was a feisty woman of near sixty who had been cursed by a bad heart for over a quarter of those years. She was born and raised in the Springs and had never left the state of Colorado in her entire life. She seldom even left her house except for council meetings and could be found at virtually any hour of the day or night listening to an old radio and working her way through needlepoint after needlepoint. Her whole house was covered with her creations, few of them any good since her eyes started to go, the stitching sloppy and the colored patches running into each other to create an inadvertent impressionism. Clara refused to accept glasses and relied instead on an antique magnifying glass for her meager reading needs.

"Whoever they are, they thought this out plenty good," put forth Dog-ear McCluskey. "Knew just where to cut the power and phone lines. Even had a list of all the registered ham radio operators."

"It's public record," Clara told him.

"You know," started the mayor, "I had a friend once in the Signal Corps and it seems to me there's a way to convert a standard radio receiver into a transmitter. Damned if I can remember it, though."

"Even if you could," said Clara, "I doubt you could round up all the necessary equipment without them catching on. Lord knows there's enough of 'em to watch our every move, even when we make those rounds of the people they let us make today."

"I counted a few over a hundred," said eighty-two-year-old Isaac T. Hall. "Been counting for two days solid now. A hundred's the number all right. Seventy to eighty always working on the hillside or the gulley and the rest watching the town."

"Lots of men," muttered Sheriff Junk. He brought his knees up to his chest and there was a crackling noise.

"Not so many in my eyes," Ike T. Hall responded sharply. "Been through the two big wars myself. Seen things that'd turn your stomachs so far around you'd be shitting through your belly buttons. The Nazis were the worst. Rode over people 'cause people let 'em. The ones that fought, like in them ghettos, had a chance anyway. We could do the same," Hall insisted, pushing his thin wispy hair from his forehead. "That'd be my suggestion. We got 'em outnumbered. Hell, there's 700 of us. Was up to me, I'd strap on Uncle Wyatt's six-guns and have a go at the bastards. I get three or four 'fore they get me, we're ahead of the game."

Isaac Hall had lived in Pamosa Springs all his eighty-two years, half of them served as marshall. His greatest claim to fame was a distant relationship with Wyatt Earp himself. How he was related varied from great-nephew to cousin to great-grandson. Ike's flesh had been wrinkled and sagging for as long as most people could remember. The hair got thinner and wispier as the years went on.

"It ain't just the numbers, Ike," Sheriff Heep told him. "It's the weapons. To have any chance at all we'd have to come up with plenty more than your six-guns, and the town's armory's not exactly well stocked."

"What about *their* armory?" suggested Clara.

"Huh?"

"Their armory. If we can find out where they set it up, we could 'borrow' some of their weapons."

"And assuming we do, how many people in this town you think could make 'em work to any decent degree?" challenged Dog-ear. "Nope, I'm thinking along different lines. We ain't so isolated we couldn't get one person out to bring back help."

Junk's arm went *pop* as he slapped his thigh in disdain. "You thought out in which direction to send this person,

Dog-ear?'' he challenged. "I mean, you can forget the road the way it's guarded and the only walk that's even conceivable is east over the San Juans. That's five days in the best of conditions for someone who knows what they're doing.''

"Gotta be someone like that in town.''

"Gotta be nuts to want to chance it. This time of year I'd wager his chances of making it across the San Juans alive were no better than fifty-fifty.''

"Which might be better than our chances if we sit around and do nothing.''

A large blast sounded on the hillside, silencing the town council's voices and stilling their hearts.

"Might help if we knew what in hell it was that brought 'em here,'' said the mayor.

"Seems obvious to me,'' responded Heep. "There's something in that hillside that's plenty valuable and they're here to steal it right from under us.''

"Yeah,'' agreed Clara Buhl, "that explains their digging on the hillside. But anybody got an idea what they're building in the gulley?''

The soldier was bored. He hadn't known what to expect from this mission, but he was sure it would be better than patrolling an empty street by himself after midnight. The M-16 slung over his shoulder clapped against his hip, begging to be used. The soldier yawned. The prospects for action tonight, or anytime soon, were dismal. His walk had become mechanical now. The shift had been substantially reduced at midnight and the full moon proved a blessing for some, although the soldier would have preferred a fog-shrouded night when at least some of the local assholes would try to flee through his grid. Just let them try. . . .

A flash of movement caught his eye, a tall, thin figure moving on the outskirts of town, keeping to the shadows. The soldier was about to shout out, then elected to remove the M-16 from his shoulder instead. He brought it up as he dashed silently forward to better his angle. Standing square against a building, he pushed his eye against the infrared night scope and recognized the man superimposed in the cross hairs as the town's sheriff. No matter. His orders were open to interpretation in such situations. He would tell the commander he thought the man had a gun. The soldier started to reach for his trigger.

He didn't hear the footsteps coming up behind him until it was too late. He swung, expecting to see one of his fellows, but what he saw was the face of death itself.

The soldier felt himself trying to scream, feeling a horrible burst of agony in his back as a smelly hand closed over his mouth. That was his last thought—that the hand was big and that it smelled bad. The creeping figure extracted its blade, pulled the corpse between a pair of buildings, and slipped off into the night.

CHAPTER 15

WHEN McCracken woke up stiff and cold on the floor the next morning, Natalya was gone, the single blanket she had tossed over herself folded neatly at the foot of the bed.

"That antique dealer was right about Megilido Fass's sexual tendencies," she said when she returned twenty minutes later.

"What about taking advantage of those tendencies?"

"I'm not sure." She shrugged. "Thursday is the day Fass's contact makes his weekly delivery, but I'm not sure what we can do with this."

Blaine felt sickened by the perverted world of the reclusive and powerful Fass. "Learn anything about this contact?"

"Plenty."

Blaine smiled.

Two hours later, with Natalya's help, the disguise required for Blaine's impersonation was complete.

"Lucky this guy's got a beard," he said, rearranging his hair. "I really didn't want to shave mine." He looked to see Natalya gathering up her things. "Where you headed from here?"

"Bangkok," she replied matter-of-factly, "to meet with

an apparently desperate aide of Raskowski who seems eager to talk. I would have been there already, if not for the detour necessitated by your involvement."

"Please accept my apologies."

"Only if you'll accept my hand in good luck. One of us has to succeed. Otherwise both our countries will pay."

McCracken emerged from the run-down hotel dressed in baggy white trousers and a slightly soiled white, unstructured jacket. He had combed out his beard to give it an unkempt look and picked his wavy hair for the same effect. A series of makeup shades mixed together produced the necessary native flesh tone and hid his more noticeable scars nicely. He would have to be careful about smiling, though, for the man whose place he would be taking had a gold tooth in the front. Blaine had wedged a crinkled, floppy hat into his back pocket, ready for wear as the final element of his disguise. The real delivery man was not known to wear one but some improvisations were needed if he was to get close to Fass.

Natalya's information had spotted Megilido Fass on a huge estate in the Khania section of the island of Crete, specifically in Sfakia. Every Thursday a man named Manolokis took a ferry from southern Greece across the Mediterranean to the port of Khania. He always drove a white van, the windows of which were darkened to keep the curious from observing the merchandise he was retained to deliver once a week. Blaine would be waiting for him to arrive in Khania after flying in from Athens. The switch would have to be made with a minimum of fuss and even then Blaine would still have his work cut out for him in gaining access to Fass.

His parting with Natalya had been stiff and wholly professional. He admired her ability to distance herself from her mission. She had come to Greece only to save Blaine's life and set him straight on what they were facing. This done, she could leave knowing they would in all probability never meet again. Blaine couldn't accept that, though he sorely wished he could. After the pain of finding T.C. in New York, he felt certain he would never be able to feel close to a woman again. And yet, strangely, Natalya reminded him of T.C. so much that he couldn't help but be attracted to her. She was strong, independent, and mysterious in the same ways that Blaine had always thought of T.C. He tried to probe Natalya's mystery by comparing her to himself. While he wore his emotions like an old suit, tattered but open to view, she held hers within, her stoic seriousness as much a survival mechanism as his often misplaced sense of humor. Blaine didn't doubt she was hiding a hurt so deep that it powered her single-mindedness.

Blaine started down the street, doing his best to blend with the large number of people out on a beautiful Athens Thursday morning. He had plenty of time before catching his flight across the Mediterranean and figured his best use of it would be to phone Sundowner. The best means to do so was to make his way to a top-rated hotel with a smooth-working long-distance service. Twenty minutes later, he had checked into the Athens Hilton. It was another twenty minutes before a long-distance line was available.

"Good morning, Blaine," Sundowner said cheerfully from halfway around the world.

"Hope I didn't wake you."

"The Toy Factory never sleeps. How goes your search for Atragon?"

"Not in hand yet, but drawing closer. Actually I'm calling about some complications I've encountered along a different line."

"Such as?"

"Suffice it to say I've linked up with a foreign operative with as big a stake in this as ours. She told me an interesting story about a Farmer Boy the Soviets placed in America and have been running ever since."

"A *child* spy?"

"Now all grown up with the ear of the President."

"Christ. . . ."

"I think we can safely rule *him* out for the time being. But the existence of a mole would explain our problems in New York, Sundance. In fact, it would explain a hell of a lot. Go over the members of the crisis committee for me again."

"William Wyler Stamp, CIA director. George Kappel, Secretary of Defense. And Edmund Mercheson, Secretary of State."

"Eliminate Stamp. He fell into this position by accident and no one goes anywhere after running the Company these days. Tell me about Kappel."

"Very hawkish. His philosophy's a bit archaic in view of the proposed treaties, or maybe it isn't since the whole peace process has fallen on its ass. In Washington they call Kappel a survivor. Administrations come and go, but he always manages to hang on."

"And Mercheson?"

"A dove. Next to the President, he's the most unpopular man in the country, according to polls, since the disarmament treaties collapsed. People feel he cheated them, made the country give up too much only to be taken in by the Soviets who didn't want peace to begin with. I guess people look at him and expect him to work the same magic Kissinger did. No chance."

"I assume Mercheson is career Washington as well."

"Not as openly as Kappel but, yes, that would be an understatement. He's been around forever and promises to be around a while longer. I'm pretty good with a computer, Blaine," Sundowner added after a pause. "I can quietly go over their full files with the proverbial fine-tooth CRT screen."

"Don't bother. The truth's been buried too deep for anyone to ever find. This is the Soviet version of the deep-cover plant. They wouldn't have made any mistakes with their Farmer Boy."

Something occurred to Sundowner.

"They may have made one," he said. "Mercheson grew up on a farm in Michigan."

* * *

Manolokis was sweating inside the steaming white van as the ferry rolled over the waves of the Mediterranean. The port of Khania had finally come into sharp view. Manolokis dreaded these Thursday voyages, but he kept making them because the pay was impossible to refuse. So much for so little work. Every week a new shipment and another cash payment. He sometimes wondered what happened to the previous week's shipment, but he tried to think about it as little as possible. Part of his job was to ask no questions.

Manolokis gave in to temptation and rolled down the window on the driver's side of the van.

"Stay silent," he commanded the young passengers behind him, "or I'll cut off your balls."

He would round them up from various Mediterranean cities over the course of the week for delivery on Thursday. They were beggar boys willing to do anything for a decent meal and a few pennies. Manolokis promised them much more. A home. A life. For a time anyway, though he never elaborated on that. Four or five every week between the ages of eleven and fifteen. Since they were homeless or runaways, no one noticed when they disappeared.

Manolokis did his best never to consider the ramifications of what he had become involved in; it was too late to pull out in any event. His employer was not a man to cross, nor were the men Manolokis dealt with directly. Megilido Fass kept a tight net over the goings on in his Sfakia villa. News that came in never went out.

The same could be said for the merchandise Manolokis was charged with delivering.

He dozed briefly in the heat, until he was awakened by the bump of the ferry grazing the dock of the port. *At last*, he thought. Manolokis stretched, his sweat-soaked pants and white linen jacket clinging to the seat. He rolled up the window, turned on the engine, and switched the blessed air-conditioning back on.

There were never any questions when Manolokis drove off the ferry. The authorities who might have raised them were almost certainly on Fass's payroll as well. This was Crete, after all. Fass owned it.

The van bucked slightly as it passed from dock to roadway. Manolokis would be in Khania proper only briefly, soon swinging east to Vryses and then toward the south coast to the region of Sfakia and Fass's villa. At the end of the port district a shepherd was driving his goats across the road. Manolokis sat back to wait for the herd to pass.

A knocking came on the window. Manolokis turned to see a beggar wielding a tin cup. He shooed the man away without paying further heed. The knocking came again. Manolokis looked longer. The darkened windows made seeing out almost as difficult as seeing in and he decided it would be best to deal with the beggar through an open window anyway. Bastard deserved a good smack in the face for bothering him. He should report him to Fass's people. Bastard would probably lose his hands for the effort.

"Look," Manolokis started, "I don't know who—"

And stopped, just like that. Because the man outside the van was no beggar. It was . . . *him*, could have been a twin. The same face he saw regularly in the mirror except when it smiled no gold tooth flashed. Manolokis saw the twin's hand lash forward through the open window. He remembered trying to recoil and nothing else.

An instant later Blaine McCracken opened the door and climbed inside. Swiftly he pushed the unconscious Greek's body from the seat and took his place behind the wheel.

Blaine checked the rearview mirror. Five frightened faces glared back at him, teenage boys cowering in their seats. A few began to spit words out quickly in Greek, too quick for Blaine to follow them.

"Sorry," he shrugged, "don't speak the language too well, but I do speak another."

He pulled the van onto a side street and climbed out, beckoning the boys to follow him. They resisted for a moment, confused, even angry, but one by one they came forward. As they stepped toward Blaine, he handed each boy five worn

American dollar bills, more money than any of them had ever seen before. The beggar boys gathered together to share their shock and then glee, jumping up and down and babbling away joyously, ultimately hugging McCracken with thanks all at once. He fought them off as best he could but they stubbornly clung to him. Blaine finally managed to force them off with instructions in decent Greek for them to be on their way. The boys resisted, then at last moved off together as McCracken climbed back into the van.

Five minutes later, the bound and gagged body of Manolokis abandoned in the nearby brush, Blaine headed south. The ride would be long and the roads unfamiliar, but the route to Fass's villa outside of Sfakia was reasonably straight and Natalya's directions were precise. His Heckler and Koch was history, lost the night before on some Athens street, and Natalya had done her best to fill the gap with a pair of Brin 10 semiautomatic pistols. The substitution was acceptable and Blaine had stowed both of his fresh pistols under the seat.

He knew little about the part of Crete he was heading toward. Natalya had mentioned only a countryside rich in history and containing a subterranean well of ancient caves. Of Fass's villa little was known other than its hugeness. Fass himself was a mystery man, a smuggler of anything if the price was right. His perverted sexual leanings were the only thing known of him for sure and this the authorities did nothing about. Crete was his territory, its lavish beauty in direct contrast with the evil of a man who many believed to be a direct descendant of the devil.

It was two hours before McCracken found the private road that would take him to Fass's villa. Video cameras rotating from their tree posts signaled its location even as they tracked his arrival. He guessed there would be plenty of guards lining the road as well, but they would be well hidden and would appear only if the vehicle seeking entry was deemed a threat.

Several miles back Blaine had stuffed the Brin 10s in his belt beneath his baggy linen jacket. His last touch was to put on the floppy, crinkled hat and tilt it just enough over his eyes to put them in shadows. He steadied himself with a deep breath as the entrance to Fass's villa, a huge white stone gate, appeared before him. The guards on either side seemed to recognize the van and paid it little heed as he approached.

He cracked the window a few inches as he drew closer, braking the van to a walking clip. The guards never moved. The gate began to swing electronically open and they waved him through.

The courtyard is very large. A fountain, beautifully manicured lawns and shrubbery. Follow the driveway to the left where it winds in a semicircle before Fass's mansion. The procedure is for the guards to meet the van and take delivery of the contents. From that point you're on your own.

Natalya's description of the villa was absolutely precise. She had left out only its true magnitude. It was certainly one of the largest houses Blaine had ever seen, built entirely of white stone.

McCracken speeded up the van as he headed toward the circular drive in the front of the mansion. At the same time, he lifted one hand from the steering wheel and pulled a razor blade from the dashboard where he had left it. For the rest of his plan to work, the mansion guards would have to be distracted enough not to notice he wasn't the real Manolokis. Bringing the razor blade to his forehead, he made a quick slice in an old scar. Blood began pouring out instantly, dripping into his eyes. Perfect. Nothing beat blood for a distraction.

He was honking the horn when he screeched the van to a halt directly before the double entrance doors.

"Help! Help!" he called, throwing himself clumsily out of the van and making sure there was ample blood on his sleeves as well. The guards were running up. "They forced me off the road, took the boys!"

"Who?" the lead guard demanded in Greek.

"Fass! I must see Fass!"

McCracken was counting on the element of surprise once

he was escorted into Fass's chamber. A quick motion to draw his guns or knife and the Greek would be at his mercy. All the guards in the world would do him no good.

The guards were leading him into the mansion.

"He'll be angry, I know," McCracken continued, making no effort to clear away the blood from his face. "But it wasn't my fault. He'll have to understand that. . . ."

They had reached a huge circular stairwell and ascended it toward the mansion's second floor. The hallway at the top was long and curving. Guards flanked him on either side as they led him down it. Blaine kept his breathing rapid in mock panic but inside he was calming himself to his task.

"In here," the lead guard signaled, throwing the door open to what must have been Fass's chamber.

Blaine picked up his pace just a little as he entered, ready to spring now, hands already starting for his guns.

The sight of a half dozen men wielding automatic rifles froze him in his tracks. Behind the guards was a huge desk, and Blaine caught a glimpse of the man behind it.

"Welcome to my home, Mr. McCracken," said Megilido Fass.

CHAPTER 16

"PLEASE," Fass continued, "make yourself comfortable, but first drop your weapons on the floor."

McCracken emptied his belt deliberately, one of Fass's white-clad guards on either side of him. Both moved closer for a frisk.

"Be careful of this one," Fass warned them. "He could strip your rifles away in the blink of an eye."

"It's nice to have my skills appreciated for once," Blaine said, the frisk nearly complete.

Fass rose from behind his desk. "Here," he said, tossing a towel to McCracken. "The blood is most unbecoming to you."

Blaine caught the towel in midair and swiped away at his forehead, noticing for the first time a television monitor sitting atop Fass's desk.

"I recorded your performance outside on tape," the Greek explained. "Most impressive."

"I'm expecting royalties every time you show that."

"And rest assured I will show it often. It will be added to my permanent collection."

Blaine surveyed the scene before him, searching for options. Fass was not at all what he expected. The Greek smuggler was tall and gaunt, dressed in a white suit, white shirt, and white silk tie. His flesh was bronzed by the Mediterranean sun and his jet-black hair was slicked down close to his scalp. His eyes were hidden behind a pair of narrow sunglasses. A young boy, dressed in white shirt and pants, stood behind him against the back wall next to a dry bar. The servant had long curly locks that tumbled to his shoulders and couldn't have been older than fourteen.

"You were expecting me," Blaine said.

Fass chuckled, grinning devilishly. "An old friend of yours made a number of phone calls telling us to be on the lookout."

"Vasquez . . ."

Fass nodded. "I'm sure he'll be pleased you remember him. He called me twice. For some reason he was sure I would be your next target."

"You could have killed me downstairs if you wanted to."

"Of course I could have." Fass beamed. "But there would have been no sport in it." He tilted his stare toward the monitor. "No permanent recording of your exploits for an epitaph." Fass grinned again and pulled something from his pocket as he summoned the boy from the dry bar to his side. "Human life is nothing but a possession to be dealt with and replaced accordingly. Man is an intrinsically dispensable creature. Life and death are merely relative states of being I control within these walls."

Fass grabbed the boy by the hair and jerked his head back. In the same instant, Blaine saw the object he had pulled from his pocket was a small blade that he now whipped up and across the boy's throat.

"No!" McCracken screamed. But it was already too late when the guards on both sides moved to restrain him.

Blood poured outward from the neat slice in the boy's throat, rushing down his white shirt. The boy staggered backwards, eyes empty and glazing over, clutching for the wound futilely as he crumbled to the white carpet behind Fass's desk. Blaine heard the hideous, airless gurgle as death claimed him. He saw the boy's blood pooling on the carpet.

"As I said," Fass proceeded calmly, "people are mere possessions. You, meanwhile, have stripped me of this week's allotment. I've had to figure out a way for you to make compensation."

McCracken stopped pulling against the guards. "How about we dismiss the rest of your 'possessions' here and you try to slit *my* throat?"

Fass laughed and moved out from behind his desk. "Your reputation, as they say, has preceded you, Mr. McCracken. Vasquez warned me to keep my distance. He said you knew a dozen ways to kill a man with your bare hands in under two seconds."

"Fourteen. I've picked up a few more these last few years."

"Vasquez has not forgotten the debt he owes you."

"I suppose he wants you to deliver me to him."

"No," said Fass, "he just wants you dealt with. He left the specific manner up to me."

"You haven't even asked what brought me here."

"Because it doesn't matter. Whatever your pursuits, I'm afraid they won't be completed."

"Pity."

"Not totally." And Fass stepped still closer, baiting McCracken to move. "It's difficult to find a specimen like you these days. Many have crossed these walls but never one with your physical abilities and prowess. Vasquez asked only that I kill you. He left the choice of means up to me but, as I mentioned, death should be regarded as sport just as life is. Have you ever heard of the mythical Labyrinth, Mr. McCracken?"

"As in the Minotaur? Sure."

"Good, because you're going into it now."

* * *

"I've reconstructed it, Mr. McCracken," Fass told him as the guards escorted both of them down the corridor. "Here."

They reached a stairway at the end of the long, curving hallway and began to descend.

"Let me review for you the myth you are about to become part of," Fass resumed. "King Minos had the Labyrinth built to house the Minotaur. Born of the unholy union between a bull and the King's wife, who lay hidden within a wooden cow, the Minotaur was a creature with the head of a bull and the body of a man." When they had reached the bottom of the stairway they walked down another corridor and out a back door of the mansion. "Athens was annually required to send a host of youths and maidens as tribute—and food—for the Minotaur. Finally Theseus sailed from Athens to slay the dreaded creature. And this he accomplished with the help of Minos's daughter Ariadne, who gave him a ball of wool. He unravelled it on his way into the Labyrinth and then used it to find his way out." They stopped at a break in a huge row of thick green bushes. "How would you like to play Theseus in my little game today, Mr. McCracken?"

"Only if I get to win like he did. But I suppose that depends on what you've got for a Minotaur."

Fass grinned and led the way through the narrow passage in the bushes. Blaine saw a domed building, circular in design, perhaps sixty or so yards in diameter, though his angle made it difficult to judge. They moved toward a crowd of white-clad armed guards closer to the dome.

"Allow me to introduce *my* Minotaur, Mr. McCracken," Fass announced proudly.

The guards parted, and Blaine felt himself grow cold. It was a huge man. No, more than huge, monstrous. Naked to the waist and wearing only what might have been a loincloth and sandals, the giant was as muscular as he was tall. Bulging bands of sweat-shined flesh rippled across his arms, shoulders, and chest. His thighs were layered with knobs of muscles. He stood like a statue, pectoral muscles popping slightly with his even breaths.

"Here is how the game is played, Mr. McCracken," Fass explained. "You will enter the Labyrinth first, weaponless of course."

"Not even a spool of wool?"

"It wouldn't help you defeat my Minotaur. He will enter at his leisure from below, through a trapdoor. Defeat him and you win your freedom."

"And let me guess," Blaine said. "You've got plenty of your hidden video cameras down there to record every instant of the proceedings."

"Of course. Without spectators, there is no sport. You should be grateful, Mr. McCracken. I'm offering you a chance to live."

Even if that were true, the chance was minute, Blaine thought as he watched Fass's Minotaur pull on a pair of gloves decorated with rows of sharp spikes protruding a half inch or so outward. Last the giant donned a bull's-head mask complete with pointed horns which would make a formidable weapon for a man who knew how to wield them, as this one undoubtedly did.

"I must warn you, Mr. McCracken," Fass told him, "that my Minotaur has never even come close to being defeated. But, then, he has never faced a challenge as worthy as the one you will pose. Remember, victory means your life. I expect a good show." Then to his guards, "Lead him inside, but search him again first."

The men ruffled Blaine twice over, until they were satisfied he had no other weapons. Then they led him up to the Labyrinth's front door and shoved him through. The door slammed and echoed behind him. Blaine's first thought was that the lighting was dim, little more than the glow off a digital clock in a darkened bedroom. He would make as much use of it as possible. Not waiting for his eyes to adjust, he began walking. Fifteen feet down the corridor he reached an abutment that forced him to take a right, then a left. He was totally at the mercy of the Labyrinth's construction.

The problems it raised were many, and Blaine contemplated most of them in the seconds before the Minotaur's expected entry. To begin with, there were the walls of the structure itself. If he became trapped in a false passageway, backed up against a corner, his chances of defeating the spiked and horned giant would be reduced significantly. He had to make the maze's construction work *for* him somehow, perhaps taking the monster from behind. That task in itself would be close to impossible without a weapon. A man that huge and heavily muscled would feel little pain from a blow that would fell an ordinary man. Only a perfect strike would have any effect at all and McCracken wondered if in the near-darkness he could muster one.

Even if he managed to defeat the Minotaur, he had no illusions that Fass would in fact grant him his life. The *prospect* might appeal to the sportsman in Fass by providing motivation for McCracken to put on a good show. But no man in the Greek's position would ever dare cross Vasquez. McCracken had to die here, at the hands of the Minotaur on videotape, or by the guns of Fass's guards. It didn't matter. Not only did he have to slay the Minotaur, he also had to escape the Labyrinth by a means other than the entrance—a problem far greater than what Theseus had faced even with his ball of wool.

Blaine kept walking, at first trying to memorize the twisting corridors for future reference. But each turn brought him to a corner he swore he had seen before yet knew he couldn't have. He was totally confused, his sense of direction completely gone. He might have covered the entire swirling length of the Labyrinth or he might have gotten nowhere at all. Impossible to say.

There was a soft echo of a door being snapped back into place and McCracken knew the Minotaur had risen from the subterranean corridors beneath the structure. He strained his ears to hear the monster's footsteps approaching, then recalled the giant's feet had been clothed in light sandals that would not produce a sound. He could stay in the same place and wait for the Minotaur to make his move, but inaction was not part of McCracken's nature. The thing to do was hunt the monster, who would expect that least of all. Fass would get a better show on his video than he could have possibly imagined.

The cameras! If he could find and disable them, he could blind Fass to whatever escape he chose after slaying the Minotaur. . . .

Wait, Blaine urged himself. He was getting ahead of himself, way ahead. First he had to deal with the creature, which promised to be a near impossible task in itself.

Not creature, he reminded himself. *He's just a man and that's how I've got to think of him. . . .*

McCracken swung right and found a wall before him. A quick turn to the left brought him to another. He had trapped himself and would have to double back. Damn! How could he hunt the monster hunting him if he couldn't even find his way? He supposed the giant had memorized these corridors, but perhaps there were coded signs on the wall or floor.

Blaine felt the pounding of his heart intensify and fought to steady his breathing. He tried to listen for the sounds of the giant approaching, but his own thoughts got in the way.

Relax! he urged himself. *Release! . . .*

Advice and training from Johnny Wareagle. Release everything, the big Indian had counseled him, and surrender to the forces. Feel what lies around you. Don't wait to see or hear it. *Release!*

McCracken stopped. He had come to a point in the Labyrinth where he could go left or right. He calmed himself and let his feelings take over. Going left would take him back in his own path. Going right was the answer.

He stayed on the move, thinking now that the best strategy would be to lure the Minotaur into a closed-off corridor and then attack. He came to the end of a small corridor and turned to reverse his footing.

The noise was slight, flesh grazing wood, but he had heard it. Blaine *released*. The Minotaur was three turns away, coming directly for him, aware of his presence.

A weapon, I need a weapon. . . .

McCracken pulled up his shirt quickly. Fass's guards had searched him but neglected to strip off his belt with its heavy brass buckle. He had forgotten about it, just as they had. Wielded properly, it could make a potent weapon indeed.

Blaine yanked it through the loops and wrapped it twice around his arm, leaving a foot-and-a-half or so extended with the heavy buckle dangling free. He could feel the Minotaur closing now, and he imagined the sharp glove spikes and head horns. Others in this position would have waited to jump out when the giant was close. Waiting was what had gotten them killed.

McCracken headed toward the Minotaur's position, felt him just around the next turn and lunged forward at the instant he expected him to appear.

The timing of the move was perfect. The Minotaur glided round the abutment just as Blaine swung his belt into violent motion. It lashed upward against the side of the giant's mask. He grunted, and Blaine wasted no time in whipping the belt again. The Minotaur ducked late and the belt buckle snapped into his eye. This time the giant howled in pain and staggered, blinded and instinctively bringing the back of his spiked glove up to his brow.

McCracken continued his assault, blasting the much bigger man several times in the kidneys. Then he leaped behind the Minotaur and looped the belt around his throat. He pulled both ends tight, taking up the slack and tightening the noose. Blaine heard the rush of air trapped in the monster's throat and felt certain he had won.

But Fass's Minotaur had managed to sneak one of his spiked gloves upward and wedge it between his flesh and the belt. One of the spikes was close to ripping through it. McCracken managed to close off most of his air but the Minotaur was conscious and still struggling.

Blaine yanked backwards on the makeshift noose, and the giant's huge throat emitted a watery sound. Blaine drew closer, trying to increase pressure for the kill.

A mistake.

The Minotaur sensed his position and sent his free glove, the one that wasn't fighting desperately to tear through the belt, hurtling backwards. The tips of the spikes ripped through the flesh of McCracken's midsection. The pain was enormous, blood spreading through the ragged rips in his white shirt and jacket. Now it was McCracken who screamed, easing up enough for the Minotaur to tear free from the noose.

He swung the spiked glove at Blaine and McCracken managed to duck at the last possible instant, feeling the steel whistle over his head. The main problem now was to neutralize the monster's deadly hands. McCracken wrapped his arms around the Minotaur's waist, locking the bulging arms at his sides, and drove the massive frame backwards against one of the walls. The whole structure seemed to tremble and Blaine felt the monster struggling futilely to pull his spiked gloves free of the lock, while Blaine angled himself to ram his knee into the giant's groin.

The huge testicles, a bull's indeed, made a welcome target and Blaine pounded them twice. The Minotaur, gasping in pain after McCracken's second strike rammed home, lowered his head, tensed his neck, and thrust the sharp horns directly at McCracken.

Blaine felt them pierce his back and screamed in agony. The giant tore them out, taking a measure of flesh with them. Then with one swift motion, he tossed McCracken to the floor.

Even in the darkness, Blaine could see the spiked gloves converging toward his head. He shrank back and the steel clanged together. McCracken backpedaled as the beast stalked him for the kill.

The belt! The damn belt! Where was it? Blaine needed a weapon, and he needed it now.

The monster had slowed his pace to regroup and ease the

pain in his groin. He moved with his legs closer together, involuntarily protecting his ruined testicles. McCracken retreated until he reached a dead-end wall. He could almost feel Megilido Fass ogling in expectation of the kill. Well, it wasn't going to come as fast as he thought. . . .

McCracken tore off both his loafers and pushed his hands into them. In the next motion he moved away from the wall, in order to meet the Minotaur where he would have the advantage of his greater mobility. His strategy was simple. He could not possibly hope to fend off the spiked gloves with merely his hands. He needed more, something to parry with to buy himself time.

The Minotaur hesitated, unsure, then came at Blaine fast and hard. His right glove lashed out for Blaine's throat. McCracken deflected it with the shoe and launched a kick into the giant's knee. The Minotaur grimaced and limped sideways, swishing the other glove through the air. This time McCracken stepped to the inside and extended his shoed hand to block the spikes. With the second shoe he rammed the Minotaur's solar plexus. Again the giant gasped and staggered backwards. For the moment the advantage was Blaine's.

What do you think of that, Fass?

The taunt was only in his mind, but it was enough to disturb his concentration. The Minotaur swung out wildly with a spiked glove and Blaine tried to reroute the force and lodge the spikes in the giant's midsection. But in doing so he totally neglected the second glove which pounded his left side with fiery pain as the spikes tore in and then out. McCracken closed in reflexively to prevent the giant from fashioning a killing blow, but the Minotaur was equal to the task. He heaved McCracken upward by the throat with his two huge arms, then slammed him into the wall. McCracken could see him angling the spikes for a simultaneous sweep across his throat. But before they found flesh, Blaine was able to smash the giant's ears with his forearms. His balance shaken, the Minotaur dropped Blaine to the floor.

Blaine hit the floor hard and rolled, out of range of what he felt certain would be a countermove. But the giant was still struggling to get his balance back. He was in pain and breathing hard. McCracken, though, held no illusions he could finish the beast even on these terms. He was just too big and too strong. And Blaine had suffered too many injuries to generate the kind of blows that were required. The Minotaur swiped wildly at him once more and McCracken ducked under the blow and rushed back into the Labyrinth.

He knew the monster was giving chase, knew it even as the pain exploded through his sides and back. He could feel the warm blood soaking him everywhere. He realized he had lost his shoes back there, and he started to feel dizzy. He wavered as he ran, crashing into a wall.

No! Release! *Release!*

He fought to recall all of Johnny Wareagle's lessons. What would he do faced with the same predicament? Probably rip out the Minotaur's throat with his bare hands. Blaine had no doubt he could do it. Without Johnny's superhuman strength, Blaine would have to find another means.

Release!

His breath came more easily, and he negotiated the twisting turns and corners with surprising ease, only once turning into a dead end.

Wait! A dead end was just what he needed, a corner the Minotaur would have no choice but to follow him into. Through all the blood and pain, McCracken concentrated on something he had noticed about the structure of the Labyrinth. The top of the inner walls had a space of an inch or so between them and the ceiling, indicating the ceiling itself must be false. The panels snapped into steel girders and would be removable. Yes, that was it!

The Minotaur's labored breathing was around the corner from McCracken. Just a few more turns to negotiate!

Blaine scaled the wall, virtually running up it until his fingers locked on the ridge between partition and ceiling. His feet against the wall enabled him to raise one of his hands, knock aside a ceiling panel, and grab one of the steel girders. He pulled the rest of his frame upward, legs hoisted high to his chest, prepared to spring. His hands held fast, feet pressing hard against the side wall for leverage. If the darkness was sufficient, he would have one chance to pull off what he planned. One chance . . .

The Minotaur turned the corner and headed down the corridor just far enough to see that the dead end did not reveal his quarry. He swung around.

McCracken dropped upon him, pushing his legs out hard to cover the distance. In one swift motion he had grabbed hold of the bull's-head mask by the horns and yanked it off. Then he fell to the floor as, disoriented, the giant reeled backwards, bellowed and charged him with both spiked gloves raised overhead.

He never saw McCracken drive the bull's-head mask forward horns first, into the rippling flesh of his abdomen. The Minotaur's insides spilled outward—blood and flesh pooled with steaming intestines—and the giant collapsed in a heap.

Breathing hard, McCracken slid back against the wall. The bloody headpiece fell to the floor. God, the pain racked him, but he had beaten Fass's damn monster.

Still the Greek would have seen it all on the monitors. Even now his guards would be heading into the Labyrinth to finish the Minotaur's job for him. Blaine needed a way out, and it had to be now!

The Minotaur would have been able to use more than one entry from the subterranean tunnels, but how could he find these entries? Where were they?

Blaine could hear the heavy footsteps of Fass's guards charging into the maze. Their pursuit would be slowed considerably by the twists and turns which would provide some time for him. He had to make it enough.

McCracken dropped to his hands and knees, the motion sending bolts of pain through his wounded sides and back. His hands probed the floor beneath him as he crawled in search of a slight space indicating the presence of a passage from below.

The heavy boots were almost upon him when he found it. Blaine wedged his fingers tight into an opening and lifted upwards. The trapdoor came free. Beneath him the darkness was total. McCracken started to lower his frame in and then dropped down into the blackness.

CHAPTER 17

"WHAT do you mean he's not there?" Megilido Fass demanded from the safety of his office. "I saw him drop into the passageway myself! I have it on tape!"

"We have searched everywhere and found no sign of him," the captain of the guards reported.

"Impossible! Bring him to me or I'll cut *your* throat instead!"

"I cannot deliver that which is no longer here."

"He couldn't have escaped! He couldn't!"

"Sir," the captain said as placatingly as possible, "please don't forget that the Labyrinth was constructed over several ancient entrances to the Sfakia caves. McCracken could have found one of these entrances before we arrived and plunged into it to escape."

"Impossible, I tell you, impossible!" Fass persisted, his tone one of panic.

"So was defeating the Minotaur . . . or that was what we thought until today. Rest assured that the man is out of miracles, though. Once in the maze of caves underlying this area, no man could ever find his way out again."

"I want you to send teams into the caves just to be sure."

"Sir," the captain begged, "it is too easy for them to lose their way. *They* might never make it out again."

"Tell them to take along a spool of wool," Fass joked madly, but the humor was lost on the captain.

Night fell with the passing of hours. Fass's guards searched the underground chambers beneath the Labyrinth again and again; team after team of men emerged dirty and frustrated. Several groups were ordered into the maze of caves, connected to their entrances by ropes that permitted entry up to three hundred yards. The lighting was insufficient, the air stale and dank. By nightfall, it seemed hopeless and the search was called off. Somehow Blaine McCracken had found a way to elude them. Fass insisted that the guards around the villa compound be doubled. The captain agreed, knowing in his own mind that there was no way a man like McCracken would ever return so soon after leaving.

In fact, though, Blaine had never left. The pain from his wounds convinced him he was in no shape for anything but rest. But tending his wounds would have to wait. For now, all that mattered was survival.

He was betting that Fass would have moved to alert his guards as soon as he saw Blaine drop through the entrance. Fass would not be paying close attention to his monitor screens. So upon landing, Blaine counted to five, climbed back up into the Labyrinth, and ducked safely behind another partition just as the guards reached the trapdoor he had left propped up. Later he had moved deeper into what he judged to be the center of the Labyrinth. The guards would never think to check it. There was clearly no reason to, since he had been seen escaping.

In the ensuing hours, Blaine cared for himself as best he could by ripping his shirt into strips for bandages and tourniquets. Without medical supplies, all he could do was stay still and let the wounds close naturally. It took three hours for the pain to subside and another one for exhaustion to give way to sleep. When Blaine awoke, night had fallen. His built-in clock told him it was between eight and nine o'clock. Any sounds of men searching beneath him were gone.

But his business with Megilido Fass was by no means finished.

Blaine knew his wounds would prove extremely restricting but with stealth and cleverness he could do what *had* to be done. McCracken wanted Fass now more than anything, including the Atragon. He neither enjoyed nor loathed killing. But taking the life of a man who placed no value on life, who had slit the throat of an innocent boy just as easily as he would have swatted a fly, would give Blaine satisfaction. He could not lie to himself about that.

Near midnight, Blaine eased gingerly out of his position. He made his way to the Labyrinth entrance and opened the door a crack. The night was moonless, but light poured out of the house, making a direct approach impossible. Blaine's first thought was to short out the fuse box, but he realized such a move would only result in Fass's tightening security to an impossible degree.

That left a one-man commando assault as his only option. Blaine opened the door a bit more.

There was one guard posted between the Labyrinth and the tall row of bushes enclosing it. What a blessing! Blaine sighed slightly with relief; he would not have to kill the man to move on to the next phase.

He eased himself through the door, careful to make sure it closed softly behind him. Keeping his frame low and avoiding the light as much as possible, he glided soundlessly over the mist-coated grass.

The man's head was turned the other way when McCracken lunged and seized him in a hold across the carotid artery designed to shut off the flow of oxygen to the brain. Ten seconds was all it took for a well-skilled professional, and the guard was disabled silently with a minimum of fuss.

Seconds later, the guard's white uniform had been pulled over Blaine's bloodied clothes. He left the rifle but pocketed the man's knife and stuffed his pistol into the tight belt. The shoes were tight as well, but they would do. McCracken took up the man's post and at the last second elected to sling the rifle over his shoulder on the chance that he was seen. He peered out through the narrow break in the bushes toward Fass's mansion. The sight distressed him. Three guards were in plain view, all too well spaced to be simply overcome. With no time left for further consideration, Blaine left the rifle behind and passed through the opening into the mansion's backyard, again keeping his frame as low as possible.

The light was his greatest foe now, as he studied the routine of the guard closest to him on the right. The man's territory seemed to run from the start of the veranda to the far edge of the kidney-shaped swimming pool. He could tell this guard's steps were bored and laconic. That would work for him.

Staying close to the bushes for as long as he could, Blaine edged on, closing the distance to the pool as directly as possible. Then he waited for the guard to finish his patrol of that area and start back for the veranda before sprinting toward the cover of the cabanas. The rest was a matter of waiting . . . and moving at the correct moment.

The guard turned at the veranda and started lazily back, almost retracing his steps. Blaine counted the seconds to distract himself before lunging at the precise instant the guard passed into the shadows. A sharp blow to the rear of this guard's head, followed swiftly by a second blow to ensure unconsciousness. The only sound was a muffled gasp, barely finished when McCracken began dragging the frame into the cover of the cabanas. Now the next step.

"Over here! Over here!"

Blaine's voice was raised with concern, not panic, nothing that would make the other guards use their radios before approaching. Blaine would have said more if his knowledge of Greek had not been so limited. He had to hope it was enough.

He heard the remaining two guards' feet pounding toward him, and he didn't look back for fear they might see his face in time to respond. As it was, they realized nothing until Blaine swung. They were very close together, which made his task even easier. He lashed out at the nearest just to stun; a stiff blow to the nose was more than sufficient to buy him the time required to launch a crunching kick into the groin of the other. The first was staggering when Blaine finished him with a knee rammed into a face forced downward to meet it. The second was on his knees going for his pistol when Blaine cracked an elbow across his temple and ear.

All obstacles to the mansion were now eliminated. He had to hope the uniform would be enough to get him by once he was inside. A quick, painful sprint brought him to the rear entrance. The door was locked but a knife blade lifted off one of the guards was narrow enough to work between the gap. Then he was inside, searching for the steps he had descended under armed escort hours before.

He found them quickly and ascended at a restrained pace. He was certain there would be a guard at the top and wished to do nothing which might make the man confront him. As it was, Blaine simply walked by the staircase guard, who seemed not interested at all in another uniformed figure. Blaine headed directly to Fass's office and found two guards before the door with rifles at the ready. McCracken fought against hesitation and kept walking.

They regarded him only briefly as he moved by them, dismissing his presence much too early. Blaine pivoted and lunged in the same instant, driving his blade into the nearest man's chest as the man on the other side of the door swung his rifle up and around. The move was foolish because it took much too long to execute; rifles were too bulky to be effective in close. Blaine rammed a set of rigid knuckles into his windpipe, shattering cartilage and forcing the man's Adam's apple into his airway. A second blow to the head forced the guard into unconsciousness.

Fass made the rest easy for him.

McCracken heard the door being unbolted from the inside and pressed himself against the wall.

"What's going on out—"

Still clad in his white suit but lacking the tie now, Fass stuck his head out just far enough to see his guards on the ground. He was attempting to pull back and close the door when Blaine sprang, cracking him in the face with an iron fist which propelled the Greek backwards. Seconds later, the corpses of both guards lay against the wall in Fass's office, and McCracken was grasping his slick hair to yank him to his feet. Trembling with rage, he pressed the bloody edge of his knife against the Greek's throat.

"Wanna get your death on camera, friend? Might make for good viewing later."

"No!" Fass pleaded. "Anything! *Anything!*"

"Too late for generosity. Just answer my questions. First a story. A small-time bandit robbed some crystals from you. That sound familiar?"

Fass nodded fearfully, eyes bulging as he struggled to swallow.

"They were dark red, lined with many crevices and grooves, yes?"

Another nod.

"Where did you get them?" When Fass remained silent, Blaine jolted him across the room until his back was bent over his own desk. Behind it, Blaine could see the huge patch of blood left from the boy's murder. He pressed the blade a little closer. "Talk!"

"They were sent to me from Morocco. They were sent to many people in my field."

"Why?"

"To solicit bids for the remaining reserves."

"You mean you don't have any more?"

"Just the ones that were stolen. I swear!"

"Then the rest are in Morocco?"

"I don't know!"

"You're lying!" Blaine drew a thin line of blood on the Greek's neck.

"No! No! I'm telling the truth. We were told to take the

crystals to our own scientific people for testing. This is months ago, months! I learned they were an incredible energy source, with the potential for a devastating new weapon. Whoever possessed it could obtain a position of incredible power."

"An auction," Blaine realized, "that's what you're describing, isn't it? Tell me!"

"Yes! Yes!"

"And your bid?"

"Too low."

"Who won?"

"I don't know. Maybe no one. I was never told. I'm telling the truth! My correspondence with Marrakesh was general. It never got specific even when I was still in the bidding."

"Correspondence with *who* in Marrakesh?"

"A man known as El Tan."

"His address, what's his address, damnit?"

Fass's eyes darted wildly from left to right. "He can't be reached directly. There's a middleman, a snake charmer named Abidir from somewhere in Djema El Fna square. El Tan can be reached only through him."

An instant of hesitation followed in which neither man knew what was coming next. The knife trembled in Blaine's hand as he struggled to control his rage.

"I want to kill you, Fass, but that would be too easy and too quick," he said at last. "You need to suffer longer for all those boys plucked up from the streets and served up to you here in your own private hell. So I'm going to let you live. But mercy's got nothing to do with it, because when Vasquez finds out you let me escape—and believe me, he will—his means of dealing with you will be infinitely more colorful than mine."

McCracken jammed the knife harder against the Greek's throat as he stripped his belt free to begin tying him up. "Might even ask the fat man to send me a videotape of the proceedings. Have a swell eternity," Blaine said, as he laced the Greek's hands behind him. "You've earned it."

Johnny Wareagle knelt in the meadow on the spacious Oklahoma land set aside for the Sioux Reservation. Behind him Chief Silver Cloud approached warily, stopping when he could tell the huge Indian was aware of his presence.

"I am sorry, *Wanblee-Isnala.*"

Wareagle stared straight ahead over the miles of rolling flatlands alive in the breeze. "There is no reason to apologize."

"I think there is. The Sallow Souls wanted our land even though the courts ruled against them. They became cruel, angry, their spirits dark and rank. I had nowhere else to turn."

Wareagle turned to look at the old man. He smiled reassuringly. "I am here. Nothing else matters."

"I should have told you the truth, *Wanblee-Isnala,*" Chief Silver Cloud muttered, his bronzed, leathery skin looking suddenly all of its seventy years in the hard sun. His long gray hair flapped lightly. "Instead I invited you to a nonexistent convention. I knew you could not refuse that. I worried you could refuse involvement if the truth was made known." The chief came closer, the way a wary hunter might to an animal he thinks is tame. "You are a legend among our people, Johnny. Your manitou evokes memories of the warriors of legend."

"The hellfire did not make legends. It made memories," Wareagle told him.

"What will you do?"

"Sit among you today."

"And if the Sallow Souls come?"

"Then they will come."

Wareagle had learned only yesterday of the hoax played upon him. Chief Silver Cloud explained that oil had recently been discovered on the reservation and the locals were enraged over the Indians' stubborn refusal to sell off the mineral rights which would have brought prosperity to a depressed area. Today the locals were coming in with their own heavy equipment to clear the meadow. The local police had disassociated themselves, and the Indians were honor-bound not to turn outside their ranks for help.

So they had turned to Johnny.

He sat in the center of the two-lane road leading up to the reservation. Around him were a hundred other Sioux of all ages, men and women. The locals would have to run them over to get their equipment past, and while Wareagle felt certain they would not go that far, he knew they might come close. In his hands was a four-foot-long wooden staff that might have been a walking stick to someone seven feet tall. The staff was made of birch and he had finished fashioning it himself last night.

The convoy of heavy equipment passed over the last ridge and rolled toward them. Fifty feet away brakes squealed, and the convoy rolled to a halt. Wareagle saw that the first two trucks were packed with two dozen men who were now climbing down with chains, bats, axe handles, clubs, and assorted other weapons.

Wareagle rose with the eyes of all his people upon him, and with the staff held lightly in his hands, he approached the semicircle of men who held their ground before the idling trucks. He stopped a yard away from a mustachioed man with a baseball bat.

"You and your friends be best to move out and let us through, Indian."

"It's our land."

The man smirked and gazed around for support. Wareagle towered more than a foot over him, but he had more than twenty backups who had now closed into a circle.

" 'Our'? Seems like 'your' since you're the only one standing here. Don't want to see you get hurt now, do we?"

"Then leave."

"Can't do that, Indian."

The man's bat came overhead fast, but Johnny's staff rose even faster, deflecting it with one end and striking the man on the side of the head with the other. Three men charged from the rear, their weapons in motion, but Wareagle swung his staff in a wide loop that smashed one against another and took them all to the ground.

A man attacking from the front with a club was met with a savage thrust to the midsection while another closing from the rear was halted by an equally savage thrust backward. The biggest of the locals came at Johnny whipping a heavy chain roundhouse fashion. The Indian leaped in to close the gap and caught the chain in his fist as he launched a sizzling kick into the man's groin.

Seeing an opening, another local swung an axe handle high for Johnny's head. Wareagle avoided it by dropping to one knee as he brought his staff around hard into the man's ribs. He was vulnerable on the ground and a pair of men sought the advantage by bringing their clubs straight overhead from both front and rear. Johnny angled his staff upward and blocked both at the same time, wood clacking against wood. The men raised their clubs again, but Johnny pushed his staff like a pool cue into the front man's solar plexus and then sliced it backwards into the other's groin.

The man with the mustache was scampering back for the cab of his truck, bleeding rather badly from the mouth and cursing up a storm.

Three men came at Wareagle with weapons flailing. Johnny ducked, lowered his staff, and tripped two of them up. Then he brought it back up fast enough to block another blow and follow with a combination strike to the man's face and ribs.

The rest of the locals backed away fearfully.

The man with the mustache had pulled a pistol from his glove compartment and was bringing it up to aim it.

Wareagle never even seemed to look at him. In a blur the staff was out of his hand and flying. It cracked into the man's wrist at the precise moment he squeezed the trigger. His single shot flew hopelessly errant, and he scrambled back into the cab of his truck.

Wareagle stood his ground and watched the others rush by him, a few stopping to drag their downed fellows along with them. Johnny backed away and returned to the throng of Indians who rose as he approached, gazing on him with awe. Chief Silver Cloud sought him out as the members of the convoy fled in their trucks.

"The spirits shine on you, *Wanblee-Isnala*," he said, as mesmerized by what he had just seen as all the others.

"They shine on all who heed their lessons."

"The Sallow Souls will be back."

Wareagle shook his head. "I don't think so. Word of this will get out. The authorities will not be able to stand aside again."

"But you will stay with us for a time. Let us find a means to repay our debt."

"No action requires debt. Each exists unto itself, an entity alone. I must leave."

Chief Silver Cloud nodded sadly. "I understand."

"It is not your doing, Chief. You did just as the spirits wanted. But last night they came to me with a message: an old friend will soon need me again."

The chief looked at him reverently. "Keep note of the road back, Johnny."

"There is only one road, Chief Silver Cloud, and it passes everywhere twice."

CHAPTER 18

GENERAL Vladimir Raskowski hated Bangkok. He had been able to survive thanks only to his air-conditioned townhouse outside the city. Plenty of wealthy locals shared the beautifully landscaped area with him but he spoke to none of them, seldom venturing out.

Years before the city had held promise, but then westernization had set in. Now the American capitalists were spreading their cancer to yet another region that should have belonged to the Soviet Union. The result was a miserable, teeming, overcrowded city where consumerism ruled above all else. In the spring heat, the collective stink of the hordes inevitably wrinkled his nose. Raskowski was so sensitive about the smell that he felt the necessity of bathing three times a day, even on days when he didn't set foot out of his townhouse.

He was even more sensitive about his height. Of course, at just over five feet four inches he was hardly a dwarf, but he knew that compared to other Soviet generals from past and present, he was a victim of the legend. All Soviet military leaders from Peter the Great on were supposed to have been large, strapping men, and Raskowski had risen through the ranks ever conscious of the fact that the more power he obtained, the more his height would betray him. He became obsessed with it; he ordered three pair of leather boots with custom-elevated soles. He had his desk placed on a platform. And when his curly, salt-and-pepper hair began to fall out in clumps, he had a transplant. Baldness would unfairly steal several centimeters of his height.

He had spent his younger years trying to compensate for his lack of height by building muscle. With the aid of a trainer for Soviet Olympic weightlifters, he had developed a body that was much too big for its frame. His arms were huge and knobby with muscle, his chest barrel-shaped. Raskowski had always been proud of the fact that all his uniforms had to be custom-tailored; that this was still true at almost age sixty made him even more proud.

Of course, he could no longer wear his uniforms in public, not while in exile, for they would draw too much attention to him. The few times he was forced to venture out into Bangkok he did so in Western clothes and did his best to look like a tourist. It made his flesh crawl and made him feel dirty. It was those rare hours outside his townhouse that set his expression so tight that his pointed chin seemed to curve upward for his nose. It shouldn't have come to this. By all rights he should be General Secretary at this moment. He had worked for it and deserved it, but they had stolen it from him. He was a man from a different time they said, a relic from the past. Raskowski did not disagree. But times were the product of the people living in them. They were whatever those people made them and Raskowski knew exactly what he was making them now.

After stepping from the shower he used two towels to dry every inch of his frame. He put on a freshly pressed uniform. With the shades of his townhouse carefully drawn he could smell the fresh wool and see himself in the mirror as he was meant to be seen. Soon he would be free to wear the uniforms at his leisure once again. Soon his position within the Soviet Union would *require* him to. The wrongs were going to be set right. He was going to make them so. He was a man totally in control of his own destiny.

And the world's.

The general towel-dried his hair once more and combed it neatly. The meeting he was about to chair would take place by conference call instead of in person, but he had showered and changed for it nonetheless. He pulled on his elevated boots and headed downstairs toward the windowless back room where the technological implements for these meetings had been set up.

Raskowski's starched uniform snapped stiffly as he quickly passed the large bay window he had forgotten to draw the curtains over. No one saw him. No one was looking. Soon the whole world would be watching.

It didn't have to be this way. He had brought the results of his Alpha project to the Politburo in loyalty and good faith, and he had suffered only embarrassment and heartache as a result. Raskowski refused to take their rejection lying down, but there were just too many of the weak old men and younger ones calling themselves "reformers" to beat back. He accepted his exile with enough grace to assure the opportunity to enact the "disappearance" he was planning. He had already recruited men in all levels of the Soviet government and military who felt as he did. When he made his move, they would be with him.

The key, though, remained the death ray. Once all tests were pronounced successful, Raskowski managed to launch the satellite that made his plan operational. All over the Soviet Union his people began laying the foundation for the tumultuous upheaval to come. Every phase of the operation, every minute detail, had been thought out to the letter. The destruction of Hope Valley went off brilliantly, as did his indirect contact with the Americans. All was perfect.

Until the unthinkable occurred. A scientific miscalculation, not his at all, threw the entire plan into jeopardy. It was left to Raskowski to lift it from the heap, to reform his strategy in a daring and nearly impossible plan. Impossible for others perhaps, but not for him. The true basis of brilliance, he had always believed, was the ability to deal with change. On the battlefield especially, and that was what the whole world had become. Only a handful of people were privy to the revised operation, and that was the way it would stay. Timing was everything now. The slightest slipup or miscalculation would destroy everything.

The back room contained only a single table and chair. Atop the table rested three speaker-phones: white, red, and green. Each of his main Soviet subordinates spoke over the same one every time and Raskowski had come to think of them, as they themselves did, in terms of the color of their speakers. Raskowski sat down in the single chair and eased it gracefully under the table, careful not to wrinkle his uniform.

"Green, are you there?" he asked at precisely eleven A.M. Bangkok time.

"Yes, sir," the voice answered in Russian.

"White?"

"Here, sir."

"Red?"

"Ready, sir."

"Very good. Then let us begin. My report, comrades, is simple. Everything is proceeding on schedule, as planned."

"What of the American response to our second message sent through Turkey?" asked White.

"Befuddlement and fear. Did you expect any less?"

"I expected considerably more," White said. "I feel we are waiting too long to use the ray to its full capabilities."

"The reasons for that strategy have already been discussed. Let us not waste time reiterating."

"You had planned to provide us with the details of the final stage today," Red reminded him.

"I'm afraid that must be put off for a brief time."

"So this continues to be a question of trust," noted Green. "You ask us to trust you, yet you do not return the favor."

"Moscow is too small a city to take the risk. I've learned that already in my career. I do not intend to make the same mistake twice."

"All the same," said White, "if we are in possession of the means to destroy America, it seems foolish not to employ it before the Americans have time to formulate a more active response."

"At least a larger demonstration," suggested Green.

"Comrade Green," Raskowski started, groping for the advantage, "you have already informed me that your override of the Omsk communications facility cannot take place for at least four more days. At that time the Russian people will be informed of the ultimatum the true leadership of our country has issued the United States. With that time frame in mind, what could we possibly gain from escalating matters now? I would suggest, then, that you, all of us, remain concerned purely with our own individual roles. Time can only work for us. The more we give the U.S., the more she will realize her hopelessness. If she accedes to our demands, then her surrender will pave the way for our ascension to power. If she does not and we are forced to destroy her, the Soviet Union will be left as the lone superpower, and the present impotent leadership will have no choice but to abdicate to us."

For a few moments only breathing emerged from the speakers. Finally Red spoke again.

"When do you plan to inform us of the precise timetable for the final stage?"

"In two days. Three at most."

"I can accept that," Red told him.

"And I."

"And I."

Raskowski smiled, relaxed now. "Then I believe our

business for today is concluded, comrades. I will contact you again soon through the usual channels. *Das Zvedanya*."

CHAPTER 19

"BANNA *es su sei! Banna es su sei!*"

Natalya Tomachenko shoved through the crowd of young Thai children who continued to plead for money with their hands outstretched. She had arrived in Bangkok yesterday afternoon and checked into the Siam Intercontinental Hotel to await contact from Raskowski's underling. His name was Katlov and the intelligence reports she had read before leaving Moscow had no trace of him. He would be checking for a certain name daily in the hotel register, and when it appeared a letter would soon arrive with further instructions for her.

True to his word, it had arrived just one hour before, instructing her to wear a blue hat and to walk from her hotel to Taa Phra Chan Pier and then take a boat to the Thonburi Floating Market. She had obtained the hat from a shop in the hotel and set straight out into the hot and humid Bangkok day. Thunderstorms were in the forecast. She loved the city for its vitality and pace, and also for the way it clung to ancient traditions and manners. The streets were crowded but locals generally moved aside to let tourists pass.

As she walked Natalya's thoughts turned to Blaine McCracken. She was attracted to him mostly out of admiration for his personal honor. Natalya knew what he had been through, knew what his government had done to him. In a sense it was not much different from what her government had done to her. The difference was that in America McCracken had found room to slide out. It was Natalya's lot to have to make her own room.

Even before he and his former employers parted company, though, McCracken's career had been marked by a relentless individualism. In one respect he was a mercenary, a hired killer. Yet in another he was a liberator, a man who stood for something. Somehow these two opposites had meshed within him, creating a man of incredible complexities who was quite comfortable with himself.

His physical appearance personified this. Not handsome, maybe not even good-looking, but still attractive and sensually appealing. He didn't try to be anything and ended up being much. Natalya could admit only to herself that Friday night she wanted more than anything to invite him to her bed. But she hadn't let herself. It would have revealed more of herself than she was prepared to. Her shields were her greatest resource. In a world of men, she needed them always. She was an outsider in their world, tolerated by her superiors and feared by her enemies who inevitably underestimated her. But Blaine McCracken hadn't tried to estimate her at all. His only personal comment stung her for the insight he possessed, as if he could look into her soul and read its message.

What have they got on you, Natalya?

She hadn't told him because as much as it hurt to think about it, it would hurt even more to discuss. She had come from a family of soldiers, heroes whose coffins were weighed down by many medals. Her father had been the lone exception, an outspoken professor of philosophy whose frustration mounted with each book that was refused publication in the Soviet Union. For a time Natalya could barely tolerate him herself, considering him an embarrassment to the State. It had been a pair of uncles who had secured her appointment for her, one of the conditions being that she renounce her father, which she did willingly and with a minimum of guilt.

The guilt came later, for he never disowned her, respecting her choice as she had never respected his. The early years of her work brought them closer, as she rose through the ranks and saw increasingly that the opinions that had branded him an outcast were justified. She had just had her request for reassignment out of the field accepted when her father was sentenced to a gulag, and her KGB superior quickly made it plain that his only hope for a pardon lay in her agreeing to continue to work on "wet" affairs, the wettest in fact. They promised her just one mission would do the job and she agreed. Her father, they said, would be waiting at home when she returned.

Natalya could barely get her key into the door, she was so excited. At last they would have time together to make up for the lost years. When the door swung free her eyes fell on her KGB control, seated in any easy chair flanked by a pair of his mindless henchmen.

"My father," she said flatly.

"Some legal problems," came his businesslike response. "Nothing to concern yourself with. The paperwork tends to be slow in these matters. In the interim we have another mission which you might want to consider. Not part of the deal of course, merely a show of good faith on your part."

The control didn't elaborate; he didn't have to. His message was clear. She resisted, and he kindly offered to let her visit her father. In three short months he had aged a dozen years. But still he bore her no ill feeling. She promised him he would soon be out without telling him that to assure his release she had sold herself to the forces he hated most.

At the end of her next mission, she was greeted with the news that he had, in fact, been released. She was taken straight to him, but not to his home of thirty years near the university. More technicalities, her control explained, which led to his being placed in a small guarded flat in Gorky. The implication was clear. A return to the university could come only after she completed yet *another* mission. That was it. They had her. Then, after two further missions, when he was finally allowed to return to teaching in a much lower position, the news came that he had progressive heart disease and only a visa to the United States could save his life. Just one more mission and he'll have it, her control had told her three missions back.

Well, this was the mission that would finally win her father that visa. If she could add a few years to his life, perhaps it would make up for the years they had lost together. Natalya had become a child of the State instead of her father. She had realized too late the bitter lesson that the State was a loveless parent that cared for its children only as far as those children could provide for it. But Natalya was providing only for herself now. This time she would complete the mission with the means to finally end their extortion. Her conversations with the General Secretary had been recorded, and she would use them against him unless he cooperated. Eventually this might mean her death, but she owed it to her father to try.

Her thoughts had so engrossed her en route to the pier closest to Thammasart University that she barely noticed the thunder and pelting rain which drove a hot scent off the asphalt and had soaked through her clothes in seconds. A three-wheeled gas-driven taxi known as a samlor pulled up alongside her.

"Need a ride, miss?" the rain-soaked driver asked her.

Natalya was about to beg off when she realized the man had addressed her in English.

"And might you offer a suggestion as to where I should go?" she answered in Russian.

He smiled, teeth full and white. "The floating market, miss, of course!" In Russian.

Natalya climbed into the back of the samlor. The driver started off, leaning on his horn to clear the muddied streets of the hordes spilling off the sidewalk.

No further words were exchanged. Natalya knew now that the route to Katlov would be long and intricate; the defector from Raskowski's ranks was not about to take chances. The complexity was unnerving yet reassuring. Precautions had been taken. The chances of a run-in with the general's people seemed substantially reduced.

The nameless samlor driver delivered her to Taa Phra Chan Pier. In the klong below sat endless rows of rickety boats with single drivers waiting for potential fares. They began beckoning to Natalya as soon as they saw her approach.

"I will handle everything, miss," the driver whispered and led her to a boat near the end of the row. Its driver sat placidly in the stern with a straw hat tipped over his eyes.

"Aye!"

The boatman pushed his straw hat back, and Natalya saw he had no front teeth. The samlor driver helped her down into the bow.

"Thonburi Floating Market," he told the boatman in Thai. "And be quick about it."

The boatman started to ease out from the pier, and minutes later they were drifting slowly south, their boat hugging the side to keep the center clear for larger boat traffic. Much of the city of Bangkok is crisscrossed by canals known as klongs, some as wide as a street, others barely two meters, and many marked for extinction by the demand for more roadways. Many of the klongs are lined by shops where the tourist can dock his boat at a private jetty. The klongs recede deep into the Thonburi district, where they finally reach the floating market: a collection of narrow skiffs packed to the brim with fresh fruits and vegetables advertised with screams and shouts by the boat merchants seeking to sell them. Cheap jewelry and pottery are available as well.

In years past the floating market was a necessary element for survival in Bangkok. Locals did all their shopping there, and the ebb and flow of the economy was tied directly to the weather. But more recently it has become a tourist attraction more than anything else.

The Thonburi Market lies within a serpentine collection of narrower klongs in the northwest section of Bangkok. Natalya saw the first of the shops thirty minutes into the ride. If the weather had been better, boat traffic would have been as thick as a New York rush hour. The rain, though, had kept most tourists away, and Natalya's boatman was able to easily negotiate through the waters.

The rain had slackened to barely a drizzle as Natalya's boatman pulled to a halt next to an old woman selling an assorted collection of fresh vegetables. The boatman spoke with the old woman briefly, and she proceeded to pack one box full of her best merchandise.

"Baht 500," her toothless driver called to Natalya.

She handed him the proper collection of bills and he exchanged them for the box of vegetables, stowing it just before Natalya as he swung his craft back around.

"Your next instructions are inside," he said in English, not looking at her.

Natalya eased herself forward and removed the top of the box. When no note was immediately visible, she began to move the vegetables aside until a sheet of yellowed paper was revealed. She left it in the box as she read.

Dusit Hall of the Royal Palace.

Natalya sighed. The grounds of the Royal Palace were located back near Taa Phra Chan Pier, where she had embarked for the floating market. She was being run around in a circle, but she was in Katlov's hands and subject totally to his whims.

The toothless boatman deposited her in almost the very spot he had picked her up, and Natalya walked the short distance to the Gate of Wonderful Victory from which a wide street led into the outer courtyard of the Royal Palace. There were more than a hundred individual buildings situated on the grounds, starting with a number of government-occupied ones. As she moved further into the complex, the buildings grew older and richer in history.

Dusit Hall was an art gallery located within Dusit Maham Prasad, an elegant white building. The hall was actually a large inner chamber, the only part of this building open to visitors. She walked about past the various paintings, murals, and statues, trying to keep herself patient. Suddenly a blue-suited Asian was at her side readying his camera before a massive painting.

"Your next stop is the Wat Phra Kaeo," he said, regarding her briefly. "Go to the Chapel of the Emerald Buddha."

The man snapped a series of pictures and moved on. Natalya turned and headed back for the door.

The Wat Phra Kaeo was the most sacred of all buildings in Thailand, accessible through a side gate from the palace courtyard. Natalya paid a separate admission and was immediately awed by what lay before her. The complex, with gold-layered domes and pillars of white marble, was like nothing else here. Its beauty lay in its simplicity, as if it had been built with humility but with great reverence to the spirit housed within.

Natalya passed down a long corridor lined with murals, at the end of which lay a staircase flanked by bronze lions. Visitors were requested to remove their shoes before proceeding up and Natalya complied. At the top, directly before the entrance to Buddha's chamber, a larger pair of lions maintained their eternal vigil between golden pillars. Natalya walked between them and into the chamber.

Before her rose the pale-green jasper statue of Buddha. Beneath a nine-tier canopy, he was huge and breathtaking, garbed in his summer shoulder cloak and headpiece. The crowd in the chamber was small—just a few tourists circling about and a Buddhist monk kneeling on a cushion before the statue. Natalya paced leisurely around, finally drawing near the monk who turned his head toward her.

"Come closer."

The words had been spoken in Russian! *Katlov!*

"Kneel on one of the cushions," he continued. "Act as if you're praying," he added when she was kneeling. "No, better yet, pray for real. The world could use it."

"That's why I'm here," Natalya said softly, glancing over

at Katlov's face, which was framed by his orange robes. She saw he wore a patch over his left eye.

"Don't look at me," he ordered. "Keep your eyes on the Buddha. Lean over. Pray. Do it!"

Again Natalya obeyed, but her impatience got the better of her. She whispered, "Enough precautions."

"No! With Raskowski, there can never be enough." Katlov silenced himself as an American woman with twin daughters passed just behind them. "The general is everywhere in this city. Everything I've put you through today reflects that. Believe me, it was for both our sakes."

"You have been with him from the beginning?"

"Yes, under the auspices of the Scientific Bureau working on the Alpha project. I had a different name back then, a different identity. He insisted I become who I am now when I followed him in exile."

"Others followed him as well."

"Yes, several. But many stayed behind to await the call. Besides those specifically connected with the scientific aspects of Alpha, no one else was *allowed* to leave. They can do more damage from within—once the time comes."

"Raskowski gave the Americans three weeks to unilaterally disarm. Is that his timetable?"

"I don't know. Only he does."

"Were you always this frightened of him?"

"In awe, originally. He gave me a purpose in my work on the Alpha death ray, made me feel what I was accomplishing was crucial to the fulfillment of Soviet destiny." Katlov paused. "It was spending so many hours close to him in the weeks prior to the initiation of the plan that made me see the truth."

"Hope Valley made you see?"

"Was that the name of the American town we destroyed? My God, I'd forgotten it. I'm becoming as insensitive as the general." Katlov gazed at her. "I joined him in his crusade because I honestly believed we were doing something noble. But lately I have come to see the general was only interested in doing what was best for himself. Our homeland means nothing to him, comrade. He will kill anyone who stands in the way of his plan. He will send his tanks rolling through Moscow if that's what it takes to seize power."

"Where can I find him?"

"I don't know. Our meetings are always arranged by him. If I need to reach him there are drops, signals, but he never appears personally unless the advances come from him. This madness can still be stopped, though, by destroying his weapon." Katlov paused. "You are familiar with the massive American early detection satellite *Ulysses*, launched six months ago?"

"Of course. But what— No, it can't be!"

Natalya stopped. Katlov didn't say a word. He didn't have to.

Raskowski's death beam had been deployed aboard an American satellite!

"It was all accomplished through the Farmer Boy," Katlov explained. "I don't know the specifics, only the results. Once Raskowski was exiled it was the only means of getting his death ray into space. The Farmer Boy took care of all the scientific arrangements; complicated to be sure, but obviously worth it."

"Then if the General Secretary can convince the President to deactivate *Ulysses*, it will be finished. He is in a position to deal from strength now. He'll do it, I'm sure. This will all be over."

"Not quite, because Raskowski will still be out there and only I can lead you to him."

"I thought you said—"

"I have learned much from the general during the course of Alpha, comrade, including what to hold back and for how long. I have furnished you with the general's death ray, but unless he, too, is dealt with, the weapon will surface again." Katlov stopped as a man entered and began snapping pictures of the Buddha.

"So what do you want from me?" Natalya asked Katlov.

"Raskowski arranged resettlement of our families. It was a benevolent gesture, but as with everything the general does there was an ulterior motive. By resettling our families, he controls them and, accordingly, us. If we cross him, we will be punished with far more than the loss of our own lives. That was never stated, but the implications are there." He paused to steady his voice. "Get my family to safety, comrade. Then and only then will I . . ."

Katlov was still talking when Natalya recalled that no picture taking was permitted in this chamber. She turned toward the man behind them. He was drawing his gun in that instant. Natalya dove at Katlov and shoved him to the side, but it was too late. The man had already begun firing. She heard Katlov gasp as the bullets hit him.

"Traitor!" the killer shouted in Russian over the terrified screams of the other tourists who scrambled frantically for cover.

Natalya wasn't sure whether the gunman was addressing her or Katlov's corpse. She had whipped her pistol from her handbag and fired it just as the gunman turned his weapon on her. Natalya's barked first; one bullet to the head, a second to the chest. The killer reeled briefly, then crumbled.

Natalya gazed fiercely around her. Procedure dictated a backup be present. Perhaps outside the chamber, though. She charged out before the cowering, still-screaming tourists recovered their senses enough to note her face. She had to move and keep moving. Somewhere more of Raskowski's assassins would be waiting for her. She had to outthink as well as outrun them.

She slowed her pace only when she had reached the bottom of the stairs and replaced her shoes. Temple security personnel would be charging past her any second, alerted by gunshots and the witnesses who had escaped ahead of her. She had to be far off the grounds before news spread. She had what she needed.

Raskowski's beam weapon had been deployed on board an American satellite!

But the general could be stopped now. She would contact the General Secretary, and he would contact the Americans. *Ulysses* would be deactivated. Out of near catastrophe, a new dialogue would be initiated.

Natalya left the grounds through a gate behind the Temple of the Emerald Buddha. Back in the crowded streets, she felt safer. Her hotel was a brief walk from the grounds and walking was her safest means of travel now. She gave any of the gunman's possible backups plenty of opportunities to move on her but none were taken. Still, she did not let herself think it could be finished this simply.

She slowed as she approached her hotel. Something was wrong, something she couldn't identify at first. She continued to survey the scene as her pace slowed to a crawl.

The bellhops. Suddenly there were too many of them and few seemed interested in toting the bags of arriving or departing guests. Of course. Raskowski's men hadn't followed her from the Royal Palace because if she survived they knew where she would go.

Natalya couldn't risk anything that would draw the eyes of the bellhops to her. She doubted any of these men knew her from anything but pictures. A subtle disguise would be effective.

She stooped her shoulders and bent slightly at the knees. The result was to make her appear older and shorter. If she kept her head down and walked without hesitation, the fake bellmen would have no reason to take notice.

She was never sure if they even looked at her because she kept her eyes down as she passed in front of the hotel and continued on. Other problems faced her. Her hotel possessed long-distance phone service with which she had intended to get word of her discovery to the General Secretary. She would need an alternative. The Post and Telegraph Department, as its name indicated, possessed mail and telegraph facilities in addition to phones. A wire sent in code to the proper drop point would get the news to Chernopolov in a matter of hours.

Up ahead, a pair of buses were approaching a stop. On

impulse, Natalya dashed toward them. If she had been spotted upon passing the hotel, this would certainly tell her. She rushed forward as the buses squealed to a halt one behind the other and squeezed herself on. Looking behind her out the windows, she saw no one sprinting to give chase. The stampede of others pushing themselves on forced her into the center of the bus, pressed against bodies on all sides. Two stops later she climbed out and began walking the few remaining blocks to the Post and Telegraph Department. She found herself breathing easier.

The building was modern in design, almost western, and Natalya walked calmly inside. The telegraph windows were off to the right. There were counters complete with pads on which messages could be drafted. Natalya had the code memorized. She worked out the proper sequence for her message in her head and got the wording right on the first draft, double and triple-checking it just to be sure. She added the drop address from which it would reach the General Secretary directly and presented it with payment at one of the windows.

In her haste to leave, she almost forgot to retrieve the change. Pocketing it, she moved away. Best to make use of a different door in leaving, she thought, and made straight for an exit in the back of the building. She threw open the door and started out, muttering an apology to a man she had nearly collided with.

General Vladimir Raskowski smiled at her. He was holding a pistol aimed at her face.

"I trust your message to the General Secretary is on its way now," he said. Then he stepped back so Natalya could see the armed men on either side of him before she had a chance to act rashly.

It was his tone that confused her more than anything. "You let me send it," she realized. "You *wanted* me to send it. . . ."

"Guilty as charged," Raskowski said. His perfectly transplanted hair whipped in the wind as he turned to indicate a man standing directly behind him.

She recognized the man well enough to know what she was seeing was impossible. But within the impossible lay the heart of the madness.

The one-eyed Katlov smiled at her, no longer dressed in his monk's attire and very much alive.

"You're dead!" Natalya said quite surely. "I saw you shot!"

And General Raskowski began to laugh.

PART THREE

ROUNDING UP THE USUAL SUSPECTS

Pamosa Springs; Friday, five P.M.

CHAPTER 20

BY five P.M. Friday the streets of Pamosa Springs were quiet. The town had been divided into sectors, and residents were allowed to venture out for supplies only in escorted groups. A number of guards patrolled the small commercial district on foot, while others made slow, careful loops in jeeps.

The work on the hillside, meanwhile, continued at a non-stop, frenetic pace. Whatever the invaders were mining was being transferred into the hidden gulley where even more labor was concentrated. At night huge sparks would dance into the air, evidence of massive welding equipment. Cables had been run from various power stations into the work area to provide the vast amounts of electricity needed. Something was being constructed in the gulley, the residents knew, and whatever it was, the fruits of the invaders' mining labor must have had a great deal to do with it.

Mayor McCluskey and Sheriff Heep, en route to Doc Hatcher's office, watched the sparks climbing toward the sky. A team of guards was escorting them there under orders from Colonel Quintell, leader of the occupying forces. Quintell met them in the waiting room. He looked harried and tired, eyes drawn, his beret off for the first time in the four days of occupation.

"We have problems," were his first words.

"I'll say," returned Dog-ear.

"Why do you choose to make this so hard on yourselves?"

"It's a tendency we have when some murdering bastards take over our town and steal what's ours," came Sheriff Junk's reply.

"If we put aside our differences, we can get through this, all of us. I would be willing to go as far as to forget the events of the past two nights."

"What events?" Dog-ear questioned.

"Please, gentlemen, do not insult my intelligence."

"What events?" from Heep this time.

Colonel Quintell nodded to himself. "Follow me."

He opened the door to Doc Hatcher's examination room, and a pair of soldiers escorted Dog-ear and Sheriff Junk inside after him. There, laid out on three tables, were three sheet-covered corpses.

"Three of my men," the colonel started with repressed rage. He drew back the first sheet. "This one was knifed in the back." To the second corpse now. "This one had his throat cut." And the third. "This one's neck was snapped. It takes a tremendous amount of strength to break a man's neck in this manner, strength and training. Do you have any idea who in your town has the training to do such things?"

"Yeah," replied Dog-ear. "Hal Taggart, but I think we can safely rule him out."

Quintell ignored the remark. "A victim was claimed Tuesday, a second on Wednesday, the third last night. If you won't help me find the murderer, at least stop him on your own. I beg you. It would be for your own good."

"Own good?" Sheriff Junk repeated. "What the fuck? You rode into town, and we came out into the street. A guy with a rifle that couldn't shoot straight comes along after some rats, and you gun him down without a single word of warning. I'd call *you* the murderers.''

Quintell surprised them by nodding. ''Denials on my part would be pointless at this stage.'' The pain in his face seemed honest. ''I loathe this sort of work. I loathe losing men even more, though, which is why you must understand that I cannot allow it to go on.''

''You want a list of suspects from us?'' asked Dog-ear. ''Just go to the town hall and read the rolls.''

''I want a list of men with recent military service or other training in weapons. This killer is an expert. After losing one man on each of our first two nights here, I doubled the patrols but he still managed to kill another. Men like that cannot go unnoticed in a town as small as yours.''

''Apparently they can,'' Dog-ear told him.

''Maybe he's just getting settled and hasn't met many folks yet,'' said Heep.

''This is nothing to joke about,'' snapped the colonel. ''Believe me when I say it is best for you and your town to cooperate with me. I'm simply an underling, just as frustrated and just as anxious as you are. If I do not produce the results my superiors desire, I will be replaced.'' Quintell hesitated. ''There is talk of a man being sent for, a man whose approach you will find considerably less cordial than mine. An enforcer, not a soldier.''

''You know this man?''

''I know his type and I hate it as much as I hate this type of work. Cooperate with me, help me find the murderer of my men. My superiors are not patient. There is no telling what steps they are liable to take. Please, I beg you, for both our sakes.''

''Don't look to us to get your ass out of the fire,'' Dog-ear said harshly.

''Your own asses will be charred far blacker than mine if the worst comes to pass.''

''Look, friend,'' said the sheriff, ''we couldn't help you

even if we wanted to. The killer you're describing don't exist in Pamosa Springs."

Colonel Quintell stood over the third murdered soldier. His eyes were open, and a hideous grimace froze the instant of incredible agony when his neck was snapped.

"Tell that to my men," the colonel said grimly.

A soldier appeared in the doorway and snapped to attention. "Sir, Post One reports that a man has arrived at the roadblock with clearance papers."

"*Clearance* papers?" The dread in Quintell's voice was obvious.

"Yes, sir."

"Send him through," the colonel ordered softly. He steadied himself against the table where the soldier lay.

"What's it mean?" wondered Dog-ear McCluskey.

"That it just became too late for all of us."

The President had listened to the General Secretary's words in shocked silence. The fact that no interpreter had been employed, thanks to the Soviet leader's fluency in English, made the tale even more startling and ominous.

"I don't suppose you can tell me, Mr. Chernopolov, how your death-ray found its way onto *our* satellite."

"It's not our weapon. It belongs to General Raskowski, as I explained. Please, this has not been easy for me to admit."

"Any easier for me to listen to, you think?"

"Mr. President, Raskowski was no longer one of our own. He was an outcast. The Kremlin underestimated his resources and contacts . . . even within your own military community."

"I suppose you will want to blame all your aggressions on Raskowski."

"He has made every effort to create hostility between us because he knew that open communication might prove the best weapon against him."

"Can 'open communication' prevent another Hope Valley?"

"It can if we refrain from thinking in the manner he expects us to. If we are to survive this crisis, if true peace is ever to be achieved, we must rise above the inclination to accept the sentiments of those with a grasp of only part of the picture. The stakes demand it."

"I can't disagree with you there."

"What will you do, Mr. President?"

"You'll be among the first to know."

General Secretary Chernopolov held the phone to his ear for a time after the connection had broken off. His eyes fell again on the communiqué received just hours before from Bangkok.

Natalya Tomachenko had saved her country, perhaps even the world. In doing so, however, she had placed herself in a position of power no Soviet citizen could be allowed to hold. A delicate balance was at stake which the slightest weight could throw off. Her knowledge, if used properly, could be as devastating a weapon against the Soviet Union as Raskowski's plan itself. She had been used for so long against her wishes, and now she had the means to swing that balance in her favor.

Chernopolov replaced the receiver and lifted the communiqué in his hand. He slid an ashtray over and placed the single sheet of paper in it. Then he struck a match and dropped it down. In seconds, the communiqué was gone and with it all record of this operation.

Soon Natalya Tomachenko would follow.

General Raskowski was glad when the phone was picked up after only a single ring.

"I have reached Pamosa Springs," a familiar voice reported.

"Your assessment?"

"It's even worse than you were led to believe. The previous leadership was ineffectual. The plan was botched from the beginning and then a single incident escalated into a major complication. There are rebels afoot here, General. I can feel it.''

''But you will flush them out, won't you, Major?''

''That is my specialty.''

Raskowski nodded. ''I've always liked you, Major. I've followed your career since we met four years ago. I helped gain you the command that was recently stripped from you.''

''I know that, sir. And if I've dishonored you, please—''

''You haven't dishonored anything! Not yourself, not me, and certainly not your adopted motherland, the glorious Soviet Union. Your career was ruined by fools just as mine was. But there's still a place for you by my side, if you can put this town back on a tight leash. You know the stakes, Major.''

''Yes, sir. I do.''

''Six days ago I pulled your career off the scrap heap because you are much too fine a soldier to be sacrificed for the errors of the inefficient lot that surrounded you in that steaming hot box you were born in.''

''And forced to return to . . .''

''Not by my orders. But fate has been generous with us. It has given us a chance to work together again, perhaps indefinitely.'' Raskowski paused, just long enough for his words to sink in. ''But that, of course, depends on your performance in Pamosa Springs. Don't prove me a poor judge of character.''

The major's voice stiffened. ''I assume I am permitted to use any means at my disposal to return the situation to reasonable order.''

''Anything you choose, Major. Just get it done.''

And on the other end of the line, in Pamosa Springs, Guillermo Paz smiled.

The new commander had issued fresh instructions to the soldiers patrolling the streets of Pamosa Springs after dark:

they were to shoot on sight any figure they could not identify. No questions asked and no accounts to be made. The new commander, Major Paz, scared them, seeming to have little more regard for his own men than for their hostages. No man wanted to face him with failure.

The soldier on patrol between the general store and the post office had no aspiration other than to finish his shift. Dark clouds had rolled in hours before, blocking out the bright moon. But there was some light. The new commander had ordered the few streetlights throughout the town to be turned back on.

Antsy as his shift reached its halfway point, the soldier switched his rifle from his left shoulder to his right. He was stretching to shake himself alert when he heard a shuffling sound. He swung quickly.

A shadow darted through the circle cast by one of the streetlights. A dark shadow. Nothing more. A trick of the wind perhaps, or of his own fatigue.

Then came another sound. A door whining stubbornly closed. The soldier ran toward where it came from and emerged at the rear of the town grill. He knew he should report this and wait for reinforcements. But if the murderer was seeking shelter within, he wanted him all for himself. He tried the latch. It hadn't caught. The door came open with a whining sound. The same whining.

The soldier yanked his rifle from his shoulder and held it in one hand with his flashlight in the other. Before him lay a hallway leading toward the kitchen area. To the right was—

A shuffling sound found his ears from . . . below. The soldier moved to the door on his right. It opened onto a narrow flight of stairs, dropping down into the basement. Flashlight beam swaying before him, he began to descend. At the bottom he saw crates and boxes stacked everywhere. The shuffling could have been rats, he told himself. Then again, it couldn't have been rats that opened the back door.

The silence was deafening now. He started walking about,

flashlight beam carving holes in the dust-coated darkness. Everything seemed as it should have been. *But wait*. Directly before him was a . . . He approached cautiously. Yes, a door, finished in the same color as the walls so as to be virtually indistinguishable from them except for a single brass latch. Wasting no time, the soldier yanked the door open. A musty, rotten scent filled his nostrils, a scent of dirt and rot and death. The flashlight beam poured into the blackness.

"What the hell . . ."

The soldier stepped through the doorway mesmerized, flashlight sweeping about. He couldn't have seen the figure come up from behind him, and heard only a whistling sound like a scythe whipped through the air. He was thinking he should scream to draw attention when a tingle crossed his throat and he couldn't breathe.

For the briefest of instants after his head was severed from his body he could still see, though he felt absolutely nothing. The rest of his frame spasmed before tumbling into the gush of blood that was everywhere, and his head plunked across the floor leaving a trail of red behind it.

CHAPTER 21

"Do you believe him, Mr. President?" Secretary of State Edmund Mercheson asked after Lyman Scott had completed his report on his conversation with the General Secretary.

"I'm not sure. It's all a bit too convenient, and it comes down to us believing in a mad general who's part Napoleon and part Alexander. But Chernopolov's point about *Ulysses* doing us no good when it came to the first attack is well taken. Why should we hesitate to deactivate a satellite that is useless against this threat we're facing?"

"But how do we know this is the only threat?" challenged George Kappel from Defense. "Let's not forget the Russian penchant for disinformation. Let's not forget the very real possibility that everything we have witnessed was part of a plan leading precisely to this end."

"Disinformation didn't destroy Hope Valley," Lyman Scott reminded him.

"No, a renegade Ivan general did, if we're to believe Chernopolov. One town—no more—because maybe that's all their superweapon was ever capable of destroying. A single demonstration to make us think they've got more than they really do."

"That's stretching things, George."

"Is it? We all know the purpose of *Ulysses*. We put it up there to provide immediate *verifiable* warning of a missile launch from anywhere in the world. Effectively, the message to our enemies was that the best they could hope for was a simultaneous launch on warning. Stalemate. Suicide. But then the Soviets come up with a one-shot demonstration and we deactivate it, thereby exposing ourselves to the full brunt of their nuclear arsenal."

The President turned to Sundowner. "Have you checked out *Ulysses*?"

Sundowner nodded. "All systems functional."

"What about the beam weapon?"

"Without a detailed, in-person inspection, I couldn't tell if it had been placed on board or not. It's possible. Size is the greatest restriction, but the death beam wouldn't have to be terribly big."

The President turned to Stamp. "What about security surrounding construction and deployment?"

"There are inconsistencies present in the logs," the CIA chief reported, "and I can't swear to the proficiency of the security employed. All scientists directly involved have been interrogated and they all admitted that *Ulysses* could have been under light guard when the various snafus arose."

Sundowner remembered something. "Snafus set the project back nearly a year at the outset. Some of this was before my time, but as I recall, the first prototype of *Ulysses* didn't fit all the specs and was replaced with the model now in orbit. But we've still got the prototype. Since the modifications required are mostly cosmetic, we could have it ready to launch within ninety-six hours, seventy-two if we're lucky and if the records are up to date."

Lyman Scott nodded. "Then we could delay deactivation of *Ulysses* until we can get a temporary replacement up."

"And we can make sure the Russians know it," suggested Kappel, "so if I'm right about their intentions, they'll know we've managed to stay one step ahead of them. Beat the bastards at their own game."

"Mr. President," began Mercheson, "if we are agreed on this subject, there is another that should be raised. We now have a rogue agent operating in the field, not formally working for us, pursuing a substance that has become superfluous to our needs, and possessing more information than we can afford to have released."

"Yes," the President sighed, "I'm aware of that, along with McCracken's means for dispensing that sort of information. We needed him before. We don't anymore."

"Sir?" Ryan Sundowner spoke tentatively.

"Nothing melodramatic, Ryan. I just want him brought in and isolated until we can explain everything to him. The longer he's out there, operating on his own, the greater the threat he poses, not just because of what he might say but because of what, under the wrong circumstances, he might be *forced* to say. We can't survive the truth of this coming out any more than we can survive the death beam itself. McCracken's reputation as a rogue is well earned. We can't trust him out there. He'll understand our reasoning."

"And if he doesn't?"

"Why wouldn't he?"

"You're forgetting the woman who was killed, Mr. President. That's what drew him into this in the first place, and it's my guess he won't be able to pull out so easily until he's settled that score."

The President's eyes went cold. "Then we'll have to find some way to persuade him."

"So when he calls in, I should—"

"For the reasons you just alluded to," broke in CIA chief Stamp, "it should be someone else whom he reaches, someone well versed in such matters."

"McCracken trusts me."

"The stakes have changed," said the President. "It's a matter of convincing him, and if that falls short, knowing instantly what other steps to resort to."

"Other steps," Sundowner echoed, but his mind had strayed to a fact he didn't dare raise now: one of the men in this room was a Soviet mole. How would that affect Blaine's response to being called in?

Natalya came awake, groggily aware of being in motion. Her eyes cleared slowly to the sight of the straps which bound her to the seat of an eight-passenger private jet. A few seats ahead sat a pair of guards, absently watching her. Her head ached horribly from serums and sedatives. But the rest of her seemed whole, though slowed significantly.

She closed her eyes tight again before the guards noticed she was conscious.

Think! Put it together piece by piece in your head. Retrace the passage of time. . . .

Her last lucid sequence of thoughts had come at Bangkok's Post and Telegraph Department. She had seen General Raskowski first and then Katlov, a man she had seen killed in the Chapel of the Emerald Buddha. But obviously he hadn't died at all. Obviously everything that had occurred, starting with the initial contact in Moscow, had been by the general's direction. So Katlov was alive and had passed information to her which she in turn passed to General Secretary Chernopolov, again by Raskowski's design. Deception on top of deception.

But why? Where was the sense?

After her capture, the fuzziness began. She was taken to a warehouse on the outskirts of Bangkok where truth serum was administered. She had been trained to resist it, but she could only hold back so much, letting go when the strain shook her insides. General Raskowski had questioned her personally. When he was satisfied with her responses he began to feed her a constant diet of sedatives, with the most recent one administered just prior to takeoff.

She was fully awake now, though her reasoning process continued to function lazily.

"Paz will straighten things out. I have faith in him." It was the general's voice. He was emerging from the front cabin, with another man by his side: Katlov.

"I'm still worried," Katlov said. "I haven't been comfortable with our troop deployment in Pamosa Springs from—"

Raskowski silenced him as they drew closer to Natalya. He leaned over and shook her shoulder. Natalya opened her eyes, forcing herself to look even more dazed than she was.

"And how are you doing, my dear?"

Natalya tested the straps and felt the uncomfortable dryness in her mouth as she spoke. "Your concern for my comfort is refreshing."

"I couldn't allow you the temptation of starting an incident which could only result in further harm to yourself."

"You wanted me to make my report to the General Secretary," she offered lamely.

"Of course I did, my dear," he said in a gentlemanly tone. "And you were most obliging, relayed to him everything I wanted you to."

"Which you relayed to me through the walking corpse Katlov over there."

"Shot with blanks."

"I killed a man who had *blanks* in his gun. My God. . . ."

"I'm impressed by your show of guilt," Raskowski said. "But you perceived exactly what was expected of you."

"Would you like to know what I perceive now, General? I perceive a man who has betrayed his country."

Raskowski's features reddened, nostrils flaring back like a bull about to charge. "*Me* a traitor?" he said, incredulously, almost shouting. "You are the traitor, you and all the spineless dreamers whose visions will drive our country into the ground. There is a cancer in the body of the Soviet Union, a cancer that must be cut out if our people are to survive and prosper."

"With you as the surgeon, I'll take the sickness over the cure. It's your vision that will destroy us and the rest of the world. History has already judged your kind, the power-crazed madmen convinced they alone have the answers. Like you they're all small men with small plans because all they can see is what lies immediately before them."

"Small?" blared Raskowski. "Is that what you think? Is what you saw yesterday the work of a 'small' mind?"

Natalya seized the opening. "You wanted the General Secretary to know your death beam was deployed aboard *Ulysses*. Why?"

"Because it isn't."

"What?"

"Listen to the progression of a small mind's thoughts," Raskowski ranted. "Through great pains I managed to launch my own satellite several months ago. That satellite destroyed Hope Valley, but a power surge overloaded its circuits and it self-destructed. I would need something, wouldn't I, small man that I am?"

"A new means of deploying your weapon."

"Impossible, though, for me to launch another satellite of my own. A message had already been sent. The Americans were on notice. So I sought out help. From you. I *used* you, so I suppose you must be even smaller."

Natalya made herself look angry so he would continue.

"Through you Chernopolov was deceived into believing that my weapon was on board the American early detection satellite. Then what?"

"He would contact the Americans and urge them to deactivate it."

"And would they?"

Natalya thought briefly. "Under the present state of tension, only if they had a replacement."

Raskowski's taut grimace spread into a smile. He nodded and kept nodding, suddenly subdued.

Natalya's breath left her as quickly as from a punctured balloon. "No! The replacement . . . *The replacement*!"

The general's grin grew still wider. "Does such a deception sound like the work of a small mind? All of Alpha has become a deception since the loss of my first satellite. Believe me, it wasn't easy fitting all the pieces together, but I had come too far to be denied."

"But you couldn't possibly get another beam weapon on board the replacement satellite!"

Raskowski rose and pulled a syringe from his jacket pocket. "There is an explanation for everything, my dear, including giving you this sedative as we begin our descent. I understand the risks involved to your life but they would be far greater if we left you to your wits. Rest assured," he said as if offering comfort, "that this will be the last shot you need ever receive. I promise."

Natalya was groggy when the plane landed. She had no idea where she was, but she guessed it was the place Raskowski was moving his headquarters from Bangkok.

She kept her eyes closed as the plane's wheels met the runway, bounced, then settled again. Surprise was her only hope now. The general's men had to be induced to underestimate her, or better yet, not estimate her at all. Escape, if it was going to happen, would have to take place before she reached Raskowski's new stronghold. In transit maybe, or . . .

A pair of guards approached her. She could hear their heavy shoes pounding closer and she concentrated on convincing them that the sedative was still enjoying its full effect. Like many drugs, the effect of too many doses often lessened the net effect. Furthermore, a veteran Soviet operative had taught her about such drugs, advising her to cause herself pain at the moment of injection, to induce her body to release powerful antineurons which would, in turn, block at least some of the drug's effects. The theory had never been proven, but the old spy was unyielding in his conviction. She had not had the opportunity to test the theory until now.

The guards unfastened the seat straps and eased her to her feet. Natalya stirred slightly, as would a sedated person. She made sure her breathing was shallow, almost mechanical, eyes open now as narrow slits. She felt that her mind was at full capacity, but what of her body?

The guards gripped her tightly as they led her down the aisle toward the exit door. They would be the last ones out. Not good. Too much would already have transpired outside the plane. Not enough time to make something out of nothing.

Natalya found herself well in control of her motor capabilities as she and her guards reached the steps leading down to the tarmac. It was dusk, the grayness suiting her chances. She walked unsurely, waiting for the men to lead her. Twenty feet from the portable steps a trio of limousines waited on the tarmac. Natalya felt her heart quicken with hope. One of the cars, meant surely to take her to her death, could similarly provide her with a means of escape. She would have to act in the shadow of an instant, and the circumstances would have to be just right. At least there was a chance.

This was Algiers! She recognized the airport clearly!

More of Raskowski's guards surrounded the cars. The general himself was not to be seen. Three guards stood near the limousine to which she was being led. Her mind sharpened all the way. She fought to push blood into her lagging muscles. Speed would determine survival.

A plan, a hope, she had it! One of the guards by the limo held a small machine gun at the ready. The others were wary but not yet handling their weapons. What of the driver? Was he inside or was he outside the car? If he was inside, her plan would be in jeopardy. In the half-darkness she could see nothing through the darkened limousine windows.

Almost there . . .

Natalya stilled her thoughts. The rest she would have to leave to reflex.

Ten feet from the limo she could see one of the guards reach for the back door latch. The big car's engine was idling. Perfect.

The man was holding the door open when Natalya drew

within a yard. She acted in an instant. A quick lunge both separated her from her escorts' grip and closed the gap to the limo.

The force of her body weight crashed the back door inward, pinning the man's hand against steel. He was screaming horribly when Natalya went for the machine-gun-toting guard who was starting to aim the weapon at her. She didn't stop him from firing. Instead she grabbed the barrel and aimed the bullets where she wanted them.

The escorts and final guard went quickly, and she aimed next at the guards outside the other limos to keep their fire erratic. The guard was trying to pull his machine gun free now, and Natalya let him while she pounded his back hard against the frame of the limo, grasping his hair and yanking his head viciously backward. His skull rammed hard into steel and he stiffened. Natalya went for the front door and threw it open.

The side window shattered and glass rained over her. More bullets peppered the windshield, carving jagged holes which quickly spread into spiderweb patterns. Natalya didn't care. She jammed the idling limo into gear and lurched forward with her head beneath the dashboard.

She didn't think of fleeing yet. She couldn't with two fully able cars intact and plenty of men in them. The first thing was to make sure they were reasonably disabled before proceeding.

Windows were lowering. Gunshots blazed at her from both the other cars. One of the drivers had the sense to move. The other stayed as he was, so when Natalya drove into his rear passenger-side fender, the sudden impact stripped his transmission and left him with an engine-racing shell. Tires screeching, Natalya threw her limo into reverse as the last car came for her with bullets flashing from within. Her back window exploded and more glass showered the rear seats, a few shards nipping at the back of her neck. Screaming down the pain, she backed her car hard into the front of the last limo. Steam burst from its radiator.

Gunshots followed her as she floored her car. Despite an incessant screech and a strong smell of gasoline mixed with friction-burned rubber, Natalya concentrated on the tarmac. Airport security would be responding, but that was hardly a bother. She sped along the cement, swerved to avoid one parked jet, and headed for an open gate that would take her to freedom.

The Toy Factory never slept; there were not enough hours in the day to accomplish all of its tasks. The past week had seen the normally hectic activity turn frantic. With little chance that stores of Atragon sufficient to power Bugzapper could be found in time, the search was on for an element to take its place. So far that search had yielded nothing.

The man in charge of these labors was Robert Tibbs, who had been with the Bureau of Scientific Intelligence for seven years. His devotion to his work was total, and many days came and went without his leaving the grounds. Because he often worked well past normal hours, the Toy Factory staff had christened Tibbs "Captain Midnight." He was known to become so obsessed with a particular assignment that for days on end he wouldn't sleep, eat, or change his clothes.

The last week had seen him whipped into the most unyielding frenzy of his career. He had not left the lab once in two full days, other than to refill his canteen from a cooler of water down the hall. He had assigned himself the task of sifting through those few substances deemed by his subordinates to have any chance at all of serving as a surrogate power source. Thus far all those that had passed into his lab had passed into the waste basket.

But the latest substance intrigued him, resisting his attempts to dismiss it. True, there were dozens more tests to be performed. At least, though, there was hope, and Captain Midnight was ready to grasp at anything.

He returned to his lab with freshly filled canteen in hand

and flipped a single switch which illuminated a trio of pinkish crystals on his work table.

"Okay, fellas," he told them, "let's get back to work. . . ."

CHAPTER 22

THE plane bound for Madrid from Athens started into its descent and McCracken shifted uneasily in his seat. Whatever over twenty-four hours of rest had done to soothe the wounds he'd suffered at Fass's villa had been offset by the cramped, uncomfortable flight. It had been early Saturday morning before Blaine felt well enough to travel and to discover that the quickest way to reach Marrakesh was actually to fly first to Madrid and then switch planes.

Escaping from Fass's villa on Thursday night had not proven difficult. Still wearing the uniform of one of the mad Greek's guards, he moved from one group to another until the simplest opportunity to walk out presented itself. Returning to Athens had yet to be considered and with the wounds inflicted by Fass's Minotaur, the trek promised to be rough. He stayed off the roads but near them, since he would need to appropriate a car.

He found one on a hill overlooking the Sfakia River. Two young lovers were busy in the backseat and Blaine, with the help of his gun, had little trouble talking them into a loan. The next few hours were spent driving to a port. He was back in the Athens hotel room he had shared with Natalya by early morning on Friday.

Taking care of his wounds was the next order of business and inspection of them revealed a doctor would not be required. For the most part they were puncture wounds, already closed but still extremely painful. Blaine paid the hotel clerk to fetch antiseptic, bandages, and other implements and then spent the next hour cleaning, stitching, and dressing the wounds, after which he collapsed at last on the bed.

He awoke nearly an entire day later with the realization that his first task was to call Sundowner with an update on his progress. Some more bills pressed into the clerk's hand gained him use of the hotel's only phone. He waited an hour after requesting an overseas line and another twenty minutes before the operator called back with the connection to Sundowner's contact exchange.

"*This is a Deep Seven Cover reroute,*" a mechanical voice greeted him, a tape recording obviously. "*Reinitiate at the following exchange. . . .*"

McCracken memorized the exchange as he'd been trained to, forming immediate patterns in the numbers to keep them from sliding from memory. Something was wrong. This wasn't the procedure, wasn't what he had set up with Sundowner. But the scientist was calling the shots.

"You have reached Deep Seven Cover station," a real male voice greeted this time.

"I want Sundowner. Get me Sundowner."

"Negative. His line is down. I have alternative—"

McCracken hung up the phone, face flushed with anger. Something had happened in Washington and whatever it was it had isolated him from Sundowner. They wanted him to talk to someone else. Why? He thought of the Farmer Boy. Was he getting so close to the Atragon that Raskowski's mole had maneuvered the crisis committee into a change of strategy? He didn't know.

But he knew that matters had taken a turn for the worse. He was being cut off. It was a truth he constantly had to face. There was no one he could trust.

No one except . . .

He picked up the phone and repeated the whole lengthy procedure, an hour this time, of putting through a call. He reached the contact number for Johnny Wareagle. A message would be sent to the big Indian, and Blaine could only hope his friend would be in a position to receive it.

All this accomplished, he set out for the airport and the first flight he could catch for Madrid.

Victor Ivanovitch gathered up the morning papers to read with his coffee, as he customarily did at the start of each day. The Soviet chargé d'affaires at the Syrian embassy in Algiers was actually a career intelligence officer with twenty years' experience in the KGB. The increasingly strategic importance of Algeria over the last few years had called for a man of Ivanovitch's seasoning to be stationed here. Though the Soviets carried on few "wet" missions in the port city, they needed to keep an eye toward future manipulation. Ivanovitch was an expert in such matters and he infinitely preferred the Algerian desert climate to that of Moscow. A Soviet who hated snow might be unpatriotic, but for Ivanovitch the warm sun was as natural as his morning ritual with papers and coffee.

The phone on his desk buzzed twice.

"Yes?" he said in Arabic, a language he had come to speak as well as his own over the years.

"You have a call, sir. Line ten."

Ivanovitch stiffened. The Syrian embassy had only nine official lines. The tenth existed only for direct, and unusual, contact by a mission operating within his sector. Strange, he had not been informed of any. . . .

"I'll take it," he told the operator as he reached for a second phone and lifted the receiver to his ear. "How may I help you?"

"All happy families resemble each other," said a female voice, "but each unhappy family is unhappy in its own way."

Ivanovitch stiffened even more. The first line of *Anna Karenina*! How could it be? Alerts were signaled by reciting the agreed-upon first line of a Russian book. *Anna Karenina* was the current code.

"I'm afraid you have the wrong number," the KGB man told the caller. "Try the party at . . ." He proceeded to provide a drop point address. As soon as the call was terminated a messenger would be sent to the drop with a note telling the caller when and where in Algiers to meet him. Something must be up, something very big. Ivanovitch's flesh tingled with excitement. Only the deepest Soviet agents were furnished with the regular alert code. He was finally about to see action again.

"Thank you very much," said Natalya Tomachenko, and she left the phone booth.

The drop point to which Ivanovitch had sent her was an ancient hotel struggling for its existence against far more luxurious competition. Natalya's instructions for the meet were contained in the room box belonging to a nonexistent guest whose name the KGB man had passed on during the course of their conversation.

The instructions stated that she should proceed immediately to the National Museum of Fine Arts, specifically the African exhibit on the second floor, where Ivanovitch would meet her. Natalya hoped to arrive before him, to give her an opportunity to make sure all was clean on the premises. But as soon as she stepped into the second-floor hall she found the KGB man standing before a tapestry of an ancient warrior.

"Long time no see, Victor," she said softly.

He stared at her in shock. "Natalya . . ."

"I didn't mean to scare you," she told him, aware it was difficult *not* to, given the numerous small cuts on her face from shattered car glass.

"No, no. It's just—"

"You're surprised to see me."

He calmed a bit. "It's just that I was expecting it to be someone else."

"Who?"

"Anyone." He paused, settled down even more. "An agent of your clearance is a rare find in Algiers. Small pickings, as the Americans say."

But Natalya was not convinced. The KGB man still seemed nervous, as if his thoughts were not his own.

"What is it I can do for you?" he asked.

"I need a direct line to the General Secretary. You know the codes and clearances."

"The . . . *General Secretary*?"

"The explanations don't concern you. Suffice it to say I had a private channel but it's been disconnected."

"No, it's not that. This sort of thing is new even to me. You're asking a lot."

"But you can deliver. I know that. The problem is procedure. It must be a direct link, no middleman involved."

"My channel will have to be red flagged. There'll be questions."

"Which you won't be able to answer. All you'll have is my name, but that will be enough. The General Secretary will understand the importance of contact, rest assured."

"If not, my career, my reputation . . ."

"Neither is in jeopardy. My latest assignment," she said, almost whispering, "was uncoded. My channels were closed upon completion, but completion was not achieved. Am I making myself clear?"

He smiled. "Of course not. But I'll do what you ask." He thought briefly. "We are set up for this here. The hardware is in place. You know the Sidi Fredj holiday resort?"

"At the far end of the Bay of Algiers, yes."

"The complex contains a marina. Many boats are docked there this time of year. One is called the *Red Tide*."

"How fitting."

"In terms of color as well. A thirty-six-foot cabin cruiser. You can't miss it. The equipment is on board. We had to move it out of the embassy when the CIA set up shop around the corner.'' Ivanovitch checked his watch. ''I'll meet you there in three hours. Go below as soon as you arrive.''

''The call came from Greece,'' CIA chief Stamp reported to the President. ''Athens specifically. We've flooded the city with agents, focusing on all avenues of potential transit.''

''But you don't expect to catch him, do you?''

Stamp paused. ''Honestly, sir, no.''

''This cloak-and-dagger business was uncalled for,'' Lyman Scott said. ''You should have simply got on the line and laid out the situation for McCracken to see.''

''If he'd refused, we would have had nothing.''

''And what do we have now?''

Natalya arrived at the Sidi Fredj marina ten minutes before the three hours had elapsed. She had taken a route which provided her the opportunity to view the marina from the other side of the bay. She saw the red cabin cruiser. Something was wrong, but she couldn't figure out what. Ivanovitch's tone had been off. There was too much shifting in his voice. Why?

It didn't matter. The *Red Tide* held a direct line to Chernopolov, and the General Secretary would be waiting for her call. But something *still* felt wrong.

Eight minutes remained to her rendezvous with Ivanovitch when she started down the dock for the *Red Tide*. Several men were at work on their boats, and they eyed her as she passed. Any of them or none could have belonged to the KGB man.

She stepped lightly from the wharf down a set of steps leading from the gunwale to the deck. The entire boat was spotless. She gazed around her for signs of something wrong but found nothing. The *Red Tide* was just as it should have been.

She opened the door to the cabin and descended the three steps into it. Somewhere in the exquisitely furnished interior was the communications equipment to effect a patch-through to Moscow. Technologically, that road would be long and complicated, the transfers made in milliseconds from channel to channel and all originating here.

Like the exterior, the cabin was spotlessly clean. Except. . . .

The thin carpet covering the cabin floor was damp in patches, with the outlines of footprints visible. Not sneakers or boat shoes. Loafers, with thin, slippery heels. And the wet footprints had to be recent, left by men who had departed only minutes before her arrival.

Yes! She should have seen it earlier. Ivanovitch had so much as told her, not with words but gestures, tones—subtle indications she should have picked up then. But there was still time; there had to be!

The explosion came seconds later. It obliterated not just the *Red Tide* but a good portion of the dock and boats two deep on either side of it. Showers of flaming wood and steel covered the area, falling up to two hundred yards away, out to sea, onto the parking lot, and into the nearby Sidi Fredj recreational area. The nearby hospitals took in seven emergency patients suffering from lacerations and contusions.

Fire officials were reasonably quick to appear on the scene, but they could do nothing more than watch as the last remains of several ships sank into the bay dragging the dying flames with them.

CHAPTER 23

AFTER learning that the bastards occupying the town had turned his jailhouse into their armory, Sheriff Junk knew there was only one option available to him for spiriting some of the weapons out.

Much of Pamosa Springs was built over mining veins whose hidden entrances had been sealed for generations. Heep had located several as a boy, including one which lay directly beneath the jailhouse. Years later he had covered up the entrance himself so this latest generation of kids wouldn't be tempted by it. Since the front of the jailhouse was well guarded, his sole chance for gaining access to the weapons stored in the rear was to approach the building from the abandoned mines beneath it. Once inside, he would grab as much as he could carry and then retrace his path out.

The soldiers' new commander, like the old, agreed to let town council members move freely through Pamosa Springs during the day, mostly to keep people at ease as to what was going on. Such permission not only served to keep the leaders separated, but it also cast them in the role of being unwitting accomplices to the takeover. The other residents would resent their freedom of movement and inwardly hold it against them. Thus, subtly, their authority was undermined. If it came down to depending on their orders, the people would resist. The strategy was one of factionalization, a classic of occupational forces.

Sheriff Junk didn't give much thought to that as he meandered through his appointed rounds. His plan was to sneak out the back of Nellie Motta's house, which was a scant twenty yards from the covered entrance to the tunnel leading to the jailhouse. If everything went as planned, he would enter the house, exit unseen through the back, and make his way into the tunnel. After finishing in the jailhouse, he would store all pilfered weapons back at the start of the tunnel for easy access later. Junk figured if things went well he could repeat the process on almost a daily basis.

He entered Nellie Motta's house, explained briefly what he was up to, and then moved quickly to her back door. The entrance to the tunnel was clearly in sight, and no soldiers were anywhere in view. This didn't put Heep particularly at ease because he knew that plenty of bad things could happen in the time it would take him to cover the ground. Nonetheless, he steadied himself with a deep breath and bolted out Nellie Motta's back door.

The short dash seemed to take forever, and his war-ravaged joints and bones creaked and cracked in protest. He plunged the final yard into the brush that camouflaged the tunnel entrance and chewed down the pain long enough to begin stripping the brush away. A few minutes later the passage into the depths of the earth was revealed. A twelve-foot descent by ladder would take him into the tunnel and then he would follow the serpentine route to its end beneath the jailhouse where there was another ladder.

Holding the flashlight in his right hand, Sheriff Junk lowered himself down the first rungs after testing the strength of the old wood. It creaked but held his spiny frame and, trembling a bit, he gave it all his weight and started down.

He was halfway to the bottom when the ladder seemed to crumble, wood snapping and the whole apparatus tearing itself from its delicate perch. The rung he was standing on gave way and his fall tore the others beneath him out as well. He took most of the impact on his lower back, but one leg twisted beneath him and a fiery pain erupted in his ankle. He located his flashlight and pulled himself to his feet to check for other injuries, cursing the ladder silently. The rest of him was whole, which was more than he could say for the ladder. He could forget all about climbing back out this same way, a reality that shot his entire plan to hell.

Heep brushed the dried dirt from his clothes and, limping slightly, pressed on down the dank corridor. The tunnel was barely high enough to accommodate his height, as if it had been constructed for the herd of children that had played here years before. In a few spots, the ceiling was so low he was forced into a crouch which placed more pressure on his twisted ankle and made the pain even hotter. The walk seemed endless, but at last his flashlight caught a dirt wall and a second ladder that would take him up into the rear of the jail. He inched his way up the rungs deliberately, distributing his weight as evenly as he could manage. He hadn't stopped to consider just how he was going to get out yet, nor what he might do with the pilfered weapons. One step at a time, just one step at a time. . . .

At the top of the ladder, the floorboards forming the bottom of the century-old jailhouse rose before him, the original hatch long since covered over. They had been loose and rotting for years and he had little trouble working them free with a tire iron lifted from the back of a car with a midget spare tire. The hardest chore was balancing himself on the ladder while he worked. He had survived one fall already. Another from a full fifteen feet would be disastrous.

When the first board started to come free in his hand, Heep stilled his own breathing to listen for boards creaking nearby. The absence of that sound told him no soldiers were walking above. That didn't mean they weren't close enough to hear him but he had to chance it. He pushed the loosened floorboards aside and hoisted himself up through the portal.

Since he would not be returning by the same route, he covered the hole again as neatly as he could. The lighting was dim as always but there was enough to pick out just what he had come for: rows of large crates containing plenty of ammo and weapons. A quick inspection revealed grenades, Laws rockets, and automatic rifles. But what good would they do now with no place to hide them? He had to come up with a fresh plan.

Ahead, in the jail's front section separated by a short corridor and a heavy wood door, there was stirring, and Heep pressed himself behind some crates. If they came back here and found him now. . . . Well, there was no sense in even considering that; he was better off not thinking about it. Sheriff Junk padded forward as lightly as he could. He had the rudiments of a plan, his eyes falling on the pair of never-used jail cells, each with moth-eaten wool blankets tossed over a pair of rusted cots. Yes, yes! It wasn't much, but it was something. The next best thing to storing some of the weapons in the tunnel would be to store them where they might be removed at some later point.

Heep felt his back muscles spasm as he hoisted upward a box marked GRENADES. Careful not to drop the crate, he took it to the never-locked cell and opened the door, which squealed so loudly that Heep felt certain at that moment he was done for. But no soldiers appeared, so he proceeded to slide the crate under one of the cots and then replace the blanket to cover it. The soldiers had enough supplies stacked back here so they certainly wouldn't miss four crates, and one beneath each of the cots was all he could safely fit. How they might be retrieved later was open to further consideration. But at least he had separated these from the main supply, and if it hadn't been for that damn ladder. . . .

Sheriff Junk was ready to lift the fourth crate upward when he heard a key being turned in the door. He froze for an eternal second, was about to duck again behind the slightly shorter stack of crates when something else occurred to him. He hurried across the dusty floor and pinned his shoulders against the wall behind where the door would open, thus shielding him and perhaps offering him a way out if he moved fast enough.

The locks came free, and the door swung open. Heep saw the backs of a pair of soldiers as they started toward the stack of supply crates. That was all the time he wasted. Not looking back, he slithered around the door and into the short corridor. Almost to the front room, he heard a loud congestion of voices, four at least, and swung back toward the cells, striding down the corridor again as if he belonged.

A pair of men with one box each appeared before him.

"Hey, what are you doing here?"

"Looking for your commander," Sheriff Junk said without missing a beat. "You know, the Latin guy who's always playing with his mustache."

"He's not here." The soldier grabbed hold of his arm with his free hand. "Come on, get out. How'd you get in here anyway?"

"Walked. How 'bout you?"

"I could report you."

"Gaw 'head. Might be the best way I got of finding that miniature shit of yours."

A pair of them escorted Heep rudely from his own jailhouse and Sheriff Junk waited until he was well away before letting his smile break.

The smile was gone a few hours later when Guillermo Paz summoned him and Dog-ear to the command post he had set up in the fire station.

"Gentlemen," Paz said with a pair of fingers working his mustache, "how rude it has been of me not to get formally acquainted with you since my arrival two days ago. Contrary to what you have heard, I am a reasonable man."

"Where's the other guy?" Dog-ear wanted to know.

"That would be Colonel Quintell," Guillermo Paz reported with a thick Spanish accent. "He met with an accident and had to leave." The major rose from behind a desk and paced before McCluskey and Heep. "I would have hoped the precautions enacted upon my arrival would have rid this town of the misinformed faction that had taken to killing my men. Unfortunately this has not been the case. Two more nights have passed and three more have died. Six in all, gentlemen."

"You're a regular whiz with math," observed Mayor McCluskey dryly.

Paz ignored him. "My predecessor failed to make his point with you. The leaders of any group are responsible for that group's actions."

"We ain't a group, friend. We're a town you got no business bein' in."

"Your point is academic. Mine is not. My predecessor was lax in his response to problems, and the problems festered. I had hoped the kind of response I had planned could be prevented in view of increased vigilance on your own parts. Obviously I was mistaken. Unless you produce for me now the man who has been killing my men, I will have no choice but to act."

"We don't know anything," said Dog-ear.

"And if we did, we'd piss in our soup 'fore telling you," added Sheriff Heep. "Whoever it is got the only sense in this town. At this rate, a few more weeks and there won't be no more of you bastards left."

"Now it's I who must compliment *your* math, Sheriff," said Guillermo Paz, lifting his hand from his mustache to pat the taller man on the shoulder. "But since we are on the subject of subtraction, perhaps you gentlemen should follow me outside."

Heep and Dog-ear gazed at each other as they exited, with a half-dozen soldiers following close behind. What they saw stole their breath away and set them trembling. Across the street, lined up against the front of the boarded-up K Mart, were six citizens of Pamosa Springs with their hands tied behind their backs. Fifteen feet before them stood three soldiers armed with automatic rifles.

"Six of your people," Pax explained. "One for each of mine lost so far. But I am willing to forego this equalization if you give me the killer; at least tell me who you think he might be."

"Damnit, we don't know!" pleaded Dog-ear. "Can't you see that?"

"What I see is that someone in this town is an expert at what he does. He has penetrated our security and killed without ever being seen or leaving a trace, only bodies. Such a man could not go unnoticed by men in your position."

"But there isn't anybody like that in the Springs," ranted McCluskey. "Hasn't been for years. Maybe after Korea but we all got old. Look at us. See for yourself."

Paz cocked his head toward the six figures lined up before the building. "I'm looking at *them*. They are about to die."

"You can't do this!" screeched Dog-ear, starting forward until he was restrained by two soldiers.

"Tell me who is killing my men."

"We don't know! I swear it!"

Paz turned to the rifle bearers. "Ready!"

"Please," begged Dog-ear, "take us instead!"

"Aim!"

"We don't know! We don't know!"

"Fire!"

The bursts from the rifles lasted barely five seconds, slamming three of the victims up against the store front and dropping three as they stood. Blood spread and pooled, seeming to form one splotch across Main Street. A jean-clad leg and sneakered foot kicked once more. A red-smeared dress fluttered in the breeze.

"Oh God," sobbed Dog-ear. "Oh God, oh God, oh God. . . ."

"Others will die," Paz promised. "Ten for every one of

my soldiers who meets the same fate as the other six. And I think, gentlemen, I will accept your offer as well. Take them," he ordered the men behind Dog-ear and Sheriff Heep. "And lock them in the jail."

CHAPTER 24

THE trawler rode the waves listlessly, protesting each bit of speed McCracken requested of it with a rumble that led him to ease back on the throttle. He stood on the exposed bridge in the morning winds, steering for the Moroccan port of Tangier en route to Marrakesh and the shadowy El Tan.

With Washington no longer supporting his quest, and in fact probably pursuing him, he decided it would be safer not to make a continuous journey by air from country to country. Customs details would accumulate on a man of McCracken's description traveling from Athens, where his enemies in Washington now knew he had been. A rental car and then a boat were the safest and fastest means to flee Spain and reach Morocco. He almost fell asleep at the wheel several times before reaching a port in Tarifa on the Strait of Gibraltar. Arriving there at the peak of darkness in the early morning hours of Sunday, he was able to steal the trawler and set out to sea.

Through the long hours he had only his thoughts for company, and the company wasn't pleasant. Fatigue, and lingering injuries courtesy of the Minotaur, added to his anguish. He felt confused, no longer sure what exactly he was after. He had started out on the trail of Atragon, hoping it would bring him to T.C.'s murderer. Natalya brought Raskowski into the picture and the trails separated. And yet he had continued on his probably hopeless quest. Why?

The question had plagued him throughout the long voyage and in the end he supposed the answer was that there were millions of people, innocent people like T.C., who might die if he failed. He knew he could just walk away and let the world take its chances. His arrangements were made: There was plenty of money in discreet Caribbean banks. But then the buffer he formed between the masses and the fools who ruled them would be gone and, no matter how hard he tried not to, he could not help but feel for the people who were as much victims of the fools' decisions as he was. He was still fueled by T.C.'s senseless murder. But he realized that she could be best avenged by stopping Raskowski from killing millions of others like her.

He docked at Tangier just past noon, abandoned the trawler, and made his way to the airport where flights for Marrakesh left regularly. The terminal was jammed, though, and it was nearly two hours later before he squeezed on to an eighteen-passenger turboprop plane.

Upon arriving in Marrakesh, McCracken took a cab from the airport to Djema El Fna Square, center of activity in the city's ancient sector. Since it closed at nightfall, his major concern all day had been that he wouldn't make it in time and would waste the entire night as a result. But he arrived with an hour to spare and set about locating Abidir the snake charmer.

The square was a haunt for both tourists and locals. The merchants screamed prices that were four times too high, screamed as if to drown each other out. Bargaining had become an art here at Djema El Fna, the merchants enjoying it as much as the tourists. They sold their wares from the backs of horse-drawn carriages or beneath canopied shops set up in the morning and occasionally toppled by the wind. They knew only as much of a given language as served them, always the conversion tables for francs and dollars. To listen to their claims, they made up a uniformly generous lot whose children frequently went to bed hungry due to the generosity of their fathers' merchant souls.

Blaine walked among the shops and stands. Distinct sections of the square were reserved for storytellers, acrobats, fire-eaters and sidewalk musicians who left large tins about in which passersby might deposit money for the "free" entertainment.

Abidir's spot turned out to be separate from the other snake charmers, down a small side street lined with shops already closed for the day. The charmer sat stubbornly on, as if to arouse the pathos of those passing by to gaze at a blind man who could not tell the time of day. A cobra dangled around his neck and an empty silver cup sat before him.

Blaine approached and saw that both Abidir's eyes were covered by black patches. Those parts of his face left exposed by his cap showed ancient skin, dried and wrinkled, scarred by both age and the elements. The eyes of his cobra twitched as Blaine stepped before him and blocked out the sun.

"Test your courage, my good man," the blind man offered. "Pet the snake for a few pennies. For a few more, I'll play a tune and have him do a dance."

"You knew I was a man."

"The blind see much when they're careful about it. I can sense much about you from this wretched frame I'm stuck in. A brave one you are, you might pet the snake near its fangs."

McCracken dropped a pair of coins into the cup. "I would have dropped bills but the sound might not have caught your attention."

"You'd be surprised, my friend. Enough of your American bills and I'll change the snake into a woman for your pleasure."

"It's information I'm after. I'm looking for a man who calls himself El Tan."

Abidir's expression remained the same. The cobra stirred briefly on his shoulder. "I know no such man."

"I heard different."

"You heard wrong."

"I'm prepared to pay."

"Only if you don't mind receiving nothing in return."

"What a pity. . . ."

McCracken was in motion very fast, lunging behind Abidir and grabbing for the snake. He used the beast to drag the charmer backwards behind the cover of his wagon. Then he pulled the snake tighter, using it the way he would a rope.

"Don't worry," Blaine soothed, "I won't hurt him any more than whatever drug you've got him on."

"I can't . . . *breathe*!"

"You can talk. That's good enough."

"Please, you can't rob me. I'm just a poor blind man. Have compassion!"

McCracken felt the tranquilized snake make a futile effort to free itself. "You're no more blind than I am. But you *will* be, unless you talk. Where can I find El Tan?"

The snake charmer gagged for air. "I can't direct you without the proper signal. It would mean my—"

McCracken shut off more of his wind. "This should do. . . ." Finally he let the pressure up and Abidir slumped over, gasping.

The snake charmer caught the breath Blaine allowed him and gave up his resistance. "Le Club Miramar. Pass a note to the dancer Tara with El Tan's name written on it. She will take care of the rest."

Le Club Miramar, Blaine learned upon entering, featured exotic dancing all day long. Exotic in Marrakesh might have been referred to as topless back in America. Add to that a bit of sexually explicit posturing thrown in for good measure and you have the definition of "exotic."

The club was located in the modern section of the city, but the streets nonetheless maintained a flavor similar to that of the market square. The bargaining proved just as intense and the crowds almost as numerous even at night.

He arrived at Le Club Miramar in time to snare a front-row seat for Tara's performance. She stepped onstage to the applause of the audience, dressed in a green bodysuit that looked like the skin of a snake. Blaine recalled Abidir and his drugged cobra and wondered if the connection might have been intentional. Intentional or not, it lasted only as long as Tara's snake suit stayed wrapped round her body, which was not long at all. She peeled it off in great reptilean strips, much to the delight of the audience, which was composed half of locals and half of tourists, all of whom were eager for a chance to slide currency into Tara's G-string, which before long was the last bit of clothing she wore. The more money, the longer Tara would stay before the customer. One customer paid enough to have his entire head swallowed in the radiant beauty's giant breasts.

At last Tara made it over to McCracken and gazed at him as if genuinely interested. He leaned a bit forward over the stage to slide an American bill into place, making sure Tara saw the note sandwiched within it. The dancer nodded slightly, eyes telling him to stay where he was.

Blaine waited through her set and that of another dancer. The next approached him early in her routine and eyed McCracken seductively. He took the hint and came forward to slip her the standard gratuity. She grasped his hand tenderly, and drew his face to hers. While kissing him, she passed a note into his left hand. He completed the kiss without even acknowledging the presence of the paper. He gazed at it only when the dancer had parted from him and he was certain all other eyes were fixed upon her. It was a cocktail napkin with an address printed upon it:

Dar es Salaam, Derb Raid Jerdid . . .

And beneath that, in English:

Table five in three hours. . . .

McCracken rose from his seat, and another eager patron

took his place before he even had a chance to slide the chair back under the counter.

Three hours later to the minute, Blaine entered the Dar es Salaam restaurant, which featured authentic Moroccan cuisine such as *couscous* and *pastilla*. The dinner rush had long wound down and the maître d', dressed in formal robes, approached him straightaway.

Blaine interpreted the bulge of his eyes as disdain for the ruffled appearance the long day had given him, but those same eyes froze when Blaine produced the note directing him to table five. Without further hesitation, the maître d' led him to a private booth in the rear of the restaurant. He pulled back a curtain and beckoned Blaine to enter. This done, the curtain was drawn closed again. Behind it was a semicircular booth designed to accommodate four or five people and Blaine slid into it.

Minutes later he caught the sound of footsteps approaching before a shadow reached up for the curtain.

"Mind if I sit down?" asked an older, graying man with a British accent.

"Sorry. This booth's reserved."

"So I was told," the Brit came back, pushing his disheveled hair from his forehead. He stepped into the private booth and drew the curtain behind him.

Blaine tensed. "I have a meeting here."

"Yes, with the infamous El Tan. Well, ease up, old boy. You're looking at him."

The Brit sat down across from McCracken in the booth. He was wearing a loose-fitting, crinkled beige suit stained by sweat at the underarms. His shirt was yellowed white and his beard as much from yesterday as today. His eyes were dull and listless. He breathed heavily.

"The name's Professor Gavin Clive," the older man told Blaine. "The El Tan business is just a cover. Keeps people off my back when I don't want them there, eh?" He pulled a pocket flask from his suit jacket and poured part of its contents into the empty water glass before him. "Never been one to trust what someone else pours for me. You read me, sport?" A sip and a pause. "You buying or selling?"

"Depends on how you answer a few questions."

Professor Clive stopped the water glass halfway to his mouth and gazed at him knowingly. "One of those, eh? Yes, I suspected this latest business would bring your kind out of the woodwork."

"And just what is my kind?"

"Fixer, repairman; what's in a name anyway?" Clive finished and sipped from the glass. "Don't care much, either." He started coughing and kept at it until his face purpled. The spasm over, he lifted the glass back to his mouth in a trembling hand and drained whatever contents hadn't slid over the sides. "The liver's gone, lungs too. Cancer and plenty more eating them away. I've got six months. The last two won't be pleasant."

"I haven't come here to kill you."

Professor Clive looked almost disappointed. He sighed loudly. "I guess Sadim probably knows letting me live is a greater punishment for my sins."

"Sadim?"

"The man behind what I suspect you're after. The man I've been fronting for. It's what I do, old chap. Front for other people. Got no identity of my own I care to talk about much. Used to, though." Clive refilled his glass and held it up to the booth's dim light in order to stare at the brownish liquid reflectively. "A college professor, would you believe it? Specializing in artifacts and gems. Did favors for people, appraisals. Lost my job teaching and went into it full-time. Began fronting for people who didn't want their identities made public. Lost my identity in theirs. It worked for a while."

"But not anymore."

"Maybe the cancer started it, I'm not sure. I tell you, you look back on your life at my age it'd be nice to be able to take something out. Me, well, all the withdrawals been made already.'' He started on his second glass and gazed warmly across the table. ''You're an easy man to talk to. Hell of a thing, since I gotta figure you got your own problems.'' Clive took three more hefty sips. ''Along with a pretty good notion of what brought you here. It's in your eyes, old boy, the uncertainty. And the fear.''

''Atragon,'' Blaine muttered.

''Sorry, didn't get that.''

''Atragon. The name given to certain crystals with inexplicable powers and properties.''

Clive nodded. ''You reached me through the same channels as the others. They've been inactive for months now. But this is my 'post' as they say and I decided to see you for curiosity's sake, knowing the kind of man you'd be. These crystals have changed you, that much I can tell.''

Blaine started to speak, then stopped.

Clive's whiskey-stained voice turned distant. ''Can't deny it, can you? Everyone who comes into contact with the crystals says the same thing. There's death in them, has been ever since they were discovered. Everyone who's ever gotten close has died.''

McCracken thought of T.C., and his stare was telling.

''Been that way for thousands of years, old chap.''

''I didn't come here to learn about curses, Professor, and if you really want to help me, you'd—''

''I didn't come here to teach you about them. But I'd be selling you short if I didn't try to persuade you to abandon whatever quest you're on.''

''It's too late for that,'' Blaine said almost bitterly. ''There's a madman out there, and these crystals might be the only way to stop him.''

Clive nodded knowingly, the glass an extension of his hand now. ''It always seems to come down to that. History runs in circles, and the circles keep repeating.'' His eyes sharpened. ''The crystals aren't your answer. Stay away from them.''

"I've already seen what they are. I had a sample in my possession until a few days ago. They're just stones."

"You don't believe that. I can tell by your voice. You're too damned sensitive to be so naive. You looked at those crystals and felt something. I can bloody well tell."

"Where can I find the reserves, Professor? Tell me that, and I'll leave you to your misery."

"It's not that simple!" Clive blared, nearly spilling his whiskey. "For thousands of years they lay hidden until seismic changes brought them closer to the surface where once again they promised destruction. An entire civilization has already perished from the abuse of the power they hold. Don't you know that?"

"If you're talking about Atlantis, I don't buy it. Myths have nothing to do with what I'm after."

"They have everything to do with it, old boy."

"Professor—"

"Just listen," Clive said rapidly. "Hear me out. What harm can it do you?" He leaned forward and let the glass of whiskey go. "The people of Atlantis harnessed the power of ıat they referred to as a 'firestone'. They found that when angled properly in relation to the sun, the stone could harness the sun's rays and redirect them as a source of incredible energy. The closest thing we have to this process is the laser beam, but in Atlantis they harnessed the power totally. You called the crystal Atragon."

"Yes, dark red crystals with many ridges—no one section totally symmetrical with another."

"Yes! And each individual section, dozens on each crystal, is its own reflector. Sunlight channeled through the various chambers of these crystals created an energy source which powered the civilization of Atlantis through domed buildings which served as massive solar receptors. The amount of energy created, stored, was immeasurable."

"I said I don't believe in all this—"

"It doesn't matter what you believe. Just listen; you've got to," Clive pleaded. "The people of Atlantis attained technological heights even we have yet to achieve. But something went wrong. The power of the great crystals you call Atragon was abused. Whether this was intentional or not is not definitely known. It was probably unintentional at first, the reserves overloaded which led to a tragedy. But then the potential of Atragon as a weapon was revealed. Factionalization resulted. Various parties in Atlantis struggled desperately for control of the crystals which alone could assure their unhindered rise to power. The fanatics got hold of them first. Fanatics got hold of the crystals and brought about the destruction of the entire society."

"And sank the continent into the Atlantic, right?"

"It would not be beyond the power of the crystals. You've seen them. You know it as well as I do."

"What I know has nothing to do with imaginary continents sinking into the ocean. And nothing to do with miraculous reappearances."

"There was nothing miraculous about it, as I said. Seismic changes occurred. Atlantis, parts of it anyway, became accessible once more. The crystals emerged unhindered by the passage of time, prepared to cause destruction yet again."

"Or prevent it in this case." McCracken leaned over the table. "Those crystals, Professor, may be the only thing that can prevent a cataclysm just as bad and maybe worse than Atlantis sinking into the sea. They've already cost the life of a woman I loved, and unless I find them she'll have died for nothing. So I really don't care if they came from the black depths or some kid's marble collection, I've got to find them and you're the only one who can help me."

"I'm not a fool, old boy," Clive said softly as he poured the rest of his flask into his glass. "Listening to my ravings might lead you to believe I am, but the title of professor real. I studied gems and their origins for years. My theories about Atlantis are based in fact."

"The reserves of the crystal, Professor, where can I find them?"

Clive sipped his whiskey and then squeezed both hands

around the rim. "I only know the general area: an island in the Bimini chain off the coast of Florida."

"Which one?"

"None you've ever heard of."

"You just said that—"

"I know what I said, but it isn't quite that simple. There's an island in the Biminis with no name. None of the natives ever talk about it, and tourists are steered cleverly away. There's a graveyard of ships off its coast. Plenty of vacationers and treasure hunters have disappeared after venturing too close."

"First Atlantis and now the Bermuda Triangle . . ."

"No, old boy, this time it's a sea monster."

"A *what*?" McCracken asked incredulously.

"The natives who talk at all call it Dragon Fish. Legend has it that the Dragon Fish protected the island's shores from pirates centuries ago and apparently hasn't lost its appetite yet. True or not, the legend's done wonders at keeping all curious parties away."

"And this unnamed island contains the Atragon?"

"More specifically, its coastal waters do. The crystals were discovered relatively recently in the wake of those seismic changes I mentioned. They were forced up from the ocean floor, them and some sort of structure housing them."

"Where's this island, Professor?"

"That I can't tell you. Would if I knew, old chap, but the specific coordinates were never made known to me, nor did I especially care to learn them if the truth be known. It would take you days at the very least to find the island on your own. The Biminis stretch further out than you may think."

"But somebody must have the precise coordinates. Maybe this Sadim you spoke of earlier."

Clive nodded reluctantly. "Abib El Sadim, the most mysterious man in all of Morocco. Nobody knows much about him, and I know more than most. From what I can gather Sadim not only discovered the reserves of the crystal but was the only man brave enough to challenge the Dragon Fish in its home waters."

"You don't really believe there's a sea monster, Professor, do you?"

"Don't be confused by my bloody title, old boy. I had an open mind for these things long before the booze turned my brain to mush."

"Let's stick to reality," Blaine told him. "Where can I find this Sadim?"

"You'll never get close to him. No one does."

"But there's got to be a place, a means of contact."

"Indeed. His bar in Casablanca: the Cafe American."

McCracken stared across the booth in disbelief. "If the piano player's name is Sam, I won't be able to take any more of this."

"I wouldn't be surprised if it was. Sadim has recreated the bar almost entirely from the classic film. It's become one of Casablanca's hottest spots, especially this week with all the festivals taking place. He has quite a sense of humor, I'm told."

"You've never met him?"

"No, never. I'm sure you've learned that after discovering the potential of his find he sought to sell it to the highest bidder. I fielded offers for him from terrorists and cutthroats alike. Sadim wanted to remain out of the picture. I received bids and simply passed them on to him."

"Were any ever accepted?"

"Not to my knowledge but, then, I would have no way of knowing what happened after I passed the bids along or how far along the process had gone before I came on the scene. Nor did I want to know."

"Spoken like a man not exactly happy with his work."

"I wasn't a fool, old boy. I knew that the groups represented by men like Fass were bidding purely because of the crystal's potential as a weapon. It made me realize how low I'd sunk. Didn't care much about the cancer after that. I just stayed here and waited for Sadim to send someone out to kill me."

"Which you thought was my role."

Clive nodded. "Better this way, eh? You've given me my chance at redemption. Sadim's the only man who knows exactly where the crystals can be found. You'll know what to do with them. You'll do what's best. It's the kind of man you are. It almost makes me hope I'll live long enough to see the results."

"I appreciate the support."

"You'll need a bloody hell of a lot more than that to succeed, old boy. Getting in to see Sadim in Casablanca isn't going to be easy, convincing him to cooperate even less so."

"In which case," Blaine winked, "I'll just have to round up the usual suspects."

"Then you'd better know something else about the man you're after," Clive told him. "Sadim wasn't always known as Sadim. He had another name for the better part of his life: Vasquez."

CHAPTER 25

It was too late to leave for Casablanca by the time he finished with Professor Clive, so McCracken submitted to his exhaustion and spent the night in Marrakesh. He overslept slightly Monday morning but was unbothered by it; he needed to be at his best if he planned to face Vasquez.

Blaine had been to Casablanca only once before in his career, and his impressions of the vast Moroccan city had been formed mostly by the classic Bogart film. Arriving at the airport after flying in from Marrakesh, he still half expected to see characters with resemblances to Peter Lorre and Sidney Greenstreet, but he would be more than happy to settle at this point for sight of a different fat man.

To think that somehow Vasquez was behind all this. McCracken wasn't surprised. There was plenty of money to be made from the crystals, a fortune, and money had always been the fat man's first love. The problem at this point was how to gain access to him, and Blaine could cover that only after inspecting the layout of his headquarters.

The Cafe American was located in a quarter of the city reserved for hotels, shops, and exclusive clubs. Almost there, the taxi became snarled in traffic.

"The festivals," the driver shrugged.

"I'll walk from here," Blaine told him, adding a generous tip to the amount tallied on the old-fashioned meter.

He climbed out and started down the streeet. Vasquez's establishment was just three blocks away, but those blocks were jammed with people watching the festivities. The streets had been closed off to traffic and were now filled with various displays of Moroccan culture, from Arab acrobats to Berber horsemen riding with both hands on their long rifles, firing occasionally into the air in demonstration of their famed *fantasia* rituals.

From the outside the Cafe American was a perfect reproduction, right down to several exclusive canopied tables on the sidewalk. All that was missing were the Nazi spotlights combing the area with their crisscrossing beams. It was midafternoon, and Blaine had no problems in gaining entry.

The building's interior was even more detailed. There were several rooms, separated by majestic archways. Private tables, undoubtedly available only at a premium rate, sat apart in the many alcoves, and the soft light of regularly spaced imitation candelabras cast the rooms in the kind of murky haze that might have been called atmosphere. The tapestries and artwork were detailed replicas, the squat white piano a twin of Sam's with a young black man sitting behind it playing his hourly rendition of "As Time Goes By" minus the lyrics. McCracken half expected Ingrid Bergman to come sauntering in at any moment.

He took a seat at the bar and continued to gaze around him. The backmost room lay beneath a balcony accessible by a small flight of steps which undoubtedly led to what had been Rick's office in the film and what was Vasquez's now. The only things missing were the gaming tables so crucial to the movie's flavor. Gambling had been permitted by Captain Renaux, but obviously his real-life counterparts had more scruples.

Blaine ordered a club soda and sipped it while considering what his next step should be. The staircase held his best chance for reaching Vasquez, but how could he know the fat man was even here? His eyes fell upon it once again. How to get up the steps without being seen? McCracken knew a number of the patrons seated at the tables were actually the fat man's soldiers. Vasquez left nothing to chance, and under the circumstances, he would be prepared for McCracken's expected intrusion. Accordingly, Blaine kept his face turned toward the bar, concealing it as much as possible.

He turned again only when the impossible appeared in the mirror in the form of a woman being escorted across the floor toward the staircase by two beefy guards. It wasn't Ingrid Bergman.

It was Natalya!

Of all the gin joints in all the towns in all the world, she had to walk into this one. . . .

McCracken's feelings were mixed. He was overjoyed to see Natalya. Clearly, though, she was here as a prisoner, and that was a dangerous situation for both of them.

A change of strategy was called for, and to pursue it Blaine headed for the door.

Two hours had passed with Natalya's handcuffed form seated before the huge desk of the equally huge Vasquez.

"He won't come," she told him again. "He'll know it's a trap."

"Ah, dear lady," began the fat man, patting his cheeks with a handkerchief that was already grimy with sweat, "my sources place him in Casablanca, and he will come because I represent the end of the trail he's been following."

"The crystals . . ."

"Remarkable, aren't they?"

"You don't know—"

"I know when McCracken arrives I will have you to use against him to provide me the advantage I need." He sighed mightily, his bulbous stomach stirring beneath his suit jacket. The fat man's receding hairline made even more prominent the excess flesh which seemed to stretch out his jowls. He breathed noisily. "I'm starting to feel, though, that this is not the best of places to bait a trap for my old friend McCrackenballs." He nodded to the four guards gathered around her. "I will have these men escort you to another of my establishments, eminently less cultured than this but better for our purposes." He nodded to himself. "We'll wait a few more hours. After that, I promise you a quick death since I remain a gentleman."

The guards led her from the room and Vasquez followed them down the hallway to the top of the landing that overlooked the back section of the Cafe American. Natalya knew her move would have to come quick, but she also knew that Vasquez's guards would be scattered among the cafe's customers. And who knew how many there might be in addition to the four she could identify?

They started to lead her down the steps, handcuffs carefully concealed, and Natalya was ready to feign a trip and take her chances with one of the guards' purloined guns, when a sound very much like thunder shook the smooth walls of the Cafe American. The chandeliers trembled and patrons grasped hold of glasses atop their tables to prevent them from toppling.

A pair of door guards had just reached the main entrance when the double doors crashed open in one savage thrust to allow a troop of Berber horsemen to charge through. They negotiated the various alcoves quickly, passing under the arches into the back section in just seconds. And Natalya caught a good look at the man garbed in robes at their lead, horse braying, rifle in hand.

The only Berber sporting a beard.

McCracken had gone straight up to the horseman he had identified as the Berber leader and uttered the three words taught him long ago when he had done a favor for the Berbers, a people he had always respected. The man looked down at him in shock. The words formed a bond, a pact, signifying a debt owed to any man who spoke them, words never passed to any but the bearer. Honor for the Berbers rose above all else.

The Berber leader climbed down from his horse, walked with McCracken off to the side of the road, and asked him there what his bidding might be.

Blaine told him.

Natalya threw herself into motion as soon as her eyes locked with Blaine's. She tore free of the guards' grasp when the commotion distracted them and hurled herself down the steps, just as the Berbers, expert marksmen without peer, began firing away with both hands clutching their rifles. They bellowed above the blasts, playing out the *fantasia* ritual for real.

McCracken leaped from his horse and used it for cover as he made for Natalya. He shielded her with his body and fired his rifle toward the soldiers left standing near the steps. More of Vasquez's guards appeared about them, from behind every alcove and wall it seemed, but the Berbers were more than equal to the task. Incredible as it may have seemed, several of the fifteen horsemen who had rushed into the Cafe American handled single-shot rifles which had to be reloaded after each pull of the trigger even as they continued in motion on horseback in the narrow confines. Tables toppled over and crashed to the floor. Glass shattered. Through all the chaos, the cafe's patrons did their best to make for the door or find areas of cover. The chaos allowed some of Vasquez's men to make good on their targets, but most of these shots required exposing their positions, and inevitably there were Berbers ready to fire at them.

Blaine threw off his robes and led the handcuffed Natalya across the floor, dodging behind a series of horses en route to the exit. The Berbers realized his plan when he was almost to the first archway and pulled their horses into a new formation. A few of the animals rose on their hind legs and kicked at the air, their heads just missing the ceiling.

On the main floor, Sam's counterpart was long gone but

the melody of "As Time Goes By" continued, revealing a player piano.

Blaine reached the second archway and hoisted Natalya atop a white Berber horse behind one of the group's leaders. The horse was off instantly, knocking over a pair of tables and lunging through the ruined entrance doors. McCracken pulled himself on board while the animal was running, still searching for purchase while the horseman urged the animal on, holding on to Natalya for dear life when they leaped onto the street.

But a bullet found their horseman. He was hurled off and the animal rose in fright, tossing Blaine and Natalya to the street as well. At first McCracken thought the bullet was a stray but more shots started up immediately from positions of cover across the street. Damn, Vasquez must have had men already in position, leaving nothing to chance.

Blaine shielded Natalya on the street, bullets flying everywhere as the festival erupted in chaos. Participants in elaborate sets and displays, many costumed, all fled. Tables full of souvenirs and foods were upturned, contents dumped to the ground. Amidst it all the Berbers continued to rise tall on horseback, negotiating through the crowd while firing as best they could at the gunmen across the street.

Blaine realized that with more of Vasquez's men starting to emerge from the Cafe American, the Berbers were about to be caught in a crossfire. Their only option was to regroup and rush en masse across the street to turn the tide of the battle. The Berbers' incredible organization amazed McCracken. The best shooters among them continued to return enemy fire while the rest made it across the street as best they could, discarding their rifles and drawing long, curved swords instead.

As the first of Vasquez's men appeared from within the cafe, Blaine and Natalya lunged back to their feet, each grasping a rifle belonging to a felled Berber, M-1 carbines dating back forty years at least, and took cover behind a toppled fruit stand in order to buy the Berbers the time they needed across the street. The old-fashioned bolt-assembly rifles required that they make each bullet count, which they did at the outset by dropping the first four of Vasquez's men to emerge from the door.

"Like to get back in there and find the fat man himself," Blaine yelled to Natalya between rounds. "He's the only one who knows for sure where the crystals are."

Natalya was aiming again, with great difficulty, since handcuffs still bound her wrists. Vasquez's men had stopped emerging but plenty had taken cover behind the iron cocktail tables outside the front of the cafe.

Across the street, the Berbers had used their razor-sharp swords on the supports holding up the awnings over the shops where Vasquez's gunmen were stationed. The strategy forced the enemy to show themselves, and the battle turned hand-to-hand where the Berbers' swords were infinitely superior to automatic rifles. Their horses charged through debris as the riders' blades whistled in deadly arcs that sent ribbons of blood through the air.

Blaine pulled the trigger on an empty chamber. Natalya was already starting to scurry for a replacement rifle ten yards away in the open. Blaine reached to the side and grabbed her, something else in mind. The chaos had spread through the festival well beyond the scene of the battle, and people rushed in panic everywhere, an occasional horse-drawn float or moving market cart charging wildly by.

It was one of these, pulled by a team of horses and packed with breads, that Blaine focused on. He called to Natalya and, with bullets tracing them, they leaped for it as it passed. Blaine's purchase was better than Natalya's and he crawled for the reins. She, slowed again by her handcuffs, barely pulled herself onto a stack of bread loaves.

McCracken saw the reins fluttering near the ground and found he could reach them only by lying prone and lowering his arms and upper body between the hurtling beasts.

"Grab my legs!" he screamed back to Natalya.

She did as best she could and he lowered himself between

the charging hindquarters of the horses. The reins were a blur beneath him but he managed to grab hold and precariously right himself in the same motion. He was still lying flat on his stomach, though, and from this position he attempted to gain control as the cart continued to rush madly.

"Hahhhhhhhh!" he screamed at the horses, tugging at the leather reins. "Hahhhhhhhhh!"

But the horses kept thundering on, heedless of his commands. John Wayne himself would surely have been at a loss by this point. All Blaine could do was keep pulling on the reins, until the horses slowed and finally came to a halt directly before the Sijilmassa, one of Casablanca's most elegant restaurants.

"Table for two please," Blaine said to the dumbstruck doorman.

CHAPTER 26

BLAINE picked the lock on Natalya's handcuffs in the basement of a smaller restaurant further down the street.

"Mind telling me where those Berber horsemen came from?" she asked him.

"I did a favor for them years ago when a radical group was infringing on their cherished privacy. When I saw you rudely escorted through Vasquez's establishment, I figured the time had come to call in my marker."

"And they remembered? They were the same ones you helped?"

"A few were. And Berbers never forget. As a matter of fact, the ones who volunteered were happy to be of assistance. They've been warriors for generations. This kind of stuff is in their blood."

"They spilled plenty back there."

"But ours was left intact." Blaine licked at one of his fingers. "Unless you count getting bit by a horse."

"My government is to blame for much of this," Natalya told him. "I managed to escape Raskowski and telegraph Chernopolov again but apparently I am no longer wanted."

"Escape Raskowski? Would you mind telling me what's happened since I saw you last?"

"It's a long story and not a very pleasant one," she began, and by the time she reached the climax Blaine was completely stunned.

"Just seconds before the *Red Tide* exploded,"Natalya explained, "I dropped into the water through a porthole. I still have a ringing in my ear but the water cushioned me from the blast. I stayed under as long as I could and swam away. When I finally came up, I had to rest. I needed help and decided to call in an old favor to get it." She paused. "It was Vasquez's men who showed up."

"Fat man's got them everywhere. Must have put the word out on you after he found out you were palling around with me. Vasquez likes to think ahead. Figured you'd come in handy and he was almost right. Okay," he continued, "let's take it by the numbers. Raskowski wipes out Hope Valley to illustrate the existence and potency of this Alpha weapon he devised and has managed to deploy within a satellite."

"Only something went wrong and the satellite self-destructed."

"So he has to get another beam weapon deployed fast, and with no chance of arranging another launch on his own, he deceives the U.S. government into launching his death ray for him."

Natalya nodded. "The general is undeniably a genius. Coming up with this contingency plan so quickly proves that but there's even more. All the manipulations of our two governments were his work as well."

Blaine nodded. "He had to control and use differing degrees of trust. All his machinations depended on that."

"And he's got both our nations perceiving what he wants."

"There's one man left I trust in my government," Blaine told her, "who could blow the lid off this whole thing. Trouble is they've cut me off from him. Might just have a friend, though, who can cut me back in."

* * *

They checked into the El Mansour Hotel as a married couple. Blaine chose it because it offered long-distance service from each room.

The contact procedure he had initiated with Wareagle would necessitate the big Indian's waiting by the same phone in Maine for thirty-minute periods five times a day. The next began in a half hour and it took almost that long for the operator to find an open line over which to place the call. Blaine held his breath as it went through, one ring sounding, then a second.

"Hello, Blainey," Wareagle greeted.

"You're in Maine!" Blaine wailed happily. "Goddamnit, you got the message!"

"The spirits warned of another disturbance and told me in my sleep you would be sending word."

"What about the convention?"

"I stayed long enough to learn that a man's manitou is as much forged by the impressions of others as his own. We cannot change what we are because others will not let us."

"It's bad this time, Indian."

"When was it not? Our existence has always been scorched by the flames of others' greed and lust. We escaped the hellfire only to learn that it wasn't a place, it was a condition."

"You avoided it. For years."

"A temporary reprieve in which the spirits revealed to me my true shape. We get what we want, as well as what we need."

"The world doesn't need what's about to happen to it, Indian. I'd love to deliver that message myself but I've got sort of a problem over here. You up to traveling?"

"The travels of the spirit are endless."

"What I need is for your spirit to lead you onto a plane bound for Washington. Your destination is Virginia, the Toy Factory."

"I know it, Blainey."

"The director's name is Sundowner, and if he's still alive

you've got to reach him. Tell him Washington's been duped, that this whole shitty business isn't over yet, not by a longshot. Get him to call me at this number. I'll be waiting."

"A direct line, Blainey?"

"It'll be the last thing the bastards are looking for. Besides, I haven't got much of a choice. This is the only way. But speaking of ways, finding one into the Toy Factory isn't going to be easy."

"The spirits say that the invisible man is he whom no one bothers to see."

"I could use a dose of that magic myself, Johnny."

"Your manitou is restless."

"It will continue to be as long as I'm on the trail of the only substance that might be able to save the world. The spirits ever mention anything about the continent of Atlantis, Indian?"

"Only through my ancestors, Blainey. They spoke of a paradise and an awesome power which eventually destroyed it."

"It figures."

"How can we go somewhere that doesn't exist?" Natalya asked when Blaine had finished the tale of where he was headed next.

"It's not that the island doesn't exist; it's just that we don't know exactly where to find it."

"Sounds like the same thing."

"Not at all."

"Even so, I don't see how its existence could have remained secret for so long."

"Not secret, just that you won't find it on any of the tourist maps. It's somewhere in the Biminis, though, and the *real* fun starts once we reach it."

"How so?"

"Based on what Clive said, we've got to figure that the Atragon reserves lie somewhere offshore of the island, within some underwater formation."

"Atlantis?" Natalya posed hesitantly.

"Not *you*, too. Please."

She regarded him closely. "Your strength comes from being able to remain detached. It's how you have stayed in the game so long."

"You've been doing pretty well yourself. A boat explosion and Vasquez in the same week. You get high marks for survival."

For a moment the only break in the hotel room's silence was the rattle of the air-conditioning system. Then Natalya spoke tautly.

"Did you ever think this life wasn't right for you? Did you ever question your choice?"

"Once," Blaine replied without hesitation. "It was when I was going out with T.C. She took me into her world and for a time the simplicity of it enchanted me. She was just getting ready to graduate Brown and we went to a party there. That was '82, '83 maybe. To make a long story short, I've never been more uncomfortable in my life than I was around her friends. Age was part of it, but mostly I realized the real world was as foreign to me as mine would have been to them. I just didn't belong. I belonged out here. I had come to see the people I dealt with in the field as normal. At least to me. I didn't fit anywhere else, and I saw that."

"But it was the woman who broke the relationship off."

McCracken looked stung. "Is my file that complete?"

"It was in your eyes. And your tone. All this is still about guilt, isn't it? You think it's your fault she died, and you'll do anything to avenge her."

"That's the way it started," Blaine conceded. "But I don't really give a shit about Raskowski anymore. It all comes back to the world I've chosen to exist in. If Raskowski is successful with his death-ray plot, then the door will be opened to more like him. The best way I can avenge T.C. is to stop that from happening."

"It seems we have both stopped fooling ourselves recently," Natalya said and proceeded to tell the story of her father. "It was only recently," she said at the end, "that I realized there will be no freedom for him. I wanted to believe them for so long that I wouldn't let myself see the truth."

"Don't blame yourself," Blaine soothed her. "These men are experts at turning us against ourselves. They find areas of weakness and exploit them. It's what they do, what they are. The trick is to avoid becoming the very same thing."

"You should have been a philosopher," she told him, almost smiling. "Or a poet."

"Yeah, people have been calling me a lot of names lately. Thing is I'm the same as I always was. It's their perception of me that's changed."

She came closer to him, knelt on the floor, and held his knees. "I like you just fine the way you are."

"Hmmmmmmmm . . . should take Wareagle quite a while to get to Washington and reach Sundowner. Think of any ways we can pass the time?"

"Plenty," she said, closer still.

"I think this is the beginning of a beautiful friendship."

Captain Midnight couldn't believe the results of his own tests.

The pinkish stones held a potential as a power source on a level approaching Atragon. It was impossible unless—

He would run more tests, cover every angle in triplicate before he contacted Sundowner. The enormity of this discovery humbled him, so he had to be sure. He could not risk error.

Captain Midnight stole a sip from his canteen and went back to work.

Ryan Sundowner arrived in his office at virtually the same time every morning. Since he was early Tuesday, he was not surprised to find his secretary had not yet arrived. Sundowner unlocked his office door and felt a slight chill as he stepped into its dismal coldness.

He saw the huge figure standing by the window an instant before he flicked on the light switch.

"Who the hell are—" Sundowner stopped when the man's true size became clear, along with his . . . appearance. The man was dressed in blue jeans, work shirt, and leather vest. His hair was tied up in a ponytail and his flesh was leathery and dark. An Indian . . .

"It was important that I come in unannounced," the stranger told him calmly.

Sundowner stayed near the door, wondering whether he could get out before the giant reached him. "This building's got the best security of any in the government."

"The eyes of your guards see only what they are permitted to, Mr. Sundowner," Johnny Wareagle told him. "They are easily deceived by one who walks with the spirits. But don't blame them. No harm has been done. I am simply a messenger."

"Oh?" from Sundowner, moving further from the door, more intrigued now than frightened.

"You have a phone call to make."

"We've got problems, Sundance," Blaine said by way of greeting.

"So I gathered from your large friend here."

"Just tell me if the replacement for *Ulysses* has been launched."

"No, but how did you—"

"Tell me if I've got this reasonably straight. The President gets word from the Soviet General Secretary that a mad, renegade general's death ray is deployed on board *Ulysses*. Of course this means the satellite has to be deactivated but not until a replacement can be launched just in case the whole scenario has been a setup for a Soviet sneak attack. Am I close?"

"On the money and I've got a feeling you're not finished yet."

"Not even close. You guys blew it, Sundance. The death ray's on board the replacement."

"My God . . . Blaine, it's my fault. *I* suggested using the replacement."

"Forget it, Sundance. If you hadn't, someone else would have—the Farmer Boy probably. You're only guilty of doing what was expected of you. Predicting responses seems to be Raskowski's specialty. His first satellite went bonkers after knocking out Hope Valley, and he needed a replacement. We played right into his hands."

Sundowner steadied himself. "No," he insisted. "I checked out the replacement satellite myself. No way anything on the scale of a beam weapon was on board."

"Raskowksi would have expected such precautions. He'd have planned for them."

"It doesn't matter. I'm telling you that satellite is . . ."

"*What*, Sundance? I get nervous when people don't finish their sentences."

The scientist still wasn't talking.

"Sundance?"

"He wouldn't need to launch a death beam at all, Blaine," Sundowner said almost too softly to hear. "All he really needs is to get a reflector up there, something non-carbon based like sodium or aluminum. Put it into orbit and fire his death beam from a generator on ground level. The beam would strike the reflector, which could be angled by computer to bounce the beam back to any area in the country. Just pick a target."

"Could the general have gotten such a reflector on board?"

"A dozen different ways and I would have missed all of them because I wasn't looking."

Blaine glanced at Natalya. "And what about the generator gun, could it be placed anywhere in the world?"

"Most definitely not. It would have to be the continental United States or possibly one of the islands, Cuba for instance."

"Wait a minute, if this is so simple, why'd the general bother with a satellite in the first place?"

"It would be more effective and easier to control, and a ground-based ray would be a hell of a lot easier to lock onto and shoot out than a satellite twenty thousand miles above the earth."

"Back to my original question, Sundance: has it launched?"

"It's on the pad. Six hours to liftoff."

"Then it should achieve orbit . . ."

"Thirty-six hours after that. But it doesn't matter, Blaine, because I'm going to stop the launch. I'm going straight to the President as soon as I'm finished here and lay it all out for him. He'll understand. He has to."

"That's the hope, Sundance. Now put Johnny back on."

Blaine could hear the receiver changing hands.

"Hello, Blainey," said Wareagle.

"You're a man of many miracles, Indian. I thought I'd asked the impossible of you this time."

"A state of mind," Wareagle told him, "easily overcome."

"Of that I'm sure. Up to another journey?"

"Life is but a collection of random journeys."

"I'm headed for the Biminis, Indian, specifically an island with no name. We still may need the Atragon to get this over with. This nameless island is supposed to be guarded by a sea monster."

"A new challenge for us, Blainey."

"See you there, Indian."

Sundowner was about to phone the White House when the call came from Captain Midnight. He signaled Wareagle to follow him.

A descent of six floors by elevator brought them to the cavernous bottom floor of the Toy Factory and the personal lab of Captain Midnight.

"You're sure?" Sundowner demanded, moving straight for the pinkish crystals placed atop the lab table.

Captain Midnight nodded. "It's Atragon, all right."

Sundowner ran his fingers over one of the crystals. He glanced over at Johnny Wareagle whose stolid expression showed no sign of surprise. "Not the same consistency as the ones we got from Earnst," said Sundowner. "Smoother, less ridges. More gemlike."

"Some people in Colorado were probably hoping for gemstones when they sent these to the National Assayer's Office. They sent them down here when they couldn't identify them."

"But you have."

Another nod, even surer. "It's less refined and developed but every bit as potent as Earnst's Atragon. The lighter color seems indicative of a smaller storage capacity, but the difference so far as we're concerned is negligible. If we still need this kind of power, the wild-goose chase is over."

Sundowner headed for the door. "I'll let you know in an hour."

Ordinarily, Ryan Sundowner was a patient driver. But while driving to the White House, he couldn't help charging through yellow lights with horn honking. He imagined himself explaining to a traffic cop that if he didn't deliver certain information to the President fast, the entire country would be facing destruction. Probably the best excuse the cop would ever hear.

Traffic was moderate from Bethesda to the outskirts of Washington, but once in the city the snarl of vehicles seemed to stretch forever. Sundowner fought back the gnawing in his stomach, chanced a few darts through red lights, and was certain the sound of an approaching motorcycle belonged to a traffic cop about to nail him.

He had actually relaxed a bit when the sideview mirror revealed a leather-clad civilian rider with darkened visor who had pulled his bike up right alongside the car as if sifting through traffic.

The machine pistol bullets shattered the window and most of Sundowner's brain with it. His last reflex was to jam down on the accelerator, which sent his car crashing forward, starting a chain of collisions the motorcyclist quickly left behind.

And in the backseat of a limousine far back in traffic George Kappel dialed an overseas phone number.

"Sundowner has been eliminated," the Farmer Boy reported.

Johnny Wareagle stared intensely at the phone, willing it to ring. Sundowner's call was now more than an hour overdue. Several explanations were possible, but Johnny considered only one.

Sundowner was dead. The scientist's aura had felt pale, depleted, and now Wareagle understood why. The spirits had been trying to warn him then, but he had disregarded them and now the price for that would have to be paid.

The deadly satellite would be launched.

PART FOUR

THE DRAGON FISH

The Biminis: Wednesday, nine A.M.

CHAPTER 27

THE Biminis lie fifty miles off the coast of southern Florida. They are composed of two major islands sandwiching many small cays little more than a quick sprint apart. The chain offers fewer pleasures than many of its sister islands in the Caribbean. But for big-game fishing it is one of the most sought after locales in the world.

The Biminis are isolated, nearly two hundred empty miles west of the major Bahaman islands. The Biminis' only airport lies in South Bimini, which provides easy access to all manner of boats and fishing equipment, rented or sold by people totally dependent on tourism for their survival.

McCracken and Natalya had watched the sun come up Wednesday morning on board the plane that had taken them to Miami. There they boarded a small commuter flight which landed in South Bimini just after eight A.M.

"I blew up a whole island last time I was in the Caribbean," Blaine told her when their small jet at last taxied to a halt.

"You know what they say about playing with matches."

"Yeah, you get burned. And right now we better get out. The Dragon Fish is probably just waiting for his breakfast."

"Shall we feed him?"

"Least we can do."

A small cab took them from the airport to South Bimini Harbor where they planned to rent a boat and plenty of scuba equipment. Of course what they needed most of all was a concrete destination.

"Need a detailed map of the area," Blaine told the rental shop's proprietor.

"No problem," the man returned, reaching into a drawer next to the cash register. He came out with one and spread it atop the counter. "I can recommend some of the best fishing areas."

Blaine studied the map closely. "What I'm looking for seems to be missing." And with his eyes fixed on the clerk, "Your map's one island short."

The man pretended not to grasp his meaning. "Just tell me exactly what kind of sport you're out for and—"

"What kind of sport? Say a bit of exploring. My wife and I have this Star Trek fetish. We like going where no man has gone before . . . and lived to tell about it."

"I don't know what you're talking about."

"I think you do."

The man lowered his voice. "Fortune hunters, eh?"

"In a manner of speaking, I suppose."

"Well, I won't help you get killed," the man told them, shaking his head. "And there's my equipment to consider. I doubt you carry enough cash to put up the deposit for the stuff's full worth and that's what it'll take 'fore I send you to what you're looking for."

"You've seen the island then."

The man hesitated. "Never close up. Few of us locals have. When I was a boy my friends and me took a sailboat out and felt brave." The man's black face lost its sheen. "Storm came up out of nowhere. They were lost. I got rescued."

"See any sea monsters?"

The man's eyes bulged. "You know what's good for you,

mister, you'll turn around and head for home. I seen plenty like you pass through these parts chasing after legends and mysteries. What I say is some things is better left alone." He started to fold the map back into sections.

Blaine restrained him with a grasp on his forearm. "Just point me in the right direction. I'll get the equipment somewhere else."

The man shook his head, half to say no and half to show his disbelief. "You wanna die that much, mister, I got a shotgun right here under the counter. Put you out of your misery real fast."

"I'd rather let the Dragon Fish do it. That would make my vacation."

The man regarded him strangely. "You're different from the others. I don't know how, but you're different." He tried to hold his stare into Blaine's black eyes but looked quickly away. "You just might be a match for the Dragon Fish, but don't expect me to help you find him. Know someone who can, though. Name of Captain Bob. You'll find him in Alice Town, at the End of the World bar."

"The name's symbolic, I assume."

"You go looking for that island, mister, and it might be more than a symbol."

Blaine and Natalya took the hourly seaplane from South Bimini over to Alice Town and walked the brief stretch from the airfield to the End of the World bar in the center of town. They did not hesitate before entering but perhaps should have: the End of the World, even at this early morning hour, was two-thirds full with patrons, all of them locals. Many regarded the strangers with hostility as they made their way across the floor in the bartender's direction.

"We're looking for Captain Bob," Blaine told him.

"What'd you want him for?"

"Got a job for him."

"Captain Bob's kind of retired."

"Like to charter his boat."

"It's drydocked."

"Just like its owner," came a voice from the rear of the bar. Blaine turned and saw a flabby black man with a graying Afro pouring a water glass full of bourbon. "Wet docked would be a better way of putting it in my case, though." His golfball-sized eyes, the whites creased with brownish-red streaks, turned toward the bartender. "Let the kids come over here. Maybe they'll buy me a drink."

McCracken slid a twenty-dollar bill across the bar. "Give me another bottle of whatever he's drinking."

"Cost you two of those."

"Steep," Blaine returned and reached into his pocket.

"You're paying for the atmosphere."

McCracken grasped the bottle by the neck and moved toward the old man's booth, with Natalya right behind. Too much booze had made Captain Bob's age indistinguishable.

"If you wanna join me, you'll have to get your own glasses," he greeted.

"No thanks," said Blaine, sliding into a chair.

"What about the lady?"

"Too early in the day for me," Natalya told him.

"Yeah," said Captain Bob in what seemed to be the local accent, "me too. Too early in the day but too late in life to worry about it much. Suppose I know why you're here."

"Somebody tell you to expect us?" Blaine wondered.

"Didn't have to. People like you come around regular enough. They heard of me somehow and, like you, they buy me a bottle. Then, like you're going to, they leave disappointed."

"We haven't asked you anything yet," said Natalya.

"Don't have to. Questions is always the same. Usually they pulls out a map and offers me a fee to point out what they're looking for. If I likes 'em, I just says no. If I doesn't, I sends 'em in the wrong direction. Either way they makes out ahead 'cause they stays alive.'Course that's not the way they sees it. They comes here to get rich, they figures, and I'm keeping 'em from it."

"We've come to charter your boat," Natalya told him.

"For a guided tour of the surrounding islands," Blaine added.

Captain Bob looked surprised. "Well, that's a new one. Usually I doesn't come included in the deal. People is usually too smart to bother asking me. They figures with everything I know, I doesn't need partners."

"We're not here to make our fortunes, Captain," Blaine told him with as much conviction as he could muster.

Captain Bob studied him briefly. "No, I doesn't suppose you are. You isn't like the rest, not as demanding but a hell of a lot more desperate. What you's after's got little to do with yourselves, I'd wager."

"It's got to do with us all right and with you too and with the whole goddamn world."

"There's something out there we've got to bring back," Natalya added. "Millions of lives are at stake."

"You's a pretty good actress, little lady."

"The part's real."

"I've got a map here," Blaine said, fishing through his jacket pocket. "Just point us in the right direction. You'll be paid well for the effort."

"Like I says, it ain't the money. If it was, I could be a rich man without puttin' up with the bullshit that walks through the door here. And I can't just point you in the right direction 'cause the reef formations tear the bottom of your boat out 'less you know by heart where they lie."

"Our first choice is to have you come with us," Blaine reminded him.

"And I can't do that neither. Ain't been back that way for a couple years now when the last of the island folk pulled up stakes. Won't find any of 'em left in these parts. They just up and vanished. I's the last one left, far as I know. Don't know enough to move along. Guess a man oughtta die where he got himself born, 'cept I was born on the . . ."

"The island?" Natalya finished for him.

"Raised there, anyway," Captain Bob told her. "Ain't

much to the island 'sides the lighthouse. My daddy first and then me manned it, sweeping that big light to warn ships away from the reef and the shallows. Them waters been a graveyard for ships longer than any of us can possibly imagine. Goes all the way back to Spanish galleons with enough gold pieces still in their hull to buy Miami. Plenty of people tried salvagin' them and died for the effort even before . . ." Captain Bob's voice tailed off, then picked up again. "Worst times started with the quake. That's what stirred the Dragon Fish awake most in these parts figure."

"Quake?"

"Sea quake, friend. Awful bad one too, shifted the undersea formations all over the goddamn place. Things that'd been unreachable for centuries suddenly rose. Vast treasures the eyes of man was never meant to see again. Floods of people started streaming into the waters, challenging the reefs, once again. Most never made it. Them that did, well, the Dragon Fish took care of them while they was tied up at night, sometimes during the day, too. Thing come up from the depths with the hunger of centuries. Fishermen was the first to disappear, my two sons among them. I used to sit in my boat at night with a harpoon hoping the Dragon Fish would surface. Never thought I could kill it but I had to try. But it never appeared. So I gave up and moved off the island." Captain Bob paused. "Become sort of a pact throughout the Biminis that the island just don't exist, plain and simple, but once in awhile people like you come round knowin' that it does."

Blaine assimilated Captain Bob's story. "This sea quake, would it have occurred about five years ago?"

"Yup, that would be about right, though the years ain't meant much to me for too long now."

McCracken turned to Natalya. "Professor Clive said seismic changes in the Earth's crust forced the Atragon crystals up from where nature had stored them for centuries. That sea quake fits perfectly into the scenario. They're out there, all right."

"If there are any left," Natalya said. "Vasquez could have been a very busy man."

"Sure, but the well hasn't run dry *yet*, because as of five months ago the fat man was looking for fresh buyers. That's how Fass came upon his." Blaine paused. "Question is, how did the fat man mine all that stuff underwater without anyone being aware of it, including the captain here? That Dragon Fish might have needed all of two swallows to get Vasquez down. Maybe that's what saved him."

Natalya's face was somber. "You know all this fits perfectly with the legends of the Lost Continent, don't you? The waters of Paradise Point right here in the Biminis are lined with precise rock formations that many feel are the remains of its road systems."

"The only thing lost right now is my patience." Blaine swung back to Captain Bob. "You're right, Captain, we can't make it to this island alone. But you could take us here."

He shook his head. "Lots of people asked me to over the years. Offered me more money than you ever seen to do it too. What makes you any different?"

"Because if you take me there, I'll kill the Dragon Fish for you."

"You're the first man I ever seen might be able to do it," Captain Bob said then. "I suppose I been waitin' for ya. Never did want to die scared of a place I lived most my life. Always figured I'd be going back one last time. . . ."

Four hours later they set off from the Alice Town harbor where Captain Bob's cruiser was docked. It was a thirty-three footer that had once belonged to a rich couple from the Florida Keys. They'd beached it one summer evening, and Captain Bob got it off the insurance company for a song and rebuilt it himself. That had been ten years back and the cruiser didn't get out to sea much anymore. He lived aboard it, though, and empty or half-empty bourbon bottles were the only decorations he'd added.

The captain had plenty of scuba equipment and tanks but they needed refilling, which Blaine accomplished in town while the old man and Natalya got the cruiser sea-ready. Captain Bob repeatedly refused to accept money for the charter, nor did he ask for any further elaboration on what it was they were looking for. He seemed quite content to simply head his cruiser out from the harbor and settle it gracefully into the sea. Blaine and Natalya could sense in Captain Bob a resigned acceptance of fate. He seemed to have regained a measure of health.

Captain Bob had already confirmed that the island with no name was approximately 175 miles east of Alice Town. With the cruiser's top speed at thirty miles per hour, a six-hour voyage was in store at the very least, which, Captain Bob was careful to point out, would leave them precious little daylight. Night was the Dragon Fish's time and nobody in their right mind would tempt the waters then. But he said it knowing they would anyway and he was glad of that. If he could just see the vile creature that had stolen his sons away destroyed, he would be ready to leave this world.

The island came into view through binoculars about five hours into their voyage. Soon, Captain Bob positioned Blaine and Natalya at opposite sides of the cruiser's forwardmost point to watch for reefs his bourbon-soaked mind had forgotten about. The formations were treacherous, but the captain squeezed by them, with the hull occasionally scratching against one. In some places the reefs seemed to have gathered like sharks. Blaine had done plenty of diving through the years, including a stretch at the Great Barrier Reef, but he had never seen anything like this. The reefs seemed strategically placed to deter precisely the kind of journey they were making. There was a man-made quality about them.

Gradually the island with no name sharpened in view. It was surprisingly small, no more than a half mile across. It was decorated with lavish green flora and dominated by the center steeple of the lighthouse Captain Bob had manned for years, which poked up above the trees at the edge of the shoreline. The beach was smooth yellow sand. As they drew still closer, Blaine could make out the remains of shacks abandoned years before. The whole scene had the feeling of a graveyard, albeit a lush one.

"We'll anchor here," Captain Bob announced three hundred yards from shore. "Beneath us lie the corpses of a thousand ships. Riches and treasures beyond imagining." He bit his lip. "And this is where the Dragon Fish took my sons."

"What about the center of the quake?" Blaine asked him softly.

"Right abouts where we are now. I remembers 'cause of the whirlpool. Never forget that sight. A tunnel whipping through the sea, sucking down anything which was anywhere near it."

"And the depth?"

"Hundred feet at the deepest point."

"I'm going down," Blaine told Natalya and started to climb into his wet suit.

Natalya reached for hers. "I can't let you have all the fun."

Blaine smiled at her, not bothering to argue. Together, he and Natalya donned their scuba equipment, starting with the life vests a simple tug on a string would inflate. There was also a tubular sprocket fitted for an extension out of the tanks to draw air with a simple press of a plunger. Next came the weight belt and finally the bulky tank which on land was nearly impossible to tote. Captain Bob helped Blaine pull his over his shoulders and then moved on to Natalya while McCracken worked the straps tight beneath his groin, making sure the tank was centered properly. He and Natalya then rubbed water on the insides of their masks to prevent them from fogging up, adjusted the straps to the proper tightness, and checked both their main and auxiliary regulators.

"You's got one hour of air each," Captain Bob reminded them. "If I gets no sign of you after that, nothin' saying I won't pull up anchor and leave."

"Fair enough," said Blaine, pulling on his flippers.

"Hope you finds what you's looking for, friend."

"If it's here, we'll find it."

With that, Blaine and Natalya grabbed hold of their spear-guns and tossed themselves over backwards into the black depths below.

CHAPTER 28

THE sights beneath them were breathtaking. Through the crystal-clear water they could see a paradise of sea creatures and plants springing from the nearby reefs. The fish seemed almost friendly, coming forward as if to be petted.

McCracken had always loved diving. The feeling of being underwater soothed him. It was a world where time seemed to stand still or at least pass more slowly.

The depths darkened as Blaine and Natalya kicked with their flippers and angled their bodies to swim lower. They were using the standard set of hand signals, never expecting to be far enough away from each other to actually require them and hoping not to need their spearguns and the underwater knives sheathed on their calves.

Down further now. . . .

Captain Bob had told them that the depth of these waters was between ninety and a hundred feet. The angle of the sun was strong enough now to provide them plenty of light. But each had a powerful underwater flashlight attached to their weight belt.

Blaine wasn't really sure what he expected to find or what he was going to do with it if he found it. Clearly, even if he could locate the Atragon crystals, salvaging sufficient stores of them would require a professional team like the one Vasquez must have employed. At this point, with time increasingly of the essence, he questioned whether such an operation could be mounted, especially with him being temporarily cut off from forces in the government. Still, an attempt had to be made.

Natalya grasped his shoulder and pointed hurriedly down and to their right. There, almost directly beneath them on the ocean floor, lay the remains of a ship from centuries back. The wood frame had long since fossilized, providing an eerie, ghostlike appearance. McCracken could tell from his maritime background that it was a Spanish galleon dating back to the late seventeeth or early eighteenth century. A good chunk of the bow was missing, but otherwise the hull and masts looked reasonably whole.

It grew progressively darker as they swam lower for the wreck, necessitating the use of their flashlights. The beams made a neat dent in the blackness, enough for them to notice the corpses of more dead ships. The island's reputation was well deserved. Calling its waters a graveyard was an understatement.

What made things even more eerie was the various levels of fossilization the wrecks had undergone. McCracken felt he could date each by the amount of the original frame that was visible. But many of the oldest ships had lain entombed beneath what had been the sea floor until the quake had changed the entire undersea structure. While they were entombed, fossilization had been arrested so some of the oldest relics in view had maintained the most original detail.

The graveyard stretched as far as Blaine could see. The sum of riches buried here would be enormous. No wonder Vasquez had staked a claim to these waters. . . .

They hovered over a partially fossilized frigate, rough on the outer edges with what looked like extensions of the reef above. Blaine guessed it was two centuries old, an escort to protect merchant ships from pirates as they sailed across the Atlantic. Blaine hesitated behind Natalya, as if the frigate were sleeping instead of dead and might stir if touched by human hands. There were plenty of cracks in her hull, but Blaine's flashlight locked on one that he signalled Natalya to steer toward. Something set it apart from the others, something that didn't seem right. . . .

Blaine reached the ship and felt first along its fossilized hull, kicking his flippers to hold his position in the water. Even through his glove he could feel its brittleness. He could easily have torn huge chunks away with a minimum of exertion. At last he came to the hole and felt along its perimeter. Totally smooth and unfossilized, the hole itself was, incredibly, a perfect circle. He looked to others for comparison. All were jagged and irregular, victims of the long years. This particular hole was obviously the victim of something else: man. The hole was large enough to allow passage for a diver and could have been carved by an underwater torch. That would explain the perfection of its shape, all of which led Blaine to an inescapable conclusion.

Someone had entered the frigate through this hole, in pursuit no doubt of the treasure it might well have contained. Probably it had been Vasquez.

Blaine stroked the inside perimeter of the hole and drew the flashlight up close to check the shading. It was significantly lighter than the remainder of the hull's fossilized exterior, so Vasquez had been here fairly recently. Blaine did his best to convey his discovery to Natalya and she nodded her understanding, pointing to the next nearest ship to suggest they check that one out as well. This time she took the lead, and Blaine followed.

She swam for a ship thirty yards away buried up to the halfway point of its hull in the sandy bottom. McCracken saw it was a British clipper ship, much smaller than the frigate and younger by a century at least. The clipper fleet dated back to the time of the American Revolution and several ships like this had, in fact, been used by the British to transport arms, men, and the gold coins on which the colonies were based. Conceivably a great fortune had recently been claimed from her by Vasquez.

Blaine and Natalya probed closely about her fossilized sides with their flashlights. It was Natalya who found the hole, almost identical in size and design to the one they'd found on the galleon. Again, using the rest of the ship's corpse for comparison, he was able to date Vasquez's intrusion to the last several years. So the fat man had been busy in these waters well after the appearance of the Dragon Fish.

Blaine checked his watch. Fifteen minutes had passed, leaving forty-five minutes of air. No problem there. He felt Natalya grasp him suddenly with her free arm and point frantically ahead with her flashlight. McCracken looked in the beam's direction and he saw in the darkness ahead of them a shape far bigger than any of the ships they had already passed. From a distance it looked like a circular pile of rocks and debris gathered high upon the ocean floor, but as they drew closer the shape gained definition and clarity.

It was some sort of sphere, also fossilized but with strange smoothness, a smaller version of what the top of an indoor sports stadium would look like if severed from its base. It could have been many things, all of them logical, but Blaine felt a gnawing inside his stomach which told him that they were seeing this thing for what it had always been.

Huge solar receptors placed in domed buildings . . .

Blaine recalled Professor Clive's words, then blocked them out for the distraction they might cause. He and Natalya slowed up as they drew closer to the dome, as if to respect whatever it was they had happened upon. They saw now that the dome was actually sloped low for the ocean floor at its most distant point and rose at the point closest to them. Drawing still closer, they saw the cause of this to be some sort of support system at the dome's front, a series of what looked to be pillars; two were whole, though fossilized, and a third, half the size of its neighbors, tilted precariously.

McCracken tried to form a logical explanation for the dome's presence. Professor Clive had spoken of domed buildings scattered all over Atlantis which when opened drew the great power of the sun into crystals to create the raw energy. The fabled continent used this energy to reach incredible levels of technological proficiency.

The only way to prove whether this dome was part of the myth was to enter its structure and see what it held. Half of Blaine hoped to find great reserves of the scarlet crystal Atragon. The other half hoped that closer inspection would reveal the entire sight to be a trick of the dark, deep waters.

The problem soon became academic. Maybe if Blaine's attention hadn't been directed so intensely forward, he would have sensed sooner the pursuit coming from behind. He did catch the disturbance of a sudden cold sweep of water rolling upon him, and he turned around just as a dark shape fired its spear.

Blaine shoved Natalya to warn her. At the same time he kicked his legs upward and flipped his body into a somersault. The spear passed just beneath him.

By his count, five divers were coming forward, four passing the first as he pumped his flippers in a holding position to reload. McCracken pointed down at the huge corpse of a Spanish warship which was immediately to their left, and he and Natalya kicked for it desperately as the divers gave chase.

Two of the opposition stopped to fire but a moving target, especially a swimming one, is virtually impossible to hit. Distance is almost impossible to judge and by how much to lead the target is almost impossible to estimate. A hit can be accomplished at a fleeing target only by the best or luckiest shot.

The two shooters proved to be neither. One of their spears streamed over Blaine and the other beneath Natalya. By the time all five in the enemy's party were giving chase again, Blaine and Natalya had reached the deck of the warship, where fossilized cannons were still in place behind their firing portals. There was clearly nothing that could provide sufficient cover here, leaving them no choice but to take their chances in the the belly of the long-dead warship. Natalya found a large enough hole in the deck twenty feet from the cannons, and Blaine followed her through. Since their pursuers would have to come through this portal in single file, the advantage had swung temporarily to them. But they would still have to make their shots count.

Paddling backwards now, speargun in hand, Blaine saw the first black shape drop headfirst through the portal. He and Natalya moved as far into the darkness as they could while waiting for a second figure to appear. To make the most of their meager arsenal, they would have to eliminate two of the enemy here and now. But the wait, with one target easily in range, was agonizing. At last a second figure slid through the portal and joined the first in giving chase. Blaine and Natalya fired their spearguns at the same moment.

Natalya's spear tore through the first man's leg while McCracken's ripped straight through the throat of the second. The first managed to get his spear off but the shot was hopelessly errant and lodged in the rotted wall behind Natalya. She swam for it, thinking she could use it herself. She had gotten her hand on it when Blaine saw her gesture to him. He swam to her and looked where she pointed, to an insignia printed on the shaft of the enemy spear. It was Russian.

Their attackers were Russians!

Blaine motioned for her to forget the spear and continue on. More figures were pushing through the deck opening now to give chase. Blaine and Natalya swam as fast as they dared through the serpentine corridors, the sensation reminding McCracken of his experience in Fass's Labyrinth just days before.

Their luck held. A slight brightening up ahead signaled Blaine they had located another way out. The plan was obvious now. Climb back out of the warship and take their chances with a mad surface dash. If they could outswim their Russian pursuit and reach Captain Bob far enough ahead of them, they would have a chance.

Too many "ifs," thought McCracken, none of which took

into account that these Russians hadn't swum all the way from the Biminis. They surely had a ship nearby with plenty more firepower than the single shotgun Captain Bob had brought along.

Natalya went up through the escape hole first, but her progress was arrested by an arm snaking around from behind her. She swung in time to stop the man whose leg still held her spear from cutting her throat but not her air hose. Bubbles lurched through the water and she knew the horror of having her breath taken from her. She fought against panic and turned the severed air hose on the man, blinding him with bubbles, which gave McCracken enough time to emerge from the portal with his own knife. The Russian turned toward him much too late, seeing only a glimmer as Blaine's blade whipped across his throat. The blood gushed out in a sudden burst, then swirled slowly through the water.

Blaine paddled fast for Natalya, who had drifted away, and jammed his auxiliary regulator in her open mouth. She breathed gratefully and signaled him to start a rise to the surface. Blaine yanked the cord on his vest which inflated it all at once, then did the same to Natalya's. *To avoid an embolism, never rise faster than your air bubbles*, went the popular scuba teaching, but now that seemed the least of their problems.

The remaining three Russians were already even with them fifteen yards to their left. Blaine and Natalya fought to rise faster but sharing air from the same tank proved cumbersome and slowed them up considerably. Blaine looked toward the Russians, and saw yet another shape beyond them coming fast. Oh no, not another one. This figure was not wearing a wet suit, and he moved through the water as gracefully as if it was his home. He might have moved even faster if not for the spearguns he held in both hands. He fired both from twenty yards behind the Russians.

The Russians were unaware of the figure's presence until his spears sliced through two of their midsections. The two who'd been hit pawed around them as if to grab fistfuls of water, then sank toward the bottom. The third turned and aimed his speargun in the same motion. It would be impossible for him to miss from such close range. The spear leaped dead on target, and what Blaine saw next would have been unbelievable if he hadn't watched it himself. At the last possible instant the figure reached out a hand and redirected the spear away from him without slowing his pace. Then the figure had his knife out and was upon the last Russian before the man could try anything else. McCracken didn't see the rest from this distance but he didn't have to. The sight of the final black-suited figure floating toward the bottom was enough to tell him the results.

Blaine turned his eyes back on the figure drawing closer to them and saw the long hair dangling free. The figure grasped a closed fist to his heart in an underwater signal not of the standard, but of the Indian, variety.

It was Johnny Wareagle.

McCracken steered for a dark shape on the surface with Natalya by his side. They surfaced not more than ten yards from the cruiser.

"We've got visitors," Captain Bob shouted at them. He pointed off the stern of the cruiser.

Blaine started swimming for the boat while he looked where Captain Bob pointed, toward a fishing trawler about three hundred yards away. Now that its occupants had seen them surface, the results of the underwater battle would be obvious and they were certain to attack.

Johnny Wareagle surfaced just as Blaine pushed Natalya up to Captain Bob's helping hand. A small powerboat lay a hundred yards off their bow, obviously the vehicle the Indian had miraculously steered to their rescue.

"Who the hell is that?" Captain Bob wondered as Blaine joined Natalya on the deck.

"Charlie the Tuna," McCracken told him. "Starkist finally gave him the call."

Captain Bob's mind was elsewhere and he moved for the

bridge. "I'd better get this heap moving 'fore the shootin' starts."

"They've probably got enough firepower on board to sink another fleet of ships," Blaine shouted at him grimly.

"Won't do 'em no good nohow if I can run 'em onto the reef." He gunned the engine and gazed up at the sky reflectively. "Night's comin' and we's headin' straight into the feedin' waters of the Dragon Fish."

If there was regret in the captain's voice, Blaine couldn't find it. "That's the least of our worries," he told him.

The fishing boat was already steaming forward, chancing the reef, and Johnny Wareagle was barely halfway on board when Captain Bob finally gave his cruiser gas.

"Spirits guide you out here, Indian?" Blaine asked Johnny.

"Not this time, Blainey. I just followed the men in the boat behind us. Their presence in Bimini seemed too great a coincidence."

"Sure beats Club Med if you ask me."

The humor failed to impress Wareagle. He was breathing hard. "The scientist Sundowner is dead, Blainey."

"*What?* How?" Blaine shook his head. "Never mind. The Farmer Boy must have got to him, probably *before* he reached the President with the truth about the replacement satellite. Damnit, I should have known. . . . "

"No, you couldn't have, because there's more. Just before the scientist left, he learned that Atragon has been discovered in Colorado."

"Colorado?" It was Natalya, numbed to the bone.

They both looked at her. Wareagle spoke.

"A town called Pamosa—"

"Springs!" completed Natalya abruptly. "In the plane to Algiers I overheard Raskowski and Katlov speaking about that town! Troops mobilized to hold it. But what would he want with—" She stopped, the realization striking her at the same time it struck McCracken.

"The Atragon!" he exclaimed. "The source for his death beam!" Then, thinking it out as he continued, "His first satellite blows up, and all of a sudden he needs more. The Farmer Boy somehow learns it's there in Colorado, so Raskowski takes the town over. Mines all of the crystals he can use." A puzzled look crossed McCracken's features. "Only what does he do with it then? He used his deception to get his reflector into orbit but he still would need—"

The first bullets started blazing from the fishing boat, a few smacking into the sides. The three of them dove for cover.

"Their boatman's damn good," Captain Bob called from behind the wheel. "Knows these waters almost as good as me. But he won't know the shallows. Ain't a man alive who knows 'em like I do."

Blaine watched the Soviets draw to within a hundred yards. Winds and currents were playing hell with their aim, though the narrowing of the gap would take care of that before long. If they were going to survive, it would depend on Captain Bob's savvy. The captain was making sharp maneuvers to avoid the reefs; a few times he miscalculated and the shrill grinding sound of reef rubbing against boat frame was frightening to hear.

"Blainey, I sense something," Wareagle said suddenly.

"Probably just our boat getting a massage."

"No, a disturbance in the great fields, a large imbalance. Listen close and even you will be able to hear the warnings of the spirits."

Blaine and the others watched as fifty yards back their pursuers' boat was jostled steeply to the side, the Soviet gunmen losing their balance. It wasn't hard to figure out what had happened. The underside of the Russian boat had hit the reef and a good portion of its underside was probably torn to shreds. The pilot tried to veer aside at the last instant and succeeded only in crashing his stern into a huge reef near surface level. The fishing boat turned lazily, desperately, starting to sink into the sea. Blaine and the others watched in silence. The remaining Russians dropped their weapons in favor of life jackets and inflatable rafts. The boat was dying.

"Told ya, didn't I?" Captain Bob beamed from the bridge. "Told ya, told ya, told ya so, I did!"

"There's your imbalance, Indian."

"No, Blainey, what I feel is still . . ."

Wareagle stopped when a huge swell of water rose over the dying Russian boat. It came with incredible fury. Then the very ocean seemed to open up beneath it, revealing a huge shape rising claws-first from the depths.

The Dragon Fish had finally arrived.

CHAPTER 29

Captain Bob began chanting words in a language Blaine couldn't understand, his grip on the wheel relinquished as he moved forward in a daze. The boat began to spin with the currents as he ripped his shotgun free of its perch. The rest of them watched transfixed, unable to move.

The creature had the look of a giant black crab with twin claws on either side, one of which was swooping down toward the largest concentration of the doomed Russian crew. Their screams almost covered the awful crackling that resulted when the claw splintered what remained of the fishing boat.

Captain Bob rushed to the bow, raised the shotgun, and squeezed off a pair of shots.

"Don't waste your bullets or your time," Blaine advised. "You'll only let him know we're here."

"He knows," Captain Bob said madly. "He knows." And he fired twice more before pausing to reload.

The creature's claws continued to sweep the waters for Russians. Blaine estimated the Dragon Fish to be over two hundred feet from claw tips to its strangely shaped tail. Wait a minute, the tail . . .

His thoughts were interrupted when their ship at last struck the reef, lodging there and pitching all its occupants violently to the deck. Natalya struck the gunwale hard and would have gone over if not for the quick hand of Johnny Wareagle who reached out and grabbed her. Captain Bob was not as lucky. The collision pitched him to the deck on his head. He was plunged into unconsciousness as the creature which devoured his sons loomed close.

Off their stern, the Dragon Fish continued to compress the dying boat and crew within its claws, more interested in pure destruction than dinner. Wareagle concentrated on the regular rhythm with which its claws opened and closed, opened and closed. . . .

"It's not alive!" he shouted.

With the screeching of the cruiser on the reef, McCracken didn't hear Johnny, but he was forming his own conclusions. The monster moved too stiffy and its tail—yes, its tail. It remained unexplainably stiff. There were no bends in the monster's joints, none of the supple motions one would expect from a seagoing beast. It seemed . . . mechanical.

"It's a fucking submarine!" Blaine realized.

Which seemed to make little difference as water gushed through the gaping holes in their boat's bottom. As the deck lowered beneath them, Wareagle propped up Captain Bob against the cabin which was the cruiser's highest point. The Dragon Fish was swinging toward them now, snapping together its outstretched claws and making the hollow sound of steel meeting steel. Blaine could see the mouth now, could see that the huge teeth, which had looked razor sharp and deadly from a distance, were merely painted on.

It was a submarine all right, and now it was slowing to a drift before them as they clung to whatever parts of the deck remained above water. The body of the beast was a near-perfect sphere, perforated by holes for piston jets to promote drive on the surface. It had oblong windows for eyes and lines in its hull marking hatch points.

Blaine's eyes returned to the claws, raised high, when a hatch at the top of the Dragon Fish's head opened and a pair of machine gun wielding guards appeared. Behind them was a figure McCracken recognized all too well.

"Please," said Vasquez, "come aboard."

"Welcome to the *Dragon Fish*," the fat man said politely after the last of them had climbed down into the submarine's bridge followed by a pair of guards carrying the unconscious Captain Bob. More armed guards watched them from every angle. "I had thought about devouring you, McCrackenballs, but I was worried what you might do to my baby's digestion."

"You were never one to turn down a good meal, fat man."

Vasquez made himself laugh. "You're too tough for my taste. At least you used to be."

The belly of the beast was oval shaped and lit by a soft orange glow. Blaine gazed around and saw the most advanced computerized equipment available for any submarine. Diodes and display gauges stood out everywhere, with Vasquez's technicians manning their stations in neatly starched, lime-green uniforms, totally uninterested in the action around them. A technician moved slightly to his right and the soft green glow of a CRT screen cast a dull light over Vasquez's expression.

"Steal this from Electric Boat, fat man?"

"No, McCrackenballs, but they were generous enough to furnish most of the parts."

"Your own private Trident . . ."

"And then some, as you have already seen." Not a strand of Vasquez's slicked back hair was out of place as he patted his cheeks with his ever-present handkerchief. The sweat was starting to soak through his jacket. "Professor Clive was kind enough to reveal your destination. Imagine, coming all the way to the Biminis in search of those mysterious crystals. . . ."

"Since you weren't about to part with the ones you'd already lifted, I didn't have much choice. Yup, it all makes sense, even those holes Natalya and I found in the old wrecks down there. After that sea quake made their treasures accessible again, you created—or resurrected—the myth of the Dragon Fish to assure yourself of sole salvage rights."

Vasquez gazed around him fondly. "Far more than a myth, as I'm sure you can see."

Blaine feigned looking about in order to meet Johnny Wareagle's eyes. The Indian, never one to give up easily, was obviously gauging methods for a possible turning of the tables. McCracken's unspoken instructions held him back.

"So the island with no name becomes your exclusive territory, thanks to this contraption here. I guess it doubles as a damn good salvage vehicle."

The fat man nodded, impressed with the analysis. "Parts of its lower frame are detachable: smaller robot and manned submersibles with incredible range and equipment. We've been able to plunder just about every treasure chest."

"But you've stayed around."

"Because there's still a fortune we haven't gotten to yet, McCrackenballs. Strange things were happening in these parts well before the Dragon Fish was even conceived. Someday I'll find a way to bring up the rest of those crystals."

"You mean they're still down there?"

"Besides some modest reserves that were relatively easy to salvage."

"Which you offered to the highest bidder."

Vasquez nodded. "A shame I didn't have more, though. One party paid an astounding price for my meager stores. Big Russian with a patch for a left eye."

"Katlov!" Natalya said loud enough to draw the armed guards' attention to her. Her eyes locked with McCracken's.

"Then," Blaine realized, "Raskowski was after the Atragon here as well. Unlike him to give up so easily."

"He didn't give up," Natalya said. "He found what he needed in Pamosa Springs. The Biminis became superfluous.

If anything he'd want the reserves here buried forever, so we wouldn't be able to get to them either."

"Stop the games!" Vasquez barked. "All the stories in the world won't save you this time, McCrackenballs."

"No story this time, fat man. I was after those crystals to power an energy shield, against a death ray controlled by a Russian madman. Once he wipes out America the rest of civilization will fall like dominoes. Think about it."

"You're lying!" Vasquez insisted, but his voice sounded tentative. "Holding to tricks, deceptions, till the very last."

"The deception's not mine this time, fat man. It belongs to a mad Russian general named Raskowski to whom you so kindly delivered your reserves of Atragon." McCracken stopped to put things together for himself. When he spoke again, it was mostly to Natalya. "That shipment must have powered the satellite he lost. When the need for more came up, he turned to Pamosa Springs. He could launch his reflector on board the replacement for *Ulysses* and save himself the bother of moving the crystals by constructing the generator gun right in the town. But one thing doesn't fit. The second communiqué he sent, the one containing the three-week ultimatum, was sent *after* he lost his first satellite and way before the work in Pamosa Springs was finished. I don't get it."

"Another deception," suggested Natalya. "He wanted to make your government believe they had more time than they actually did, so the element of surprise would return to his side. There won't be any more ultimatums or messages. He's going to begin firing just as soon as his reflector achieves orbit."

"Twenty-four hours from now," McCracken said. "Maybe less."

"Stop!" ordered Vasquez. "Very well rehearsed, I grant you, but—"

"Give it up, fat man. The story's true and you know it. Think about the fact that we weren't the only party to end up in your private waters. Or have you forgotten those Russians you devoured a few minutes ago?''

''Russians?''

Blaine nodded. ''Raskowski's men, as I see it. He's not just after us anymore, either. He wants you and your Atragon out of the way, too, and it's my guess we'll have proof of that before long. If I penetrated your guise as Salim, it's a sure bet he did as well. Once I arrived on the scene you became too much of a liability. He's probably had you under watch since the very beginning.''

Vasquez's huge jowls puckered in grim determination. ''Fitting, since I have kept tabs on his one-eyed bandit all this time too.''

Katlov! Natalya and McCracken thought together.

''Then you have tabs on Raskowski!'' she blurted.

''Only if they're together. The information's a phone call away, that's all. But that assumes I—''

The sonar operator broke in, turning toward Vasquez as he spoke. ''Sir, I have three aircraft coming up on our position. Range, 5,000 meters and closing.''

''Prepare to dive,'' ordered Vasquez, and a bell chimed three times within the huge belly of the *Dragon Fish*. He waited a few seconds longer, giving the armed guards ample opportunity to solidify their positions around their captives at what promised to be a most vulnerable moment. ''Dive.''

The *Dragon Fish* dropped gracefully beneath the sea, lights growing immediately dimmer and hazing over with red.

''Aircraft 4,000 meters and closing,'' reported the sonar operator as three additional blips appeared on his screen. He gazed back at the fat man once again. ''I also show three large ships steaming this way. Range four miles. Speed increasing. Trying for a signal fix now. . . .''

''Join us, fat man,'' Blaine urged. ''There are some things important enough to bring even you and me together.''

''Planes closing,'' sonar reported. ''Range now 2,000 meters. Range of boats three-and-one-half miles.'' He checked his screen, punched in a few commands onto his computer console, and read the results out loud when they flashed across his screen. "Sir, I have a signature now on those approaching ships. They're trawlers, big ones." He swallowed hard. "Soviet H-class complete with several high-powered deck guns and missile launchers. Warships in disguise."

Vasquez looked at McCracken, then at nothing in particular. "Maybe they know I'm here, McCracken, but they couldn't possibly know about the *Dragon Fish*." Then, to the uniformed figure standing by the periscope, "Commander, set an intercept course for us with those trawlers and prepare the surface-to-air missiles. Our baby is hungry again."

CHAPTER 30

"WOULDA baked you a cake with a file in it," Clara Buhl had told Dog-ear and Sheriff Junk six hours earlier at five P.M. "But I forgot the recipe."

"How's things in town?" the mayor asked her.

"Real quiet since you boys became jailbirds. Our mysterious killer seems to be taking a break."

"You and Isaac T. been around to the people?"

"Yeah, and I can tell you . . ."

The conversation was held within earshot of three of Guillermo Paz's soldiers. And it was all a front for Dog-ear to figure out a way to slip Clara the note he and Heep had composed on a tattered piece of newspaper they found under one of the mattresses. They had actually composed it two days before, but Clara had been the first visitor they were allowed.

They were under watch almost all the time and had stolen the minutes required to write the note, with Heep distracting the guards. Paz had jailed them in the right cell, the one nearest the street, where Heep had stowed two crates, one each of grenades and Laws rockets. He'd had plenty of experience with bazookas in Korea and these damn things couldn't be much different. He'd seen how they worked on television. Problem was figuring out what to make them work on. Oh, they could do plenty of damage from here before Paz's men caught on, but what would that accomplish? No, what they needed was to get the hell out of jail and get word to the outside world that they needed help. Neither man knew exactly how they were going to accomplish all that.

Dog-ear kept coughing into his hand as he spoke with Clara. He hoped the guards would be bored with the small talk and the gesture which was meant to disguise his passing over the note at the proper time. He was just about ready to figure that the proper time was never going to come when Clara, bless her, feigned a slip on the slick floor and had to use the bars to hoist her beefy frame back up. As she gripped them low at the start, before the soldiers had a chance to approach, Dog-ear slipped the note into her hand. She accepted it without expression, figuring all along the mayor would have plenty to say he wouldn't want heard and attracted by his coughing into a bit of white crumpled in his fist.

"I always wanted to be mayor, you know," Clara said at the end.

"Looks like you got your wish," said Dog-ear, forcing a smile.

Clara waited until she was back home before reading the note; she had to, really, since the printing was too small to manage without her magnifying glass. She ran it over the wrinkled page methodically, shocked and excited by the enlarged letters passing before her:

> Not enough space to explain everything. We got weapons to use in here but they won't do the town any good unless we can get out and bring help. Need two things from you and Ike T. if we're going to pull this off: a distraction to draw the attention of the guards here in the jail. And a jeep parked somewhere near enough to reach in a hurry once the shooting starts. I know you got lots of questions I wish I had the space to answer.

But I know you'll get this done somehow anyway. We'll be waiting. Try to make it tonight after ten when the guard shift around town drops a little. See ya then.

Clara sat back to think.

Dog-ear and Sheriff Junk had almost given up hope by eleven, but a commotion in the streets at 11:15 drew them to the barred window of their cell. It wasn't easy, but if they strained their necks they could see almost the whole street.

And coming down it right now, six-guns strapped to his side in an ancient leather holster, was Isaac T. Hall. The pistols were his prized possessions, said to have once belonged to Wyatt Earp himself, and there wasn't a better use for them than the one he was about to provide. He'd nodded his head dimly at Clara's plan for his original role in the distraction, knowing all the time that the whole plan stood no chance of working. So he'd come up with this alteration by himself without telling her because he knew she would have argued him down.

He used to practice with the guns every day until the arthritis got too bad and the best he had been able to manage for the past few years was once a week when he remembered. The guns were oiled and loaded, twelve shots at his disposal. If he got them all off he'd consider it a victory even if none found their mark.

"Look, it's Clara!" Sheriff Junk whispered to Dog-ear.

There, across the street, Clara was waddling in the shadows toward one of three parked jeeps. She ducked down out of sight when she reached it.

Down Main Street, in front of the bar, Ike Hall had stopped and drawn his pistols outside the fringed jacket that was probably a century old.

A dozen or so soldiers on patrol in the streets had sighted their rifles on him, waiting. One ran to get Major Paz.

Outside the jail cell, the three on-duty guards' eyes were glued to the proceedings. Sheriff Junk slid away from the cell window and moved to the cot, beneath which lay a pried-open crate of grenades.

Ike Hall didn't know where he found the strength to draw both guns in a single motion or why he chose that particular moment to do so. The swiftness of the action surprised the soldiers, and they hesitated long enough for Ike to get a shot off from each as he dove to the ground and rolled for cover behind a parked jeep. One of his shots actually winged a soldier in the instant before a dozen of them opened fire. Ike might have been shot; he hurt so much already he couldn't tell.

Inside the jail cell, Sheriff Junk pulled the pin on the grenade he had lifted from the crate and rolled it across the floor toward the three guards by the window. It exploded with Heep and McCluskey pressed tight into the corner with their faces covered. The explosion rocked the jailhouse and caught the attention of the guards who were moving on Ike.

It was then that Clara settled her bulk low in the driver's seat of the jeep and felt blindly for the key. She'd driven jeeps plenty of times back in the old days, but she hadn't driven anything in the six years since her eyes went, so it was with eyes closed and a silent prayer in her mind that she depressed the clutch and gunned the engine.

Ike T. Hall felt the bullets. A burst of energy surged through him, and he swung around with both guns firing at the same time. Wyatt himself would have been proud. He thought he might even have hit one of the soldiers, but he crumbled over before he could be sure.

The soldiers were rushing the jail from all sides now, some appearing in T-shirts and still zipping up their pants. But Heep already had an armful of Laws rockets ready and as expected they were simpler to use than any bazooka he'd ever seen. He flipped a catch, extended a stock backwards from which the thrust exhaust would belch and aimed the Laws for the middle of Main Street. A single squeeze of the trigger and the projectile hit on macadam and sent debris showering upward. A number of soldiers went down writhing and screaming.

"Another!" Heep yelled to McCluskey, who tossed a second Laws up to him.

Sheriff Junk had it cocked and ready an instant later, his target the empty K Mart across the street from which a number of soldiers were still emerging. The whole front of the building went up in a single blast of orange and black, with shattered glass flying in every direction. The soldiers were on the defensive now, searching for cover instead of culprits. But Junk wasn't finished with them yet.

As he readied his third Laws, Clara Buhl brought the jeep around in a screeching U-turn to the front of the jailhouse. Heep's third target was the telephone pole containing the junction box for all of Main Street. The pole shattered as if struck by lightning, and all of Pamosa Springs was plunged into total darkness. With that, Heep rushed to the door and hoisted a heavy boot into the latch. The rusted catch gave on contact, and the cell door flew outward. He started to grab crates.

"You mean, we coulda done that anytime since we been here?" wondered Dog-ear.

"I don't tell you everything, Mayor."

By then they were out the cell and heading for the front room. Heep toted crates under both arms, barely feeling the sting in his ankle, while Dog-ear grabbed a pair of the guards' scratched-up rifles. They seemed in good enough working order and he led Heep forward with one ready in either hand.

Outside the jailhouse, Clara had just screeched the jeep to a halt. But the soldiers were regrouping and the mayor found himself with plenty of targets when he led Sheriff Junk out of the building. Both rifle barrels blazed orange, aimed at similar colors flashing in the darkness or at moving shapes. By the time the clip of his first rifle was exhausted, Heep had gotten the crates into the jeep and was signaling him forward.

"Come on!" Sheriff Junk screamed, and Clara backed the jeep up alongside him.

McCluskey leaped in and bumped his head on the extended stock of an attached .50-caliber machine gun.

"Well, I'll be damned. . . ."

He yanked back the bolt and balanced himself precariously as Clara spun the jeep around for the other side of town. The .50-caliber had more of a kick than he remembered—or maybe he had just gotten older—but with the jeep picking up speed, McCluskey kept pointing the weapon toward anything that moved, holding the trigger and feeling his teeth gnash together from the gun's kickback.

The soldiers were giving chase now. Up ahead was Bill Hapscomb's filling station and from there a road that would lead part of the way into the San Juans.

McCluskey was still firing, the clip melting into the machine gun and shells flying everywhere, when Sheriff Junk grasped another Laws and popped the stock out as they drew near Hapscomb's. He fired as they moved, aiming at the first of the three gas pumps. His aim was good enough.

First a flash of flame and then a huge mushroom of black smoke sprouted from the pump island. Gasoline sprayed outward from the ruptured lines, spreading the flames, until a wall of fire stretched across Main Street between their fleeing jeep and the charging troops, effectively blocking the enemy behind it. The flames climbed higher as numerous secondary explosions added fuel and heat.

"Heeeeeeee-yahhhhhhhh!" screamed Dog-ear and Sheriff Junk together.

The wall of flames had shrunk in the distance behind them when they saw a jeep charge through it. It wavered for a few seconds but then straightened, a soldier in it rising to his feet to steady its machine gun. The jeep was coming fast, gaining, bullets churning outward in a continuous stream, a few clanging off the leading jeep's frame.

"Shit!" yelled the mayor, ducking low. "We're out of ammo."

"Not quite," said Heep as he reached for another Laws. "It's up to you now, Clara."

Clara didn't say anything, just kept on driving. The road ahead seemed one big black blur and she was squinting like crazy just to keep the jeep reasonably straight. She hoped her expression wasn't giving away the knifing pain she felt in her chest. She thought at first she'd been shot but the tightness down her whole left arm all the way from her jaw told her the old ticker had finally had enough and was calling it quits. *Just hang on a little longer*, she urged. *Keep pumping. Come on!*

She saw stars from the pain and her vision clouded over even more. The jeep wavered slightly as the narrow road that would take them into the San Juans came up fast. Sheriff Junk had managed to steady another Laws with the bullets just clearing his head, but Clara's sudden turn into the mountains made him drop it.

"Shit!" he wailed, feeling for it desperately.

Clara clutched and downshifted into the hairpin turns, afraid to use the brakes and sacrifice their lead over the trailing jeep. Her vision had been reduced to simply steering her jeep between the mountainside and the deadly edge. She was gasping for breath now and each thud in her chest stole more of it away. The pain felt like bubbles bursting inside her. She could feel her hands stiffening, and the night was starting to go from dark to black. The jeep keeled left and sideswiped the mountain. Clara overcompensated and almost plunged them over the side.

"Easy!" screamed Dog-ear.

She got the jeep straight again, holding her breath now because it seemed to keep down the pain. Sheriff Junk had the Laws steady once more. The trailing jeep was now ten yards back. But the steep grade and sudden turns confused his aim and denied him the certain kill shot he felt he had to have.

"Fuck it," he said and rose in the jeep with Dog-ear clutching his knobby legs for support.

Heep's knees cracked and popped. He fired as Clara swung over a rise, which forced his shot down too low. But the jeep was close enough for the powerful explosion to send road fragments crashing upward into it. The driver struggled with control only briefly before the jeep smashed first up against the mountainside and then careened wildly across the road and over the edge.

Junk and Dog-ear failed to see any of this. They had both fallen to the floor of the jeep, which came slowly to a halt. Both men struggled to their feet, looked back and saw there was no more pursuit.

"We did it! Goddamnit, we did it! Got those bastards good! Hey, Clara, we—"

Dog-ear stopped when he saw Clara Buhl slumped over the wheel.

"Oh shit," he said. The San Juans loomed ahead of them, and Pamosa Springs was nothing but a dark patch below.

PART FIVE

THE BATTLE OF PAMOSA SPRINGS

Pamosa Springs: Thursday, eight A.M.

CHAPTER 31

GUILLERMO Paz completed detailing his orders to his individual unit commanders and dismissed them. In the havoc of last night he had lost a dozen men, a *dozen* to an old geezer with a pair of six-guns and a trio of middle-aged bureaucrats. Paz cursed himself for underestimating the lot of them, for not killing them when he could have. But his orders had been to stabilize the town and until last night the execution of the six citizens and jailing of the leaders had accomplished precisely that. Even the mysterious murders had ceased, and, if not for lax security, all would still be under control.

Worst of all, a rocket fired during the escape had knocked out the telephone substation containing the outside line on which General Raskowski had been calling him. But his priorities were clear: keep the townspeople where he could control them, and keep the generator gun safe from all possible harm.

With that in mind, Paz had stationed his heaviest artillery at opposite ends of the town to create a grid capable of shutting down virtually any attack from ground or air. Not that it mattered. The generator gun was encased in a shield of tungsten steel, impenetrable and easily defended in its position between two sloping hillsides. Paz gazed toward it stroking his mustache almost continuously in his anxiety. Strands came out in bunches, and he mindlessly tossed them aside. The end was near, just hours away now.

Paz could barely wait.

Blaine McCracken lay low on a rise overlooking the town of Pamosa Springs. What he saw through the binoculars made him gasp. Beneath him in the center of town, men dressed as American soldiers were continuously herding groups of residents forward at gunpoint toward the town's largest building: a steeple-fronted white church. He watched as dozens upon dozens of townspeople were wedged like cattle through a set of double doors, prodded along with automatic rifle barrels. At the same time, he noticed more soldiers packing plastic explosives against the side of the church, enough to bring down the whole town, never mind that single building. The message to the hostages inside was clear; any attempt at escape would lead to their own destruction.

He turned his attention northwest of the town center, to another phalanx of soldiers standing guard upon a ravaged foothill. In the gulley beyond it, he knew, had to be the generator gun that would fire the particle beam. Once the reflector achieved orbit twelve hours from now, the beam could be bounced anywhere Raskowski chose from his base across the Atlantic.

His mind drifted back to his last moments aboard the *Dragon Fish* after Vasquez's custom-made submarine had systematically destroyed the rest of Raskowski's Bimini forces.

"The general's not finished with you yet, fat man," Blaine charged, still uncertain of Vasquez's intentions. "Me, Natalya and the Indian are the only ones who can finish him off."

"You've forgotten someone, haven't you, McCracken? Me. I caught you. I won. Now I'm ready to move up to more challenging competition: this Russian who played me for a fool, who dared to enter my waters. . . ."

The discussion continued as they surfaced and steamed fast for Vasquez's private port in the Biminis. Foremost on Blaine's mind was that the failure of Raskowski's assault teams here would alert the general that there still existed a dangerous threat to him. The element of surprise on all fronts was gone. Their best approach now would be a three-pronged attack in which at least one of the prongs would be assured of success.

Blaine would proceed from here straight for Pamosa Springs. Wareagle would head to Washington with a plea to get troops to the area while there was still time and to abort the satellite launch at all cost. Natalya, meanwhile, would travel back to Europe with Vasquez. The fat man would provide a commando team to be used in an assault on Katlov's current position and what must certainly be Raskowski's headquarters—in Zurich, as it turned out.

"Are you sure your men are reliable?" she asked him.

"Reliable, my dear? They are all my sons, ten from six different wives, and they all take after their father."

They had gone their separate ways only eighteen hours before Raskowski's murderous strike on the United States would begin. In his position atop the small rise, McCracken knew Natalya must still be on her way to Europe. His would surely be the first blow struck.

Shifting his body slightly, McCracken checked his watch: eight hours to go. He swept his binoculars through the small center of Pamosa Springs, and his eyes locked through the lenses on the short and cocky figure of Guillermo Paz.

Paz's reputation alone had nearly led Blaine to cancel his recent Nicaraguan mission to hijack the Hind-D. And now the little man was here, fingers toying with his mustache as always, linked obviously to Raskowski and forced to prove his mettle yet again. Challenging the same man twice in so short a time was not something Blaine looked forward to. One of the things that had kept him alive this long was not tempting the law of averages.

In this case, however, Paz seemed the least of his problems. He had counted ninety soldiers and enough firepower to hold off ten times that many. He had only an Uzi Vasquez had given him and the nearly full tank of gas in the rented compact he'd driven in from Durango.

What he needed was a miracle. And it was just a few minutes later that it occurred to him where one was waiting for him.

Sheriff Junk and the mayor hadn't gone very far into the San Juans at all. The concentration of Paz's forces searching for them would have prevented it, even if a bullet wound in Dog-ear's leg hadn't. At first he pleaded with Heep to go on without him but the sheriff was hearing none of that. He cut down a great pile of thick branches and used them to camouflage a sheltered space between three large rocks. This hideout kept them dry and safe. They had to move their shelter only once in the hours since their escape, but on several occasions they had actually held their breath while Paz's troops searched close by.

Before the pursuit began, they had buried Clara in a makeshift grave of rocks and branches. Her efforts had saved them and they said their own silent prayers for both her and Isaac T. Hall before pressing on. Further up the trail, Dog-ear's leg stiffening, they had found a spot to conceal the crates of rockets and grenades which were too bulky to carry. As time went on, McCluskey's wound grew more and more painful and swollen, and Sheriff Junk had to carry him most of the way to the place where he built their shelter.

They didn't talk much because there wasn't much to say. They had escaped but done their town no good in the process. They may even have made matters worse. With two men free now to tell the world what was happening in Pamosa Springs, Paz was capable of anything.

What they needed, Sheriff Junk supposed, was a doctor to set Dog-ear's leg just right. Then they could take the rest of the grenades and rockets back down the pass and wage their own private war on Paz's troops.

But what they really needed was a miracle.

Three hours after leaving Pamosa Springs, Blaine pulled up to the gate of the Air Force Research and Testing station in Colorado Springs. He had no clearance to enter, but he managed to convince the guards at the front gate to put in a call to Lieutenant Colonel Ben Metcalf who, thankfully, was listed as present on the base. After learning his visitor was McCracken, Metcalf instructed that he be immediately passed through.

The base was generally simple in design, composed as near as Blaine could tell of little more than several barracks, a dozen hangars, numerous runways and assorted stations for drilling.

Metcalf met him outside the tri-level office building and pumped his hand happily when he climbed out of his grimy compact.

"Have you switched to the economy model?"

"My Porsche is in the shop. You know how it is."

"Sure do. Temperamental engines are what I deal with all day." They stood facing each other. "So what the hell brings you back here so soon?" Metcalf asked him.

"I need a favor."

"God knows we owe you. Just name it."

"Don't say that until you hear what it is."

"I'm listening."

"Let's go into your office."

When Metcalf had closed the door behind him, Blaine picked up again. "Tell me about the Hind-D."

"Not much to tell. We haven't done a hell of a lot with it yet besides pasting American instructions over the Russian ones. Apparently there's been a jurisdictional snafu. Everyone in the armed forces is claiming it belongs to them."

"Then you haven't disassembled it yet."

"Hell no. The only thing we've done since you dropped it off was give it a fresh fill of fuel for testing that hasn't been conducted yet."

"That's just what I needed to hear."

"Why, Blaine?"

McCracken hesitated. "Now comes the favor I told you about. I need you to lend me the Hind . . . just for the afternoon."

Metcalf's face turned serious for the first time. "Blaine, what's going on?"

"I won't bother with explanations because they wouldn't make any sense to you. Can I have the bird or not?"

Metcalf shrugged. "Everything else aside, I'd love to help you. Problem is, I haven't got the authority to check the Hind out to anyone; nobody does until this jurisdictional dispute gets settled. I'd like to help you but I can't. Christ, Blaine, I know you wouldn't be here if you didn't have a damn good reason to be, but I just don't have the authority to fill your request."

Blaine pulled out his gun. "That's what I figured."

"You don't need that," Metcalf told him calmly.

"It's for your own good that I brought it along. This way, all the cooperation you're going to give me can take place under coercion. Might save your career."

"And fuck yours royally."

"Mine doesn't exist anymore. Less so now than ever, believe me."

Metcalf started with him to the door, then stopped. "Whatever you're going up against, you're obviously going to need help. Let me—"

"No offense, Ben," McCracken interrupted, "but you're just a bureaucrat now and I haven't got time to go through channels. The *country* hasn't got time."

"That bad?"

"Oh yeah."

"At least tell me where you're headed. I might get lucky and—"

"No, can't do that either, but thanks just the same. That kind of exchange would make you an accomplice for no good reason I can see. The wheels spin too slowly to take the risk. This one's mine."

"Then put your gun away and follow me."

"I'll keep it out, Ben, just for show."

Every day this time of year, Cleb Turner, Sergeant Major in the United States Army, took a stroll around lunchtime to the first hot dog vendor he could find. Turner would take a pair of dogs and a can of diet Coke into the shade and linger over them lavishly before returning to his stale office in the Pentagon and the start of equally stale afternoon meetings.

Cleb Turner was never meant to be a bureaucrat. Damn business was too confining, especially for a man who'd served in both Korea and Vietnam. Just as bad, Cleb knew that as the first black sergeant major in army history, his appointment had been earned on the political battlefields as much as the real ones. But what the hell? He'd earned the appointment on his own merit; he just didn't like the job, kept at it mostly because he figured that having more real soldiers behind the desks might help avoid future debacles.

It was the bullshit he had to go through en route to this goal that made lunch outside the Pentagon his favorite part of the day. Since the morning had been relatively quiet, he allowed himself relish along with the usual mustard on his pair of hotdogs. He was trying to balance them in one hand and handle his soda in the other, when he turned smack-dab into a huge figure whose chest was even with his head.

"What the hell. . . ." Then Turner saw the figure's face. "Johnny Wareagle?" he said in amazement.

"With regards from the spirits, Sergeant."

"I thought you were dead."

"Only for a time."

CHAPTER 32

McCracken kept the Hind-D low, beneath the reach of air defense radar which was constantly watching for out-of-place and potentially dangerous aircraft with no registered flight plan. It was well over two hundred miles from Colorado Springs to Pamosa Springs and Blaine figured he could cover that easily in just over an hour.

Blaine insisted on leaving the colonel bound and gagged in the Hind's hangar to further promote his cover. Metcalf reluctantly agreed after pointing McCracken in the direction of the airstrip he had already reserved. By the time anyone realized something was wrong, Blaine would already be over Pamosa Springs.

He had spent two months of his life learning everything there was to learn about the Hind-D before activating the Nicaraguan operation. Then escape had been his only goal. Today's mission was considerably more complicated.

He spent the balance of the flight refamiliarizing himself with the setup of the Hind's cockpit. It was designed as a three-person aircraft but had been outfitted to allow one man to both fly it and operate its weapon systems in the event of an emergency. The English labels Metcalf had stuck over the Russian ones made life much easier in this respect, for at least on this flight Blaine wouldn't have to guess which button was which. Extremely sophisticated weapons counters gave him precise data on his laser-guided air cannons and his rocket and missile launchers. He had ninety of the .27-millimeter missiles remaining, and well over half the ammo left in his air cannons, which followed the line of his eyes once the guidance system rigged into his helmet was activitated. He would save the full complement of six antitank missiles for the generator gun.

His greatest concern at this point was how to make all this technology work for him. His target, of course, was the guarded gulley where the generator gun was set up. But with heavy artillery at either end of the town, a direct attack was impossible. High in the air, at a standard altitude, the guns would chew him to pieces. But if he . . .

Blaine swallowed hard. His only hope lay in doing the unexpected, however dangerous it might be. A low-altitude run would significantly reduce the effectiveness of the gun batteries while exposing him to potential destruction from ground level. It was a chance he could live with, though. Come in and take them by surprise. Knock out the main gun batteries and the generator gun was his.

McCracken shifted uneasily in his seat. The Hind could be controlled either by wheel or joystick, both containing firing buttons for the air cannons. He would have to launch missiles and rockets with his free hand when required, leaving him only one hand for all the rest of the controls. As Pamosa Springs drew closer, Blaine practiced the procedure again and again without engaging the weapons systems. According to his instruments he was barely five minutes from the town. The Hind's controls felt smooth and easy, tight as a sports car.

The San Juans came up fast and Blaine had to climb substantially to rise over them, keeping the Hind's bottom precariously close to their tips. The gunship obeyed his commands with immediate grace, bucking just a bit as if aware of what lay over the next ridge.

* * *

Guillermo Paz was quite proud of himself. All things considered, he had stabilized matters in Pamosa Springs so brilliantly that his few failures were certain to be overlooked in the face of his undeniable success. The last of the townspeople had been herded into the church, which was wired and ready to blow. That would keep his captives still while his guards at the gulley would easily fend off any assault the escaped mayor and sheriff might put together.

Paz stood proudly erect in the center of Main Street with one hand on his hip and the other stroking his mustache affectionately. His men saluted as they passed and Paz genially saluted back. All in all things were going to turn out pretty damn well. Soon the death beam would be fired and Paz would be among the only witnesses to actually *see* it.

The shallow whining sound confused him at first. It sounded like a chain saw echoing in the stiff wind. Then it grew louder. With a shudder Paz realized what it was and at the same time knew it couldn't be. *It couldn't be!* His eyes scanned the sky.

The Hind-D roared out from the cover of the mountains. Paz's eyes locked on it as it dropped to tree level. He knew it must be the one he had lost in Nicaragua, knew it had been flown here to be used against him. And its pilot had planned his strategy well. He was coming in beneath the range of his main guns.

Paz could see the air cannon chambers turning an instant before the *clack-clack-clack* reached his ears. The Hind's first spray bore into the area of his first gun battery, clanging sharply against steel where it connected and kicking dust up where it didn't.

The Hind came in still lower. You're crazy, Paz wanted to scream at the pilot, but this flier knew exactly what he was doing Paz realized as he watched the steel bird drop straight for him. He dove to the ground behind the cover of a jeep as the first sound of cannon fire came. It shattered the jeep and sent pieces of metal showering down on Paz. A small group of his men who had roared into the street at the first sign of fire had their frames torn apart by the warship's huge bullets.

Paz crawled out from behind the burning jeep and made for the armory, prepared to defend the generator gun himself if that's what it came to. He wouldn't fail now.

He couldn't.

McCracken had picked out Paz as soon as he cleared the ravaged front gun battery. He cut back the warship's speed to steady his aim and might have hit Paz with his next burst. He wasn't sure. Of the other men who had rushed into the street with their rifles ready, there was no question. McCracken saw their punctured corpses as he came round for his second pass, amazed at the accuracy of his air cannon fire.

Halfway to the second gun battery, he turned his attention to the thick barrels struggling for a bead on him from the foothills on the town's western perimeter. He estimated they could not possibly sight down on him before he was over and past them. Instead, they should have anticipated their fire ahead for the gulley as he soared over it. They were opening the door for him, and damned if he wasn't going to move right on through it.

McCracken fired a rocket and one of the truck-mounted guns exploded in a wall of flames. He followed up immediately with a barrage from the air cannons. This gained him the advantage he needed as he swept over the battery and climbed over the hill on the other side of which was the gulley.

The guards on the hill pelted him with rifle fire as he soared close, but the armor-piercing shells made barely a dent in the Hind's reinforced steel carcass. He drove the big bird past the gulley to facilitate a turn. He wanted to come straight over his target with plenty of time to assure himself of accurate missile launches. He figured he could fire three times before having to pull up again and three should finish the generator gun for good.

Blaine brought the Hind around and was chilled as he gazed downward. From this angle, the generator-gun complex had the look of a massive turret with an exposed barrel poking upward. It was of vast size, a dome encased in dusty gray steel. It amazed him that such an impregnable defense could have been erected so swiftly.

Blaine gulped down air as he punched in commands to the missile-targeting computer. Finger on the firing button now, one hand steadying the wheel.

He had asked for only one chance. He was about to get it.

Fire from the gun battery at the far side of town exploded in the air near him, a close call. McCracken drove the Hind into a weaving pattern as he fired his three missiles in rapid succession, the laser guides doing the rest. He was actually over the generator-gun complex and past it before he was certain of impact, but he banked the Hind back so he could see the effect of three direct hits.

Nothing! The only evidence of any impact was a few scattered fires sprouting from minor splits in the steel over-skin.

Blaine's stomach sank. He had struck the generator gun dead center with three shells that could level a city block, with no apparent effect. Already his mind was working in another direction. His only hope was to bide his time over Main Street long enough to ready another pass, and this time he would fire his missiles straight for the exposed barrel from which the ray would be emitted, a far more difficult shot but his only hope of knocking the weapon out.

He plunged closer to the ground as he crossed over Main Street again, firing his air cannons in random patterns just to buy himself time. Hitting the barrel would be a tough shot. He narrowed the firing grid at the small computer display screen on the console just to his right. The warship was fitted with an infrared camera on its underside, which broadcast the shape of whatever the missiles were aimed at on the monitor. When his target appeared on the screen all he had to do was lock into it and a missile would trace for the target from wherever it was fired.

McCracken dropped the Hind as low as he dared, barely fifty feet up, firing his laser-aimed cannons at windows where gun barrels protruded. The greatest congestion of resistant activity had been centered around three buildings in the town's center, obviously headquarters and perhaps armory for Raskowski's men.

The first, unbeknownst to him, was Sheriff Junk Heep's office, the facade of which was obliterated by his first rocket. The second was what looked like a general store. He gave it a missile and enough of the building exploded outward to make the soldiers in the street dive to the ground.

When he neared the eastern edge of town, the regrouped gun battery aimed a volley at him which missed the mark widely. He sped up and peppered the guns with as many missiles as he could fire until he passed them, leaving smoke and flaming steel behind as he headed back west to deal with the second battery.

Four of Paz's men rushed into the street beneath him holding what he recognized as Laws rockets. He aimed his helmet at them and fired, but his increased speed had the warship already beyond the shooters and his cannon bullets dug chasms out of the street's fresh tar surface. He was boxed in, the Laws behind and the western battery ahead.

He wasn't sure how many of the rockets actually struck the Hind-D. The controls seemed to lock up in his hands just for an instant. When the give came back, they were stiff. A pair of red lights flashed on his console board indicating aft fires too large for the automatic systems to fight. Blaine drove the warship on, faster, halfway to the gun battery now.

He could see the gun operators had gotten it right this time. Three of the four big guns were already aimed toward the gulley to lay down suppressing fire that would make it impossible for him to cross. The fourth fired token rounds which forced him to climb sooner than he would have wished. His maneuverability was reduced, as well as his chances of avoiding the blasts once over the gulley again.

His target, the exposed barrel, was frozen in his mind, but it needed to be equally frozen on his CRT grid if he was going to have any chance at all. The gulley came up fast as he crossed over the western battery. Blaine's hand moved to the targeting computer to lock in.

The fire of the three guns came and kept coming. He was headed straight for the generator complex now, seconds away, with the barrage of shells exploding everywhere around him, the percussion ringing in his ears as the Hind buckled. He adjusted its nose angle lower for smoother release and focused on the narrower target grid waiting for the gun barrel to lock on.

There it was, square in the center! McCracken went for the firing button.

A huge blast tore into the Hind from the rear, kicking it skyward. The warship fluttered in midair, seeming almost to stall, and smoke began to flood the cabin. Red lights flashed up and down the instrument board.

The missiles hadn't fired! They hadn't fired!

Paz's gunners had beaten him by an instant, but Blaine wasn't giving up yet. He still had three missiles and intended to find a way to fire them. He coughed through the smoke and struggled to regain control of the Hind. More blasts rocked him as he brought the sputtering bird around in a wide bank that took him back over the San Juans. More red lights flickered to warn him all his weapons systems had shorted out and the fuel line was ruptured. The Hind was limping in the air, refusing to go further. He was flying it to its death. And his.

With the last burst of strength he could grab from it, Blaine veered deeper over the foothills of the San Juans. The huge artillery shells followed him every inch of the way, a final one finding him just as the foliage of the mountains was beneath him and he had begun to try some sort of landing.

But that final blast had finished the ship. Black smoke instead of gray flooded the cockpit and filled his lungs. Blaine was aware of a terrible grinding noise and of a tumbling sensation as the brave bird plummeted. He dimly recorded the whiplash of collision, certain at that point he would never know anything again.

CHAPTER 33

ZURICH'S Bahnhofstrasse is unquestionably the city's most fashionable and elegant avenue. Combining the qualities of Wall Street and Fifth Avenue along a three-mile stretch bordered by lime trees, the Bahnhofstrasse houses numerous banks, investment firms, insurance companies and brokerage houses. It is lined from one end to the other with business and commercial buildings of various sizes and architectural styles, the more modern ones seeming to compete with each other for uniqueness of design.

In one of the largest, the Kriehold Building, the top three floors are leased by a computerized mail service that specializes in a worldwide investment newsletter. In reality, the newsletter does not exist. The mail service is a cover. The three floors contain the technological headquarters of General Vladimir Raskowski.

Raskowski had chosen the Zurich locale personally, believing that his enemies wouldn't expect him to set up shop in one of the world's busiest business centers. Besides, Raskowski found directing his project from Zurich entirely fitting, for soon even the Bahnhofstrasse would belong to him if he desired. He could have it all, he could have anything.

The computers that controlled the generator gun in Pamosa Springs and the aluminum reflector soon to be in geosynchronistic orbit were on the top three floors, encased by concrete and steel on all sides. In effect, the control room was a massive vault a hundred feet square and employing three dozen men and women.

Raskowski inserted his command card into its slot outside the control room. The huge entry door parted electronically from its seal and swung open. He entered, men rising to attention as he passed. Raulsch, the old German scientist who had designed and built the entire headquarters, rose and saluted crisply. Raskowski's favorite post was a chair from which he could gaze up at a huge electronic map of the United States. Now the map showed a rising green light—the path of the satellite containing his reflector as it climbed toward its deadly orbit. The various angles required of the reflector to achieve the destruction of specific American targets had been preprogrammed, and now those targets appeared in the form of dozens of flashing red lights all across the country.

"How long?" Raskowski asked Raulsch.

"Three hours, twenty-nine minutes, seventeen seconds," the scientist replied.

The general settled back and fidgeted in his elevated chair. Word from the Biminis had not been good. Somehow McCracken and Tomachenko had found the means to defeat the force he had dispatched to the islands. This meant they were still at large, though cut off from their respective governments. They would therefore have to stop his operation on their own, which was impossible of course.

Raskowski still fidgeted.

In the end, the trees had saved his life. That's what Blaine figured as he gazed back at the Hind's smoking, twisted carcass, one wing protruding upward in imitation of Johnny Wareagle's wooden one in Nicaragua. The treetops had torn out the warship's bottom, then accepted its weight long enough to cushion his fall. He had maintained consciousness through it all and had made a quick escape, aware that Paz would be sending troops out to finish him. He had no choice but to flee, even if he had to stumble and crawl to get away, clinging to the hope that either Natalya or Wareagle could succeed where he failed.

Twenty yards into the woods his balance failed him and he slid to the ground. He wiped blood from his brow, but the warm fluid drenched him again as quickly as he cleared it. He tried to grab hold of something to pull himself to his feet but his strength was gone. His vision was clouded and hazy. The ground spun beneath him. Blaine clutched at it to make it still and fought to remain conscious. Back on the ridge, the carcass of the Hind went up in a final explosion and in that instant everything was clear to him again.

He had somehow made it to his knees when the first of the figures appeared before him. He didn't know where they had come from but he knew they must be Paz's men come to finish him off. Then his vision cleared long enough for him to see a pair of grizzled characters, one with a gut hanging well over his belt and the other whose frame amounted to flesh wrapped around a beanpole.

"Afternoon, friend," one of them said.

Everything had gone well for Natalya until the private plane holding her and Vasquez's commandos neared Zurich. The soldiers, also his sons, were as well schooled as any she had worked with. They possessed all of their father's arrogance but none of his girth and had little in common, physically, except cold staring eyes. It was as if the fat man had fathered many sons just so he would have at least this many expertly trained and trustworthy killers. In his business, you could never have too many.

She and Vasquez had made it to Morocco from the Biminis in just over ten hours. The commandos were waiting with another fueled jet on the runway. After a brief inventory of equipment, they took off with their plans to be detailed as they flew.

Their intended landing at Zurich three hours later proved unsuccessful when they learned the airport there was hopelessly fogged in. The plane had no choice but to divert to another airport at Winterthur, where Vasquez would have vans waiting to spirit them by road into Zurich. It would take three hours to reach the city and another twenty minutes on top of that before they reached the Bahnhofstrasse. By Natalya's calculations that would leave little time to demolish Raskowski's base of operations and destroy his means of ordering the generator beam in Pamosa Springs to fire.

The centerpiece of the plan was surprise. All of them were dressed as Swiss electrical workers. Their blue uniforms would permit them easy, casual entry to any building especially at night.

The final deception. And perhaps the most important.

"Don't tell me, let me guess," Blaine started wearily, speaking to both of the apparitions. "You're out collecting for the Red Cross, right?"

"If we were," said Dog-ear McCluskey, "we could do a helluva lot better than you."

The men moved to either side of him, one of them limping, and helped lift him to his feet.

"Mind telling me who you are?" Blaine asked them.

"We were about to ask you the same question," said the one with the limp.

"Just a guy who had a few drinks too many and missed a turnoff."

McCracken felt better on his feet, the world seeming more balanced. Still, he had to throw his arms around the men's shoulders for support.

"A few good belts might be in order when we tell you what's been going on down in our town," said the one with the limp.

* * *

"We saw what you did," the man Blaine had come to know as Mayor Dog-ear McCluskey told him when they had reached a clearing higher up the mountain. "If the crash didn't kill ya, Sheriff Junk Heep and I figured you might be the kind of man who can help us."

"Help you what?"

"Get our town back."

Blaine listened to their whole story with a compress of cold spring water pressed against his fresh head wound, feeling much better already. Mayor Dog-ear was careful to stress the bestiality of Paz and the unexplained killings that had riddled the town.

"Now it's your turn," McCluskey beckoned him. "Since you're here, I gotta figure you got a line on what's really going on."

Blaine nodded. "Actually, you boys have put it together pretty good yourselves. The element they've been digging out of that hillside isn't a gem. It's something called Atragon."

"Atragon?" raised the sheriff. "What the hell's that? Is it worth much?"

"Until recently no one even knew it existed. But right now, conservatively speaking, I'd say it's the most precious mineral on the face of the earth."

"That's a relief," sighed Junk.

And Blaine told them everything, as best he could, from the beginning, ending with his failed attempt to destroy the generator gun using the Hind-D.

"So this Russian general blows up a town," said Dog-ear when he was finished, "and his satellite gets fucked in the process."

"Yup," said McCracken, "so he's got to resort to a new plan and he's got to do it fast. First he needs more Atragon to power the beam weapon, then he needs a new means of delivering it."

"And we helped on both accounts," noted Junk grimly.

"My guess," said Blaine, "is that he caught on to your reserves after you sent samples to the National Assayer's Office."

"Pretty short notice to put a hundred men together, especially considering this is all super-high tech," noted the mayor.

"Raskowski already had the men and plenty of them were very likely already inside the country. Besides, the man's relentless. The word *impossible* doesn't exist for him."

"So he mines this Atragon stuff," started Sheriff Junk, "and then what? Can you just pack it into that gun like batteries?"

"No, he'd have to store power in the crystals first in order to generate the beam. You said the power into town was rerouted into the hills. Lots of that went straight into the crystals, immeasurable amounts."

Junk looked at Blaine closely. "Be nice if you told us the cavalry was waitin' over the next ridge for your signal to nuke the sucker."

"Be nice, but it'd also be a lie. I got word out but it's a big country, and lots more than distance is probably holding the cavalry up. I gave it my best shot with the chopper. Came up a little short, though."

"Would you try it again?"

"Sure, Dog-ear. Just lead me to the nearest army weapons surplus store and we'll have a go at it."

Mayor McCluskey smiled.

Just to be on the safe side, Guillermo Paz had posted guards in the freight yard between the mountains and the town. If the sheriff and mayor, the last threats to his command now that the flier had been killed, were still close by, he wanted to be in a position to thwart any efforts they might mount to disrupt the final stages of General Raskowski's plan. The generator gun was impregnable, true, but too much had already happened that defied the odds. First, the strange murders, then last night's escape, and finally the return of the stolen Hind-D.

Paz wasn't about to let a fourth mishap ruin this command.

McCluskey spoke as Blaine inspected the crates full of grenades and Laws rockets Sheriff Junk had retrieved from their hiding place.

"Way I see it, friend," explained Mayor McCluskey, "the only chance we got of disablin' that monster gun is to borrow some of the explosives those bastards got stored in town. Means we gotta launch a raid. Might as well save the townspeople while we're at it."

Blaine nodded. "Your strategy's not far off. We've got to knock the gun out all right, but we won't stand a chance of even getting close until we eliminate Paz's troops. Not that the three of us have a prayer of accomplishing that by ourselves. . . ."

"Don't like your attitude," snapped Junk.

"You didn't let me finish. There's a whole church full of reinforcements waiting for us—if we can free them. Way you boys have described it, there's plenty of people in your town who'll know what to do if given the opportunity."

"And the rest might not have until ten days back."

"Especially since a few leaders, example setters, will be all it takes," Blaine explained. "That's what subversive activities are all about to an extent: making people rise up and be noticed themselves."

Dog-ear almost laughed. "So we become the subversives in our own town."

"I've been all over the world," Blaine told him. "It's not as strange as it seems."

"So all we need now is a plan," advanced Heep.

"The progression's simple," Blaine told him. "We take the town back first and then use whatever we can to blow the fuck out of that generator gun." He checked his watch. "A lot to accomplish in just under ninety minutes."

"Three of us ought to give 'em a run for their money."

"I'm starting to think we just might, Sheriff. Let me lay it out for the two of you. . . ."

Blaine explained the details of the plan to them as quickly and simply as he could. The operation had several independent components, each of which must be successful if all were to work. McCracken's job was to infiltrate the town and free the residents trapped in the church, so that they might join the battle. To accomplish this, he would need plenty of distraction and cover in the form of grenades and Laws rockets. This task was given to Sheriff Junk, whose specialty was munitions. First, he would use grenades on the soldiers in the railroad yard. Then he would fire his Laws rockets down into the town, hoping to create total havoc. He would then use the rest of his armaments to disable the still intact western battery of guns. With those still functional, they stood no chance of reaching the gulley, no matter what else transpired.

Similarly, Blaine could not let the fifteen soldiers remain on the mountainside. Not only could they provide a strong defense of the stronghold from that position, but they also could rush back into the town to lend support from the rear. The mayor, a crack shot, would come in here. As soon as Junk began hurling his grenades, McCluskey would begin picking off the soldiers guarding the gulley. He would remain up there to shoot any more of the soldiers who rushed to the gulley's defense after the battle began. Junk, meanwhile, would join McCracken in the town center, once his rockets were expended, to take charge of the eager mob freed from the church.

McCracken calculated that little more than an hour remained for them to accomplish their plan before the generator gun fired its beam of death. The mayor and sheriff of Pamosa Springs nodded their understanding.

There were fifty-four minutes left by the time Blaine worked his way around to the other side of town. He had circled to better his position in relation to the church. He expected to find a rear entrance, guarded but not nearly as well fortified as the front.

The best he could do for proximity was fifty yards, his cover being a doghouse in somebody's front yard, which, thankfully, was empty.

The guards posted around the church were superfluous when measured against the hugh mounds of C-4 plastic explosives that had been packed close enough to the windows for all to see. Clearly if his plan was to be successful the explosives had to be disabled. Cutting the fuse line at any point would do the job since a continuous current was required to set this type of *plastique* off.

Blaine checked his watch. It was 3:26. In four minutes Dog-ear would begin shooting and Sheriff Junk Heep would start hurling his grenades. The rest would be left to him. He had anticipated the timing up to this point and took that as a good omen.

Omens . . . Ah, to have Johnny Wareagle and a team of Indian warriors to help him now. . . .

He was glad the timing provided him only a few minutes to be alone with his thoughts. He had spent so many years living with violence that he believed he had become inured to it. He could excuse such acceptance in himself because he realized his actions were necessary. But now he was using innocent people, and was willing to sacrifice their lives.

To rid the world of senseless killing, he had become a killer. The knowledge chilled him. But in this case, he told himself, the only hope the people had was to fight back themselves. In the complex code of ethics he lived with and so often had nearly died with, nothing was clear-cut; there was plenty of gray but almost no black and white. And now he was having trouble with the gray.

He could see the whole world in Pamosa Springs. He would save Pamosa Springs.

His watch moved to 3:30.

* * *

Dog-ear and Sheriff Junk had taken cover within sight of each other to ensure their assaults would begin simultaneously. Heep had left all his rockets and most of his grenades in the brush twenty yards back because there was no sense in lugging them with him, and his damn creaky joints forced him to rest every other yard, or so it seemed. He'd stuffed his pockets and shirt full of grenades to hurl, even slid one into his mouth and dangled another from the dogtags he had never shed since Korea, jingling in soft counterpoint to the creaking.

A simple nod from Dog-ear was all it took for him to yank the pins out of his first pair of grenades. They were in the air an instant before McCluskey began picking off the soldiers watching over the gulley and the promised death it contained.

Lyman Scott was reaching for the phone even before Sergeant Major Cleb Turner was finished relating the story passed to him by Johnny Wareagle.

"Get me NASA, Ben," he said nervously into the receiver. "Now!"

Turner stopped. The President eyed him.

"I'm not sure what to make of what you said, Sergeant, but I'll be damned if I'm not going to check it out. An Indian named Warbird, you say. . . ."

"War*eagle*, sir."

NASA came on the line.

The President knew there was trouble as soon as NASA failed to report back that they had carried out his orders. Four minutes passed before his phone rang again.

"Sir," the NASA mission chief of the satellite launch said at last, "we have lost control of the satellite."

"I didn't tell you to control it, son," the President snapped. "I told you to blow it up."

"Yes, sir, I'm aware of that, but the problem's a bit more

complicated. The satellite isn't responding to *anv* of our commands, including self-destruct.''

''Then just abort, damnit, abort!''

''We tried, sir. No response on that one either.''

''What about shooting it down?''

''It's too high up, sir, prepared to achieve geosynchronistic orbit in . . . forty-nine minutes now.''

''So you're telling me you put the damn thing up there and there's not a damn thing you can do to get it back under control?''

''Sir, we may have put the satellite up, but someone else has got control of it now.''

''We have forty-nine minutes left to mission activation,'' Raulsch said into the microphone which channeled his voice throughout the huge control room. ''All personnel begin engaging final control tests.''

On the electronic aerial map before him, the single light representing the aluminum reflector flashed over the center of the United States.

''Prepare to jettison protective cone,'' said Raulsch.

''Ready, sir,'' responded a technician.

''On my mark . . . now.''

A single button was pressed. Twenty thousand miles above the surface of the Earth, the top part of the satellite launched to replace *Ulysses* jettisoned and fluttered into space, a fact recorded by a series of green lights in the command vault.

''Prepare to open reflector,'' Raulsch ordered next.

''Ready, sir,'' followed another technician.

''On my mark . . . now.''

This time a series of switches were flipped. In outer space, the exposed aluminum spread out to the sides like a fan, a full seventy yards across at its widest point, its precise angle of tilt controlled by the preprogrammed targeting computer.

General Raskowski sat in his elevated chair just behind

Raulsch's station, observing it all the way a father might the birth of his first child. His attention focused primarily on the flashing lights which indicated the preprogrammed selection of targets. Before him, on a small control desk, was a single black button. As soon as the reflector achieved orbit, he would press it and the beam in Pamosa Springs would begin to fire. The initial strikes would center on the eastern seaboard, starting with Washington. In a matter of a few short minutes, nearly forty million people would perish. Black carbon dust would swirl over vast metropolitan graves, soon to encompass the entire dying nation. He shifted impatiently in the stiff confines of his uniform, stopped from enjoying these final moments by concern over the whereabouts of McCracken and Tomachenko. They were out there, aware of what he was about to do, and until he at last depressed the black button he would not feel safe.

"Forty-seven minutes until system activation," announced Raulsch.

Natalya's vans made great time through the night from Winterthur to Zurich, but late-night road construction had shut down all three lanes on her side of the road. Natalya felt the grip of frustration. She breathed rapidly, fought to steady herself. The road was a sea of headlights, shining ahead into the murk for as far as she could see. On the other side of a six-inch median strip, sparse traffic moved in the opposite direction. She reached over for her driver's shoulder.

"Cross it!" she ordered.

"We'll be going in the wrong direction. No turnoffs for—"

"Cross it and go in the *right* direction!"

The man looked at her only briefly before turning the lead van's tires over the strip and against the flow of oncoming traffic, with the other van close behind.

It had been over thirty years since Sheriff Junk had lobbed grenades, and these felt totally different from any he had handled way back then. He was glad they were lighter because had they been too heavy the best he'd have been able to manage was three before his arm went. His first two lobs were right on target in the abandoned freight yard and the next four almost as good. Troops crumbled from left to right; the rest scattered in the direction of the town instead of offering resistance. Heep scrambled back for his rockets.

McCluskey, meanwhile, met no resistance at all. The soldiers on the hillside seemed numbed by inactivity and they fell like the targets in a shooting gallery. Dog-ear loved the feel of the M-16. Its gas-propelled shells made it a breeze to control. No kick whatsoever. He'd read all about the problems with the M-16, how the gas got stuffed up somehow and the thing would jam or misfire. Well, *this* one was behaving *just fine*, thank you.

He had taped a pair of clips upside down against each other, so when it came time to reload, a quick snap in and out and he would be ready to keep firing. A second or two was all it took but even that was too long, for it allowed a soldier who had found his rifle along with his senses time to put a bullet in Dog-ear's side followed by a second which grazed his head. Dog-ear gritted the pain down long enough to sight down on the bold gunman and send a dozen bullets in his direction. Enough found him, the rest Dog-ear saved for those soldiers searching futilely for cover.

The pain had him down by the time the second clip was exhausted but, lying prone, he managed to snap a fresh one home and maintain his vigil. He could forget all about joining the others in town but, what the hell, you can't have everything.

From his position of cover in Pamosa Springs, Blaine had no way of knowing just how successful the efforts of Dog-ear and Sheriff Junk had been. He knew little for sure until the Laws rockets started jetting in. From his doghouse, he couldn't see the immediate blasts, just the smoke, debris, and flames kicked up in their wake. Four came in rapid succession, a pause, and then two more blasts on Main Street itself. Perfect!

Blaine saw Paz's soldiers spilling into the street, firing their rifles blindly through the showering debris. The three soldiers charged with guarding the church's rear, though, held their positions stubbornly, only their eyes cheating around the corner.

Move, Blaine urged them silently. *Move*!

He had hoped to avoid using his rifle on them for fear the resulting clamor would drag reinforcements to the area. But if he timed the shots with the backlash of the rocket explosions, the rest of Paz's men would never hear them. Blaine estimated the angle involved. From his present position, he did not have a clear shot at the soldiers as they were standing. And there was the fuse line that needed to be severed to be considered as well. A rush into the open was called for. Three men to cut down before they got him or, worse, managed to set off the *plastique*. . . .

McCracken timed his charge into the street for the next rocket blast which came fifteen seconds later and hurled blasted debris high into the air. He rushed forward and sideways, directly into the line of possible fire from the church guards and did not fire himself until he was sure he had them. The guards saw him but took too long to react. Blaine hit his trigger and rotated the barrel of his gun. All three crumbled. One dropped to the base of the steps and two spilled down from the porch. Blaine pulled the fusing down toward him and snapped it with his teeth. The wire dug into his lip but with the explosives disabled the blood didn't faze him.

McCracken lunged up the steps and crashed his shoulder against the door, turning the knob as he did. The door was locked and took his charge without so much as giving. Blaine heard heavy boots clacking down the side street adjacent to the church and reached back for his rifle.

For his part, Sheriff Junk figured his depleted supply of Laws rockets signaled it was time to turn the remaining ones on the primary targets composing the artillery battery on the western edge of town. The firing of the rockets had become routine. It was the numbness of his ears that bothered him along with a stiffness in his arms and shoulders he fought down. The range to the battery was longer, but Junk was expecting no problems. He adjusted the range meter accordingly and raised another of the disposable bazookas over his shoulder.

Biting his lip against a sudden bolt of pain in the joint area, he focused through the sight on the guns. They were big and menacing, yet as a demolitions man, he knew disabling them was as simple as knocking out their stands to send them crashing downward.

Heep fired the rocket and watched a black streak whisk through the air, gathering speed. The expected burst of flames was brief and hardly dramatic, but the first of the big guns tumbled sideways like a slain giant. He got even luckier on his next two shots, finding ammo dumps with both of them, which coughed fire and smoke high into the air.

"Fucking A," Heep muttered through his pained grimace, starting another Laws upward.

No time to play it safe . . .

Blaine leaped over the church's porch and met the charging soldiers head on. There were just two of them but they were spaced apart and firing as they ran. McCracken caught one in his first spray and exhausted his clip in the other's direction as he rolled out of line of that man's burst. His arms were scraped raw by a poor dive and he looked up to see huge mounds of plastic explosives wedged into the church's brick construction.

The sight seemed to recharge him. He rolled behind the cover of an adjacent building as rifle bullets kicked cement fragments up everywhere around him. He came to a halt with his pistol out and aimed at the shape still moving toward him. He took the man down with two shots, then lurched back to his feet and bolted for the church's rear doors once more. The windows were too high to utilize as a viable escape route so he was left with the heavy, chained doors.

"Stand back!" he screamed and stripped a grenade from his belt, hoping those inside could hear him.

He pulled the pin and rolled the grenade across the porch, lunging to the ground for safety.

The explosion coughed splinters and shards everywhere. From inside, the door was ripped off its hinges. A stream of humanity started out; a screaming, wild pack with no clear path or destination, though a clear purpose lay before them.

"Follow me! Hurry!" McCracken shouted and took the lead toward Main Street.

A soldier staggered before him with his guts hanging out as Guillermo Paz made his way in a crouch across the street to a shop containing additional weapons. He was halfway there when the front of the building exploded outward. All of Main Street seemed to be burning, buildings reduced to flaming shells that sent splinters into the smoky air. The crackling continued, easily mistaken for gunfire, causing still more confusion in troops still rushing about the street looking for someone to shoot at.

All the jeeps he could see were demolished. Worst of all, Paz had lost contact with his men on the hillside. They were either dead or disabled and could no longer be relied on for help. But the generator was going to remain safe even if he had to defend it himself.

The horrible roar of the mob crossed onto Main Street, as Paz scrambled behind a building en route to the hills.

Once freed, only a few of the residents, women carting children and old people, had veered away from the battle. And only the very first to emerge noticed McCracken at all, the rest giving no consideration to the means of their freedom, just glad for the freedom itself.

Blaine hid himself among them, blending, slowing his pace occasionally as those around him reached down for a stray rifle or one still gripped by a soldier's corpse. Others opted for sections of wooden planks or steel shards separated from the structures that had once occupied Main Street.

McCracken searched for Paz as he ran in the center of the mob. His troops had been reduced to chaos, the ones still in the streets trying hard to run from the mob once their clips were exhausted. Those soldiers the enraged citizens of Pamosa Springs were able to catch were pummeled with whatever the citizens were able to get their hands on. Buildings continued to burn and cough up fragments, smoke dissipating with the wind to reveal jagged holes in walls and roofs courtesy of Sheriff Junk's rockets. The residents seemed not to notice. Their fury continued, increased, fed on itself.

Heep had stopped firing the rockets at the first sign of the mob rushing into the street. Exuberantly, almost near tears, he stuffed a host more grenades into his pockets and grabbed his M-16. Signaling his intention to the wounded Dog-ear, he started down for Pamosa Springs, hobbling the whole way.

McCracken moved with the stride of a commander who knew his troops were winning. The fires at the western edge of town signaled the ruin of the final gun battery, which left only foot soldiers between him and the gulley containing the generator gun. And at this rate men would prove little bother so long as the tide in the battle of Pamosa Springs continued to go his way.

His greatest enemy remained time, one perhaps too great to overcome with barely twenty-five minutes to go before the beam was activated.

Before him, Sheriff Junk emerged from the side of a building, steadying himself against it with his M-16 blasting toward a congestion of fleeing soldiers. Blaine veered away and had reached Heep's side just when the spits started. Just more crackling, he thought at first, but soon all around him bodies of the residents of Pamosa Springs began to go down. Blaine hit the cement hard and rolled to the sidewalk within the cover of a still-standing drugstore as bullets traced the ground around him. He judged their trajectory and knew instantly they were coming from above, from soldiers who had strategically managed to gain rooftop positions where they could fire down at will.

Sheriff Junk hit the ground wincing in pain next to him. "What the fuck. . . ."

A squad of Paz's soldiers had charged out from positions of cover they had fled to, grabbing the offensive again, firing into the hordes of helpless who had delivered themselves into a slaughter.

Blaine saw the grenades hanging from Heep's belt. "The grenades! Quick!"

Heep passed a few over, realizing his intention, and together they rose, ripping the pins out with their teeth and hurling the promised death upward in the direction of the rooftops. Not being sure where the fire was coming from, they relied on instinct to aim their lobs. The blasts followed quickly and just as quickly the fire from above ceased.

But the issue seemed only delayed, for Paz's troops had control of the town again and were massing in the center of Main Street, moving in a fast walk forward, shooting at anything that moved. A few broke off toward Blaine and Heep, who were firing desperately in an attempt to subdue them. Blaine heard Junk's clip click empty and leaped sideways to shield him with the rest of his bullets. Hardly enough, though, to stop the soldiers, a fact Blaine had just accepted when he caught the sound of heavy-caliber machine gun fire an instant before he was ready to accept death. Nothing else registered besides the fact that Paz's soldiers were dropping all about him, cast once again in the role of the ones scurrying for cover. Blaine looked up into the sun and caught the extension of a machine gun's barrel supported by a tripod peering down from the rooftop of a building further up the street.

Who, damnit, who?

He recalled Dog-ear's story of a mystery avenger as he lunged back to his feet after casting a quick glance toward Heep who was scrambling for one of the downed soldiers' guns. Again the tables of the battle had started to turn with the residents of Pamosa Springs confronting the rest of their captors.

McCracken joined the battle at its center. He alternated between downing what soldiers he could with a stray rifle lifted from the ground, and dragging several of the wounded townspeople to safety. From the roof well beyond him, single gunshots continued to pour down, the work of an expert marksman picking off Paz's men one at a time. Blaine had been in many battles before, including firefights in Nam in which a hundred lives were lost in a minute, but this was the worst of any he'd seen. The soldiers' numbers severely dwindling, they nonetheless held the advantage of weaponry and position, while the residents relied on raw determination and the aid of a phantom from a rooftop above. Things improved for the townspeople when several grabbed the rifles of dead soldiers, but only a few of them could make the weapons work in any effective way. The hits they recorded were lucky. The remaining soldiers paid them little regard.

Main Street of Pamosa Springs was a sea of bodies, stirring and otherwise. The battle was now receding into the areas between and behind buildings, with soldiers and townspeople shooting at each other from positions as fortified as they could gain. Neither side controlled any special area. The distribution was random and the bullets blazed in the same manner. With vastly superior numbers, though, it was the residents who were now wearing the soldiers down. Blaine even had time to gaze up at the rooftop, but found no further sign of the phantom. It seemed as if things were winding down, Paz's men on the verge of surrender.

Then he heard the rumbling. He knew what it was even before he saw the squat, ugly-looking monster lumbering down the street with four machine guns blasting away in every direction from within its armored walls. The army called it the "Jungle Buster," an all-terrain vehicle featuring six-foot-high tires and a frame impenetrable to anything but a direct rocket hit. The Jungle Buster was actually of Israeli design and was used by the armed forces there in raiding the fortified and secluded terrorist training camps in Lebanon. It looked like one of those monster car-crushers with machine gun barrels poking out from where its windows should have been.

These barrels blazed orange toward all concentrations of townspeople. McCracken saw dozens felled immediately, thinking their positions to be safe and themselves victorious until the very last. Even those who tried to run were no better off, since the incredible range of the Jungle Buster's fire made escape impossible.

"*No*!" Blaine screamed and bounded to his feet as the Jungle Buster squealed closer.

He had seen enough. The shallow ache in the pit of his gut was directing him now. He could take no more. Someone was going to pay for all this and it was going to start now. In the next instant he was sprinting forward on an oblique angle with the Buster's fire. He reached it and leaped between exposed barrels on the vehicle's side and pulled himself upon its roof with a grenade poised in his hand. McCracken yanked the pin out with his teeth and leaned his arm over to make sure he wedged it through one of the thing's firing slats. He hurled himself off and rolled aside just before the blast sounded, sending bursts of flames through the openings which had spewed death only seconds before. The Jungle Buster kept lumbering forward for a time, then swung sharply to the right, where it rolled into the débris of a ruined building. And died.

McCracken lunged back to his feet. Sheriff Junk hobbled over to his side and around them amidst the rolling smoke, the gunfire had turned sporadic, fading out by the second.

"We did it!" Junk roared. "We fuckin' did it!"

"Not yet," Blaine reminded him. "The generator gun, remember?"

"Shit."

It had to be blown up, at the very least disabled. But if there had been any hope of using Paz's armaments to accomplish that, the flames and smoke seemed to smother it. There was no time to find the explosives required, even if they knew where to look. Their best bet in retrospect would have been to leave the western artillery battery intact and have a go at the monster beam with it. Blaine's thoughts spun. Explosives, there had to be something he could use. . . .

And then he realized. What he needed was right before him. Thanks to Paz.

He started to move away, beckoning Heep to follow. "Grab as many of your people as you can and follow me."

"What?"

"Just do as I say!"

Blaine glanced at his watch. There were exactly twenty minutes left to go.

CHAPTER 34

THE vans swung onto the Bahnhofstrasse, Natalya's in the lead and setting the pace for the other as it sped through the thin, late-night traffic, making fast for the Kriehold Building. Their drive on the wrong side of the road had lasted for one agonizing mile, Natalya herself squeezing her eyes closed through much of it. Suddenly she felt the brakes being applied an instant before the headlights illuminated a steel rail directly before them, blocking their way.

Damn! How could I have been so stupid?

Most of the Bahnhofstrasse had long ago been converted into a large sidewalk mall, with all traffic prohibited other than the tramcars referred to here as "Holy Cows." The vans had now come to the mall area, and it was impossible to crash their way through the steel rail fencing which detoured all traffic to the right or left. They were barely ten blocks from the Kriehold Building, with just under twenty minutes left before the reflector would achieve orbit.

With no choice, Natalya told her driver to pull over.

"We go on foot!" she ordered as the second van came up along side.

The commandos spilled out onto the Bahnhofstrasse mall, still heavily populated by pedestrians even past midnight, since its bright lights and beautiful fountained walkways and all-night shops invariably drew a crowd. The blue-garbed figures slung rifles over their shoulders and grasped knapsacks full of explosives and ammunition as they raced down the center of the mall for the Kriehold Building which nestled with a few others near the center.

Natalya managed to stay at the head of the pack, thoughts swimming frantically through her mind. She resisted all temptation to gaze at her watch, knowing its message was useless to her now. She and the others could run no faster. The best they could do was reach the Kriehold Building and hope they were in time.

Guillermo Paz had stopped to watch the end of the battle from the outskirts of town. Right until the end he had maintained the hope that his troops would be triumphant and save him the indignity of losing his command. He was horrified to see them admit defeat by stepping into the street with their hands in the air.

It was only then that Paz got a clear look at the man who, he had come to realize, was responsible for the greatest portion of his defeat. Never mind the rest of the town, this man was a one-person army. His face was familiar. The black, gray-speckled beard and dark eyes . . . but from where?

Paz shuddered with fury. It was the man who had disgraced him in Nicaragua, the very same one who had stolen the Hind-D, no doubt the very same one who had strafed the town and gone after the generator gun with it just hours before! And now he was . . .

Paz stopped his thoughts as the next phase of the bastard's plan grew clear beneath him. He went cold with fear. The gun wasn't safe yet, but if he could save it, then his entire mission could be salvaged. Raskowski would pin him with a medal. He could accomplish it by himself; he had to.

He sprinted to the hillside, clambering up the slope on his short, muscular legs. The bodies of his men were littered in the dirt and rocks. He cursed them as incompetent slugs. As he neared the top, his strategy became clear: Find the most easily defensible position and use it to slow the coming approach of the townspeople. Just minutes was all he had to buy.

"Drop that rifle and turn around real slow," a familiar voice ordered.

Paz did as he was told, coming face-to-face with the mayor of Pamosa Springs. The man was crouching on one knee and bleeding rather badly from his left side. He was breathing hard.

"Kick that rifle away from you now."

Again Paz did as he was told. His exposed, stubbly head poured sweat, and he fought to keep the rage from showing on his raw-boned features. He positioned himself so the mayor had no hope of seeing the pistol holstered in his belt.

"I been waitin' for this for the longest time, you bastard," McCluskey said and Paz knew in that moment the man wasn't going to kill him right away, which meant he wasn't going to kill him at all. "Put your arms in the air," came the next order. "Straight up so the fingertips touch the sky."

Paz started to oblige, smiling warmly to display his submission. When his arms were almost fully outstretched, he launched his taut body into a dive and used his left hand for leverage as he rolled across the ground with his right going for his pistol.

The wounded mayor sprayed the dirt with fire, bullets coming close but not close enough. Paz felt their heat as he brought his pistol up and fired it repeatedly. The first bullet spun the mayor violently around and the next two dropped him. Paz smacked one more into his writhing frame just for good measure and lurched back to his feet, grasping his Kalishnikov on the way. Beneath him the people of Pamosa Springs were rushing toward the hillside, a large stream collectively holding the potential instrument of his failure in their hands with the bearded bastard at their lead.

Paz scrambled into position.

* * *

"You really think this is going to work?" an out-of-breath and hobbling Sheriff Junk huffed to McCracken, catching up to him en route to the hill.

"*You're* the demolitions man. Why don't *you* tell *me*?"

"Fuck. . . . You would put it on my shoulders, wouldn't you? 'Case you haven't noticed, they're not in the best of shape."

"They'll do," said McCracken.

On Blaine's orders, a throng of residents had lifted the mounds of C-4 plastic explosives from the church's perimeter and hurried after him toward the sloping hill which overlooked the gulley containing the generator gun. His plan was to plug the hill with the *plastique*, wiring it in a way that would bring the whole bulk of land mass down upon the huge gun. Thousands of pounds of rocks and dirt and sand entombing it just might stop the generator from firing its beam, redirect it at the very least in a direction where it would do no harm.

So long as Sheriff Junk could get it wired properly.

So long as there was time for him to try.

"Fifteen minutes to system activation," announced Raulsch in his gravelly voice.

Activity in the command vault had stabilized. As long as all readout lights continued to flash green, there was little the personnel could do other than wait for a dreaded malfunction as they sat attentively behind their monitors or CRT screens.

For Raskowski, the minutes had already passed into an eternity. He should have been savoring these final moments, but instead he was nervous, on edge, a feeling of foreboding filling him with the certainty that the enemies he had let slip from his grasp had one final card to play.

He was so caught up in these thoughts that he was not aware of Katlov's breathless presence until the man grasped his shoulder.

"General," came his agitated report, "deployed ground

security spotters have just reported armed commandos rushing down the Bahnhofstrasse in our direction. Just blocks away now."

Raskowski rose from his chair, still towering above the one-eyed Katlov who had spoken from floor level. "Who?" he wanted to know.

Katlov swallowed hard. "Tomachenko is at their lead."

"The bitch!" Raskowski roared drawing attention from nearby technicians but not seeming to care. Fighting to calm himself, he turned to Katlov. "Deploy all our defenses. Condition Red. You know the procedures."

"Da," Katlov replied and rushed out after making the semblance of a salute.

Raskowski waited for the electronic door to close behind his security chief before speaking again. "Seal the vault," he ordered Raulsch.

Raulsch began flipping switches on his console, deactivating the mechanism that permitted entry and switching the vault's air supply to its own tanks, so that no foreign gases could be introduced. The vault could now be opened only from the inside and only with the special cards that both Raulsch and Raskowski possessed.

"Twelve minutes to system activation," Raulsch announced.

The general leaned back, confident. With all these precautions taken, Natalya Tomachenko and whoever her friends were stood no chance of getting in to stop him now.

The shooting began when Natalya and the commandos were still a block away from the Kriehold Building. The building was fronted by a giant fountain adorned with falls and spouts. The first line of Raskowski's defenses had taken cover behind it, cloaked by the night.

"They were expecting us!" one of Vasquez's men screamed as he ducked for cover.

"It doesn't matter!" Natalya shouted back.

The commandos responded instinctively. With their firepower infinitely superior to that of the guards, they knew this resistance was futile. But any resistance took time, and time was the one weapon they didn't possess. They hurled grenades immediately, a pair landing in the fountain and ripping away parts of its structure. Water gushed everywhere, adding to the chaotic rush of people screaming and charging for cover. More grenades followed the first and a path was cleared through the floodlit darkness to the building's main entrance.

A lead phalanx had already lunged ahead of the grenade hurlers and encountered more enemy fire from inside the Kriehold's lobby. This, too, was ended with a few grenades that shattered the glass in the huge doors, demolishing them. Natalya was impressed with the ruthlessness of Vasquez's men. Their loyalty was fierce. Their orders were to help penetrate the madman's stronghold and nothing was allowed to get in their way. The commandos were of one mind, one purpose. With Natalya just behind the first group, they rushed into the lobby and used their machine guns to fell the remainder of Raskowski's inadequately armed security guards, hardly prepared to deal with such a full-scale assault.

"What floor?" one of them screamed at her.

"Fourteen!" Natalya returned, and they rushed along toward the elevators.

One of the commandos pushed the UP arrow again and again. At last the doors slid open. Only Natalya's surprisingly strong grasp stopped the first of the men from entering.

"No!" she ordered. "No elevators! We enter them and he turns the power off in mid-flight. The stairs, it's got to be the stairs!"

Raskowski watched all this transpire on one of the seven miniature closed-circuit monitors on the console directly before his chair. The enemy was coming up the stairs. His men could not possibly hold them off. But they would still have to find the command center and even then there would be the vault door to contend with.

Impregnable. He had won. *Everything was on his side.*

"Ten minutes to system activation. . . ."

Including time.

The resistance within the stairwell was heavier than expected. Grenades were dangerous to use in so narrow a space because of their percussion qualities and potential to roll back or send clouds of deadly debris showering in their wake. It came down to hand-held weapons, then, and the commandos were well up to the task, seeming to find it preferable.

They never stopped, even when the enemy fire was at its strongest. Soon Raskowski's forces were pinned with their backs against the exit door from the stairwell onto the fourteenth floor. They were out of bullets and fighting to reload when the commandos killed them. The door proved only a small hindrance to them and they were through it in an instant to the sound of more enemy fire trying to cut them down as they surged into the corridor in what had to be single file.

The first two out suffered wounds, sacrificing themselves to pinpoint the positions of the gunmen. This accomplished, more grenades were hurled to clear the way for a rush by the others. Raskowski's security troops were severely depleted now and the commandos met with only sporadic resistance as they funneled through the corridor in search of a room suitable for what they knew must be the command center.

"My God," muttered Natalya when she came upon the huge steel vault door bearing an electronic entry system. "This must be it!"

One of the commandos whose speciality was demolitions felt the steel. "We'll never be able to blast through this," came his grim report.

"Try, damnit, try!"

Paz readied his machine gun, sighting on the men and women trudging up the hill. Somehow he had lost the bearded bastard who'd been at their lead and now must have melted into the center of the crowd. No matter. His spray would do the job well enough and even if the bearded one was spared, he would be powerless alone.

Paz pawed the trigger, waiting for his targets to draw a little closer. No reason to rush. Every reason to be sure.

Just a little bit more . . .

A branch snapped behind him. Paz spun. And froze.

Ten feet away McCracken held a pistol in line with his face.

"Thought I'd leave you a chance," Blaine told him.

Paz tried to bring his rifle up to fire. McCracken's gun exploded twice and Paz's face disappeared.

They found Dog-ear's body not far from where Paz ended up after tumbling partway down the hill. The sight of his murdered best friend seemed to charge Sheriff Junk with a fresh resolve. All doubt vanished and the pain with it, as he determinedly directed the packing of the C-4 plastic explosives into the side of the hill looking down over the gulley.

"You sure this is the right way?" McCracken asked Heep as together they strung the fusing which linked the individual mounds of *plastique* together.

"Look, bud," Heep snapped, joints and limbs cracking up a storm, sounding like popcorn over a fire, "this stuff might be more advanced than what we had in Korea, but principles is principles. Mountains still fall the same way they used to."

With all the explosives packed into the gulley side of the hill, the idea was to create a landslide that would move only in the generator gun's direction, the hope being that the rubble would be enough to bring the big gun down. Blaine gazed down upon it yet again. The steel casing must have been a hundred feet in diameter, the circle almost perfect. Extended from its top and poised at a seventy-five-degree angle upward (in line with the reflector no doubt) was a huge tabular extension. It had looked more like a gun barrel from above but from closer Blaine could see its bore was finished with a honeycomb pattern, indicating the crystals would actually generate a dozen or so individual beams which would join up as soon as they blazed from the tube stretching forty feet into the air. Wrapped around its one-meter circumference was black, lead-encased housing which would undoubtedly maintain a constant pumping of water to keep the tube cooled while the incredible energy in the form of the particle beam was pulsing through it. Inside the vast superstructure, resembling a turret, would be the self-contained computers which communicated with Raskowski's headquarters in Zurich to accept commands and then instruct the gun to execute them, all of which took place in a fraction of a second.

But long enough to assure the deaths of millions.

"Six minutes to system activation. . . ."

Another of his closed-circuit monitors showed Raskowski the feebly futile efforts of the commandos in the corridor to gain entry to his command vault. He actually laughed at their desperation.

After a few seconds the woman Tomachenko gazed in the camera and their eyes met. It seemed as if both of them knew it. Raskowski grinned. Natalya hoisted her Uzi upward and shot the camera out.

"It's like I told you," the demolitions specialist told her after two attempts to blast through the door had failed. "No way."

Natalya's thoughts were already moving in another direction. The computers within the vault controlled the generator gun but not directly. There had to be some sort of dish that would beam the command signals to a receiving device in Pamosa Springs. And knowing Raskowski, the dish would have to be close by. . . . The roof, Natalya realized! Had she noticed a large dish from the street? No, the roof was flat, impossible to pick anything out from ground level.

"Half of you come with me!" she screamed. "The rest keep trying to get through that door. Throw everything we've got at it!"

And then she was sprinting down the corridor back toward the main stairwell. Just one flight up and the roof was hers.

The commandos were at her side as she charged up, the door already in sight. One threw his shoulder into it as he worked the knob.

It was locked.

McCracken and Heep were working feverishly now. They had separated to easier facilitate the joining of the many individual mounds of the plastic explosives together with the fusing. Once completed, the end of the wire would be connected to the electronic detonator they had found among the invaders' mining equipment, the switch to be turned once all the residents were free of the blast zone and the hill itself.

Most had already fled to a safe distance, and now Blaine and Sheriff Junk were alone. They reached the hill's top again at the same time, Heep twirling the individual ends of their fusing together and taping them tight. They had two hundred yards of fusing left, plenty to give them a safe pillow from the blast. The ends joined, they hurried down the hillside, almost tumbling, Blaine holding fast to Heep so he wouldn't fall. At the bottom, the sheriff dragged his feet quick as he could parallel to the town, already looping the wire around the conduits that would channel the signal through the hill and bring it down upon the generator gun.

Heep had to pause with hands on his knees when the fusing lost its slack. Again Blaine supported him, taking the detonator until Junk was upright again. He was still huffing as he turned the switch all the way to the left. The red test light flashed on.

"Wanna do the honors?" he asked.

"All yours," Blaine told him.

Heep turned the switch to his right, flinching against the expected jolting series of explosions.

Nothing happened.

"Two minutes to system activation. . . ."

Raskowski had seen Tomachenko rushing down the corridor through another of his monitors. He knew immediately she was headed for the roof and only wished he had placed cameras up there so he could have seen the expression on her face when she came upon his final surprise. He had anticipated her moves perfectly, anticipated *all* their moves perfectly, always one step ahead. It was fitting that his mind should be the one charged with remaking civilization with the proper rules in place. He had never lost sight of the goals set for himself, never failing to accomplish them with only one remaining unfulfilled.

But not for much longer.

"Give me an explosives pack!" Natalya ordered one of the commandos who produced it instantly. Before it was even firm in her hand she had jammed it against the heavy door's latch area and stuck a five-second delay fuse into it.

The group backed halfway down the final flight of stairs to avoid the spraying of fragments. A *poof* followed and the door opened outward onto the roof. Natalya rushed through.

And gasped.

McCracken reached the first mounds of *plastique*, eyes and hands working feverishly, both ablaze with sweat. When the turn of the detonator had brought no explosion, the obvious explanation was a break somewhere in the fusing. He had to trace down the break, the time frame buried in his consciousness because consideration of it was pointless, could only lead to frustration and from frustration invariably to failure. He knew he didn't have time enough to cover the entire swirling length, and so elected to focus his search at the rockiest part of the hillside, where a sharp shard could easily have split the fuse.

Almost back to the hilltop, his hand following the fuse was sliced by something that felt like a knife. He drew it back in pain, saw the blood first and the break in the fusing second.

There it was!

The jagged rock had cleanly severed the steel. Blaine twisted it together, ripping the flesh of his fingertips in his resolve to get it tight fast. He never considered there might be another break somewhere else; it was pointless to. Instead he lunged to his feet and waved his arms as he started running back down the hillside.

"Blow it!" he screamed to Sheriff Junk below. *"Blow it!"*

Screamed in full awareness that the rubble might kill him even if the blast didn't, his tomb shared with a gun that might otherwise have taken millions of lives.

Heep closed his eyes and turned the detonator switch.

McCracken's ears seemed to shatter at the initial explosion, the earth giving way with a rumble beneath him. Then there was only air.

"Twenty seconds," announced Raulsch. "Eighteen, seventeen, sixteen . . ."

And Raskowski leaned back with the feeling of triumph warm within him and edged his hand over the button that would activate his beam in Pamosa Springs.

Natalya had frozen for an instant upon reaching the rooftop. The satellite dishes were everywhere before her, at least fifteen of varying sizes. But which was Raskowski's? With a shudder, she realized they all were, placed up here to disguise a single one. Still she had to try. Knowing only seconds remained, she ordered the commandos to hurl their grenades to destroy *all* the dishes in one final effort.

Perhaps forever.

* * *

After the initial burst of rubble upward, the hillside seemed to settle in motion, rolling downward for the gulley like floodwaters after ten days of rain, gathering speed and mass as it tumbled. The pile grew, absorbed, became huge in scope as it neared the generator gun's huge steel housing and rose over it like a *tsunami* ready to crash.

Heep held his breath, forgetting in that long instant that the rubble had swept away the man responsible for saving him and the town and wondering if the generator gun was going to perish beneath the tons of earth and rubble pouring down.

"Four seconds, three, two, one . . . System activation has been achieved." With those words spoken, Raulsch turned back to General Vladimir Raskowski.

The general had already depressed the button, finger frozen there to savor the moment. The signal had been beamed at the speed of light to his generator gun in Pamosa Springs which in the next second would fire its beam upward at his reflector. All lights flashed green signaling the process had begun, impossible to stop from this point on.

His satellite dish was hidden on the roof, disguised as a ventilation outlet, with all the others serving as decoys.

Victory was his.

The generator gun and its housing had been utterly buried by the mound of earth and rock which continued to roll onward, settling at the lowest point at the gulley's bottom and continuing to pile up. Not even the slightest bit of its bore was visible when Sheriff Heep could have sworn he felt the ground rumble beneath him in a way that shook all his insides.

The pile of moving debris trembled, starting at the very top and within seconds spreading all the way down through the mass. Heep knew the beam had been activated and dove for cover out of fear of what was coming next.

The beam *had* fired, but as it struck the mounds of rocks and earth covering its bore, they melted instantly and drained down. Superheated to unfathomable temperatures, the liquified molten earth, much like lava, flowed in a continuous stream straight down the barrel through the honeycombed tops. The beam continued to pulse for a time until the flow reached the bottom of the bore and filled the firing receivers, which accepted the Atragon-charged beam from the generator to send it skyward. At that point, a massive overload occurred, combustion on a near-nuclear level achieved, as the tremendous energy stores broke free of their bonds and sought a vent.

Virtually all the rocks and dirt forming the mound melted into a heat-driven flow that leaped into the air like a huge splash of filthy water, settling down almost as quickly with a sizzling hiss as the vapors and liquified solids began to cool, solidifying once more.

The rubble was gone by this point, replaced by a smooth, grainy mound which glowed with a red translucence as it hardened into black volcanic glass. The hissing continued as Heep rose cautiously in the still-blowing, heated wind. The sight before him in the gulley was awe-inspiring, a lava tomb effectively encased over the generator gun and its housing.

Suddenly Heep felt chilled through his sweat. What of McCracken?

Natalya had resigned herself to failure. She was beaten, and so was the world. She had no reason for hope because she had no way of knowing what had transpired in Raskowski's command vault.

His computers in Zurich had been beaming a continuous set of commands to the generator complex in Pamosa Springs. The overload there had been so great that a huge charge of feedback sped back over the open line, tracing the path of the original command to fire. The charge was so potent that upon receiving it, everything electrical within the vault began to short-circuit. Control boards fizzled and smoked, some giving way to full-scale eruptions which showered sparks everywhere. The lighting died. All power ceased to function.

More of the circuit boards and panels crackled and smoked, fire popping up in one after the other. The flames spread quickly through the oxygen-rich air, attempts to fight them abandoned after a short time in favor of escape. But the vault remained electronically sealed. And the flames were widening, reaching outward in tentacles coated with poisonous vapors and fumes. The bulk of the personnel rushed the vault door and pushed on it futilely, coughing, dying, while the whole time General Vladimir Raskowski clung to the command dais, pressing the firing button over and over, his features contorted into a mad stare until the flames swallowed him.

By the time investigators drilled through the vault door hours later, most of the bodies were unrecognizable. Those that remained in any form were charred black and continued to smolder. The facts as to what had happened were ambiguous, and always would be.

A woman, whom each investigative authority assumed worked for another, spent only enough time in the vault to linger over a body in the center. No one saw her smile as she lowered a hand to the corpse's shoulder area. No one saw her remove the blackened gold stars which labeled the man a general in the Soviet army.

And then she was gone.

CHAPTER 35

SHERIFF Junk Heep was kneeling over the body of Dog-ear McCluskey when he heard the footsteps shuffling toward him.

"Son of a bitch," he said, almost managing a smile. "Now look who's having trouble walkin'."

McCracken stopped near him, grimacing with pain, covered with dirt and dust, flesh torn and scratched from face to ankles. He had just managed to avoid the brunt of the blast, pummeled by layers of rebellious debris that hadn't joined the molten flow in the gulley. Gazing at the mound he saw the red translucence had now faded slightly, the generator complex's tomb becoming almost crystalline black.

"Least you can do is help me back into town," McCracken said lightly as a pair of silver jet fighters soared overhead. His eyes turned to an army convoy on the access road leading into town. "Looks like we got company."

"In more ways than one." Heep gazed over McCracken's shoulder at the dirty figure moving down toward them, a number of townspeople in his tracks. Heep rose all the way up. "Shit, that's Hal Taggart's boy." The figure was closer now. "What's left of him, anyway."

The left side of the figure's body was dragging noticeably

behind the right. And the left half of his face was creased with scar tissue that covered even the eye.

"He was a marine in the Mideast," Heep continued. "We all thought he died. Taggart told us so."

"Apparently he came close." McCracken had seen that kind of appearance before. There were parts of the young man's brain that would never work again, others that were as good as ever. "Taggart must have brought him back here and hid him from the world."

Heep managed another look. "After the bastards killed his father, the kid figured he'd take things into his own hands. Had those murdering shits guarding their own assholes when he started knocking 'em off one at a time."

"Not to mention the fact that he saved our asses today. Must have been him on that rooftop."

"Guess he brought more than memories back with him from the Mideast."

McCracken shrugged at that and the motion sent a bolt of pain surging through him. Heep dragged himself over and started to lower himself under Blaine's shoulder.

"Guess it's my turn to do the helpin'," he said, grimacing almost as much as McCracken was as they started forward. "This oughtta be fun."

McCracken approached the men climbing from the lead jeep by himself.

"You McCracken?" asked the one in charge.

Blaine nodded. "Wareagle send you?"

"Don't know any Wareagle. My orders came straight from the Pentagon. Woulda been here sooner but had trouble arranging for proper air support," the commander explained as the jets streaked overhead again. He gazed about him at the bodies strewn throughout the town, littered among the smoldering buildings. "Hell of a mess."

"You missed the action."

"Looks like you had matters well in hand without us."

Blaine thought of Dog-ear McCluskey and of the son of

Hal Taggart. "You might say that," he returned distantly. "You in touch with Washington, Commander?"

"Open line."

"You made my day."

"I think the time has finally come for me to retire to the woods too, Indian, or at least to some lonely island somewhere," Blaine told Wareagle as they strolled down the mall fronting the Washington Monument.

"That was forced upon you once already, Blainey. The five years in France. Remember?"

"And every day I prayed to be let back in, to be a part of things again."

"And you think this time the same prayers would not come?"

"I think this time I'd be praying to be left alone."

Wareagle stopped and gazed down at him. "No, Blainey. You can close your eyes during the day but the light remains. And sooner or later you must open your eyes again and face that."

"I wasn't talking about myself, Indian. It's the others I'm fed up with, the mindless ones for whom day and night don't exist, for whom it's always dusk because that way there's no firm commitment in any direction."

"They exist to remind us of our own failings, to keep us in touch with what is pure and holy so we never take the words of the spirits for granted."

"That doesn't justify the way they handle things, or mishandle them."

"I didn't mean it to. Actions are their own justifications, Blainey. Do not search for that which does not exist because then you become no better than them."

"That's the point, Indian. I already am no better than the others because I've been a part of this too long. What I did needed to be done, right? My private justification."

Wareagle touched his shoulder tenderly. "Blainey, you see others in the shadow of your own reflection, believe their concerns for completion to be the same as your own. You expect their manitous to reflect the same colors yours does, and now you find that many reflect nothing because they are black, colorless."

"So what's the point?"

"The universe exists in a delicate balance as much as each individual does. They cannot help what they are any more than you can help what you are. Each of you provides the other with balance, both needed to justify the actions of the other."

"Then you're saying I shouldn't quit once we wrap this thing up, once it's finished."

"I'm saying that for you the finishing does not exist. Yes, maybe for this single affair but where this one leaves off another picks up. Extension follows extension, with the distinctions negligible."

McCracken shook his head reflectively. "I got to Washington half-certain I was going to forget about my meeting with the President. I guess there is one last thing I've got to take care of."

"At least," said Wareagle.

"You'll be happy to know the Farmer Boy business has been cleared up as well," the President told Blaine as they sat at a wrought iron table in the Rose Garden with the Secret Service guards out of earshot. "George Kappel turned himself in when the outcome was final. Figured we might go easy on him that way."

"And will you?"

"Not at all. My first inclination was to go public with everything, Kappel included. But I'm not certain the country can handle another travesty of government."

"Might stop the next one from happening."

"It hasn't yet and won't in the future. We hold our own, which is the best we can do because people are imperfect. This hasn't been easy for me. George Kappel's been my friend since I got elected to the House. He used me from the beginning. I guess that's a microcosm of life."

"Not life, Mr. President, just politics. But not mine, because I haven't got any." McCracken was silent for a while, then brought up the subject Lyman Scott was hesitant to broach. "I suppose you're interested in the coordinates of the Atragon reserves I wasn't able to bring up."

"The thought had crossed my mind."

"Perish it. I'm going to give you those coordinates, Mr. President, but not for the reasons you think."

"What, then?"

Blaine told him, making it fast.

"That's impossible!" the President roared when he had finished.

"Amazing the miracles the Oval Office can work, though."

Lyman Scott swallowed hard. "Think of the risks if we carry this madness out."

"Think of the risks if we don't," Blaine returned, his meaning clear.

"Mr. McCracken, with further stores of Atragon in our possession, we need never face a threat like this again. We should have learned that from these past two weeks, if nothing else."

"What we should have learned is that there are things in this world that are better left alone. I don't pretend to know where Atragon really comes from, but I do know plenty more innocent people will die if I let you salvage it." Then, after a pause, "We're not ready to control its power yet. I'm not sure we'll ever be."

Lyman Scott nodded to himself. "I came into office committed to peace at any cost. That much hasn't changed. What you say makes sense, Mr. McCracken. Something like Atragon, well, I'm not sure we could allow the Soviets to possess it either. If I agree to carry out your request, you'll agree to sit on everything you've got, correct?"

"Absolutely. So long as you get what I need to Miami within twenty-four hours."

"Twenty-four hours? Impossi—"

"I'm feeling generous today. Make it twenty-five."

The navy ship docked in Biscayne Bay at the Port of Miami at noon the next day. Blaine had spent most of the morning watching a few cruise liners come in and out, overcome by their size but equally impressed by the small tugs which nudged and maneuvered their vast bulks at will. He leaned over the railing to support his battered frame. The pain was bad today, and he did his best to hide his many bandages from passersby, just wanting to be left alone.

He looked up to find Natalya by his side, looking solemn and somber.

"They tell you what this was about?" Blaine asked her.

"They told me. And they must have told you about Zurich."

"Yup."

"Then you must believe in the myth when it comes to the origin of those crystals. How else can you account for what happened in Raskowski's command vault?"

"I leave the accounting to the scientists."

"And let them explain things for which there is no explanation? No, with what you've convinced your government to do, you *must* believe!"

"In Atlantis you mean? Haven't really thought about it much. I only know that those crystals Vasquez discovered and Raskowski almost blew up the world with are better buried forever."

"The same lesson the Lost Continent—and Raskowski—learned. Both too late."

"Maybe so," Blaine conceded. "And I've learned a few things lately as well, like how to see the truth. I've been at this for fifteen years, and all I've seen are the lies. They're everywhere around me and for all that time I mistook plenty of them for the truth. I haven't helped the world out of its hopeless lot; I've just added to it by accepting other people's truths, their *myths*, so maybe I'm the wrong person to speak with on the subject."

Natalya shrugged. "I think we have fooled ourselves more than we have allowed ourselves to be fooled. So full are we with ideals and beliefs that helped us accomplish the impossible. Our governments turned to us because we were more than good; we were willing. And when we aren't willing anymore, they have come to know us so well that it is not hard for them to make us willing again. My father, your romantic nature—if not these, there would be others."

There was a pause when both of them turned their attention to the speedboats splashing through Biscayne Bay.

"What will you do now?" Blaine asked finally.

"Finally I have enough on them to get my father out," she replied. "Only I will have to accept the fact that I too will never be able to return."

"Does that bother you?"

"All my work these long years would be futile if it didn't." The pain was evident in her voice. "And what about you, Blaine McCracken?"

"I'm thinking about finding an island where no one else has ever been and staking a claim for a while."

"Could be dangerous," Natalya told him. "Much safer to explore in pairs."

"That sounds like the truth to me," Blaine smiled.

EPILOGUE

THE bomb was small enough to be easily maneuverable underwater. The only problem arose when the navy ship proved too large to tempt the reefs, and the cylindrical device had to be loaded onto a motorboat and transported the last half mile to the coast of the nameless Bimini island. Another boat was required to get all the necessary equipment and personnel to the site. A third went along just in case either of these failed at some point during the journey.

The placing of the nuclear charge was totally according to McCracken's specifications. He had drawn them a detailed map of the ocean floor and was careful to include all the wrecks he could recall from his dive. They had made good time from Miami, and the weather had cooperated brilliantly.

Blaine stood by Natalya on the deck, both of them watching the motorboats negotiate the reefs and reach their destination safely. It was up to the divers now, who surfaced forty minutes later flashing the thumbs-up sign. They returned to the ship at top speed, the weather still good and nothing to impede their dash for safety. The timing device had been set for six hours—more than enough time to be far out of range of the blast's effects. The coming nuclear explosion would be extremely minor, but the consequences to immediate and surrounding waters nonetheless promised to be severe.

As it turned out, six hours later their ship was too far away from what Blaine had termed "Water Zero" to feel anything at all. No one, in fact, would know if they had been successful until divers returned to check the area several months later, when the radioactivity had dissipated entirely.

They could not see, then, the huge swell of water which blasted into the air and totally drenched the lost island of the Biminis, submerging a great portion of it. Some of this water was superheated and a steam cloud rose into the air, looking like a fog bank in search of a ship to strand on the now-ruptured reef.

It was near the ocean floor itself, though, where the greatest effects were felt. The explosion created a fissure in the very top layer of the Earth, which opened to swallow the graveyard of ships above it and seal the secrets of the sea forever.

About the Author

Jon Land is the author of THE DOOMSDAY SPIRAL, THE LUCIFER DIRECTIVE, VORTEX, LABYRINTH, THE OMEGA COMMAND, THE COUNCIL OF TEN, and THE ALPHA DECEPTION. He is thirty years old and lives in Providence, Rhode Island, where he is currently at work on a new novel.